I0652596

The Shadows of Blackbriar Academy

The Hex of Blackbriar Academy

The Blood Oath of Blackbriar Academy

The Battle of Blackbriar Academy

Sentinel Saga

By Dahlia Leigh and Olivia Ash

The Shadow Shifter

STAY CONNECTED

Join the exclusive group where all the cool kids hang out... Olivia's secret club for cool ladies! Consider this your formal invitation to a world of hot guys, fun people, and your fellow book lovers. Olivia hangs out in this group all the time. She made the group specifically for readers like you to come together and share their lives and interests, especially regarding the hot guys from her novels.

Check it out! Everyone in there is amazing, and you'll fit right in.

https://www.facebook.com/groups/LilaJeanOliviaAsh/

Sign up for email alerts of new releases AND exclusive access to bonus content, book recommendations, and more!

https://wispvine.com/newsletter/olivia-ash-email-signup/

Enjoying the series? Awesome! Help others discover the Dragon Dojo Brotherhood by leaving a review at Amazon.

http://mybook.to/DDB1

REIGN OF DRAGONS

Book One of the Dragon Dojo Brotherhood

OLIVIA ASH

No one screws with my family.

My sister and I are human orphans raised by the world's best assassin, taught to steal and kill our way through the dragonlands under her watchful eye. Grown men fear us, and no one knows we're coming until it's too late to run.

Irena and I—we're *good*. The best. In a dog-eat-dragon kind of world, we have to be. But someone betrayed us. Someone we trusted with our lives.

Irena is missing. My mentor is gone. And as for me… the man responsible for this mess thought he killed me. He kicked me into a pit, and he left me to die.

But I don't give up that easy.

In the darkness, facing death itself, I fused with dragons. I had no choice. This is ancient magic, and dangerous people want it. They want *me,* dead or alive, and they'll start a war if that's what it takes to control me.

The magic I discovered—the magic these brutal people want—it's mine, plain and simple. No one can take it from me. And I'm coming back from the dead.

For blood. For vengeance.

For Irena.

CONTENTS

CHAPTER ONE

T onight, I'm out for *blood.*

As I press my back against the mansion wall, body tense and ready for war, the modified handgun I'm holding warms against my palm. Custom scopes and attachments lie against the barrel, ready at a moment's notice.

Every movement I make, every glance, is made with intention.

Precision.

Purpose.

Find the vial of green liquid that can save Irena's life, then get the hell out of here.

Usually, I try not to slit throats unless it's a direct order. I go in. I steal. I get out. But this is different.

This is for *family.*

Sisters stay together. Always. And these bastards tried to *kill* mine.

The windows we pass show hints of a crescent moon suspended in the cold midnight sky, but I'm used to the darkness. Like the other corridors I've stolen through tonight, this hallway is empty, with only a thin ray of light streaming from around the corner to illuminate my path through the smuggler's mansion.

Some asshole named Mason Greene—a dragon shifter with a penchant for inflicting pain—owns this place.

According to his dossier, Mason's victims usually beg for death long before he's done with them. But we're here because he has one of the only known reserves of the antidote Irena needs.

That's all my mentor will tell me.

Stealing from dragons. For most, it's suicide. For Spectres like us, it's our forte.

Silent as a ghost, Zurie races ahead of me. I sprint to keep up with my mentor, forced to just follow regardless of how much I want to move faster, to get to the vial sooner, to save Irena's life and find out what the hell happened that made her so sick.

Zurie won't tell me the truth, but Irena will once—*if* —she wakes up. And I have a feeling I won't like it.

We slow as we near an open doorway, and Zurie holds up a fist, the silent order to stop. I obey. I always have, for as long as I can remember.

This life—the sneaking, the stealing, the stealth, the murder—it's all I've ever known.

With the subtlest of movements, Zurie peeks around the wall into the open room beyond. She holds up two fingers, another silent order.

Two cameras. Two voids.

Without a sound, I lift my shirt hem and unzip the thin bag strapped to my abdomen, fishing out two silver devices the size of my thumbnail. I hand her one and keep the other for myself. Silently, I shift the various attachments on my gun's scope until I get to the one I want.

Zurie hesitates, fingers spread in warning. Two seconds later, she nods.

The command to move.

In unison, we roll into the empty room, pausing only to kneel and fire the voids at the camera wiring. Our silencers muffle the thundering booms of gunshots to mere pops.

One shot each. No failure permitted.

I'm *never* allowed to fail.

And I don't.

The voids hit, sparking briefly before the little red light on each camera goes out.

Dragons have magic, sure, but we humans have tech. It's our magic, in a way. Our only means of fighting back against the supernatural creatures who have all but overtaken us as masters of the planet.

They hide behind governments and lobbyists, sure, but we humans know the dragons rule our world from behind the curtain.

With the red lights on the cameras out, we're golden. Thanks to the void devices, the cameras will play back the last fifteen seconds on a loop, giving us free rein of this part of the house. The only way a guard would've seen us is if he'd been watching as we fired, and since most watchmen have dozens of screens to monitor, we're in the clear.

Probably.

With the cams covered, I scope the room. An ornate, twenty-person dining table takes up most of the floor, stacks of cash simply sitting on the surface. I scan the piles, guessing there's probably six hundred grand laying out in the open.

Hmm. How trusting.

I'm on edge. So far, we've snuck by every guard we've seen. We're good, sure, but even we usually have to kill *someone*.

Because I like not dying, I tap Zurie twice on the back of her arm, a silent request to pause and discuss.

"What *now*, Rory?" she snaps, her voice a barely audible whisper.

"I don't like this," I say quietly, my tone hard and wary as I ignore her annoyance so I can make my point. "It's too easy."

She huffs. "No one knows we're here. Focus."

I grimace, disagreeing but overruled.

Fine.

We carry on through the mansion, slipping from shadow to shadow, never making a noise, never leaving so much as a hair behind.

Zurie is wrong. I know it in my bones and can feel it in every scar on my body from every lesson learned the hard way. I can almost feel the dragon eyes on the back on my head and can almost taste the lingering tension in the air as they lie in wait for us. Zurie calls this paranoia my imagination, the reason Irena was chosen as Zurie's successor instead of me, but I don't care what anyone calls it.

I call it instinct. And it's almost always *right.*

It doesn't matter, though. I'm not leaving this mansion without that green goo Irena needs, no matter who I have to kill to get it.

No matter how many traps I set off on the way.

Because I'm certain, now. This is a trap.

The thing that concerns me most, though? Somehow, they know we're coming. Spectres are feared because we steal through the night, silent as ghosts and just as easily overlooked.

As a Spectre, no one is supposed to know I'm coming for them until it's too late to do a damn thing about it.

Zurie leads us down another hallway, following the stolen map on her wrist display. We pause at a set of double doors, and she gestures toward the far wall. I nod and duck around her, ready to kick it in, to finally storm this place and take what we need.

I've never loved stealing, despite how often Zurie makes me do it. But this time, it's for Irena.

For her, I would do anything.

Zurie presses her ear against the door, frowning as she listens. Her brown eyes shift, catching my attention, and she shakes her head once.

Empty room.

My jaw tenses. My whole damn *body* tenses. Dragon families operate like the mafia—no kings here, no common law, just one Boss and the dragons who obey him. And this mansion belongs to an underling of the Vaer family, dragons who don't play nice even among themselves.

Smugglers.

Traffickers.

Hitmen.

They're not going to leave a stronghold like this *empty*, especially not one filled to the brim with cash and probably stuffed with stolen goods.

I grip my gun tighter, waiting for the trap to spring.

Waiting for someone to shoot.

Zurie stands, shoulders squared, eyes on the door-knob. To my horror, she's going in, even though I would rather scout some more to get a feel for what's really going on.

But my mentor isn't stupid. If she's seriously considering this despite the red flags, despite the danger I know she sees, then she must be more desperate than I realized.

Zurie saw what happened to Irena. I didn't. And whatever it was, this entire situation must be so much worse than I thought.

She nods, the silent order to go. As always, I obey.

In unison, we kick the door in and roll. I scope the room, gun drawn, and the first thing I see is the clear bottle on a table by the windows, the vial filled with glowing green liquid.

I have a fleeting moment of joy at finding the antidote before the lights go out, and my body immediately floods with cold dread.

In the darkness, time seems to slow as my other senses kick into high gear. Boots scuffle over the floor. Eight—no, nine—men. Their heavy breath, the swish of their clothes. The clink of their handguns at their waists, jostling in the holsters.

These men walk with purpose. Direction. No stumbling, no cussing under their breath.

Great, they have night vision goggles. And I *don't*.

But I've been in way worse situations than this. Hell, my *training* was worse than this. These men won't shift indoors and risk destroying their precious master's pretty house, so that gives me an advantage.

My ear twitches at the ever-nearing thumps of their

boots on the floor, and I aim into the shadows. I fire three rounds. Two hit. One smashes through a window.

Damn. A wasted bullet.

My victims fall with heavy thuds to the hardwood, and the others don't take their time anymore. The rest run toward me at full speed.

Idiots.

Zurie fires two shots as I take my next aim. I get another bullet in before the thundering boots get too close. The air around me shifts, and as my eyes strain in the utter darkness, I tap into the instinct and muscle memory that has helped me survive all these years of Zurie's brutal training.

A man grabs my hand. I twist back his fingers, breaking them. He yells out in pain. Another man's arm goes around my neck. I coil in his grip, using his own body weight against him as I fling him off of me.

One by one, they grab my arms, my neck, my waist. Quick as lightning, I throw them off, breaking bones any chance I can. A broken man can't fight back.

Rule 37 of the Spectres—always deal the first and final blow.

A Spectre never leaves home without weapons, and my body is covered with them. I'm finally able to reach the knife in my boot, and I dig it into the side of the nearest attacker. He yells in agony. I twist the blade, and he falls to his knees.

But then I hear Zurie scream.

It's short. Quick. Shattering. It's a scream of deep agony, the kind of scream that would escape my mouth during training when she broke too many bones to prove a point. The kind that got me additional punishment for revealing weakness.

A scream like that is punishable. Unpermitted. Absolutely not allowed.

If *she* screams, we're in deep shit.

I spin and bury the knife in the nearest man. He gargles, and I think I've hit his throat. I don't care.

I bolt toward Zurie, but now there are more boots thundering over the hardwood. Ten more men run in from both ahead and behind us. Great. They must have been stationed throughout the house, not entirely sure which of their traps would spring on us first.

But now they know exactly where we are.

Secret doors hidden in the walls burst open, their hinges barely squeaking as they give way to more and more soldiers.

Twenty men.

Thirty.

This entire mission is crumbling apart.

Rule 12 of the Spectres—always know when and how to escape.

The *how* is easy. I saw it the moment we kicked in the door. Two windows on the far wall, easy enough to break through, most likely with thick grass to soften my landing. Hell, my bullet already shattered one, which might make the escape even easier.

But the *when*—that's what I've always had trouble with. Zurie calls it stupidity. Irena calls it courage.

I call it... well, I haven't figured out what it really is, yet.

The boots rumble closer. More and more shifters funnel into the room.

There are only seconds left.

I have to think fast.

I have four choices: save Irena, save Zurie, save both, or save myself and get the hell out of here.

Both. Both is good.

I only need two things: the green vial and my mentor. They're both in this room. They're both within an arm's reach, but as more and more dragon shifters funnel in, my odds are getting worse by the second.

I finally reach a body lying still on the ground. My eyes are slowly adjusting to the darkness, and I can finally make out the slim silhouette of a feminine figure on the hardwood, surrounded by the broken bodies of a half dozen men. She has a pulse, but it's faint. She's barely breathing.

The vial is probably still on the table, the bait to their trap. Little did they realize they left it in the perfect spot, right by my exit.

I can still do this.

And when I do, maybe Zurie will finally let me go on missions alone.

Maybe she'll finally trust me, finally give me a bit of freedom. Finally give me my initiation, letting me graduate from a life of perpetual training and obedience to one of at least a *bit* of autonomy.

Icy pangs of adrenaline shoot through me, propelling me forward, giving me strength. With my fingers frantically brushing along the floor, I reach for the nearest dead man's face, my fingers brushing the cold metal of a set of night vision goggles.

Score.

With two swift tugs, I rip it off his head and put it on mine, my eyes adjusting quickly as the world turns bright green.

The first thing I see is a fist, aimed right for my face.

I dodge, twisting out of the way and rolling to avoid Zurie's body. The men follow, each trying to hit me. A few have knives. A few have guns strapped to their waists, but not even they are stupid enough to shoot wildly into a crowded, pitch-black room.

In the flurry of the moment, I can barely pause to breathe. Fists fly at my face. Blades narrowly pass my nose as I duck to avoid them. One grazes my jaw, drawing blood.

I don't flinch. I'm used to pain.

A fist lands in my gut. I grunt and double over,

dodging another blow, but a knee hits my side. I grimace, trying not to fall.

If I hit the ground, this is over.

I *cannot* fail.

Determined to shatter them, to do whatever it takes to save Zurie and Irena, I give my everything to the fight. Every move I make is like lightning. I give into the instinct, give into my training, and let it guide me. My fists hit throats, eyes, abdomens, groins—I don't care. Anything to take them down. To break them.

They fall. One by one, they give way. I can see the exit again, see the bottle on the table.

There's hope.

I dodge a blow to my forehead and roll, using my momentum to pick up Zurie fireman-style. She's heavy, pretty much solid muscle on a five-foot-ten frame, but I've done this before.

Something hits the small of my back as I retreat. It burns. Electricity shoots through me, rooting me in place, and I grit my teeth in agony as what can only be a high-voltage taser pulse rips through me.

It finally stops.

My legs give out on me, and I drop to my knees. Zurie rolls off my back, just five feet from the vial.

Struggling to stand, disoriented from the taser, I take a second too long to turn around, to face my attacker.

Someone rips the night vision goggles off my face.

The metal scratches my cheek as it's tugged off. Once more lost in the darkness, I fight.

When cornered, I *always* fight.

There's no surrender for a Spectre.

There's not much light, but through muscle memory and a bit of luck, I land a punch in someone's throat. Thick fingers grab my neck, and I kick at where I think his groin should be. He yelps and goes limp. Bingo.

But as the men circle me, more and more funneling in through every entrance, the tide slips out of my favor. For every blow I land, I now get hit twice.

I'm losing.

Before I can revisit rule twelve, an arm wraps around my neck, choking me. Two blows hit my stomach. I can barely breathe, and pain splinters through every inch of my body.

In the shadows, one man chuckles darkly.

"You're just too much fun, little girl," he says. "I think I'll play with you a bit before I kill you."

This must be Mason.

I am so *screwed*.

There's a whistle, like something shooting through the air toward my face. A sharp pain splinters through my temple. A quick rush of hot blood falls instantly down cheek. My body goes limp, and the last shred of moonlight fades from the pitch-black room.

CHAPTER TWO

I wake to the metallic clink of chains.

My head aches. The world around me blurs, shifting in and out of focus. Nothing but shadows. No shapes, no colors. I groan, but something over my mouth stifles the sound. A gag.

Oh, awesome. This day just keeps getting better.

"Good, you're up," a man says.

Still disoriented, all I can tell is I'm being dragged along the ground. I lean my chin upward to get a view of whomever spoke.

Above me, a dark green and gray forest canopy sways in a gentle breeze, still a bit blurry as I come to. A man smirks down at me, his dark hair a wiry mess, his square jaw covered in stubble.

He'd be hot if he weren't trying to kill me.

I yell some muffled obscenities at him, but that only

makes him laugh. He tugs a bit harder on the chains in his hands, and I feel metal cuffs around my wrists tighten in response. I'm skidding across the forest floor on my butt, my heels digging a thin trail in the dirt and dead leaves behind us.

"You shouldn't steal from the Vaer," Mason says, cracking his neck. "We aren't forgiving. Especially not of Spectres."

I stiffen, momentarily distracted from my thoughts of escape.

He knows.

How the *hell* does he know?

Mason laughs. "Oh, we know what you are. What that other woman is. She's the Ghost, and you're her little successor. Her heir."

I roll my eyes. I *wish.* It would be nice to give the orders for once, but that's Irena's future. Not mine. However, if it keeps him off Irena's tail, then fine, I'll pretend I'm the heir.

Besides, this is Survival 101—never show your cards. And this idiot is putting them down on the table, one by one, gloating as if he's won the game already even though I haven't even shown him my hand.

When dealing with the Spectres, no one wins until the other person is dead.

This is a rookie move. Either he's new, or he's cocky. He's just a bit older than me, maybe twenty-nine, but I've seen younger dragons ruling mansions like his if their daddies are rich enough. Judging by his build and the scars covering his arms, I guess he's experienced but cocky.

I can work with this.

"We were told the Ghost would show up alone, though," Mason continued. "After we got that other girl in our last trap, I was sure I'd had all the fun I would get to have. But I'm glad I have one last toy to play with. I think you'll be fun, Rory."

The way he says my name shoots chills through me. I don't feel fear—I'm not permitted to, not as a Spectre —but I *do* feel the icy dread that comes with a madman knowing who I am.

This needs to end. Now.

I rub the gag against my shoulder, slowly working it free as he continues to gloat. Before I can, he yanks me to the left, *hard*, and I roll onto my stomach. I tense as the chains tighten around my body, wriggling, trying to work my hands free of the shackles.

A boot pushes against my back, and I grimace as I sink into the layers of leaves and dirt under his weight. I momentarily pause, letting him think I'll play nice, letting him think I'm afraid.

As I go still, I glance around to get a feel for where we are. For an exit plan. Thin gray fog slinks through the dark forest, casting strange shadows against the trees. More astonishing, though, are the three statues of life-sized dragons rising from the rotting forest floor, bound in marble chains similar to mine.

Each of the stone dragons is frozen in time, howling up at the sky as their own shackles tie them to the ground. Between the figures, the forest floor caves, sloping downward as if there's a giant pit beneath the leaves.

My eyes widen. This can't be good.

"Know where we are?" Mason asks.

He drops the chains on my back, and sharp pains shoot through my shoulder blades as the heavy metal hits me. I grimace, doing my best to hide my reaction as I glare at him.

"No, I guess you wouldn't." He walks to the nearest statue, one of a slender dragon whose body coils around itself as she screams at the sky. "It's just some old dragon legend, after all. You Spectres have probably never even heard of it."

With his back finally turned, I see it—the gun at his waist. Good, I can use that. Though human caliber guns feel like insect bites to a dragon, even in human form, Mason probably carries higher caliber weapons to put other dragons in their place. I'm betting a bullet from that gun would kill him, easy. I just need to get close enough to grab it, to catch him off guard.

Subtly, with barely any movement, I begin to slip my wrists from the shackles. This angle is better, and it gives me more leverage. Any minute now, I'll break free. Though by now I could also work the gag loose, I leave it on as a distraction. If he thinks I'm still bound, maybe I can buy myself some time.

I need to keep him talking. As he looks at me over his shoulder, my eyes narrow in a ploy to make him think I feel helpless.

It works. He grins. "I need Zurie for a bit, to see what info she has for me, but our contact tells us you're disposable."

In the metal shackles behind my back, my hands tighten into fists. I burn with anger, with hatred, with the raging realization that someone betrayed us. Someone played Zurie. Played Irena. Played *me*.

Someone I know.

He leans down and grabs a fistful of my hair, that stupid cocky grin of his really starting to get on my nerves. "People die here, Rory. Ready for a little fun?"

I mutter more obscenities at him, my words still muffled by the gag, as I continue to subtly work free of the shackles.

"I've sent, hmm..." He pauses, staring at the forest canopy briefly as he thinks. "Two hundred and forty-eight people here to die. Ready to be number two hundred and forty-nine?"

Dear *God*, I wish I could just work out of these chains already.

They're so damn *tight*.

"Wait, where are my manners?" Mason feigns a

modest chuckle and stands. "I should tell you the legend first, don't you think? To set the scene."

I groan in annoyance with this idiot, the sound still muffled by the gag. Jesus, I want to kill him so badly.

He pats the chained dragon figure affectionately. "Some say there's magic beneath these statues, just waiting to break free, to find the one who's worthy. What do you think, Rory? Is it just an old story?"

He smacks his fist against the dragon statue, harder this time, and the figure's eyes burn red.

I pause my wriggling, gaping at the statue in shock.

The dragon is glowing.

This. Is. Not. Good.

No. Wait. I need to be rational. Clear-headed. Focused.

I tense, scanning the pit and statues, taking it all in and trying to see it from a new angle. While humans know very little about dragon shifters and their magic, this could all be a ruse. There's a chance this is just some theatrical death machine, a chance there's no magic at all. He could simply like to make people feel fear before he kills them, make them feel small in the face of the power of dragons that has left so many humans cowering through the millennia.

After all, his dossier did say he likes to play with his food.

Right, that's all this is. It has to be.

But if I'm being honest, a lingering flicker of doubt

burns in my gut. If this place really does have dragon magic, I am one hundred and ten percent screwed.

The ground trembles, and in a blinding flash of red light, the leaves between the three statues disintegrate into dust. Dozens of thin smoke trails swirl upward toward the night sky as the last leaves burn away, the thin black coils barely visible as they escape through the thick treetops overhead.

With the leaves gone, I can finally see what was hidden beneath them—a steep and sloping pit lined with marble, glimmering in the low moonlight of the dark forest. Evenly spaced lines of red light glow through the stone, leading toward the center fifty feet below, where the walls meet at a small circular symbol I can't make out. The base of the pit is perhaps five feet in diameter, tops.

"What do you think, Rory?" Mason's foot is on my back again, and this time I can't stifle the pained groan as the metal chains bite into my back. "Are you worthy?"

Before I can wrestle free, he kicks me. Hard. I roll over the edge, sliding down the slick marble walls, doing my best to avoid the red lights leading toward the center as heat radiates from them. Heart in my chest, my training kicks in, and I maneuver my feet to catch the brunt of the fall so that my neck doesn't break at the bottom.

My heels hit the ground hard, and I yell as my joints

ache from the force of the fall. I briefly pause to catch my breath, but there's no moment for respite.

"You okay down there?" Mason yells, laughing. "Don't want you to get hurt!"

Though I'm still chained, I work the gag free with my shoulder and glare at Mason. "You'd better kill me yourself, coward."

"I could," he said with an uninterested shrug. "But then you wouldn't make the sounds I like to hear. There's something about this pit, Rory," he says wistfully, almost dreamily. "Whatever it does to people, I just can't reproduce it myself. I've tried, trust me. I simply like the way it makes people squeal."

"You're messed *up*."

"Yeah, maybe," he says with a lazy wave of his hand. "But at least I'm not boring."

I try to climb out of the pit, to wring this asshole's skinny neck, but it's useless. I slide back down each time, barely getting ten feet before I fall again. I scan the walls, trying to think of something that will keep him talking. I need to delay this and buy myself as much time as possible.

"Who told you about me? About the Spectres?"

"And Zurie? And Irena?" He mocks the hard edge in my voice, smirking all the while. "Don't worry about that, baby. Worry about yourself."

More beams of red light shoot down the edges of the pit, and I jump back into the middle to avoid getting burned. They surround the small circular plat-form beneath my boots, illuminating the symbol I hadn't been able to make out before—a chained dragon with broken wings, trying to fly.

"I'll take care of Irena, don't you worry," Mason says, looking down at me from the edge of the pit, gloating. "I'll even make sure she wakes up before I kill her, give her the antidote myself. Scouts honor." He winks. "Hell, maybe I'll bring her here once I'm done with her. Reunite you two."

"I'll haunt the *fuck* out of you if you so much as *touch* her!" I shout, kicking the pit wall in my fury.

The marble hums. The red light brightens, almost blinding now. I squint to shield my eyes as best I can, glaring at Mason all the while, wishing I could reach up there and simply end him.

I can't die.

I *won't*.

Not yet.

The humming stops. The light fades. In the bewil-dering moments that follow, it's deadly silent. Mason's smile falters, and for a second, I wonder if it broke. If whatever he rigged up here is faulty.

But then it hits me.

A thundering boom. It shakes me to the core, rattles my bones, boils my blood. I gasp and fall to my knees.

Beneath me, the symbol burns red hot. I try to avoid it, but it's impossible. Every crease in the marble, every line around me glows gold. Singeing my skin. I curse, trying to move away from the light, but it's hopeless.

The ground beneath me drops at least ten feet, just straight down. No warning. My stomach flies into my throat as my world plummets.

The chains around me tremble, as if unseen hands are ripping at them. The shackles on my wrists shatter. The chains swirl around me like a tornado of metal, the silver slowly turning red until they burn away and dissolve into dust.

For a fleeting minute, I'm happy.

For a fleeting moment, I'm free.

It doesn't last long.

Beneath me, new chains appear. Gold ones this time. They shoot from the ground, from *nothing*, and circle me. They coil around my arms, my legs, my torso, my neck. I gasp for air, barely able to breathe as they tighten around me like snakes, burning, scorching every inch of my body.

And then they *pull.*

I'm drawn downward, toward the ground. I feel the world around me slowly ripping apart, and I'm left with that same urgent thought as before.

I can't die now.

I won't.

Not yet.

I take one last look at Mason, determined to

remember who did this to me, to get my revenge even if I have to do it from the grave.

But he isn't gloating.

He looks… scared.

Mason draws his gun and aims it at me, his face pale, his hand shaking a bit, and I realize what's happening.

I realize the truth.

The pit… the legend… it's real. He wasn't lying. This isn't some fabrication he made to scare his prey. He was meddling with real magic, real lore, and after the hundreds of people he's killed in this pit, he thought the magic was broken.

But it's not.

Whatever this place is, whatever secrets and power it holds, it woke up. After killing all those countless others, it *chose* me.

Mason aims his pistol at my head. I stare him down, in agony, unable to move as the chains around me tighten.

It's a perfect shot. No one could miss it. I'm trapped, and he can't allow me to live, not with what I am. Not with what I know.

His finger curls around the trigger, the barrel aimed at the space between my eyes, and the thundering crack of a gunshot rings through the forest as he fires.

CHAPTER THREE

I n a blistering moment of confusion, my world shifts.

I'm not in the forest anymore. The air around me shimmers, blue and white, glimmering and rippling like water. The pressure of the chains releases, and though I can't shake them off, I'm finally able to stand. My hands are bound, but I can thankfully still move a little despite the chains around my legs.

Through the glowing haze, I see glimpses of the world I came from, of the pit, of the forest far above.

Of Mason.

Every movement in the other world is slowed to a crawl. The bullet cuts through the air toward me, slipping slowly through the veil, and I try to step aside.

But I can't.

In the tiny space at the bottom of the pit, there's

nowhere to go. As I try to shift even an inch out of the way, to let the bullet slip by, the chains around my legs lock and root me in place.

No.

This can't be it.

So close to a way out, so close to survival, I refuse to die.

The bullet carves its way through the air as I struggle to bend out of the way.

It hits.

And, without an ounce of pain, it slices through my stomach. I shudder, the sensation not unlike dipping my toe in cold water, but otherwise the high caliber bullet passes harmlessly through. It digs into the marble on the other side of me, kicking up dust and leaving a small crater in the wall instead of in me.

"Holy shit," I say softly.

I just survived a gunshot to the stomach. No bleeding. No pain.

Whatever this magic is, I freaking *love* it.

So far, anyway.

I glance around this new world of shimmering light, taking it in, wondering where the hell I am or if I went anywhere at all.

"Rory," a woman's voice echoes in my mind, everywhere and nowhere all at once.

Oh *hell* no.

I flinch, wishing I had my hands free, wishing I

could be ready to break someone's nose, but there's no one behind me. I'm alone in the shimmering mist, isolated in this world I don't understand.

Worst of all, though, her voice seems to burrow into me. It takes root, like it wants to live in my bones. Her voice… it sends chills through my body. My intuition flares, and I know in my heart I don't like her at *all.*

"You now carry great magic," a second voice says. A man this time. "*Our* magic."

"The power of ancient dragons," another man adds. "The true dragons. The First."

"Others will seek you out," the woman says, her voice still grating against my soul. "They will find you. They will hunt you. Trust no one but us."

"Come to us," the first man orders.

I roll my eyes. Yeah, right. Like I'm going to seek out creepy disembodied voices from beyond the veil.

But it's probably not wise to piss off magical voices floating through an otherworldly mist. This wasn't exactly covered in my training, but I feel confident taking *that* metaphorical stab in the dark.

"Who are you?" I ask instead.

They answer, each speaking over the other, but their voices begin to fade. I can only make out a word here and there.

"…ancient dragons…"

"…you can trust…"

"…order of the…"

"Wait, what?" I say, trying to take a step toward where I think they're coming from. Even if they creep me out, this *is* their magic. Their clues might be important to my survival.

But I can't move. The pit and chains stop me, and once more, I'm stuck.

"Rory!" the woman screams, her voice shrill and panicked. It sends another cold chill up my spine, stirring up emotions I don't fully understand.

In the silence that follows, I remain still, ready to headbutt someone if I have to, breathing heavily as I wait in the eerie quiet. Ears straining, I listen for the voices that are no longer there, fully prepared for them to come back, for this to get ugly, and fast.

But no one returns.

In my training, I've survived hell. Four times in my life, I've taken on two shifted dragons at once and won. I've been locked in a room with twelve human assassins, but after an hour of blood, I was the only one left standing. I've stolen from the vaults of kings and governments to pad Zurie's pockets. And now, thanks to Mason, I've survived a gunshot to the gut.

But even after all of that, after all the horror and blood I've endured throughout my life, I hope I *never* meet *her*. This woman in the mist.

Because that voice—her presence—it feels like death itself.

When it's clear the voices won't return, I finally

relax. Just a little. One threat down, one to go. I glance over my shoulder, scanning the lip of the pit.

Mason is gone.

I cuss under my breath and try to slip out of the chains. I need to get the hell out of here, to end this nightmare and chase after Mason.

But they get *tighter*.

And just like that, my body freezes. It's as if, for a moment, someone else has control. I can't move. I can't speak. I grimace, fighting it, fighting for control of my hands, my feet—anything.

The golden chains begin to hum and shift, slinking over my skin like snakes. But this time, it's different. They don't pull me down.

They *burn* me.

It's agonizing.

The pain eats away at me, digging into my soul, carving into the last shreds of resilience I've built up over the years of torture and training.

And, slowly, a second sensation begins as well. It starts as a trickle, as the barest hint of something more, and builds to a crescendo with every passing second.

Power.

It fills every vein, every pore, every ounce of muscle. It burrows into every crevice, into my throat, my spine.

It consumes me.

For as long as I can, I fight the urge to scream. As

this foreign energy burrows into me, it burns, getting worse and worse until the agony is too much. My body can't take this. I feel as though I'm being split apart layer by layer, as if my skin will simply dissolve at any moment, unable to take the strain.

When I can't take this anymore, I open my mouth to scream—and nothing comes out.

I have no voice.

My mind fractures in the agony, and I lose track of time.

Eventually, the chains release me. In a sudden blissful rush, the pain disappears. I fall to the ground, heaving, my body trembling. I'm spent. I have nothing left. Everything aches. Everything hurts. I close my eyes, unable to take any more of the misery, my breath not coming fast enough as I try to regain my composure.

Somehow, despite the pain, I begin to slowly buzz with a numb kind of energy. Tenderly, I lift my head, examining my fingers as my vision blurs in and out of focus.

The chains.

They *fused* to me.

The gold links snake up my body, merged with my skin like glowing tattoos that climb up my arms and legs. Stunned, a tad horrified, I lift my shirt to find them there as well, beneath the bag still strapped to my abdomen.

I stammer in shock, unable to fully process how my entire body is covered in these strange chains that glow with the magic of dragons.

With each passing second, the ache subsides a bit more. A slow rush of strength fills me, like a dull heartbeat, another life within my chest. A second pulse in my throat, in my head, in my soul.

Something *other*.

Something inhuman.

Before I can piece it all together, before I can make sense of this insanity, a deafening roar shakes the ground beneath my feet.

And just like that, the blue and white mist disappears. Instantly, I'm thrown back in the marble pit, the red light gone, the statues dull and lifeless once more. I'm trapped in the hole beneath the forest canopy, alone beneath the cold crescent moon.

In the agonizing silence that follows, all I can hear is my thundering heart. Slowly, I try to calm myself—to still my pulse, to steady my breath. It barely works, but I have to get it together.

For once, I have no idea what's going to happen next.

Irena's gone. Zurie's gone. I am alone, and I'm the only one who can save them.

My world has crumbled, all thanks to Mason. I don't know what this pit did to me, but I do know I have a second chance—a chance to gut him alive.

And this time, I will not fail.

A massive shadow cuts through the darkness overhead, and I instinctively press my back against the wall of the pit to keep whatever it is from seeing me. Roars echo through the night, shrill and deadly. With a cold pang of dread and a few pats to the various pockets on my pants, I realize that I'm unarmed in a forest filled with God-knows-what.

They will hunt you, the voice in the mist said.

Fantastic. Whoever "they" are, it seems they've found me.

Time to get the hell out of here—and plan my revenge on Mason Greene.

CHAPTER FOUR

As the dark shadows circle above, my body still trembles from the pain, from everything I just endured, unwilling to move.

But I have to. I have to get out of here.

The beautiful strength I felt before, the buzzing energy, it's gone. All I'm left with is the throbbing ache that floods my veins with every heartbeat.

Out of habit, I feel for the bag around my abdomen. Good, it's still here. But as I lower my shirt, I once more catch the dull glow of the chains fused with my body.

Damn. Those are still here, too.

I shake the thought, urging myself to focus. What matters is I have my bag. It has my gear, and even though I don't have my gun anymore, it's easy to get another thanks to Zurie's connections. I'll need my tech if I'm going to fix this mess. I'll need it to rescue Zurie. To save Irena.

A dragon roars nearby, his voice shaking the trees. The trunks shiver, as if in fear, and a scattering of dark green leaves float on the wind as he flies through the night sky overhead.

Before I worry about Zurie or Irena, I should probably worry about saving myself.

I stare up at the marble pit, at the fifty feet of slick stone I couldn't scale before. I curse under my breath, desperate for a way out.

Stubborn as all hell, I try again to climb. My boots slip on the smooth marble, and in a moment of reflex, I dig my fingers into the stone, fully expecting to fall.

I don't.

This time, my fingers dig into the pit as if it's dirt. Tiny chunks of marble tumble past me, and I briefly pause to marvel at what I just did.

Breaking stone as if it's butter. And it didn't even hurt.

The pit.

The magic.

Did it really just—

Another roar kicks me from my daze. I'll have to figure this out later.

As I climb toward the edge of the pit, two shadows careen toward me from above, crashing into one of the statues. Dust kicks into the air as a silver ice dragon and an orange fire dragon wrestle each other, equally matched, their jaws snapping as they reach for each other's throat.

The orange dragon spews a stream of fire, catching the canopy ablaze. Not to be outdone, the silver dragon screeches and spits a stream of ice shards, each sharp as a dagger. Four dig deep into the orange dragon's hide, and he screams in pain.

They don't look over, and it seems like they haven't seen me yet.

I climb faster.

The dragons are fighting each other. For what? For me? For whatever magic I just awoke?

They must be.

Super.

I pull myself out of the pit and roll onto the ground, every fiber of my being begging for rest, but I push myself forward. I can't exactly have a power nap here, of all places.

Spectres specialize in dragon hunting. Solo, we can take on two fully shifted fire or ice dragons at a time. But as I glance between gaps in the trees, I count thirty. Forty. Fifty. The numbers climb as I snake through the woods, doing my best to keep my cover. At the same time, I'm trying to get my bearings.

It's a lot to process at once, but I have no other choice. This is do or die, and I'm not going to die today.

Looking around, I have *no* idea where I am. Best guess is Mason dragged me into the woods behind the mansion, but even that's just a hunch.

The trees end abruptly at an open field, and I pause beneath the trees to examine the sky. Hundreds of dragons circle the forest, their dark silhouettes blurring against the stars like a swarm.

A soft string of curses escapes me, because everything just got so much *worse.*

And there—at the lowest tier of the silhouettes, a large black dragon joins the horde. The veins in his wings glow blue, as do the spines along his back, and as he opens his mouth, I see a brilliant blue light burning within him.

A thunderbird.

Here.

Coming after *me.*

Fire dragons are deadly. Ice dragons are worse. But thunderbirds—they're the rarest dragons, the only ones to have any hint of the legendary magic that could raze cities and charm nations. If they're here, the dragon Bosses have probably been notified of what happened in the pit. That means powerful dragons with incredible connections and dangerous friends are hunting me, too.

Yay me.

"Damn it all to hell," I mutter, ready to find a different route for escape.

But as I turn to leave, the thunderbird's head tilts towards me, as if he senses me. As if he knows where I am.

Across the expanse, our eyes meet.

And it hits me.

Much like the magic from the pit, a thundering jolt shoots through me like a bullet. It shakes me, rattling my bones, and I tightly grip a nearby tree to catch my balance.

In that instant, I know.

He's dangerous.

And no matter what I try, I will never escape him.

Like a bolt of lightning, he streams toward me with the speed of a fighter jet. His wings curl, tightening, and I've seen that angle before.

He intends to grab me and fly off.

Like hell.

If he picks me up, I'll stab the shit out of him. I'm a Spectre, not some hapless damsel, and I *don't* get carried off in a dragon's claws.

Tapping into my last shreds of energy, I dip into the shadows of the forest, bolting along the tree line. I dig deep into my reserves, relying on adrenaline and muscle memory to remain unseen. All the while, I keep an eye on the thunderbird any chance I get.

But he knows. Somehow, he's tracking my movements even though he's blocked by the trees. Through gaps between the trunks, I watch him fly, angling his body to follow my movements.

As the thunderbird stalks me, another black dragon careens over the canopy above and intercepts him. They tumble to the ground, kicking up grass and dirt, leaving a crater in their wake. The thunderbird roars in frustration, the sound unnatural and eerie, but I push forward.

In the distance, across a short stretch of meadow, a coil of smoke trails into the sky. Artificial light bathes small sections of the trees, and I thank my lucky stars.

A house.

Where there's a house, there's probably a car.

Where there's a car, there's a way to hotwire myself out of this mess.

Even if it's Mason's mansion, even if it's crawling with guards, they're likely busy dealing with the dragon swarm. There isn't a single thunderbird known in the Vaer family, which means *other* dragon families are here—and dragons hate having other dragons on their turf.

Any guards I come across will be distracted. I can get in, steal a car, and get out unseen.

I briefly think about Zurie, about the vial of green goo, but Mason's no idiot. He'll have cleared out the house the second Zurie was apprehended. No one leaves the bait behind, especially when their target escapes.

No, rescue has to wait. I have to get to the safehouse, move Irena's unconscious body to a secure location, and only then can I come up with a plan.

The wind kicks up, my brown hair stinging my face in the strong gusts as more dragons join the horde overhead.

They're waiting. Waiting for a sign, for something to chase.

I have to time this right, or I'm going to have hell itself chasing after me.

When I reach the edge of the forest, right off the shortest stretch of meadow between me and the next copse of evergreen trees, I pause in the shadows and wait. Observing, timing each wing beat, guessing which direction the swarm will move.

There. It's slowly tracking south. Good... kinda. At least it's not right over where I need to go.

A chorus of roars echoes overhead, slowly getting louder as they no doubt get more and more impatient. Several of the dragons on the lower edge of the swarm begin to fight, which sets off a chain reaction that slowly trickles upward through the cloud of massive silhouettes.

They're as distracted as they're going to be.

Now's my chance. Perhaps, my *only* chance.

I bolt through the field as fast as my feet will carry me. The other trees near, and for a fleeting moment, I have hope.

A rush of wind tussles my hair, and I look over my shoulder just as the largest red dragon I've ever seen lands mere feet from me. The ground shakes as his claws dig into the grass. He charges me, too close for me to escape, and I reach for the dagger in my boot.

Only, it's not there. Mason took it, along with all of my other weapons, when he captured me.

As I reach for the other pockets, hoping that asshole missed at least one weapon, the red dragon presses his head against my torso and pins me against a tree. He tilts his head slightly, one of his golden eyes zeroing in on me as the bark scrapes against my back. A shimmering golden stripe on his forehead briefly catches my eye, the glimmering line of scales trailing down his spine to his tail.

I twist beneath him, looking for any way to escape, but he's too big, too strong. I grimace as the bark bites into my spine, forcing me to still or risk breaking something.

For a moment, I wonder if this is it. If this is how I die.

He snorts in annoyance and presses his nose against the palm of my hand. *I won't kill you.*

"Whoa," I mutter, surprised despite the rest of the crazy in this situation. I didn't know dragons could use telepathy.

This is how we speak in our dragon forms, he says

curtly, as if it's obvious and not an earth-shattering revelation for me. *Now listen closely.*

I pause, body tense, watching him warily. "I'm listening."

Go to the Dragon Dojo. It's a neutral zone that belongs to the Fairfax family. You'll be safe there, and they can help you. Ask for Jace.

I pause, watching him, his expression intent and urgent. This dragon is... helping me?

No, it must be a game. A way to play with my mind.

I'm certainly not going to trust him.

I could just take you. He leans his powerful head a bit more against my torso, and my body aches under the pressure. *I could just force you to come with me.*

"Then why don't you?" I snap, not in the mood for games. He's bluffing, and I want to know why.

To his credit, his eyes soften. *Because you would never trust me. You would never stay. I would have to fight you forever. We don't have to hate each other, and I want you to see what life could be like. You don't know what you've gotten yourself into, but I do. I need you to trust me.*

I narrow my eyes in suspicion. Well, at least he's not an idiot.

He huffs impatiently, his gaze shifting briefly toward the swarm behind him. *Not all dragons are cruel, but many here right now absolutely are. You need to leave. Now. Get to the dojo, and you will be safe.*

I want to tell him that's never going to happen, but it looks like he might let me go. I keep quiet.

I'll hold off the others until you can escape. Go now. Move quickly.

With that, the massive red dragon bolts into the sky. Every beat of his wings, every movement of his body radiates power.

Authority.

Control.

He roars into the swarm, the ground shaking beneath my feet at the sheer strength of his voice, and a dozen dragons along the lower tier of the swarm scatter in fear.

I know I should run. This is my prime chance to escape, and my training is urging me to go. But as I stare after the red dragon, I'm simply perplexed. No dragon has ever shown me kindness. Not as a Spectre. Not as a human on the street. Not *ever*.

I'm... confused.

Zurie has always told me they're evil. Selfish. Vain. That they treat human life as disposable.

And maybe she's right. After all, these dragons all want something from me. Even the red one. He said so himself, in a way, so this is most likely just some mind game.

Rule 2 of the Spectres—trust no one.

I duck into the forest, running at full speed, with all the energy I have left. I'm not out of these woods yet, and even though I have no intention of following up with the red dragon's order, I recite the name of the dojo and its dragon family in my mind as I run, wondering what his connection to them is.

Maybe he's Jace, whoever that is.

Maybe he's not.

At the very least, it's a clue that might come in handy when I can pause to reflect on this madness.

As I escape toward the house, a deafening roar cuts through the trees. It sounds pained, frustrated, a little desperate. It reminds me of the thunderbird's cry, but I don't want to find out for sure.

CHAPTER FIVE

I tear down a dirt road in a Jeep I stole from a farmhouse, and though Zurie would be disappointed in me for having emotions, I feel bad for taking it. Hopefully, the owners have good insurance, but with several dragon armies after me, I don't have another choice.

The Jeep also doesn't have a top, which isn't ideal, but at this point, I don't have the luxury of being choosy.

The wind whips in my face, my long hair stinging my skin as I floor it. The Jeep's shocks do a decent job of absorbing the rough road, and even though I only have a vague idea of where I'm headed, at least it's away from the swarm.

I shift gears and push the Jeep faster.

Inwardly, I wrestle with my next step. I ache to go

back to the mansion, to get clues on Zurie's where-abouts, and to find that damn green goo so I can wake Irena and get her help with this craziness.

I already know what Irena will do once I heal her. Wake up. Listen. Laugh her ass off at my expense. Once she's done, she'll grab her gun and nod toward the door with that trademark *let's do this* attitude I've always admired.

I chuckle at the thought, but it doesn't last long.

My body tense, my knuckles aching from the tight grip on the steering wheel, I briefly glance in my rear view to eye the shrinking swarm of dragon silhouettes against the night sky.

Yes, I will head back to the mansion to find clues, but there's no use doing it right now. Mason will expect it. He'll have a trap set for me and, given all I've endured in the last few hours, I don't have the energy to face him. I can barely stand up as it is. The only thing keeping me moving at the moment is adrenaline, and even that's going to fade soon. I can't rely on it, not with so much at stake.

Soon—very soon—I will need to rest and recharge or risk making a fatal error. But first, I have a short list of things to do.

My next steps are easy. Go to the safehouse. Move the still-unconscious Irena. Regroup. Make a plan. Rescue Zurie.

I briefly glance at my arms, at the glowing chains

sticking out from under my sleeve. I already know how Zurie will react to this whole mess, too—she won't laugh like Irena will. She won't take this lightly. Hell, she might even take it as treason.

Rule 4 of the Spectres—don't fraternize with dragons. Ever. In any way.

Except to kill them, of course.

Movement in the mirror catches my eye. I tense as two dark gray dragons loom overhead, their massive heads angled toward me.

I groan in exasperation as the escape from hell continues.

We're no longer on dragon land, so now it's clear these dragons are completely fine with breaking the rules if it means nabbing me. Per human law, no dragon can fly under five hundred feet in a human-occupied area or it's considered an act of war.

Well, they just declared war, but only time will tell if any human government is going to do a thing about it.

The Jeep can't go much faster, but I push it to its limit, careening down the road, kicking up a trail of dust and using the overhanging branches to deter the dragons as much as I can. But a dragon doesn't give a shit about a tree, and as soon as they find a good opening, they're going to dive.

They're going to try to grab me out of this Jeep, and

this is exactly why I didn't want a car with an open roof.

Damn it.

The road bends and, around the curve, the path straightens. It's a solid stretch of about two hundred feet of open road. Barely any trees line this patch, and I'm out of cover.

Damn it!

Something falls from the last tree overhanging the road and thumps in the passenger seat. I swerve in surprise, frustrated that I could be so distracted I wouldn't notice something about to fall into my car.

A guy roughly my age now sits in the passenger seat, and he shoots me a charming wink as he twists in his seat to look back at the dragons. The wind from the open car blows through his dark brown hair, I can't help but notice the dark stubble over his jaw and the strong fighter's build of his body.

This is a warrior. A hot one.

I frown, still driving, and switch feet on the pedals so I can kick him out of my stolen vehicle.

"You might want to keep going, babe." He clicks his tongue in mock disappointment and points upward at the dragons as they snap at each other, each trying to out-maneuver the other for the inevitable dive. "I'm a helluva lot nicer than those guys."

"Sure you are," I mutter.

Rule 37 of the Spectres—always deal the first and final blow.

According to my training, I'm supposed to hit him and get him out of my space. Now. But honestly, I can use him. If this is a dragon shifter, maybe I can get him to duke it out with the two above me.

He pivots in his seat and grabs a few items out of the various pockets on his vest and pants. In seconds, I realize what he's assembling—a dragon taser.

Nope, not a dragon shifter, then. A shifter would just launch up there and fight. This guy is a human, but I've never seen a taser quite like his before. Surprisingly, there are quite a few human organizations that have anti-dragon weapons like that, and I unfortunately can't narrow down who he works for. Or if he works for *anyone*.

There are plenty of lone wolves who hate dragons, too.

What concerns me most, though, is that he's here at all. Somehow, even non-dragon organizations know about what happened in the pit.

Freaking *wonderful*.

I resist the urge to bang my head against the wheel in frustration as my day spirals out of control.

The mystery man in my passenger seat assembles his dragon taser faster than I've ever seen it done. In seconds, he has a modified pulse shooter locked into his shoulder, and he fires.

Only the highest caliber bullets can pierce dragon hide, but a taser like this *will* knock them out. If the guy is a good enough shot, of course.

And damn, he *is*.

Two shots, and both fall. The ground shakes as their massive bodies hit the earth, and I fishtail momentarily as the impact screws with my tires.

"You caused a bit of a fuss, huh?" he says with a chuckle as he disassembles the taser, still braced against the seat and facing the wrong way.

"Leave that out," I demand, eyeing the rearview in case any more decide to join us. I don't trust him for a second, but at the moment, he's useful. At least he's not aiming it at me.

Heaven help him if he tried.

"Nah, it's fine." He shrugs and puts the last of it away. "I can get it out again if need be." He nestles into his seat and sets his hands behind his head, eyes closed as if he's enjoying a Sunday morning drive and not a midnight escape through dragon-infested forests.

I stare at him in confusion for a second, utterly baffled by this strange man who just helped me.

He adjusts in his seat and reaches behind him, tugging out a massive bullet from between his shoulders and casually tossing it out of the car. "You hungry? I know a good Vietnamese place about a mile from here. We'll get some takeout."

"Who the hell are you?" I ask.

He laughs as I gun it down the dirt road and leans his elbow on my seat, entirely too close for comfort. "Where are my manners? I'm Tucker Chase. I'm here to help you. We humans have to stick together, you know?"

I don't answer. It's suddenly very clear he has no idea I'm a Spectre, and that's a good thing. I was beginning to worry Mason would tell the world, but it seems the idiot can keep *some* things close to his chest.

"Anyway," Tucker continues. "You must be beat. I figure we grab some food, sleep it off, then get you somewhere safe."

"Sure," I lie, stringing him along. He's hot and charming, but he's still a fully-armed stranger who jumped into my car from a tree.

He's out of here the moment an opportunity presents itself.

We drive for another seven minutes. Seven minutes of him casually chatting like we're on a date. Seven minutes of me anxiously looking over my shoulder for more dragons.

It looks like I'm finally in the clear.

"Turn left here, babe," Tucker says, nodding to a side road about a quarter mile ahead.

"Thanks for the help," I say, eyeing the ditch on the passenger's side, looking for a soft landing that will minimize potential injury to him once I kick him out.

After all, he *was* useful. It's the least I can do.

He grins, and I have to admit he has a gorgeous smile. "You're wel—"

I unlock the doors and drift along the dirt road, angling my turn so that the force throws him out of the car. He's obviously skilled, so I trust his training will kick in fast enough to make sure he rolls along the road instead of breaking his neck.

He does.

I correct the wheel and gun it straight, passing the road he told me to take. A small cloud of dust swirls in my rearview mirror, and seconds later he stands in the middle of the road, completely unharmed and covered in dirt.

I carefully watch for his reaction, expecting cursing or a deadly glare. It'll tell me what kind of man I'm dealing with.

Instead of flipping me off, he just laughs and shakes his head, crossing his arms as he watches me drive away.

Interesting.

I'm out of the hurricane, but the storm isn't over yet. I'll ditch the car well away from the safehouse, steal a different one, and leave no trail. No trace. It's what I'm good at.

And once I've had a moment to breathe, I'm going to unleash hell on the people coming after me.

CHAPTER SIX

Though I'm finally at the safehouse, I pause outside and simply observe for a moment.

Before I go in, I need to assess the risk.

There's a traitor within the Spectres. They told the Vaer about me, about Irena, about Zurie. To the best of my knowledge, it seems like they even shared some of the inner workings about the organization. There's a chance the traitor knows about the safehouse, too, and I have to be careful even though all I want to do is run inside and see if Irena is okay.

I eye the plain white two-story cottage on the outskirts of town, the grass in the front yard over-grown from months of neglect. Thunder rumbles in the sky overhead, and I wonder if it's from a dragon or a storm.

The windows are dark, just as we left them, but that

doesn't mean anything. I scan the glass, looking for movement, but the house is silent and still.

Cautiously, I sneak toward the back door and twist the knob. Locked, just as we left it. A good sign, but not enough to put me at ease. I pull out my kit from the pouch hidden beneath my shirt and quietly pick the lock, only half-paying attention to my work as I continue to scan the shadows inside.

Moments later, I slip into the kitchen, my back to the wall as I move silently through the barely furnished house.

Living room, empty.

Dining room, empty.

Upstairs, silent.

I wait again, listening for the slightest knock of a boot on the floor, for the subtlest breath, for the crinkle of skin tightening over a metal grip as someone holds his gun tighter, ready to shoot.

Nothing.

But I'm absolutely exhausted. I can barely hold my head up at this point. I've been pushed to my limit, and I worry I'm missing something. Even though I'm good, there's a high chance I'll start to make mistakes. And in my line of work, even a small miscalculation could get me killed.

Gritting my teeth, I push forward.

I make my way up the stairs, avoiding every creaky step, not making a sound as I approach the landing.

We left Irena in the room by the stairs, and I pray she's still there. With no weapons but my own hands, I peek into the room.

Like the rest of the house, it's empty.

My heart hammers in my chest, and for a moment, I can't breathe.

I want to be wrong. I want to search the other rooms, thinking perhaps she woke up on her own, that perhaps she's out there, looking for me.

A man's boot thumps on the hardwood behind me. "Good to see you, Rory."

I know that voice.

"Mason," I say quietly, my voice brimming with the simmering hatred I can barely contain.

Emotion ruins a fight. It clouds judgment. In my training, I was taught to suppress it, to clear the mind and focus on the now.

But after everything that happened tonight, I just can't.

"Where is she?" I face him, finally understanding the depths of my own fatigue.

This is really, *really* bad. If I didn't detect him, I'm even more distracted than I feared. It doesn't matter what happened to me in the pit, in the forest, or on the drive here. This is inexcusable, something Zurie would punish me for if she knew, but I suppose it can't be helped at this point.

If only Zurie were that forgiving.

"I have a new deal for you, Rory," Mason says, step-ping into the dark hallway from one of the other pitch-black bedrooms. "Come quietly with me, and I'll let Irena go."

For a moment, I actually consider the offer. He's lying, of course, but this is my predicament—the Vaer will use Irena and Zurie as leverage against me for as long as they can.

Zurie can handle herself, but Irena isn't even conscious.

"I'm not a patient man," Mason says curtly. "Come with us, now, or we'll kill them both."

"No, you won't." I call his bluff, slowly circling him until I can get a bit closer to the stairs.

It's time to honor rule twelve and look for my escape.

He's armed, and I can guarantee he isn't here alone. I listen to the darkness again, and this time I notice the shuffle of four—no, six men in the shadows.

Honestly, I'm a little disappointed he only brought six. It's a bit insulting. He must think I'm too exhausted to put up a fight.

He's not completely wrong, but he's wildly underes-timating me. Even though it plays to my advantage, it's kind of annoying when people do this. Mainly, because it happens so often.

"Fine, you caught me." Mason sneers. "I won't kill

both of them, not yet. Zurie, I still need. But Irena is useless. Don't you want to save your sister's life?"

I frown. Jesus, this guy knows way too much.

I shake my head, fully calling his bluff. "You need her to get to me. You wouldn't dare kill the only leverage you have against me." I smirk, just to piss him off. "Or risk disappointing your precious Boss."

He scowls and draws his gun. It's apparently the silent signal for his cronies to attack because his grunts bolt from the shadows.

I take my chance to escape.

My muscles screaming for rest, I practically fall down the stairs, rolling at the end to recover. Determined to find cover, I barrel through the front door and into the yard.

Two gunshots ring through the air, but they miss by miles.

It's like they're not even trying.

I run through the grass and, in seconds, I'm gone. Mason pounced too soon, gave me too good of an exit. I hear him yell into the sky, and I look over my shoulder as I disappear into the woods around the cottage.

Behind me, the house goes up in flames as the dragon shifters pile out of it. I laugh and shake my head. Mason's such a sore loser. There's nothing useful in there, nothing significant we would keep in such a temporary place, but he just wanted to blow something up.

Somebody has an easily bruised ego. Good. I can use that to my advantage—because he and I will definitely meet again.

One street over, I jump into my second stolen car of the day as I hear the men fan out, searching the surrounding woods and houses for me.

Too late.

I gun it out of there like a bat out of hell, my laugh slowly fading as I watch smoke and flame spiral into the sky.

No Irena. No Zurie. No gear. No assets. No leads.

I always wanted freedom, and I finally got it—just not in the way I intended. I'm on my own, with more people after me than I can even count, and this isn't looking good.

Twenty miles away from the safehouse that's no longer safe, I spot an old shed on the back lot of a farmhouse. I've already ditched the car far away from here, just in case Mason saw it, and I need a moment to breathe. To process. To think all of this through.

I pick the lock on the shed and slip inside the musty space to find nothing but old tools and some wooden boards.

Good.

As the door swings shut behind me, I lean against the wall and close my eyes, waiting for my heart to settle.

They found Irena, which must mean the traitor gave them everything on us. Our locations, our missions, likely safehouses, methods, how to trap us.

Our weaknesses.

I pause, eyes slipping out of focus as I recall all the arguments Zurie and a few of her subordinates had over the years. Several of them said it was a weakness to keep me and Irena together, a weakness to endorse a bond beyond the basic Spectre brotherhood. They wanted to split us up, but Zurie never allowed it.

Sisters—family—that was weakness to them. Hell, maybe they were right. Zurie used it against us, made us train harder, run farther, work more than anyone else—for each other, to avoid getting each other punished.

I always hated the way those men and women looked at Irena and me. Usually, we spent time alone, just the three of us, but every now and again we had to meet with the others. Even after a lifetime in the Spectres, I've only met a fraction of them, and I can't think of a single one who likes either me or Irena. They would go silent as we passed, or outright glare at us, or challenge us to sparring matches beyond our skill set, ones we couldn't hope to win, ones they hoped would leave us broken.

I never understood why Irena and me being sisters threatened them so much. If maybe they hated us because we were the Ghost's trainees, which meant she would pass the reins to one of us and not them.

But now, I'm starting to wonder if their arguments against sisters training together had merit. If my love for my sister really is my weakness. If that's what Mason will exploit to take me down.

Furious, my body burning with hate and grief, I punch the wall.

The entire shed trembles, and the wood beneath my knuckles splinters into dust. A hole the size of my fist reveals a slim view of the night outside.

Oops.

Marveling at my newfound strength, I look in awe at my fingers. No cuts. No pain. Not even a bruise.

This new magic of mine—I wish I understood it.

I push up my sleeves and look again at the golden chains wrapped around my arms, fused to my skin, glowing with otherworldly light. Thankfully, I don't glow like a lantern, but it *is* noticeable.

It's also… kind of pretty.

I'm not used to having pretty things.

A dirty old hand mirror in the corner of the shed catches my eye, and I lift it to see how far the chains go. Thankfully, nothing shows on my face, but my skin has a glow to it as well, as if I just stepped off a beach with a flawless tan. My warm brown eyes have a golden tint to them. My hair bounces, full of body and curls, devoid of any frizz despite my hellish day.

Craziest of all, I look thinner. I squint at the mirror, wondering if it's just the exhaustion or if the dragon magic altered my body in other ways as well.

Tenderly, I drag my fingers along my waist, my legs, my chest, trying to take an inventory of the changes. Every stubborn pound of fat is gone, leaving behind only smooth curves and strong muscle.

Hell, even my boobs are bigger.

Most importantly, though, I once more feel that electricity bubbling under my skin, that raw power and magic I felt in the other world, where I was surrounded by disembodied voices.

I stare at my hands, wishing I knew how to control it. Wishing I knew what this magic can even do.

There's something in me, no doubt about that. Whatever happened in the pit, whatever those voices did to me, it's real.

What I don't understand, though, is why they chose *me*.

I'm just a human. To dragons, I'm a peasant. Disposable. Beneath them. Why would dragons give *me* magic, instead of giving it to another shifter?

It doesn't make sense.

Now that I can finally take a moment to process all

of this, I sit on one of the work surfaces and lean my head back against the wall. Eyes closed, I listen to my pulse until it steadies.

Zurie and Irena were up to something dangerous. They pissed off the Vaer family, but obviously this mess goes deeper than even that mission. I wonder who the traitor could be, and it's strange to think I can't go to anyone. I don't trust the other Spectres, but we've always been bound by a sense of shared purpose, if not a true brotherhood.

Rule 1 of the Spectres—obey the Ghost.

Obey Zurie.

Someone in the organization broke rule number one. The big one. One of the few punishable by death instead of a beating.

I sigh deeply, staring up at the corkboard ceiling of this little shack, wondering what I should do next.

Out there, dragons are scouring the forests, no doubt breaking laws left and right to find me. What I don't know, however, is *why*.

What they want from me.

How they even *know*.

They say dragons are connected, even if most of them hate each other. That there's magic in them we humans will never understand.

I pause, eying the golden links fused with my body, and wonder if I can really classify myself as human anymore.

My brain kicks into high gear at the thought, and it's the one piece of good news that shifts my mood entirely.

I can't help but smile.

This is *good*.

All this power, all this ability—Zurie would lose her mind, of course, if she knew about this. Irena would feel like it was a curse if this happened to her.

But me? I know better.

Everything just changed, and for once, it's in my favor. For all his obnoxious gloating, Mason said one thing that mattered—the pit chose me because I'm worthy.

And now, I have a vast supply of magic that can help me find my mentor and my sister.

They won't like it at first, of course, but they'll come around. I'm still the same person I was. This magic, this power, it only helps us continue to do what we did before.

I stare again at my hands, smiling now, reveling in the electric hum that buzzes deep in my bones. Despite my biting exhaustion, I've never felt so strong. So capable. It's like waking up and seeing the sun for the first time, knowing nothing will be the same.

And I decide, right then, to keep this. This power, this magic—it's mine, and I won't relinquish it, no matter who asks me to do so.

Mason wants it, as do the red dragon and the thunderbird. Hell, I can safely assume every dragon alive wants whatever it is I have, so my every move must be carefully planned and painfully clever.

Tapping my finger on my chin, I think through what to do next. Most likely, Mason will separate Irena and Zurie. I won't be able to save both, not at first.

I have to choose.

I grapple with the thought, debating both options. As much as I hate to admit it, it's already clear what I have to do.

Zurie is alive, awake, and experienced. Irena is unconscious, and while she's good, Zurie is the *best*. On top of that, the second step to bringing Irena back to her full power is to find the antidote to whatever illness she has, which I doubt Mason will keep anywhere near her. He'll likely keep her sick as a ploy to make me move faster, to trip me up, to keep me worried. After all, we don't know how much time she has left.

I hate to delay getting my sister her antidote, but it'll be easier to save Zurie, and then Zurie can help me save Irena.

I sigh, wishing I could go for Irena first, but logic has to outweigh emotion in this choice.

Fact is, the only people I trust in this situation are Irena and Zurie, and they're both gone.

However, I do know *one* person I can milk for information. I'll take whatever he gives me with a grain of salt, of course, but I do need a lead—and I know exactly where to get it.

And in the meantime, while he's gathering intel, I'm going to see if Mason left anything useful behind for me.

CHAPTER SEVEN

Once more, I slink through Mason's ornate manor, hating every second of it.

This time, though, there's no mentor to lead the way, and I have to say I love the freedom even if I hate the mission. I take my own route, scanning each empty hallway for signs of life, and once more feel the warning signs of a trap.

Only this time, I actually listen.

The sun will rise in less than an hour, and I prefer to work in the dark. This is just a cursory scan, a quick in and out to see if this place is even worth my time.

It's not.

So far, I've carefully avoided seven tripwires and kept to the blind spots of fourteen cams, but without my modified handgun to shoot the void devices, it's next to impossible to rove through these halls unseen. I'm not going to get far. Even if I did have my gun, most of my gear is one-time use, and I need to resupply soon, if possible.

Thankfully, most of the dragons I've seen are shifted and roaming the skies above—by now, I imagine they assume I won't be back to the mansion and am long gone.

It looks like Zurie's long gone, too, and there's not a trace of her left behind.

I curse under my breath, eye on the soft yellow glow slowly burning the horizon through one of the hallway windows. It'll be light out, soon, and I'm running out of time.

Briefly, I debate finding a low-level dragon shifter to capture and torture for information, but that's Zurie's thing, not mine. Causing someone pain, just to get information out of them—it feels wrong, no matter what I stand to gain.

But that's just one more reason Zurie insists I would be a terrible Ghost—I can't do what has to be done. She always says I'm soft. I disagree. I simply use other methods to get the same intel.

Not wanting to wait around, I slip outside and dip once more into the forest to gather my thoughts. I wait on the edge of the woods, shrouded in shadow, debating my next move.

Ten feet off, a twig snaps. I hide behind a thick trunk, my knuckles cracking as I ball my hand into a fist, ready to fight despite my deep exhaustion.

"You here, babe" a familiar voice asks in a whisper.

Tucker.

I suppress a groan, relaxing a bit but still ready to gut him if need be. If it were anyone else, I would have sprung from my hiding place and kicked him in the throat.

Honestly, I probably still should. I'm not sure why I don't. Something about him screams "harmless," despite his fighter's build and apparent expertise with weapons.

Yeah, the more I think about that combination, the less sense it makes. But hey, I have to admire the man's tenacity.

Without letting him see me, I slink into the shadows farthest from him, slipping away and heading back toward the car I have waiting by the road less than a mile off. It seems like there won't be any clues for me here, and in my fatigued state, I struggle to think of the best next move.

"I'm starting to feel like you're avoiding me," Tucker says from above.

I curse under my breath, apparently far more tired than I realized, and lean against a tree as I figure out where he's sitting. He lounges on the branch above me, back to the trunk as he watches me with that charming grin of his.

"Yeah, that's kind of the point," I say with a frustrated shrug.

"Babe, I'm hurt." He holds his hand to his heart in mock disappointment.

"What do you want, Tucker?" I asked pointedly.

I don't have time for this.

"Your name would be a good start," he says with a grin, as if we're on a blind date and not trespassing on dragon territory.

"That's not going to happen."

"I saw you go in there." He nods toward the mansion, apparently unfazed by my tone. "I thought you were crazy, to be honest. I was sure you were going to get caught and couldn't for the life of me think of one good reason to go into a dragon den." He tilts his head, a curious bend to his eyebrows. "But you didn't trip a single alarm. You got in and out of one of the most heavily guarded mansions in the state, and no one knew you were there. I respect that."

I hesitate, unused to compliments. "Thanks."

"How did you do it?" He crosses his arms, still lounging in the tree, one leg draped over the branch as the other rests on the limb.

I resist the impulse to roll my eyes. Yeah, we're done here.

But I decide to have some fun first. "I can't tell you

how I did it, but I *can* tell you *this*." I lean in, as if I'm going to divulge some great secret.

Still on his perch up in the tree, he leans toward me, one eyebrow raised in curiosity.

"Stop following me," I say in a menacing whisper. "Or I'll beat you senseless."

"Damn, you're cute." His smile broadens at my very serious threat, as if he thinks I'm joking. He adjusts his weight, ready to jump down onto the ground.

Good. This is the moment I've been waiting for. All I need is one second of distraction, and I can slip away unnoticed.

As I wait for my cue, time seems to slow. He looks down at the leaves, preparing to jump. I eye a deep thicket of trees and shadows to my right. He leaps, and I take my chance.

In seconds, I'm gone.

I wait in the darkness and watch him, wanting to see how he'll react when he thinks I'm not looking.

The whole thing was over in seconds, and I'm sure as far as he's concerned, I disappeared in the blink of an eye. He looks around, his smile faltering for a moment, eyebrows furrowed in confusion.

"How the hell does she do that?" he asks the forest. He scans the trees, but aside from a bit of confusion, his demeanor doesn't change. He's still relaxed, still goofy, still poised and ready to follow.

Tucker runs off in another direction, almost

completely silent, toward a clearer path that would make for easier running. A good choice if someone doesn't know they're chasing a Spectre. As for me, I don't need to see where I'm going to make my exit.

I continue through the shadows, headed again for the car. Tucker is certainly persistent, and I have a feeling he won't be easy to shake even after I leave this city.

What concerns me, though, is what a human like him could possibly want with me, and why he's even here.

This goofy, carefree weapons expert seems completely unfazed by dragons and is brazenly willing to trespass on their land, where human law doesn't matter. Humans disappear on dragon land all the time, and nothing is ever done about it. He could die here, burned to a crisp by dragons, and no human government would lift a finger.

Yet he stays.

To hunt me.

Because let's be real—he's charming, yes, but he's on the hunt just as much as the dragons are.

As much as I hate to do it, I pull out my phone and text Diesel for an update on our rendezvous point. Though he's a fellow Spectre, I hate him. He sticks his nose in everyone's business, but for once, that might be useful.

He might have a lead for me.

And as soon as I have some intel, as soon as I have any *hint* of what I can do next, I'm going to finally let myself sleep.

CHAPTER EIGHT

Grimacing, I stare at the flickering sign of what could possibly be the filthiest bar I've ever seen in my life.

Tucked away in the industrial area of town, this bar has a dirt lot sprinkled with a dusting of gravel. A broken door leads to the seating area, and through the windows, I can see eight men hunched over beer mugs inside despite the fact that it's almost six in the morning. Most of them wear hats to obscure their faces, and I'm quite certain most of these men don't want to be recognized for one reason or another.

"I hate you, Diesel," I mutter under my breath, pinching the bridge of my nose in annoyance as I try to settle my nerves.

I don't like this place one bit, and I wish he had picked literally anywhere else to meet. But no, in true insufferable fashion, he picks a seedy bar filled with criminals.

Trying my best to blend in, I burrow a bit deeper in the oversized maroon hoodie I found nearby, trying not to think too hard about why it was strewn over a fence or what that rank smell is.

Desperate times, desperate measures.

I fuss with the hood, trying to hide my face. As I lift my hand, the large sleeve slides up my arm, and I catch a glimpse of the shimmering golden chains fused with my skin. Frowning, I slide the sleeve back up to my wrist.

Damn, that's right. I'm practically glowing. There's no way I'm going to blend in here.

In the dim light of the coming dawn, I lean over a puddle in the parking lot and see my reflection in the murky water. I try to smudge a bit of dirt over my cheeks to hide the newfound shimmer in my skin, and it helps. A little.

It's good enough.

Eyes to the ground, I duck in the door and do my best to keep to myself and avoid eye contact as the criminals flooding this bar look up at me one by one. A classic rock song plays quietly overhead, and the low buzz of conversation slowly fades as I walk deeper into the building.

With every step, I just think the same thought over and over: *Diesel, you jerk. Diesel, you jerk. Diesel—*

"You know how many wanted lists you're on right now?" a man says as I reach the bar, his deep voice low so as not to draw anyone else's attention.

Diesel.

I sit on the stool next to him and face forward, keeping an eye on the cracked mirror behind the bar as the patrons behind us continue to stare at me. A bowl of peanuts sits on the counter, the nuts dark gray from age.

With a fleeting glare at Diesel's broad shoulders, I fidget in my seat. "It doesn't help that we're meeting in a place like *this*."

We don't look at each other. That's the rule of meetings like this—speak in hushed tones and act like strangers.

Through the mirror, he briefly glances me up and down. "You're glowing."

"No shit."

Good *God*, man, get on with it.

At the far end of the bar, the sole employee of this hole in the wall briefly looks up from a newspaper and gives me a sidelong glance. I shake my head, signaling I don't want anything to drink. He shrugs and returns to his paper.

Diesel, on the other hand, lifts a half-finished glass of whiskey to his lips and subtly points to the space beneath the bar with one of his fingers. "You owe me for this. Big time."

That's the way of the Spectres—no helping each other. Everything is a favor to be cashed in later.

Careful to be discreet, I slip my hands beneath the bar, searching for whatever he brought me. My fingers graze the burlap of an old sack, and judging by the weight, I'm guessing there's at least one handgun stored inside.

I look again at the mirror, checking behind me to make sure most of the patrons have gone back to their drinks and conversations. A few still stare at my back, and I make mental note of their faces in case they try to tail me later.

"There are notes and coordinates in the bag," Diesel says quietly, drawing my attention. "They're moving in four directions, but I only found one final destination so far. They're clearly masking movements."

"Thanks." I'm itching to dig into the bag, but I can't look at it here. I have to wait until this is over.

"Don't thank me, kid." He downs the last of his whiskey. "I'm going to ask for one hell of a favor when all this is done."

"And what's that?" There's a hard edge to my voice. Of all the Spectres I know—granted, I don't know them all—I like being indebted to him the *least*.

He just grins. "I'm not sure yet, but I can promise it'll be fun."

Oh, how *fabulous*.

I sink a little in my seat, willing this conversation to

end already, but he might have more info for me. I wait.

"You're on your own," he says, as if this is news to me. "Our kind need to know how to clean up our messes."

Duh.

I don't tell him, but he's the last person I would ask to join me on a mission. I wouldn't trust him leading, and I *certainly* wouldn't trust him at my back.

He taps the bar absently. "I'll keep looking. Every coordinate I give you is another favor you owe me."

It's not a negotiation. It's a price. He knows I don't have any bargaining chips, and I begrudgingly nod.

"Kid, one bit of advice." He looks at me finally, those cold black eyes piercing me.

With his smooth face and the tattoos crawling up his neck, he honestly doesn't look old enough to call me a kid. Maybe thirty-five at most, covered head to toe in massive muscles barely restrained by his clothes. However, it's his posture that gives him age and authority, the way he carries himself like a warrior who's seen everything already and is fazed by nothing.

His eyes scan me briefly as he pauses, maybe for dramatic effect, and he sets his empty glass on the counter. "The rumors about why people want you, about what you *are*, they're already starting, and none of them are good. I'll keep my ear to the ground, try to see *when*, not if, someone comes to kill you. But in the end, remember what you were bred to be—and remember why the dragons hate you."

A Spectre. An assassin. A deadly weapon in the shadows, bred to kill dragons. That's what I am. That's why they hate me. I frown, wondering if he knows more than he's letting on.

He stands, his stool scraping the wooden floor as he stomps his way to the exit. Listening to all the noise he's making, no one would know he's one of the deadliest Spectres alive.

Second to Irena and the Ghost, of course.

The door bangs behind him, and I feel an uncomfortable shift in the room. I glance again to the mirror and see more eyes on my back this time than before he left.

Usually, I've found it's best to wait seven minutes after the first person leaves before making my own exit. It allows the rest of the room to distract themselves, to let their thoughts wander and forget we were together.

But the way these guys are looking at me, I think I'll take my chances.

I reach for the bag and spin on my stool, only to see Tucker walk in through a side door. He waves, grinning like an idiot, and takes the seat next to me.

"Ooh, peanuts." He picks through the vile bowl of ancient nuts as I stare at him in bewilderment.

Exhausted and now in a bit of shock, I just gape at him. "How in the—"

"Ah, this one might still be good." He pops a peanut into his mouth and instantly grimaces. "Nope."

I rub my face in frustration. "You have got to be kidding me," I mutter to myself, to whatever higher power must be giving him my coordinates just to screw with me.

"You are one clever woman," he says a little louder than I'd like, pushing away the peanuts as he settles into his seat.

"How are you even here right now? Did you put a tracker on me?" I ask in a hushed tone as more heads turn toward us.

"I wish." He laughs, then pauses for a moment, staring off into the distance as if considering it for the first time. "That's actually a really good idea."

Despite striking out the first time, he reaches again for the peanuts. I grab his wrist, pinning him to the bar, and he shifts his full attention toward me, that charming grin still on his face. "Yes, dear?"

"Stop following me," I say in my darkest, most menacing voice. I lock eyes with him, shooting daggers despite my bone-deep fatigue, but those rich green eyes of his start to melt me, and I lose my concentration.

Damn, I must be *way* more exhausted than I thought.

"You can't go anywhere unnoticed, babe," he says with a nod to the men in the pub behind us, finally lowering his voice. "And the dragons seem especially fond of you, which makes you *very* important to me. They tracked you here, and I came to warn you, so a 'thank you' would be great."

"That's impossible."

I covered every track. Switched cars. Disguised myself. But as I look in the mirror, I catch the warm honey glow of my skin, and I'm reminded that there's something different about me now, something that makes it so much harder to blend in, regardless of my skills. Regardless of my training.

My next move has to be made very, *very* carefully.

Before I can stand, the lights go out. A few bulbs shatter. The music cuts off, and in the silence, men murmur in surprise. A few chair legs scrape along the floor. Several guns cock in the darkness, including what sounds like a shotgun at the far end of the bar.

Several thuds echo through the ceiling, like the footsteps of something massive walking across the roof, and I wonder how flammable this place is.

"Those overgrown lizards wouldn't dare," a man grumbles in the darkness.

Another man pipes in, far more scared than the first. "This is human territory! They wouldn't... they *couldn't...*"

"What are they *thinking?*" someone else yells.

Voices clamor through the darkness, and I hope I didn't condemn theses strangers to death just for being here.

Beside me, Tucker's muscled silhouette leans toward me. "Shall we fight our way out of here, babe?"

Call me babe one more time, I think. Instead of answering, though, I reach into the bag, grasping for my gun.

I can't find it.

The stupid thing is buried deep at the bottom, beneath loose papers and various devices I don't recognize in the dark.

Damn it, Diesel. This *isn't* how you pack a bag.

Outside, a beast roars, and I realize Tucker told the truth. Like he said, the dragons want me—and the fact that their attention makes me valuable to him does not escape my notice.

Like them, he wants something from me. And just like them, he won't get it.

CHAPTER NINE

A stream of fire blows open the front door of the bar. Men scream. Wood splinters. Several gunshots go off, shattering windows.

It's mayhem, and these men are firing wildly into the dark.

How delightful.

Seeing as I have no grasp on what weapons I have in the bag, nor any idea of how many dragons there are, I throw the pack over my shoulder and run.

Tucker is on my heels, unfortunately. Though I don't love the idea of having a stranger at my back, I have to prioritize the threats at the moment.

We sprint through the grimy kitchen as the attack rages against the front of the building. A stack of beer crates block the back exit.

"Allow me," Tucker says, rolling up his sleeves.

I don't pause long enough to answer. With my newfound enhanced strength, I effortlessly push them aside to free up the door. The crates leave skid marks in the black dust on the tile.

"Whoa." His eyebrows shoot upward. "You're a lot stronger than you look."

I groan, annoyed that he's still here, and crack the back door open. Poised to run, I pause only long enough to do a visual sweep of the back field. A thin patch of trees lines the edge of the yard, with a dumpster against the building that will perhaps be good enough for cover if it comes to needing that.

No dragons, though. They must be focusing on the front of the building, but that won't last long. They'll probably see me the moment I run out.

"You still have that taser?" I ask, gesturing for him to hand it to me as I continue to watch the grassy field.

"That's Betty, and I don't know if you and I are on good enough terms yet for me to lend her to you."

"Dear God, man, give me the damn taser!"

A dragon roars somewhere overhead, and a stream of fire billows through the kitchen ceiling. The flames lick the filthy cabinets and stained counters, encroaching on a small propane tank at the end of the kitchen line.

Shit.

I throw open the door and sprint into the field, dragons be damned. Tucker is close behind. We barely get halfway across the lot before the building explodes.

The force knocks us off our feet, and we roll. Somehow, I end up in Tucker's lap, his arm strung protectively across my chest as he grips my shoulder. We look back at the dragons circling the now-destroyed building, trying to gauge the threat.

They're looking at us.

At *me*.

Annoyed with this man I can't seem to get off my tail, I shake off his hand and jump to my feet. "That taser would be great right about now!"

"Yep, on it." Blindingly fast, he reaches into the pockets on his vest, assembling Betty as the dragons near.

I scan the horizon, looking for more, but I only count six. Likely a troop sent to verify a rumor, and most likely they'll call for backup any second.

Yep—there, the dragon farthest away from the mess bolts off into the sky, in the direction of Mason's house.

Oh great. These are probably the Vaer.

Yay me.

Without warning, the closest dragon dives toward me, and I roll out of the way with my bag still over my shoulder. He misses, but only barely. I tenderly feel through the mess of a pack Diesel brought me, searching for a gun, a knife, *anything*. I finally feel the handgun all the way at the bottom, buried under layers of crumpling paper and boxes I don't recognize through the fabric.

A second dragon dives toward me.

A crackling bolt of electricity shoots into the air, hitting the second dragon in the face. He goes down instantly.

In my peripheral vision, Tucker laughs and pumps his fist in victory.

"Can you focus, please?" I shout, rolling out of the way as another dragon dives for me.

"Come on now, darlin'! Have a bit of fun!" He shoots another blast from the taser, and it hits dragon number three. The massive beast tries to dodge it but can't. It hits, sending the dragon plummeting to the earth. Once more, the ground trembles as the beast digs a crater into the dirt.

I do a mental count. Two down, three to go, and one flying off to tell his masters where I am.

I need to end this. Now.

As I duck and dodge the dragons, I continue to reach into the bag, trying to get to the weapon buried deep at the bottom, never able to grab it fast enough. They're attacking too quickly, one right after the other, their claws razor sharp and ready to pounce, never giving me a second to breathe.

After the nonstop night I had, I'm fading. Fast. I start moving slower, and even all of my training and muscle memory won't be enough to save me for much longer.

The first dragon dives again, and I once more roll out of the way. Tucker takes him and one other down, but the last one is too quick.

For the first time, I see Tucker miss. It's enough to wipe that smile off his face. He scowls, aiming again, and misses once more.

This last dragon is *fast*.

He whips through the air like a fighter jet, always angled toward me. He dives again, and though I roll out of the way, his claw grabs my bag. The force rips the pack away from me, and I watch as it lands in a pile of gravel twenty feet away.

His wing clips me, and I fall hard on my back, skidding across the rock-strewn dirt. In the brightening sky above, the dragon swerves to avoid another blow from the taser. He banks, his eyes locked on me, and dives.

Ever the stubborn one, I lift my hands as he prepares to grab me, ready to rip open his jaw if that's what it takes to kill him.

A burst of energy boils through me, uncontrolled and wild. It fizzles and pops like carbonation beneath my skin, in my hands, swimming into my fingers.

My palms burn with otherworldly heat.

A blast of white light streams from my palm, straight for the dragon. He flinches in surprise, but even he isn't fast enough to avoid it. It pierces his heart, and he falls to the earth, lifeless.

The ground shakes as he hits, but I don't move. I can't. I simply stare at my hands in shock, completely baffled at what just happened.

It was...

It couldn't be...

"Was that *magic*?" Tucker asks, running over with his taser still assembled, and his voice snaps me out of my daze.

He offers me a hand to help me up, but I'm skeptical. I have to be. The gesture could be one of kindness, sure, but it's more likely a means to make me lower my guard. Spectres do this all the time to each other when they want something, but never out of the goodness of their hearts. I've been burned too often to fall for it.

I stand on my own, ignoring his gesture, and don't answer him. Instead, I search the skies, looking for any other dragons.

For once, the skies are clear. In the distance, however, I hear a siren. Police, from the sound of it, and probably the fire department.

"Come on, we can take my truck." Tucker disassembles Betty in a matter of seconds, neatly tucking away the sections into his vest.

I square my shoulders and look him dead in the eye. "I don't trust you. Not you, not the others who say they're trying to help me, none of you."

He nods, hands on his hips as he looks me over. "Good. That means you'll survive. Come on."

With that, he simply walks away, turning his back to me as he heads toward the parking lot.

For a moment, I'm confused. Here's someone who I've shaken twice now, who should know better than to turn his back on me because I can disappear in an instant or, you know, *kill* him.

It takes me a moment to realize this is a test, a bluff of sorts, to see if I'll stop fighting him and let him stick around.

A normal human girl would have, at this point. He's helped me fight off the dragons twice now, after all, and made it clear he won't be easily shaken.

But I'm not normal.

Though my instinct and training both urge me to get the hell out of this city, I'm running on fumes. I've pushed myself to my absolute limit, and I need to recharge. Refuel. I'll find an empty house, get some sleep, and head out tonight when it's dark.

As the sun peeks over the horizon, I run toward the bag Diesel left for me, grab it, and duck into a nearby alley. In five minutes, I'll be in a new car and on my way out of here.

Alone.

CHAPTER TEN

I stretch, snuggled deep in the soft layers of a stranger's down comforter. After a fresh shower and a good long nap, I finally feel clean after so long on the run. I even had a hot meal before climbing into bed, thanks to the half-stocked fridge, and I intend to grab another one on my way out tonight.

Do I like stealing from hardworking folks like this when they're on vacation? No. But desperate times call for desperate measures, and I won't leave a trace behind. When they get home, they'll never know they helped me.

I walk through the hall toward the kitchen, wondering what it's like to take a vacation to Greece, since that's where this family is at the moment. I've never had a vacation in my life, and I only went to

Greece on an overnight to assist Zurie with an arms deal.

Not exactly a charmed life.

The sun is finally starting to sink toward the horizon, and as much as I've enjoyed getting to know the Johnsons through their open mail on the counter and the itineraries their son accidentally left behind, my moment of rest is quickly coming to an end.

After eating a bit more of the lasagna that will expire before they get back, I empty the bag Diesel got me on the living room rug. The gun plops on the soft carpet fibers, and I suppress an annoyed grunt at Diesel's carelessness.

I've never seen a Spectre pack a bag so haphazardly. For us, everything has its place. Its purpose. Everything is supposed to be easy to grab at a moment's notice.

To shove things into a bag so carelessly—it's sloppy. It's beneath him. It almost feels like he did this on purpose, just to piss me off.

I try to make sense of the chaos. The papers he threw in here have scribbled notes and contain blurry photographs of Vaer cargo trucks. One photo of a truck has coordinates printed at the corner, and I figure this must be the location Diesel was referring to.

It's not the best lead, but at least it's something. Even if Zurie isn't there, I can at least get more information on where she might be.

Aside from the intel, there's two dozen more voids

and some attachments for the gun, though not all of the ones I'm used to. I frown, disappointed. He made such a big deal of helping me, but honestly, I didn't get what I paid for.

I'll remember this when it comes time for him to cash in the favor.

I repack the bag—properly this time—and stash the voids and a few other pieces of tech into the pouch still strapped to my abdomen and hidden beneath my shirt. The gun goes in the empty holster at my side, and I'll have to find a coat to hide it. It's going to be a cool spring day, so I can get away with a thin one.

According to my training, I should change into civilian clothes, since my recon clothes would make it harder to blend in. I briefly consider it, but in the end, I need to be ready to fight and flee at a moment's notice.

It's tough to roundhouse kick someone in the face while wearing skinny jeans.

Besides, my skin still has that subtle glow. My eyes are virtually *gold*. I don't think I'm going to do much blending in, no matter what I try. Can't say I love that, since I'm used to the shadows, but it is what it is.

As the sun finally sets, I finish cleaning up the Johnsons' house, leaving it as I found it. I briefly check their garage, hoping to find a car and keys, but the garage is empty. Looks like I'll need to find a different ride.

Dusk falls over the sleepy street, and I slip out the backdoor into the shadows.

I scan whatever cars I come across as I casually traverse the sidewalk, but they're all too flashy.

Mercedes.

BMW.

Wait—good gracious, is that a Maserati?

I pause, eyeing the beautiful black car with a bit of hunger, but I shouldn't. Yeah, it would be fun, but I'd turn the wrong heads in *that* car. I already have seven dragon families hunting me. I don't need the cops after me, too.

Across the street, a man struts onto the sidewalk from a cross street. Broad shoulders. Crooked nose. Scar over his left eye. My best guess is he's either a human thug or a dragon shifter who loses a lot. He wears a long coat with a popped collar, and though he tries to hide under his hat, I notice him watching me like a hawk.

I sigh deeply. Damn it. I just can't catch a break.

It doesn't matter, though. Getting some rest was the right move. At least now I have the energy to fight off whatever comes after me.

I turn a corner, looking for an exit. I probably won't be able to hotwire a car before he catches up to me, so I need to lose him first.

Only, there are two more guys walking toward me from this direction, both wearing loose jackets and the same scowl as the first guy.

Oh good. New friends.

Whoever these guys are, they must have fanned out to cover as much distance as possible. There's probably going to be thugs and shifters covering every inch of this city, looking for me.

Fun.

As I continue maneuvering through the suburb, I spot more men. Eight in total by the looks of it, each trying his best to look nonchalant while keeping me in his sights.

I turn another corner to find a middle school, the lights out and shades drawn. It'll be empty at this time of day.

Good. Time to see how desperate these guys are.

Without warning, I bolt toward the playground.

It's a ploy, of course. It'll make them shift into action, and that will tell me just how many goons I need to take out. As I leap over the fence, I cast a brief glance backward to count.

Yep, eight men. From their gaits, they each carry a heavy weapon on their right side, holstered beneath their coats.

Nothing I can't handle.

They're quickly closing the distance between us, and I take stock of my options. Either I can run and find a good spot to hide until they pass, or I can stay and fight. As I turn a corner, I peer again to see them getting even closer.

Fighting it is, then.

When they round the bend, I'm waiting for them. With two pops from my silencer, both men in front go down. They groan in agony, broken but not dead.

You're welcome, I think.

The area I picked for the fight gives me the advantage. They funnel in through a tight gate by a brick wall, and now two of their buddies block most of the way.

The new guy in front lifts his gun from under his coat, but I kick it effortlessly away. He jabs. I duck and counter, throwing a right hook into his throat.

He goes down.

But guy number four—dear Christ, he's a *beast*.

He grabs my neck before I can duck out of the way, lifting me off the ground as he bats away my gun. My neck screams in pain beneath his grip, and I kick him hard in the stomach.

This blow would have crippled lesser men, but he takes the hit like a pro, barely grunting as he smirks up at me.

Cocky bastard.

"You're in way over your head, kid." He cracks his neck and grips mine tighter.

I roll my eyes. I'm twenty, damn it, not some gangly preteen. Why do they all keep calling me a kid?

"We could've done this easy," one of the other guys says, cracking his knuckles. "Until you shot our buddies."

"They're fine," I say through clenched teeth, trying my best not to suffocate as the asshole continues to hold me up by the neck.

"You certainly know your way around a gun," the beast of a man says, narrowing his eyes suspiciously. "Where'd you learn that?"

"Let me go and I'll tell you," I say, unable to resist smirking at him.

One of the other men cocks his gun and aims it at my temple. He glares at me, almost sneering, and leans in close. "The Knights don't play games, kid. If you want to survive this, you need to behave. We clear on that?"

Oh, *fuck*.

They're Knights.

The Knights hate dragons even more than the Spectres, and honestly, that's an achievement. They're terrorists, mostly, using bombs and whatever guerrilla tactics they can in order to rid the Earth of dragons once and for all.

The Knights and the Spectres—well, we don't always get along.

And though they clearly don't know I'm a Spectre, even the Knights know about my new magic.

Super-freaking-*duper*.

When I don't answer, the beastly dude throws me against the brick wall. My ears ring as I hit it hard, and the back of my head aches in agony. My gun is far out of reach. In my daze, I instinctively grab for it anyway as the world spins around me.

I crumple to the ground, dizzy and disoriented. Looming overhead are the towering forms of the five remaining men, their blurry silhouettes getting closer, but my eyes won't cooperate. Nothing is in focus.

Eight on one is hardly a fair fight, and usually I'd have Zurie or Irena on my side as backup at this point. Usually, they would swoop in, Irena would crack a joke, Zurie would roll her eyes, and we'd make a clean sweep as a team.

But right now, I'm all alone.

As my eyes finally come back into focus, the beast of a man is towering over me again. He reaches for my neck. I lift my hands instinctively, and they once more burn with heat.

Oh—oh, wait.

No.

Not here. Not at a school.

Blinding white light shoots from my palms, dissolving the men, the building, absolutely anything in its path. Energy buzzes through me like lightning, stronger now than the first time it happened.

As the light fades, I blink away the spots in my vision. Only the three men I took out earlier remain, still lying on the ground. The five others are simply gone, and as I gape in shock at the aftermath, the wind kicks up a funnel of black ash from small piles on the ground where they had stood moments before. Across from me, a gaping hole about five feet in diameter cuts through the roof of the middle school.

One of the men lying on the ground, the one I punched in the throat, stares at me in horror. "What *are* you?" he asks, voice hoarse.

I stare at my hands, and I honestly can't answer that question.

Confused, maybe.

Concerned.

But definitely—most definitely—no longer human.

With the threat neutralized and the shock of this wild magic too much to process right now, my training kicks in. I grab my gun and holster it before bolting again toward the street. By now, the cops will be on their way.

None of this went according to plan, and I curse silently at what just happened. I intended to beat up a few guys in a middle school playground and get on with my day, but *no.*

Now, this will be a national event. I can already see the headlines.

Unexplained blast destroys school.

Fatal assault at local pub. Dragons to blame?

Mysterious glowing woman possible suspect.

Spectres survive because we remain unseen. We live in the shadows, and the world doesn't know we exist.

Humans know about the Knights, but not us, and that's why we have longer lifespans.

But thanks to this mess, I am very much in the public eye.

And that does *not* bode well for me.

CHAPTER ELEVEN

Thankfully, the rest of my night goes without incident. It's a nice breather, and I'm grateful. In the cold morning hours close to dawn, I drive down a remote stretch of road, lost in thought.

As the road curves along a coastline, my mind wanders. A crescent moon hangs in the cloudy sky, beaming its crackly sliver light across the foamy ocean waves below.

Without any trees for cover, this isn't the best cut of road, but there weren't any better options to get to the remote section of Vaer wilderness Diesel gave me in his coordinates.

So, I press onward. I have to.

Even though my muscles ache from sitting too long in the cramped sedan I had to steal, I have another three hours to go. I should be able to make it before dawn if I push myself.

Once I'm there, I'll get some rest. Do some recon. Make the next plan.

I've been on the road now for eight hours, and I've made good progress. The quiet kind, with no one on my tail and no other headlights for miles.

The good kind of progress. The kind that gives me a moment to think.

My life of shadows and secrets is slowly unraveling, and I hate it. I don't *do* spotlight. I don't *do* attention. A famous assassin is a terrible one. That's kind of the whole point—remain unseen.

Now, however... every dragon alive probably knows about me to some extent. That makes my job decidedly more difficult.

As the road straightens for a brief stretch, I examine one of my hands, marveling at the soft and subtle glow now radiating from my skin.

After being kicked into the pit, after what I found down there, I don't even know if I *can* avoid the spot-light, no matter how badly I want to escape attention.

Especially when I shoot pulses of magic out of my palms.

I blow a raspberry in frustration and sink deeper in my seat, resting my head on the cold window beside me as I drive.

Out of habit, I check the rearview as I always do—

once every five seconds—and this time I see four blips of shadow dart out above on the horizon behind me.

It's too far away to tell for certain what they are. They could be human-owned jets traveling in a tight formation, but I doubt it.

Not this close to dragon territory.

I tense, scanning the road ahead for cover, but with the deep curves and steep slopes of the mountain rock, I can't see more than a mile ahead of me, where the road wraps around the cliff.

It doesn't take long before I can see the movement of their wings, confirming that these are, in fact, dragons. My jaw clenches, and I do my best to keep calm.

Pulling down my jacket sleeves as hard as I can, I do my best to cover my glowing skin. I sink into the depths of the car's cabin and tilt the mirrors a bit downward, so as not to have my reflection casting up toward the dragons as they loom nearer.

At this point, my car has been spotted. They see me, a lone red blip far below, gently coasting along the shoreline. If I floor it now, I'll look suspicious, and they'll be forced to investigate even if they were simply going to pass me by.

I need to act casual. Well, as casual as one can be driving a stolen car along the outskirts of dragon territory.

The four dragons reach me quickly, coasting overhead as I try to subtly speed up. If I remember correctly from the map, this road turns away from the coast soon, and that will mean trees and glorious, merciful cover.

I hold my breath, waiting to see what will happen.

They fly overhead, well below the five hundred feet legal limit, their gold scales glinting in the low light. A gust of wind from their wings hits the car, and I can't help but swerve a bit in their wake.

Even though it looks like they might pass me by, something isn't right here.

My grip tightens on the wheel as I rake my memory, searching for the tidbit that's going to explain why I suddenly feel so uneasy. I scan them again as they continue their flight, and it takes me a tense moment to pinpoint why my heart is skipping beats.

Gold scales.

That means they're fire dragons. Pretty ones, but still.

There's only *one* dragon family with gold dragons.

And it's not the Vaer.

I watch the four Andusk dragons fly ahead of me, grateful but still suspicious of the distance they're putting between us. As they fly, their wings brush each other briefly, and I can't help but remember the red dragon's words when he first pinned me against the tree.

This is how we speak in our dragon forms, he said.

When they touch, they speak telepathically to each other.

So, the four of them—they're *talking*.

The one at the back of the pack turns his head towards me, and my heart sinks into my stomach.

He roars.

Damn. Somehow, they know it's me.

I gun it. This is one of *the* worst spots to be found, and I have a sneaking suspicion it's no accident they did a fly by here. They probably got wind of me a ways back and waited for the perfect spot to pounce.

And they found it.

On this road, there is absolutely *no* cover. A cliff on one side, the ocean on the other. Nowhere to go except forward or back to where I came from. Nowhere to run.

They bank, the four of them moving in perfect formation as they angle toward me, the low moonlight glinting off their stunning scales. The only things I have on my side right now are the few seconds it will take for them to reach me, and my lifetime of training for a moment like this.

Zurie's cruel, but at least she's a good teacher.

With one hand on the wheel, I grab the pack sitting loose in the passenger's seat and slide it over my shoulders, securing it as best I can. No matter what happens, I can't lose this.

My sedan races along the asphalt, but I save the

top speeds for my next trick. I watch them, waiting for a sign that they're going to try to grab me. It's either going to be extended claws for a dive-and-grab, or an open mouth as they attempt to roast me in the car.

And I have to say, of those two options, I'm *really* hoping for door number one. It has better odds for survival and escape.

"C'mon," I mutter, knuckles white from my anxious grip on the wheel. "C'mon!"

The huge dragon in the lead dives, only a hundred feet away, his front claws stretching and opening as they prepare to snatch the car.

Score.

I floor it, pushing the tiny car to its absolute max.

The car whines, its engine starting to overheat.

The dragon misses.

Ha!

This is an automatic vehicle, so I don't have the control I would normally prefer in a situation like this, but I make do. The road curves, and with a few deft movements of the wheel and pedals, I drift across the pavement to keep my momentum.

There's no time for brakes or blinkers when dragons are on the hunt.

But then the four of them do what I hoped they wouldn't. They split up, breaking formation and diving toward me in a carefully choreographed pattern.

One after another, they plunge toward the car, and I'm pretty much totally screwed.

I let loose a string of curses as I swerve to escape the first and second attacks. The third dragon snaps at the air by my open passenger window, missing the metal frame by an inch, and I brake suddenly to avoid the claws as they grasp the thin air where my front wheel would have been. When I gun it again, the fourth clips my bumper, and my wheels shriek as I briefly lose control.

Jaw clenched, heart pounding, I recover and floor it once more, but there's still no sign of cover.

Briefly, I debate shooting off a few rounds into the ceiling of the car to scare them off, but these aren't birds that flinch at loud bangs. Letting off a few bullets wouldn't make them leave. It probably wouldn't have a single effect, not on massive creatures like this, not when they're so hellbent on nabbing me. It would just be wasted ammunition in a time when I'm not sure when—or *if*—I'll be able to resupply.

One of them bites the tail end of the car. Metal crunches. The wheels screech and lock. The steering wheel refuses to turn, and I drift out of control down the road.

Toward the edge.

The metal barrier blocking the road from the ocean thirty feet below is most effective for side swipes, not a head-on collision at full speed.

This car is going off the cliff.

I unlock the door and roll, my skin scraping over the asphalt as my training kicks in and saves me from a gruesome, bloody death.

My bag flies through the air. Twisting my body as I roll, I reach for the pack, trying to grab it as it's flung from the car, but my fingertips only graze the fabric as it sails overhead. It smacks against the pavement, far out of reach.

That sucks, but on a positive note, at least it's not still in the car.

An ocean breeze kicks up my hair as I skid to a stop. Breathless, body aching from the tumble, I look up in time to see the car lurch off the cliff, tearing through the guardrail and plummeting to the ground below.

There's a brief moment of silence before a deafening crash fills the air, followed by the victorious roars of the four dragons above me. One of them lands on the asphalt, black smoke curling out of his nostrils as he stares me down.

Oh, how cute. They think they've won.

I debate grabbing my pack, but every movement matters right now. I'll have to grab it later, once I've kicked some dragon ass.

I've never faced four shifted dragons at once before, so it's time to find out just what I can do.

With no cover, I go full offense. I roll onto my back, bracing myself against the pavement, and aim my gun at the dragon slowly walking toward me. He roars in frustration and instantly takes off, no doubt smart enough to realize this is the caliber of gun that can pierce dragon hide.

All four take to the air, circling again, apparently starting to realize I'm not some easy mark they're going to wear down and fly off with.

Right now, we're in a standoff. My mind races through my options and, honestly, they all suck.

The best way to kill a shifted dragon isn't with a gun at all—it's with a sword or sharp blade of some kind, funny enough. Decapitation is the best bet, but I don't have anything like that on me.

But a well-placed gunshot to the skull or heart might still kill them, so I'm not totally out of options. I could slowly make my way along the road, gun trained on the dragons, until they get impatient and dive.

Nope. That'll leave me vulnerable to attack, and I'll end up in someone's claws even if I take one or two of them down with me.

I can run for it, but that would turn my back to the enemy.

Nope. That's just stupid.

I can sit here and wait for them to just get impatient and leave.

Nope. They're the ones who so patiently hunted me down, so that's clearly not going to happen.

Or…

With my right hand still gripping my gun tightly, I examine my left palm. The lines crisscross over the soft honey glow of my skin, and I wonder.

I wonder if I can control it this time. The magic. The power.

Of my sucky options, this one sucks the least.

I lift my left hand, trying to access the magic, frantically searching for the trigger deep within me. My mind sifts through the last two episodes, eager to figure out what the hell I did to make it appear before.

The largest dragon roars in frustration, circles, and dives.

Toward me.

I train my palm at his chest, willing my power to shoot through him like a bullet, willing something —*anything*—to happen.

Nothing does.

He's closer now. Five seconds to intercept.

Four.

Three.

"Damn it!" I train my gun on his chest, but from this angle, I can't get a clear shot to the heart.

I missed my chance.

Hand steady, heart racing, I shift aim to the dragon's forehead. My finger on the trigger, I search for the right spot. I'm not certain this will work at all since dragon skulls are the thickest part of their body.

There's a whistle through the air, like a missile

carving through the sky. Something intercepts the golden dragon. A blur of red scales and white teeth and anger.

One moment, the dragon's claws are reaching for me, and I'm about to shoot. The next, he's gone.

The ground shakes, and not far off, a pile of rubble in the road marks where the golden dragon hit the ground. He wrestles with another dragon, and I briefly look to the sky to count them.

Three, all circling, screeching and roaring as they seethe at the fight now happening on the trashed asphalt road.

Whoever this is, it's a new contender. I wonder if an alert went out, if perhaps a second swarm is going to descend on us at any minute, and the thought sends an ice-cold shot of dread through my core.

I have *got* to find a way out of here.

In the darkness, I can't make out any detail on this new dragon's identity. I stand, wondering if this is a good chance to make my exit, but the same problem presents itself—there's nowhere to go.

The newcomer hurls the golden dragon off the cliff and stands, digging his massive claws into the road as he roars to the sky, and I recognize him.

The red dragon with the gold stripe down his back. The one from the swarm.

He glances at me briefly before taking to the skies after the three dragons who remain. They hover, darting out of reach, clearly debating whether or not this fight is still worth it.

Apparently, it is. In unison, they dive at him.

Now with a suitable distraction to keep the gold dragons busy, I examine both ends of the road. If I continue ahead, there's still about twenty miles of coastline until I get some cover. Not ideal, but I've run farther.

I take off, but one of the golden dragons breaks free from the fight in the sky and lands on the road in front of me. He bares his teeth, claws digging into the pavement, and I skid to a stop.

Gun drawn, I aim at his chest.

He's too fast.

Digging his claws into the cliff for added momentum, he bolts toward me, ducking and weaving in almost hypnotic fashion, never in one place for more than a second, never giving me a clear shot.

As he nears, I roll out of the way before he can get his claws around my waist. The tip of his sharp claw grazes my back as I barely escape his grip, ripping a deep hole in my coat.

But I'm not in the clear.

Out of nowhere, his tail hits me hard in the gut, flinging me against the cliff wall. As my ears ring from the blow, all I can hear is the metal clink of my gun hitting the pavement somewhere in the darkness.

His tail hits my stomach again, and I double over onto my hands and knees in agony.

After yet another hit, I'm on my back, staring up at the stars. Dazed, my head spinning, I barely register the uncontrolled buzzing heat in my hands until it's too late.

He hits me once more, and a burst of white light soars into the sky. No aiming. No control. It just cuts through the air, and the red dragon swerves out of its way barely a second before it hits his wing.

Despite having his own battle to deal with in the sky, he glares down at me, those bright golden eyes narrowing in anger. A puff of smoke shoots from his nose.

"I'm sorry, damn it!" I shout at him, battling a wave of nausea as I roll to avoid another strike from my opponent's tail.

The red dragon huffs in annoyance and returns to his fight.

From the ocean below, a massive shadow soars over the cliff edge and into the sky. The large golden dragon seems to have come to, and as he hovers in the air above me, watching me, his eyes darting back and forth between me and my gun, I see him debating his choices, just as I did moments ago.

I hesitate, my attention split between him and the smaller one with the deadly accurate tail blows.

After a tense moment of internal debate, the golden

leader roars his retreat order into the clouds and takes off toward the ocean. The other three follow without missing a beat, slipping effortlessly into formation.

Seconds later, I'm left alone on a now-destroyed patch of public road, staring breathlessly at the ocean while my attackers disappear.

When they're gone, the red dragon lands. The ground trembles beneath his claws, but he gives me space. We simply watch each other for a moment, silent and cautious, before he takes off into the sky as well. The beat of his wings kicks up a gust of wind that cuts through my hair, but he leaves without so much as a word.

My adrenaline still pumping, my heart still racing, I let out a slow breath and lay my head against the cold asphalt. That was too close.

Way too close.

That's twice now he could have overpowered me, and he didn't take either opportunity. It's clear I'm not headed to his precious dojo, and at this point, any sane dragon would simply take me there himself.

I don't get this guy at *all*.

Tenderly, body sore and screaming, I stand and watch him fly away. His silhouette quickly recedes, until he's nothing but a shadow on the horizon before he disappears behind the cliff.

He wants me to go to the dragon-run neutral zone, one he simply called *the dojo,* but he has no idea who or what I am. He doesn't realize I have things to do, a mentor to save, a sister to heal.

Besides, it's just not smart. A Spectre in a dragon den… I mean, it's like throwing a match in a gas tank.

But maybe I'm wrong.

As I scan the destroyed section of road for my gun and bag, I can't help but wonder if there's more at play than I realize. More pieces moving across the board than I know of. More people after me than I thought.

Even if I *do* go to the dojo, even if I *do* believe in the alleged safety of a dragon-run neutral zone, people can still die in a place like that. There could be secret passages, bribed guards, or some other perfect storm of mistakes or oversight that gets me caught.

First, I stumble across my bag. I fling it over my aching shoulders and continue the search for my gun, which I find a short way off. Thank goodness—I can't afford to lose another gun, not right now. I holster it and begin the long walk to the next town, lost in my thoughts.

Ever since he suggested it, I've been convinced I would never go to this dojo.

But as I examine the golden chains fused to my body, as I think about the uncontrolled magic buzzing inside of me, I wonder.

I wonder how many times I'll be attacked, how long I can go unseen, and just how much the world has changed for me. Just how much of my old life I've lost.

An engine rumbles somewhere behind me, a truck by the sound of it, and I thank my lucky stars. It's usually a terrible idea to hitchhike, but in this situation, I could do with a ride. Besides, if anyone ever tries to hurt me, I'd just kick him out and steal his car.

The truck slows to a stop, and I slip my hand under my jacket, palm on my gun, just in case. I smile, trying not to look terrifying in the hopes it'll help me catch a ride.

As I approach the passenger side window, it rolls down. My smile fades as I recognize the driver.

"Hey, babe," Tucker says with a wink.

CHAPTER TWELVE

As Tucker's truck rumbles beside me, both of his windows down despite the cold night, I sigh and rub my temples. With one hand on my hip, I just shake my head in annoyance.

I don't even fight it anymore. I'm too tired, too frustrated, too astonished by his tenacity to be mad.

"How?" I ask simply, gesturing into the air. "Just... how?"

"Hop in and I'll tell you." He pats the passenger seat.

I pause. If it were almost anyone else, I'd jump in without hesitation, but the wheels are turning in my head.

Maybe he's not really a human. Maybe *he's* the red dragon. I've never seen them both at the same time, and I certainly can't tell for sure if someone's a dragon unless I see them shift. Hell, there are plenty of humans who claim they have dragon blood in them, that they can shift—but just aren't allowed to show anyone. Usually no one can call the bluff until the person submits for a test or simply disappears, as none of the dragon families particularly like having a plain old *human* pretend to belong among *gods*.

He pats the passenger seat again, that charming grin almost disarming, and I decide to turn the tables on Mr. Tucker Chase.

"I'm driving." I nod my head toward his chair and walk around the vehicle to take his spot.

"Sorry, babe. You're a delight, but I love this truck. We're not at that level in our relationship yet."

"Scoot," I demand, snapping my fingers as I reach his door.

He sighs, smiling down at me like I said something cute. "Well, okay. But only because you asked nicely."

With a few expert movements, he climbs over the dash between the two seats and into the passenger chair. Apparently settled and comfortable, he sets his hand on the back of the driver's side headrest.

Smart man. He was probably worried I would drive off with his truck if he got out to walk around.

He's not wrong.

I jump into the massive truck and don't bother adjusting the seat before taking off. The tires squeal along the pavement as I continue along the curving cliff road, eyes constantly scanning the horizon in front of and behind me for another round of dragons.

Since I can't seem to shake him, it's time to find out who this guy really is.

Tucker fiddles with the radio while I drive, finally settling on a soft rock station. His arm still resting on the back of my seat, he very lightly taps his finger on my headrest in tune with the music.

"Please stop that," I ask, a bit nicer than I intended. I don't care about the sensation—I care about having a stranger's hand that close to my neck.

"Sorry." He adjusts in his seat, arms crossed as he leans back and stares me down. "You look like you had fun."

"Oh, loads."

I return my attention to the horizon, still conscious of the fact I'm driving a truck owned by a weapons expert who is apparently also a master tracker. The music plays softly in the quiet cabin as he watches me, apparently waiting for me to speak first.

This is just weird.

"I don't do… teams." I'm not sure what to say, honestly, but the silence makes me uncomfortable. "I still don't trust you."

"Good." He says with a nod. "You shouldn't."

I can't help it. I laugh. "You keep saying that, and it's really not doing you any favors."

He shrugs. "Whatever you did back at the Vaer place, you raised a lot of eyebrows."

"Yeah, no kidding." I shift gears as we round a sharp bend in the road, deciding to be courteous and not drift his truck.

"What's your name?" He tilts his head in curiosity.

"That's not going to happen." The corners of my mouth turn upward in a slight smile, but at this point, I have to give him credit for his tenacity.

"I'll have to give you a nickname, then." He taps his finger on his chin thoughtfully.

"You really don't."

"How about Amazon? You're a good fighter. It would fit."

I shake my head, but I can't suppress the smile any more. "Pass."

"I like Wonder Woman."

"Tucker, focus." I grip the wheel tighter, my eyes on the road. "How do you keep finding me?

"You're stubborn. I could just call you Punk."

"Wait, *I'm* stubborn?" I cast a brief sidelong glance at the man who won't take no for an answer, but he's still lost in thought, as if this whole nickname thing is important.

"Yeah, I kind of like Punk," he says casually, like he's picking out breakfast cereal.

"Unreal," I mutter under my breath.

"You're kind of short. How about Half Pint?"

"I—no, man, *absolutely* not. Focus. You found me how, exactly? Because if you somehow put a tracker on—"

"Half Pint is pretty cute." He chuckles to himself and rests one leg on the dash. "Yeah, that one's growing on me."

"Tucker."

"No, that's my name. We can't have the same name."

"Tucker!"

"Oh, wait!" He smacks the dash in excitement. "What about Goldie? Since you have that weird glowing thing going on."

"Rory!" I shout, my hands tightening on the wheel as I glare at the road in front of me.

Except for the music softly playing through the speakers, the car is silent for a moment, and I can't believe what I did. Sharing my name—my real name—with a potential threat goes against all of my training.

Then again, so does calmly driving with a stranger. And, well, I just did it, so there's no going back.

"Rory," I say again softly, clearing my throat as I check the rearview mirror. "My name is Rory."

"That's really pretty." Tucker smiles, his face lighting up in an adorably annoying sort of way as he watches me. I tensely nod in thanks, and he nudges my arm gently. "Good thing, too. You were dangerously close to being called Half Pint for the rest of your life."

I laugh, shaking my head at him because I don't know what else to do. "You're such an idiot."

"Yeah, but I'm cute."

I laugh again and rub my forehead, the surreal sensation of having a conversation like this a little too much for me to handle. "Now, will you *please* tell me how you keep finding me?"

"And ruin the surprise?"

I glare at him over the bridge of my nose.

He sighs. "Fine. You're no fun."

"I'm a little fun." I shrug, thinking back to the dragons we took on together in the parking lot of that run-down pub.

"You're incredibly hard to keep track of." He pulls out a handheld radio from the glove box. "Thankfully, you're also gorgeous as all hell, so everyone sees you."

I sigh, closing my eyes for a brief moment as I process the obvious. "You used a ham radio to keep tabs on me."

"Guilty."

"Damn it all," I say softly, groaning as the realization crashes through me.

I really can't hide anymore. My shadows, my secrets —they're gone.

He laughs. "It's not just the glowing, though. There's something about you that's unique. People look. People watch you. I think with enough time, I could find you even if you wore a ski mask everywhere."

"Tucker, I'm pretty sure *anyone* could find me if I did that." I chuckle. "It's a little suspicious to wear a ski mask everywhere."

He rolls his eyes, laughing. "You know what I mean."

"Sure."

Somewhere in the car, a phone vibrates. I briefly rest my hand against the bag still on my back, but it's not mine.

Tucker holds something in the empty space between his leg and the door, just out of my sight, and my smile fades. A dim white glow reflects on his hand as his thumb passes over a screen, and though he shoots me a reassuring smile, I'm not convinced.

He's persistent, yes. But he's still not safe.

I cannot let my guard down. There's too much at stake.

I'll let him tag along for now, but he's not part of my team. I don't trust him. Not yet. Maybe not ever.

But a part of me—a very small part of me—really wants to.

CHAPTER THIRTEEN

My original plan was to get some rest before doing recon on the Vaer hideout, to be sharp and fully rested for any attempt against Mason, but the plans changed the moment I got into Tucker's truck.

Deep in the hills of California, the truck rests under a copse of evergreen trees as puffy white clouds roll through the sky above us.

Tucker sits on the hood, one leg curled under him as he watches me shed my coat and tighten a few straps on my recon gear. "You're leaving?"

I nod, wordlessly tugging the final strap around my leg.

"Where are we going?"

"You're staying here." I scan the forest, fairly certain it's safe. We're on the outskirts, far enough away to be unnoticed—and far enough away from the Vaer compound that Tucker probably doesn't know my endgame.

Yet.

I wait for him to ask more questions. To get nosey, like Zurie would. To lecture me on safety and focus, like Irena would. But he simply nods and leans his back against the windshield, getting comfortable. "Bring me back a coffee, will you?"

For a moment, I'm derailed enough to simply look at him in surprise, chuckling a bit as his eyes close.

Who *is* this guy?

Without another word, I slip into the woods and head for the Vaer compound. With each step, my focus shifts. My mind sharpens. I listen for signs that he's following me, but the farther I go, the more convinced I am that he stayed behind.

Smart man.

By the time I reach the compound, the sun is only about thirty minutes from rising, but I'm ready to get to work.

Based on Diesel's notes and confirmed by a brief circle of the place, the best entry point is around the back, over their wired fence. No cameras over here, thankfully, as I want to limit using my voids unless it's absolutely necessary.

A dragon shifter takes a smoke break by the building, sitting on an old oil drum with his gun at his side, the metal butt resting on the ground.

I roll my eyes. It's a terrible way to treat a gun.

Effortlessly, I climb a tree and tip-toe along a branch until I'm over the fence. I drop onto the ground without so much as the rustle of a leaf.

The shifter, however, looks up, as if he heard something. Thwarted, I slip behind a wall as he looks my way. Peering through tiny gaps in the metal, its ends rusted and frayed with age, I watch him scan the space where I was. His expression sours, as if he's forgotten something, and he paces along the ground where I stood seconds before.

I shake my head in annoyance. It's like they can *sense* me.

No longer patient, I take him out quietly, knocking him to the ground with a few well-placed blows. The only noise is his grunt as he's knocked unconscious. I unload his gun and heave the magazine over the fence to be safe before dragging him to a space out of sight of the doors and windows.

Using his access card, I slip inside and scope the ceilings for cameras. None.

Good for me, of course, but I'm starting to get suspicious. Mason wouldn't keep Zurie in a place with such poor security.

It's starting to feel like this will be a waste of my time.

I slink through the halls, the hair on my neck standing on end, nerves frayed. The Vaer at the pub.

The golden dragons. The shifter outside. It's as if they know where I am, as if they can feel my presence.

I *hate* that.

As I near another hallway, I pause and listen. In the distance, two men laugh, their voices muffled by a door. The scrape of metal over wood catches my attention, but it's followed shortly after by the shuffle of cards and the clink of coins.

Ah. Gambling.

Keeping close to the ground, I peer around the corner and spot a camera. Just one, but it captures the entire hall.

I hate to use even one of my precious few voids, but I have no choice.

With a quick pop of my silenced gun, the void hits the cables, and the camera goes down. I weave my way through the compound, searching for clues, looking for any hint at all of Zurie's presence.

Nothing.

This is supposed to be a recon mission, one to simply test the waters to see if this is worth my time, but my suspicions are rising. Very few guards. Very few cams. Very little likelihood of this being the building I need.

As I come to the next corner, I hear a low rumbling of voices. Men, at least six, and close. No footsteps, though, so they're possibly at their stations or guarding something.

My eyebrow raises, interest piqued, and I slip a small mirror out of the gear pouch under my shirt. Keeping close to the floor, moving as little of the mirror as possible into the hallway, I angle it down the hall.

Eight men stand two by two in the corridor, guns at the ready as they casually chat with each other. A few of them are already looking my way, at the air above me, and I resist the impulse to quickly pull the mirror out of view. If I make any sudden movements, they'll see me for sure.

But there it is again—the strange expression on their faces, that feeling as if they can sense me without me ever making a sound.

In that moment, I'm sure of it. These dragons can feel me. My magic. They seem to know where I am, and it's going to make my life and mission so much harder if I can't sneak. If I can't steal through the shadows unseen.

Thankfully, none of them act on the sensation, and they remain in place. I take a slow and steady breath, tilting the mirror to get a better view of what else is in the hall.

The hallway ends behind them at a single door embedded with frosted glass. The shifters' bulky forms block most of the doorway, but as they adjust their weight, I see a blurry silhouette of a tall female form sitting in a chair. I wait and watch, but she doesn't move. Her head is upright, but I wonder if the angle is odd and she's perhaps unconscious, with her head tilted backward. The vague hint of ropes around her arms suggest she's tied in place.

I would thank my lucky stars—if I believed for one moment that this was real.

That feeling comes again, the one Zurie calls paranoia, and it warns me this is too easy. Zurie is the Ghost, perhaps the most important prisoner the Vaer have ever had, and I don't believe for one moment they're keeping her in a facility that has an unmonitored access point.

Slowly, I lower the mirror and return it to its place in the pouch, all the while debating my next move.

Either this is some random woman who *happens* to be the same height and build as Zurie, or this is a trap for me.

Time to find out.

I think this is probably a dead lead, but I need something else to go on. I need another set of coordinates, or a plan. I'm not going to risk coming back here if my mentor isn't even in one of these rooms.

Typically, it's best to avoid the security room on recon missions like this, since it most often has the highest levels of security and is the hardest to break into.

But, seeing as I have no plan B...

I think it's time to change direction.

CHAPTER FOURTEEN

I stalk through the Vaer compound, silent as a ghost, keeping to the empty hallways.

But as I near the control room, that becomes much harder to do.

The security center is usually located in a central area. As the heart of operations for a compound like this, it has to be difficult to access and even harder to compromise.

The challenge alone would be fun if I wasn't in such a hurry.

My gun close to my chest, I push my back against a doorframe and wait as the thundering clunk of footsteps echoes down a nearby hallway. I keep hidden in an unmonitored doorway as they pass the crossroads where their hall intersects mine, staying out of sight as the troupe of four guards casually talks about the new scopes they were issued.

I patiently wait until their voices fade, scanning the ceiling for clues as to what direction to take next. A series of cables run from the room behind me out into the hall, toward where the men just came from.

A clue.

I follow the cables, keeping to blind spots and doorways when possible, and shooting out cameras with my voids when it's not. Slowly, I make my way through the Vaer compound until I reach a network of doors and hallways at the center of the building.

A faded yellow sign on one of the doors reads SECURITY.

Good. I'm finally here.

The question is, how do I get in?

I wait, watching carefully in my little mirror, until a man walks down from a side hallway. He scans his card over an access panel on the right side of the security entrance. The light turns green, and with a loud buzz that announces his presence, the door slides open.

All right. Assuming the guard outside has similar access to this room, that's everything I need.

It's a big "if," but it's all I've got.

I prepare myself for what I'll face inside. I've only been on two missions where we raided the security hole, and both times, we were nearly caught when someone tried to hit an emergency call button. It's the failsafe for them, in case the room is compromised, but it's my worst enemy.

Sometimes, the failsafe locks down the room. If that happens, I won't be able to get out no matter what I do from the inside.

Other times, the failsafe sets off a compound-wide alert, and then the entire army will funnel through every available hallway, effectively trapping and over-whelming me. And, once again, I won't be able to get out.

Either way, I can't let that happen.

To do this, I have to be completely in the present moment. Clear headed. Laser focused.

Ready to kill, but only if I have to.

If they make me.

With a deep breath, I go in.

I take out the camera over the door with a void and take a second to prepare myself before swiping the guard's stolen access card over the panel. I tuck it away as the light turns green.

The door release buzzes.

I lift my gun.

The entrance slides open.

I walk in.

In the second it takes me to get inside, I scope the place. Two levels, one flight of stairs. Screens on every wall. A large glass panel overlooks a loading dock below.

Five men in dark uniforms sit in chairs, lost in the screens, headphones blocking out the world around them. Good, I can deal with them last.

Three other men stand around with arms crossed, checking various pieces of equipment. These three turn toward me as I enter, and a brief look of utter confusion crosses each of their faces.

Their confusion doesn't last long.

As the door closes on its own behind me, I open fire, taking out the three men standing as they each reach for their own guns. Each shot is calculated to take them out, but not kill them, and I hope I don't regret the choice.

The seated men are slower to react, and I'm able to knock out the two shifters on the upper deck before they can even stand.

The remaining three on the lower deck jump to their feet and open fire, and my *goodness* they're all terrible shots. They hit the screens behind me as I leap over the railing, taking aim at the nearest one as I fall.

I shoot. It hits. He crumples to the ground.

My boots hit the metal floor the second after he does. One of the remaining two men runs out of bullets, and he throws his gun at me. I duck out of the way and lift a chair, hurling it at him. It barrels into his chest, and he slides across the floor, going limp as he hits the far wall.

The last guy sees his odds dwindling, and he races toward a giant red button on the wall.

The emergency call.

I bolt after him and tackle him to the ground, pinning him face-down beneath me. He wrestles in my grip and manages to grab a clump of my hair, tugging hard as he tries to buck me off of him. I land two sharp blows on his neck, and he's out cold.

Breathing heavily, I only give myself a moment to recover before I scan the place again, in case I missed something—or worse, some*one*.

I didn't.

With a quick sigh of relief, I kick away the men's guns as they groan. They're not threats anymore, since I won't be here long enough for them to come to.

With a wall of monitors to choose from, I quickly scan through the images until I see one I recognize— the men standing in the hallway, guarding the door with the frosted glass. They still casually chat with each other, the audio not caught by the camera, and I tap the buttons on the custom keyboard beside the monitor until I find the one that changes the angle.

At first, images flash of various hallways I don't recognize, and I curse silently to myself, hitting more keys, wondering if I broke it.

That is, until an image of the frosted glass flashes on the screen, this time at a different angle.

From inside.

It's just a shot of the door, and I lean in a bit as I page through the camera angles. This room is loaded with cams, and each one focuses on a different thing.

The door, from the inside.

The one window in the room.

The next angle reveals a clump of twenty soldiers, each of them dressed in full body suits, complete with helmets. Every single gun is trained on the door. These soldiers aren't talking. They aren't laughing. They're prepared for war.

I switch angles again, and this time I see the woman in the chair.

Only… it's not a woman at all. It's a mannequin in a wig, dressed in a baggy shirt and loose men's pants, tied to a plastic folding chair.

Furious, frustrated, I shake my head in defeat.

Yes, I avoided the trap, but I'm still no closer to finding Zurie.

Nothing. No leads. No clues. Not even a *hint* of where Zurie might really be.

It's time to get out of here.

To be safe, I check a few of the camera angles, trying to pinpoint the ones I hit with voids that are still on loop. I plan my route out of this place, holster my gun, and take the stairs two at a time on my way out.

One of the men by the door groans in pain, and I pause briefly. His eyes water with his agony, but he'll live. They all will.

Zurie and Irena, though, I'm not so sure. These assholes have both of them, and I'm left without a shred of an idea of *where*.

Again, I debate smacking one of these guys around for answers, but even if torture was something I could bring myself to do, these aren't the people who have those answers. They likely have no idea who Zurie even is, and I can't waste my time.

I'm in enemy territory, and every second counts.

I slip out the door, propping it open with a fire extinguisher as a warning sign to anyone who happens to pass by that something is wrong. Zurie would rip me a new hole for doing that, of course, but I already know my exit route, and these guys need medical attention sooner rather than later.

As I duck out of the compound and escape into the forest, I imagine Tucker laying on the hood of his truck, still waiting. If ever there was a chance to ditch him, it's now.

But like he said, I'm not that hard to find.

I kick a rock in frustration and jog toward the spot where I left him. With everyone coming after me and my dwindling resources, I could use a bit of firepower on my side.

If he remains on my side, of course. He could turn on me at any moment, and there's no logical reason to trust him.

Except that he's had my location for four hours, and there haven't been any attacks.

Hmm.

My training warns me to take this solo, but my instinct tells me I can let him tag along.

For now.

In the distance, an alarm cuts through the trees, scaring off a few birds from a nearby branch. It seems like the guys in the security room were found, then.

But most of all, Mason knows I didn't fall for his trap. He'll have to up his game if he wants to play with *me*. I won't get caught rescuing a mannequin.

If he wants to set a trap worth my time, he's going to have to bring real bait.

CHAPTER FIFTEEN

Secluded in the wilderness, far enough from the Vaer compound to remain hidden, I sit on a log and sigh in frustration.

"Tough day at work, honey?" Tucker asks as he swings open the truck's side doors.

"Cute." I rub my face, wondering what the hell I'm going to do now. What the hell there even *is* to do except sit and wait.

I relocated the truck a little bit farther out to better mask our location. Though I half-expected an ambush to be waiting for me, Tucker had barely moved from his perch on the hood.

No surprises. No battles. Just Tucker, waiting patiently for me to return.

"So, are you nocturnal, or what?" He grabs a bag of gear out of the backseat and tosses it to me. I catch it, briefly peeking inside to find what looks like a tent and sleeping bag neatly rolled together.

I shrug. "You could say I'm nocturnal, sure."

"I can work with that." He grabs another bag and tosses it on the ground as the truck door slams shut.

"Can you *try* to be quiet?" I eye the woods, altogether uncomfortable with the sheer levels of noise this man makes doing what should be fairly basic tasks. "I thought you had training."

"Yeah, but stealth isn't really my thing," he confesses with a modest shrug.

"No kidding."

"It's clearly yours, though. Where did you learn how to do, well, *this*?" He gestures to all of me in one sweeping motion.

"That's specific," I say dryly.

He laughs and points to my feet. "You know, your badass sneak thing. I've never seen anyone move like you do."

"I don't think we're at that point in our relationship yet, dear," I quip, quoting him from the night before.

"Touché."

"Are you going to tell me where *you* trained?" I lean back, doubting I'll get an answer.

"Sure, but you first."

I laugh. "That's not going to happen."

"I don't know." He shrugs. "You said the same thing about telling me your name, Rory."

My smile fades, and I stare off into the forest to avoid looking at him. He's right, of course, and telling him that was probably a mistake.

He tugs open his bag and starts to unpack, but I watch carefully out of the corner of my eye as he seems to wrestle internally with something, like he can't decide whether or not to bring it up.

"I thought you weren't coming back," he says softly. Not wounded, no accusatory, just… gentle.

"I almost didn't," I admit.

He pauses and tilts his head, the full weight of those intense green eyes focused on me. "Why did you?"

I pause, debating my answer and how much I want to share with him. Instead, I pose a question of my own. "Why didn't you follow me?"

Because he didn't. I was careful, watched every step, kept an eye out for him every bit of the way.

He could have followed me, and he didn't. He also could have ambushed me when I got back, and he didn't.

So many missed opportunities to capitalize on a fleeting thing—the knowledge of my location.

Tucker sighs and abandons the bag, instead leaning his back against my log, a few feet closer than I would have ideally liked. With one arm resting against the dead tree, he looks off wistfully into the wilderness around us. "I took a gamble."

"Let me guess," I say, leaning my elbows on my

knees as I lower my head to his level. "You want me to trust you, and following would have made me doubt your intentions."

"You *are* good," he says with a charming wink.

I don't laugh. I want to, but I can't risk liking him. There are too many unknowns when it comes to Tucker Chase, and a Spectre can never let her guard down.

"But it's more than just that." He lets out a slow breath and runs his hand through his hair. "You're… different. You're a talented fighter, easily the best I've ever seen. You have guts and fire. I respect that."

More compliments. Yet again, I'm uncertain of how to respond. I'm not used to anyone but Irena saying nice things to me.

"I don't…" He groans again, wrestling with something internally, and it piques my curiosity.

"You don't what?"

He doesn't answer, and I wait patiently in the hopes he will. In the silence, his phone buzzes again. I hear it vibrate against the tree trunk, and he quickly swipes the screen to make it stop without looking down to see who it is.

That means he already *knows* who it is.

"You're certainly popular," I say. I'm wary. I don't like that he has reception in the middle of nowhere, and I certainly don't like that he could be telling people about where I am.

He chuckles. "It's my dad. You know how parents worry."

Uh huh.

I nod toward Tucker's vest. "Does your dad know you own a dragon taser?"

Tucker laughs and absently runs his thick fingers along the stubble on his jaw. "I can't say that he does, no." He sighs. "Look, Rory..."

In the distance, I hear a faint scream. My ears twitch, and even though Tucker is speaking, my attention shifts.

At first, I think the scream is human. I stand, alert, but Tucker doesn't seem to have noticed. He's talking about family, something about duty, completely oblivious to the possible danger.

I lift my hand, a silent signal for quiet, but he either doesn't see it or doesn't care because he keeps talking.

The shriek once again echoes through the trees, only this time I recognize the distant roar of a carnivore in pain. It's frantic and sad, a wail of desperation in the otherwise silent forest.

I draw the knife from my boot and silently stalk into the forest, sidestepping twigs and dried leaves as I make my way toward the isolated sound.

Before long, I come across a large meadow. The grass comes to my waist, and there, writhing in the center of it all, is an ice dragon.

Strange. The Vaer have some ice dragons, sure, but

not many. They're mostly a family of fire dragons, and this one seems far too beautiful to fit in among them. His royal blue scales glimmer in the sunlight, bright and vivid as the ocean in the Caribbean. His powerfully massive wings stretch against the ropes binding him in place, his tail limp against the matted grass that he's flattened in his attempts to escape. From here, I can't see his face.

Ever suspicious, I scan the woods for signs of a trap. Honestly, if this is a trap for me, it's one of the worst I've ever seen. Talk about poor choice of bait.

The dragon whimpers, almost cooing in sadness, and I tense. He's a *shifter,* for goodness sake, and I can't for the life of me figure out why he doesn't just shift back into human form to avoid the ropes.

Curious, I circle the meadow, looking for any signs of soldiers or cams. One busted camera lies on the ground, shattered and covered in dirt. Aside from that, it's just me and the downed dragon, alone in this field on the edge of the Vaer lands.

I keep to the shadows of the forest as I near the dragon's head. His body heaves with exhaustion, and by the state of the grass around him, I have to guess he's been here for days. He's likely famished. At death's door.

My grip on the knife tightens, and I debate my options.

If I were to listen to my training, I would leave him

to die. He's a dragon, after all, and that's what the Spectres stand for—dethroning dragons as the masters of our world, all while reinstating humans as the dominant species.

But unlike most of the Spectres, I never had a choice to join. I've never wanted this life, never despised dragons enough to *want* to hunt or kill them. It never resonated with me, no matter how many times Zurie tried to tell me they're evil.

It's not like they demand human sacrifices or anything. To me, blaming dragons for the world's wrongs always seemed like a scapegoat, something that could unite people in their loathing.

And while I grew up with a hearty suspicion of dragons based on all they've done to my world, I don't hate them.

Carefully, my knife hidden behind my back, I creep toward the dragon. His eyes shift to me before I'm even out of the shadows, and my heart skips a beat out of habit.

I don't hate dragons, but I *do* hate it when they see me.

He, however, doesn't move. He doesn't flinch, doesn't react, doesn't so much as snort in my direction. He seems to have given up and surrendered to the ropes ensnaring him.

That's when I finally see the tiny spines on the rigging. Thin shards of metal poke out every few inches. They've dug into his beautiful scales, gouged small rivers of drying blood across his body. With every movement, they seem to dig deeper into him, rooting him in place.

"Why aren't you shifting?" I ask, looking him directly in his ice blue eyes.

He sighs in defeat and looks away, almost in shame.

An idea dawns on me, and I wonder.

I wonder if all those rumors are true.

Is he... feral?

It seems too earth-shattering to be true. If dragons can really go feral, it means they lose their ability to shift.

The truth about this is something Zurie has hunted for years. If she knew what it took to make dragons go feral, she could trigger it in them, use the ensuing carnage of hundreds of feral dragons to start a human uprising, once and for all, that would seep into every corner of the human world. Dragons are powerful, but humans have greater numbers. If we unite against the dragon race, we would win.

My mentor dreams big.

As for me, though, I don't want a war.

Tenderly, I brush my fingers along his wing. The smooth leather is soft and tight under my hand, far more supple than I imagined.

I've never touched a dragon's wing before.

In a sudden rush, I hear a garbled word echo through my mind.

Feral.

I gasp and jump back, taken off guard by his voice, and look at him again. He sighs with sadness, as if he didn't want to confirm my suspicions but has nothing left to lose.

"So, it's true," I say softly, my heart twisting for him.

He snorts, his sad eyes never leaving mine.

I don't know if I believe it, though. He's not vicious. From what I've heard, feral dragons raze cities, burn forests to the ground, eat and plunder and pillage until someone kills them. A feral dragon has lost his human side and is owned by the animal within.

But this one—he can still understand me. Still share thoughts with me, even if they're garbled and messy.

There's still some of the human in there.

"Who are you?" I touch his wing again so that he can answer me.

I catch glimpses, just moments in time, each of them a fraction of a second and too short to process.

That is, until I see a man looking in a mirror. The moment is immersive, drawing me in, and I can feel what he feels. Hear what he thinks. I fuse with him in that moment, looking into the mirror with him, completely lost in the memory.

In *him.*

The man I see is tall and dashing, with broad shoulders and a fighter's build, though his messy light brown hair is an inch or two longer than he'd like it. He rubs his hand over the beard slowly growing along his jaw, debating if it's time to shave. He leans his hands on the sink below the mirror and sighs, his piercing blue eyes staring into the reflection.

Staring at *me*.

Staring into my *soul*.

The memory releases me, and I fall backward onto the grass as I catch my breath. The knife falls to the ground, and I loosely keep track of it as I try to calm myself.

This ice dragon doesn't really speak like the red dragon did. I mean, yeah, he can talk and form sentences, but it goes deeper than that.

He *feels*.

Everything in the memory was so riveting, so captivating, drawing me in so deep I didn't know where he ended and I began.

I look at the ice dragon again, the two of us simply watching each other, wondering what will happen next.

Rule 53 of the Spectres—if a dragon's life is in your hands, it's yours to take.

In other words, kill him.

But I just... I can't.

Curse my bleeding heart, but I can't leave him here. I can't fathom the thought of him lying still in the meadow when the snows come, nothing but carcass and bone.

I groan. If I cut him free, one of two things will happen. Either he'll fly off, wounded and hungry but free, or he'll try to kill me.

Honestly, if it means a clear conscience, I can work with those odds.

Time to get to it, then.

One by one, I saw through the ropes tying him to the ground. I work furious and fast, using my shirt to minimize how many of the barbs cut open my other hand as I hold the ropes steady. They draw some blood, but pain doesn't faze me.

He stiffens as the ropes slacken around him. I toss each cord over him, and they land harmlessly on the other side, giving him his freedom.

I hesitate in my work, momentarily lost in the thought of what it must be like to soar through the sky.

It must be wonderful.

After a lifetime of obeying Zurie's orders, I've always wondered what it would be like to be truly free.

The ice dragon shifts beneath the last few ropes, snapping me out of my thoughts, and I slice through the final cables. As he rights himself, teetering on his weak feet, I step back into the forest, my hand resting on the handle of my gun in case I need it.

It would be a shame to free a dragon, only to be

forced to kill him when he comes after me, but a Spectre is always prepared.

And for all that is holy, Zurie will *never* know I let this dragon free. I would disappear into the dungeons beneath her home for a few weeks to be "reprogrammed" and reminded of what it means to obey the Rules of the Spectres.

The ice dragon stands, quickly regaining his balance after a few teetering tries, and he stretches his wings to their full length. A delighted groan escapes him, and I imagine he hasn't gotten to do that in quite a while.

I marvel despite myself, amazed at the elegant slope to his wings, the way they look more sleek and refined than any other dragon I've seen. It's as if he's built for speed and stealth, and I imagine what it must be like for him to steal through the dark sky, silent and unseen.

But instead of flying off, he shifts his intense blue gaze toward me.

My slight smile fades, and I wait. I've already defied rule fifty-three. I may as well defy rule thirty-seven, as well, and wait to see if he deals the first blow.

Slowly, deliberately, he closes the distance between us, never breaking eye contact. It's not menacing, just wary. Observant.

There are no growls. No teeth. He simply walks toward me, nimble and elegant despite the bloody scars along his body, and he sets his powerful head against my torso. His thin scales rest against my brow, far warmer than I expected. As our skin meets, I feel a rush of gratitude flood from him into me.

Thank you, he says, his voice echoing through my mind.

I sigh with relief and, on impulse, set my hands around his jaw. I can't even fit them all the way around his face.

Good lord, I'm hugging a dragon. I never thought I'd see the day, but this one melts me.

I'm Levi, he says, his voice disjointed and echoing through my mind as he speaks.

I don't answer, mostly because I'm not sure what to say. He doesn't seem to mind the quiet, though, and for a few moments, we simply stand there in silence.

My world has shifted, and this is proof. Here we are, a Spectre and a dragon, the former rescuing the latter from a snare trap not unlike one I've been ordered to set up before.

And it hits me, in this moment, just how out of my element I really am. How much I'm changing.

With each passing day, I become less and less of a Spectre. The training is there, sure, but the longer I spend away from Zurie, the easier it is to break the rules. One taste of freedom, and I've already committed a cardinal offense against the very organization that raised me.

Zurie isn't here to shield me from the truth anymore.

That there's a human side to every dragon.

As my mind races, I hold Levi a bit tighter on impulse. He leans into me, offering comfort, and yet again I'm left confused.

All my life, Zurie told me dragons are vicious and cruel because deep within, their dragon rules them even in their human form.

But Levi is proof she's wrong.

The question is—when presented with the truth, will she change her mind?

Or, like the traitor who ratted us out, did I just break rule number one?

CHAPTER SIXTEEN

In the dead-silent hush of the forest, the snap of a twig captures my full attention.

Levi and I have company.

A low growl builds in his throat, and he pulls away from me, the skin on my arms cold now that he isn't near.

Another twig snaps, and I scan the spaces between the trees until I spot him.

Tucker.

He's looking around the dense forest, probably searching for me, and I have no idea what's about to happen.

That's a feeling I neither like nor experience often.

When his head tilts toward Levi, he freezes in his tracks. His eyes go wide, shifting between me and the ice dragon, and his skin pales. "What the *hell* are you doing?"

Levi snaps. The snuggly dragon from a moment before is gone, and instantly he's a predator. He roars at Tucker, the sound as deafening as thunder. His mighty wings spread wide, and his razor-sharp claws dig into the ground as his teeth gnash the air.

Tucker reaches into his back pocket, likely for a weapon, and I realize I'm the only one who can stop this.

"Wait!" I bolt between them, spreading my arms in an effort to soothe both of them. I look at Levi first, staring down the ice dragon's piercing blue eyes. "Wait, stop. He's a—he's okay. He won't hurt you."

I almost say Tucker is a friend, but I catch myself. It's too much, too soon, for a Spectre like me to have a *friend*.

Tucker scoffs. "I *will* hurt him if he keeps snarling at me like that."

Levi growls again.

"Will you shut *up*?" I shoot an impatient glare at Tucker.

"Just giving fair warning." Tucker narrows his eyes in suspicion at Levi, his hand still dangerously close to his belt and the myriad of devices and weapons he keeps stored on his body at any given time.

"Calm down. Both of you, chill!" I snap at them, entirely done with this standoff. "Relax, damn it!"

Levi snorts impatiently, the full force of his gaze still on Tucker, his lips curling slightly as yet another growl rumbles through his body. It's a low hum, like a brewing storm, and I feel the ground subtly tremble beneath my feet in time with the sound.

With slow and powerful steps, Levi brushes past me, deftly putting his massive body between me and Tucker. I catch glimpses of the weapons expert as Levi lowers his head to attack.

Entirely fed up with this, I jump over Levi's bruised tail and try to get around him, but the stubborn dragon is faster.

Faster than *me*.

He always manages to step in front of me or Tucker at the right time, never letting either of us see the other for long.

"That's *enough*." I smack Levi's thigh.

He briefly tilts his head toward me, catching me in that intense blue gaze, his eyes narrowed in deadly focus as I interrupt him.

"Tucker won't hurt you," I remind him. "Or me."

At that, Levi finally relaxes. He hesitates a moment, briefly looking at the way Tucker's hand has slowly moved to something on his belt, but it seems to be what he needed to hear.

The ice dragon huffs impatiently, shooting one last warning glare at Tucker before he steps back and lays on the ground at my side.

For a moment, Tucker doesn't move. Jaw tense, a vein pulsing in his forehead, he watches Levi, the two of them glaring at each other in the now mercifully silent woods.

"We need to move." I scan the forest for signs of the Vaer, in case they heard Levi's little spat. We're probably in the clear since Levi has been left out here for what seems like days, but I don't take chances.

"Right," Tucker finally relaxes, though his shoulders still look a bit tense and he won't fully turn his back toward Levi.

I head off toward camp, and Levi springs into action. He follows closely behind, like he's my shadow, effortlessly ducking and weaving through the woods. He doesn't brush a single trunk, doesn't shake loose a single leaf, doesn't so much as snap a twig as he silently stalks through the forest beside me.

It's mesmerizing.

Though I continue to scan the forest for signs of trouble, I keep finding myself watching Levi's movements, entranced by the perfect grace of it all. I marvel at how a creature so massive and powerful could also be so deadly silent.

Beside me, Tucker seems equally entranced and baffled. "You know," he says softly, leaning in, his tall and solid form a little closer than I'd like. "You never cease to amaze me, Rory."

I raise one inquisitive eyebrow in answer, not bothering to ask the question I know is plainly on my face.

He shrugs. "You've clearly got ability. I mean, deadly with a gun and anything else you can turn into a weapon. You've got skills, you know a lot about dragons, and yet you continue to be full of little surprises." He gestures toward Levi. "Like Grumpy here."

Levi snorts in annoyance, flicking his ear in Tucker's direction in a motion that reminds me of all the times Irena has said, *"I heard that!"*

"Are you some kind of dragon vigilante?" Tucker asks. "Protecting them from the humans who want to kill them?"

I laugh. I can't help it.

If he only knew.

But when I look up at him, Tucker isn't laughing. He doesn't smile. He's deadly serious, and I can tell by the way his eyes subtly narrow that he's waiting. He knows I won't answer, but he's looking for something on my face, something in my body language or my tone, to give him a clue.

He's doing to me what I've been doing to him.

Just as I don't know who he really is or what organization he works for, he's trying to piece together my past from little hints in the conversation. He wants to know who *I* work for, who trained *me*.

The more time we spend together, the more clues

we'll discover about each other. And the more time I spend with this man, the more in danger he is of discovering the truth.

Because him learning the truth isn't going to put my life at risk as much as it will put *him* in the line of fire.

We Spectres value our privacy. To a lethal degree.

And, surprisingly, I'm beginning to care whether he lives or dies.

Instead of answering, I press ahead, a bit faster as I sneak through the forest. I'm careful to keep Tucker in my periphery, since I don't want to turn my back to him and his mobile arsenal of weapons, but I don't want to talk to him right now, either.

I fume inwardly about how much I'm starting to *care.* About Tucker. About Levi. Having so many feelings is just… weird.

All of this freedom is making me soft.

Or… I sigh. Maybe it's not making me soft, but rather revealing who I really am. The part of me Zurie always tried to make me stuff deep down.

Eventually, Tucker sighs and breaks off from the group.

I pause, staring at him as he branches off to the south. "Where are you going?"

"To kill our new guest a deer, babe. He looks starved." Tucker winks at me, all jokes and charm once more, as if none of the last ten minutes ever happened.

With that, Tucker ducks into the woods before I can tell him, *again,* to stop giving me those stupid pet names.

CHAPTER SEVENTEEN

As I lean against Levi's body, staring up at the sky, I am at an utter loss for words.

Levi curls protectively around me as he sleeps, and the subtle rise and fall of his chest behind me is surprisingly soothing. The tip of his tail drapes protectively over my leg, and for the life of me, I can't figure out how my already strange life could take such a surreal turn.

A gentle mist, barely even a sprinkle of rain, rolls through the forest. I rub my arms as a chill snakes through my body, but it's nothing I haven't dealt with before.

The dull embers of a fire, just enough to keep us warm, glow in a small makeshift pit between me and Tucker. He snores a little, one arm draped over his eyes to block out the afternoon light filtering through the fog. His other hand rests in his coat pocket, where I saw him slip at least one handgun before he laid down. The man is a walking armory, and I halfheartedly wonder if I should pat down a few of his pockets while he sleeps to see if I can borrow one or two of them.

My cheeks burn a bit at the thought of my hands roving down his hard torso, over the obvious muscle beneath his vest, and I glance out over the mist to distract myself from the idea of exploring his body.

I can't believe he's actually asleep. He's not faking it, judging by the steady rhythm of his breath and the light snoring. For whatever reason, he trusts me.

Actually trusts me. No experienced fighter sleeps next to someone they suspect will hurt them.

And for whatever reason, he thinks he's safe around me.

My elbow brushes against Levi's stomach, and my skin rubs against something scratchy. I twist a little to get a better view and find a massive scar that cuts deep across the ice dragon's chest. Tenderly, I run my finger along the massive gouge, wondering what could have caused this. Dragons heal quickly, most of their wounds disappearing within a day or so, but this one looks old. *Years* old. Whatever did this to him must have been truly horrible to leave such a lasting scar.

Levi hums as I touch him, his leg twitching as I gently brush the scar, and I'm once more left a bit confused by this whole turn of events.

A feral dragon nearly killed Tucker to protect me.

Me.

Of all people.

I sigh and lean against Levi's body, staring at the misty sky and wondering what on earth I should do.

I'm running out of time to save Irena, and I have neither the antidote nor an idea of what actually made her sick. Zurie is somewhere out there, locked up in a cell, probably being interrogated in the most inhumane ways possible.

All I know is the Vaer are behind all of this.

The Vaer and the traitor, of course.

I run my hands through my hair, jaw tense, frustrated and at a loss for what to do next.

No Spectre will help me at this point because of the dragon magic I possess. If I didn't get thrown into the pit, then maybe they would pitch in—begrudgingly. But now I'm on my own, and none of the so-called brotherhood will help me.

No Knight will help me, either, not that I want their help. No human governments are going to come near me with this many dragon families on my tail.

I laugh at the idea of going to humans for help. The only ones who understand my wild magic are the dragons—and the humans would sooner kill me off out of fear or turn me into a dragon family as tribute than try to train me to use it.

Absently, I stare at my palm, tracing one finger over

the lines that cut across the skin. Kind of like Levi, this magic is feral within me. Utterly untamed. I destroyed a school, killed men and dragons alike with it, and nearly took out the red dragon who was helping me, all because it's so unlike any weapon I've ever wielded.

Give me a gun, and I'll have it mastered in five minutes.

Give me a knife, and I can practically do surgery with it.

But magic…

I sigh, wondering if I'm a ticking time bomb just waiting to go off at the wrong time, at risk of hurting the wrong people.

And I *care.*

Dang it, when did I get so *soft?*

With Levi and Tucker both asleep, I figure it's time to find my own secluded spot to rest for a few hours before nightfall. Even after what I've been through with the both of them, my training won't allow me to sleep here.

Tenderly, I slip out of Levi's protective grip and duck into the forest. There's a cave about two hundred feet away, and that might—

I only make it a short distance from camp before my hair stands on end, a warning that I'm not alone.

Fine. I could do with a fight.

Careful to time my steps just right so as not to let my attacker know I sense him, I spin on my heel.

Fists at the ready, prepared to break bones and slit throats if need be, I cock my arm and prepare for blood.

But it's Levi.

The ice dragon's nose is barely two inches from me, silent as a ghost, those piercing blue eyes watching me closely.

Whoa.

I didn't even hear him move.

"How…" I relax, glancing him over in surprise. "You were fast asleep."

Without a sound, he nods back toward the camp, never taking his eyes off me.

I shake my head.

He huffs impatiently and nods again toward the smoldering embers.

Hands on my hips, I raise one eyebrow in defiance. "You don't get to boss me around, buddy."

Pushy as all hell, he forces his nose into my right palm so we can talk.

Please, he says. *For me.*

And there it is again. The twist in my heart when I look at him, that feeling like he could ask for almost anything and I would want to say yes.

I groan in annoyance. "I need to sleep."

Then sleep. You're safe.

And more than the words, I feel it. A sense of peace, of protectiveness, of unyielding strength floods through me. It takes a moment to realize it's coming from him.

It's his promise to guard me, no matter what.

But I'm a Spectre, damn it. I don't need a guardian. I never have.

Please, he says again, nudging my hand tenderly.

Maybe it's the exhaustion, or the oddities of my day, or the frustration that has slowly built in my chest since I got here, but I give in.

I go back.

And as we settle once more beside the embers, Tucker blissfully unaware we ever left, I wonder what the hell I've gotten myself into.

Levi was supposed to fly away, to live his life and be free. But now, it's painfully clear he isn't leaving. If he follows me, I can't go into any human towns to resupply because they'll kill him for flying below the five-hundred-foot legal limit. He won't listen to reason, won't stay behind, won't let me out of his sight.

And I *care.*

My options are running out, and I'm baffled that I'm so protective of a dragon. But as I run my fingers over his scales, I'm reminded of the human inside him. The one trapped, trying to get out.

After a lifetime in the Spectres, I know what it's like to be trapped.

I rub my face in frustration and stare at my palms. Diesel's help wasn't that great before, and I don't enjoy being indebted to a man like that any more than I already am. Owe too many favors, and suddenly a Spectre may find herself with a new mentor.

A new master.

He'll send me on missions, sure, but he'll demand things of me I don't want to give. Of Irena. He'll find ways to break us, body and soul. I can't fathom the idea of him ruling my life. It's too horrible to imagine.

So that lead is done. He won't get any more favors from me, and that leaves me without my last Spectre ally and no more access to tech. My one lead on the Vaer is a dead end.

All I have to go on is my hatred for the Vaer and the red dragon's insistence that the dojo is safe. Briefly, I glance at Tucker, at a loss for what to do.

Deep down, I already know where I have to go next, but I really—*really*—don't want to.

CHAPTER EIGHTEEN

Shortly after the sun sets, Tucker and I pack up the car as Levi keeps watch on the skies.

"What are you going to do?" Tucker leans in, whispering, his warm breath sending delightful little chills down my neck.

I clear my throat to distract myself from my traitorous body's reaction to this gorgeous man being so close. "You mean about Levi?"

Tucker nods.

I sigh. I spent all night thinking about this, looking for other options, trying to come up with a better plan, but there just isn't one. "I have a lead who might help us."

"That's charmingly vague." He chuckles, still too close, the heat from his body still sending warm shivers of desire through me—pulses of pleasure I try to ignore.

I shrug, doing my best to focus on one problem at a time. I'm still looking for any reason at all not to take the red dragon up on his offer.

Seriously.

Anything.

Any other plan that's even a *hair* better.

Levi growls softly, and I instinctively tense, anticipating a fight with a creature I was raised from birth to kill. But when I look at him, he's eyeing the sky, all of his focus narrowed to a few shadows on the horizon.

"Crap." I throw the last of the bags haphazardly into the back seat of the truck, not bothering to pack them. "We need to go."

"Vaer?" Tucker asks, throwing a large military pack on top of the pile that was once his well-organized backseat.

"Not sure." I shut the doors and slip my hand into Tucker's pocket, grabbing the keys before he can protest.

He grabs my wrist, pinning me against the truck, a playful smirk on his face. "If you want to feel me up, you can just ask. I don't think this is the right time, though."

"Tucker, focus." A rush of heat creeps up my neck at his touch, at the way he pinned me against the truck, at the strength in his grip. My treasonous body goes wild at the warm sensation of his strong hand around my wrist. I do my best to shove the rush of desire deep, *deep* down so that I can just focus on not dying.

He lets go, and the warm tingle of his skin on mine slowly fades.

With a nod to the sky, he crosses his arms. "What do we do, Boss?"

Huh. Boss. I kind of like that nickname.

Briefly, I debate options. The truck is parked under cover, the branches hanging over it enough to mask the vehicle from the sky. The last time I tried to outrun dragons in a car, it ended badly. Even worse, out here there aren't many places to drive a truck, so we're somewhat limited with escape routes. We would be easily spotted and just as easily hunted down.

"You have anything high-powered in there?" I tap my knuckle against the metal door.

Tucker laughs and hops into the truck's bed. "Does dragon breath reek?"

Levi snorts in annoyance, casting an irritated glare over his shoulder.

"Oh, don't be so sensitive." Tucker kneels and begins assembling something I can't see. "You know it does."

Levi rolls his eyes.

In moments, Tucker assembles a rocket launcher on a tripod and angles it toward the sky. I look it over, impressed. It's easily strong enough to pierce dragon hide, and it'll work as a backup.

"Hand me Betty." I hold out my hand for his dragon stun gun, still eyeing the sky. When nothing happens, I grimace slightly in aggravation. Without looking back at him, I groan. *"Please."*

He chuckles, and moments later, I feel the heavy weight of the stun gun in my hands.

As the dragons near, Levi slinks into the forest line beside the truck. He keeps close to me, his head low to the ground and tilted upward to keep an eye on the approaching danger, and the three of us wait in silence.

The silhouettes in the sky start to take form, and I notice seven dragons this time. The largest is at the lead, each of the others matching his flight pattern with perfect precision as he tears through the skies.

As I study their bodies, I get an intuitive itch at the back of my mind, like some old memory is trying to surface.

It takes a moment for me to put a finger on the bubbling sensation of concern that's rippling through me, but once I figure it out, it blindsides me.

The square jaws. The impossibly beautiful glimmer to their dark, almost black scales. The militant formations, suggesting clear discipline and an irrefutable hierarchy.

"Those aren't the Vaer," I say softly.

"Who is it, then?" Tucker asks.

"They're the Palarne."

"Jesus," Tucker mutters, loading the rocket launcher with a frown. "Who *isn't* after you?"

"This is Vaer territory," I say with a twinge of hope. "Maybe they're not here for me."

Tucker snorts, adjusting the scope as he tracks the dragons' movement. "Right, and I'm a fairy princess."

Above us, the dragons scan the forest. I instinctively retreat a little farther into the shadow, but I can already feel threads of their attention shifting my way.

Just like the dragons in the Vaer compound, they're close enough to sense me. They're just trying to figure out where I am.

All at once, their heads tilt toward our hiding spot, and my finger tightens around the stun gun's trigger.

They found me.

I *hate* how they can do that.

"Get ready," I warn. "This could go south fast."

"Give the word." Tucker's voice lowers, the humor gone, replaced by a cold and deadly serious tone I'm not used to hearing from him.

I resist the impulse to look over, to check on him, because I can feel the mood shift between the three of us. We're ready for war, and it's strange to think I'm not going into a battle with Spectres at my side.

Honestly, I don't know if I like this.

In almost no time at all, the troupe descends. The seven dragons land hard on the grass, kicking up dirt and small stones with the sheer force of their massive bodies. The large meadow we camped near suddenly looks much smaller, and they have to hug their wings close to their bodies to even fit.

It puts them at a mild disadvantage, but it's nothing trained killers like them can't handle.

I take a quick inventory as they grumble and growl, their eyes locked on me. The largest of them is a dark dragon with a green shimmer to his scales and a beautiful gold stripe down his spine. Of the seven shifters, he looks at me most intently. His square jaw has small spines along the edges, and as he lowers his head to my level, I notice his dagger-like teeth.

But Spectres don't feel fear. It's beaten out of us at a young age.

I lift the stun gun, aiming it squarely between his eyes. "Whether or not this gets ugly depends entirely on what you do next."

Two quick puffs of air blow through his nose, almost like a chuckle, and he takes a step back.

Huh. Surprising.

Still suspicious, I don't lower the stun gun. As a safety precaution, I'm careful to keep my attention equally split between him and my flank in case this is just an elaborate distraction.

After a tense moment of silence, with each of the seven dragons briefly scanning the three of us, their leader lowers his head again and takes a few steps toward me.

Levi growls and raises his wings, instantly ready to attack, his teeth sharp and ready to taste blood.

The dark green dragon tilts his head toward Levi and closes his eyes, nodding slightly, calm as can be.

Tucker leans toward me, whispering. "What the hell is going on?"

"An act of submission," I whisper back, a bit surprised. "I don't think he wants to fight."

"Yeah, sure." Tucker scoffs. I peek briefly behind me to find his finger hovering dangerously close to the trigger.

Beside me, Levi is equally doubtful. He takes a protective step toward me, his body nearly pressing against mine, his wing possessively placed over my head.

Even though it limits how much of the field I can see, I allow it. Not like there's a ton I can do to rein in a feral dragon, especially right now.

The Palarne leader lowers his head almost to the ground in front of me, his chin hovering inches above the grass, and stares me down. Those dark eyes of his bury into me, both commanding and calm. He pauses barely two feet away, hot air rushing over my boots as he breathes. The grass beneath him shivers in the gusts of his breath, and I imagine he's used to most creatures trembling beneath his gaze.

But he's never met *me*.

Deep down, I wonder what the hell he's doing, and it takes me a moment to guess that he wants to speak to me.

He wants me to set my hand on his nose to initiate the connection so we can talk.

My shoulders tense at the thought of lowering my weapon, but right now, we're at an impasse. They're probably not going to let us leave until I do, and since we're wildly outnumbered, I'm starting to think this might be worth the risk.

Either we have a civil conversation, or he bites off my hand the moment I lower it.

I wince. Great odds.

Slowly, I lower the taser, never breaking eye contact with their leader. Levi grumbles in protest, but he's not the one making decisions here. Still coiled and ready to spring, his body stiffens beside me, his neck arched, his wings still spread, his claws anxiously digging into the dirt.

Behind the green dragon, his soldiers shift uneasily. It's clear none of us is happy about this meeting, and no one knows what to expect.

Cautiously, I set my fingers against the dragon's surprisingly warm scales. Behind me, Tucker lets out a nervous rush of air, and I try to ignore him. He's not helping.

Hello, dear one, the dark green dragon says.

"Hi," I answer tensely, not entirely fond of the pet name he chose for me.

His dark eyes never waver, never leave my face for a second. *You obviously know the danger you're in. You know the kind of dragons who are after you.*

"Like you?" I never give an inch, matching the intensity in his gaze with the deadly seriousness of my tone.

No. We don't seek you out to harm you or use you, dear one. We are the Palarne. Do you know of us?

That, I most certainly do.

I don't answer him for a moment, merely watching and waiting to see what he'll do next. The Palarne are considered to be the most trustworthy of the dragons, raised in a culture of honor and nobility, but even noble men can make bad choices.

When I don't answer, he nudges my hand, far gentler than I expect from someone as strong and powerful as him. *I am Isaac Palarne, and I assure you I will not hurt you.*

"The *Boss*?" I barely contain a small gasp, and I know I wasn't able to hide the subtle surprise on my face. This isn't just any Palarne—this is their leader. The man who rules and commands one of the fiercest dragon families ever to exist.

Ah, so you do know of us, he says, his eyes narrowing slightly in curiosity.

My shield temporarily down, I glance away for a moment to reset myself.

Very well, he says, apparently taking my silence as an answer. *Let's try this another way. Do you know what you are?*

More than anything else he's said, *that* gets my attention.

Briefly, I lift my fingers in surprise, breaking the contact with Isaac as I wonder what he could know—and if he'll tell me the truth.

He doesn't move, instead waiting for me to once more place my hand on his skin to resume the conversation. And through it all, he continues to watch me, as if he's seeing so much more than just my expression.

It's unnerving.

I set my hand once more on his scales, and a soft growl escapes him at my touch. This entire situation sets off every alarm bell I have, and my training compels me to run him through with a sword, to do *anything* other than just sit here and talk to a dragon.

To a dragon *Boss,* no less.

"Tell me," I command.

He chuckles again, apparently tickled that a human would be so bold as to command him to do anything, but I don't let an ounce of doubt show on my face. It seems, for the moment at least, that I have the upper hand.

You are the dragon vessel, he says. *The one who possesses the ancient and dark magic of the three dragon gods themselves.*

I sit with that for a moment, not sure how I feel about it. He waits, ever patient, ever calm.

Dragon gods.

It sounds like myth and legend, the stuff of a bleak Grimm fairytale and not reality. And yet here we are, a Spectre and a dragon, discussing the magic I found at death's door in the middle of an isolated forest.

The pit.

The three voices.

The three dragon statues wrapped in chains.

Isaac could be lying, but if he is, it's a *very* convincing lie.

"Why did I get all of it, then?" I ask tentatively, testing the waters, trying to see how much he'll divulge. "Why did I get the magic of all three of them instead of just one?"

That's the benefit of coming with me.

Ah. There it is.

The catch.

I lift my hand, already done with the conversation, but he thrusts his nose back into my palm, his expression urgent. *I have answers. Ancient texts. Rites and rituals. Every question you have, I can answer.*

"No."

There are dangerous people after you, dear one. He leans harder into my hand, and I fight to retain my balance as I glare him down. *People who will kill everyone you love, destroy everything you stand for. These are people who will burn the world to rubble to find you. There are traitors everywhere, humans and dragons alike who will nestle into your heart only to cut it out.*

With that delightful little comment, he glances briefly at Tucker and Levi.

I grimace in disgust. "I'm not an idiot."

No, you clearly aren't. He growls softly. *You are also not safe out here. You are not safe anywhere but a dragon compound.*

"Yours specifically, of course." My voice drips with venom and sarcasm, as I am entirely done with this conversation.

I believe so, yes, but I wish for you to see for yourself that—

Levi tenses, growling, his head lifted to the skies. Seconds later, the dragons behind Isaac follow suit, each of them growling in warning at something I can't see.

Like a missile falling to earth, a red dragon as large as Isaac lands in the last remaining patch of space in the now-cramped meadow. He sits upright, wings tight to his body, a regal arch to his neck as he stares down Isaac without bothering to look at me or the other dragons in the field.

In a blisteringly fast moment, Isaac's mood shifts from calm and collected to ready for war. His claws slowly dip into the dirt. His muscles flex, ready for a fight. He pulls away from me, his full focus now on the red dragon who can't seem to stay away.

"Damn it," Tucker mutters beside me, glancing between the two of them, clearly not sure where to aim.

Well, crap. There goes my theory that Tucker could be the red dragon.

I quietly sigh as the air crackles with testosterone and danger, the tense standoff threatening to end in blood at any moment. The red dragon growls, the trees near him shaking from the sheer force of the sound.

"Relax," I tell Tucker. "I know this one."

CHAPTER NINETEEN

Isaac and the red dragon stare each other down in deadly silence, each daring the other to strike first.

It's tense. Uneasy. I flex my fingers, wondering how this will go.

The two regal dragons watch each other, and no one else dares to so much as growl. It feels like a meeting of kings, as though each is daring the other to act first, to be the one brazen enough to break the fragile peace that could shatter at any moment.

Isaac is nearly as big as the red dragon, and both shifters carry themselves with grace and an authoritative presence. Though their jaws and builds are wildly different, the stripes down their backs make me wonder if they share a common ancestry somehow.

The red dragon extends one of his wings toward

Isaac in a fluid, imposing motion. His gaze never shifts, never hesitates.

It's a silent command, an order for Isaac to speak to him.

Isaac chuckles, the hot rushes of air surprising me in the otherwise tense moment. For some reason, this is funny. I certainly don't get it, but I'm not about to ask questions.

Not right now.

Ever calm and commanding, Isaac extends a wing, brushing it against the red dragon's.

In the silence that follows, I subtly scan the forest for an exit. If we go now, we would have to leave the truck. The trees are too close together to drive it through the woods, which leaves only the path the red dragon currently blocks. We could hoof it, but however fast we may be able to run, dragons are faster.

We're outnumbered and cornered. Super fun.

The red dragon growls, recapturing my attention as the ground shakes with the force of his sudden anger, and I wonder if this was what it was like to watch me and Isaac speak. I have no idea what they're talking about or who this dragon even *is*.

They continue staring each other down in silence, speaking only to each other through the shared connection of their touching wings. Occasionally one of them will break the silence to snarl or huff in amusement, reacting to a conversation no one else can hear.

Levi growls softly beside me, his gaze shifting from Isaac to the newcomer, and I nod in agreement.

I don't like this, either.

The contact breaks, and I brace myself for a full battle. I lift my stun gun, training it on Isaac because he's closer, but the great green dragon simply looks at me with a blended expression of curiosity and suspicion. He doesn't lower his head again, doesn't try to speak to me. Instead, he stretches his massive wings and takes off into the skies without another word, his soldiers in tight formation behind him.

Seconds later, the Palarnes are gone, and only the red dragon remains. His attention now shifts to Levi.

It's a clear demand for answers, one Levi is apparently more than prepared to indulge.

The ice dragon slowly spreads his wings, side stepping into the field, angling himself between me and the red dragon.

I angle the stun gun toward the newcomer, waiting for him to act. The red dragon has helped me a few times, sure, but that doesn't mean I trust him enough to lower my guard.

The red dragon lowers his head to match Levi—but unlike Isaac, he does not bow in deference or respect. It's a dare, as if he's begging for a fight.

Oh.

Oh, no.

I can't get a word in, I can't even lower the stun gun before they attack each other. They snarl, their claws digging deep grooves in the ground as they snake around each other, each vying for the upper hand.

"Stop!" I shout over the gnash of teeth and the rustle of dragon wings, but my voice is barely audible over the grunts and growls from the fight.

Levi is fast, faster even than the red dragon. He ducks most of the blows, spinning and gnashing with hypnotic grace as the fight wears on.

But the red dragon has *power*. None of Levi's bites pierce his hide. None of Levi's blows draw blood. Nothing Levi does seems able to harm the red dragon much at all.

With one fierce blow, the red dragon pins Levi to the ground. The earth trembles from the utter force of the hit, but Levi doesn't flinch. He roars up at the red dragon, spitting shards of ice that cut through branches and send leaves fluttering over the air.

Not to be outdone, the red dragon hurls a stream of fire, melting every shard of ice before it can hit him.

The fire ends, dissolving in thick plumes of black smoke. He opens his jaws, his piercing white teeth glinting in the low light, and I can tell what he's going to do next.

He's going for the kill.

"Damn it, *stop!*" I fire the stun gun, the pulse hitting

his back. He roars in pain and surprise, turning the full weight of his attention on me.

In that moment, his glare, his anger, his fury and bloodlust all focus on *me.*

I'm astonished that the stun gun didn't knock him out, and now I'm not sure if this weapon will even work on him. I've never seen a dragon take a hit like that and stay standing, much less stay so focused on his prey.

But this stupid stun gun is all I have, so I'm going to make it work.

"Stop it, or the next blast goes into your face!" I aim between his eyes, fully intent on following through. "He's a *friend,* damn it, stop trying to kill him!"

There's that word again—*friend*. It comes to mind too easily, lately. Too often. I'm not sure I like it.

Still, I need to focus.

The red dragon looks at Levi and then back to me. He groans in disbelief, the grating sound, as if to say *are you serious?*

With an impatient huff, he gestures toward Levi with a sharp claw as the ice dragon rolls back onto his feet, poised again for battle.

"Yes, I *know* he's being an idiot." I shrug. "He's feral and doing his best. Chill."

The red dragon snorts impatiently. I don't need to touch him to know he's probably thinking all kind of obscenities at me spending time with a feral dragon.

Levi growls again at the nameless newcomer, coiling to spring, and I turn my stun gun on him next. "You! Stop it!"

Caught off guard, Levi turns his head toward me and briefly loses his balance, snorting in aggravation as he glances between me and the visitor. He doesn't relax at first, his body still tensed for a fight.

I tap my stun gun to recapture his attention and remind him what's at stake. "Levi, I mean it! This didn't work on him, but it *will* work on you."

Levi groans and rolls his eyes, pacing along the forest edge, surrendering to my demands all while never taking his attention off the red dragon.

"Jesus," I mutter, the adrenaline still shooting through me, sending my heart racing through my chest at a painful pace. "You all are going to be the death of me, you know that?"

Behind me, Tucker laughs. "You're like a grouchy dragon whisperer."

I glance over to him now that I finally have a moment to spare. He's still standing in the bed of his truck, lounging against the cabin with his arms crossed and that goofy smile plastered on his face, like he's watching some kind of weird rodeo.

I gesture to his body, annoyed by how relaxed he is, given what just happened. "You were a lot of help."

"You had it covered." He lazily waves me away.

The red dragon walks toward me, his intense gaze

focused and agitated. Levi snarls in warning, daring him to take another step.

Not to be outdone, the red dragon pauses and roars in Levi's direction, a clear threat not to mess with him. The two have a tense standoff, neither relaxing, both of them pissed, before the red dragon continues toward me. Levi snarls, clearly upset he has to allow this or risk a blast from my stun gun.

The red dragon, still furious, shoves his head against my hand, knocking the stun gun out of my grip.

After the experience with Isaac, I realize now that's what dragons are *supposed* to do when they want to talk. Ask. Politely.

But the red dragon isn't having it, and it seems like manners aren't even on his mind.

With our skin touching, his voice blasts through my mind. *Why are you not at the dojo? Why are you on the edge of Vaer lands, getting in trouble? Why—*

"You need to watch your tone." My voice is deadly. Dangerous.

It's *my* warning to *him*.

No one controls me. No one owns me. No one but me has any say in what I do or where I go.

No human, and no *dragon*.

He snorts, clearly irritated, the testosterone and adrenaline from his battle no doubt still bubbling through his body. I can tell he's debating something, and I wonder if he's going to try to take me by force.

I shift my weight, preparing for battle and daring him to try.

He groans and, instead of flying off with me in his claws, pulls away. He storms into the center of the meadow and shakes his entire body, as if doing so will shake off the anger and frustration burning through him.

It seems to work.

A little calmer now, he pushes his nose in my palm once more. *I need you to listen. I need to know you're going to hear me out.*

I raise one inquisitive eyebrow. "I'm listening."

You are being hunted by everyone. Everyone, woman. Every single government, dragon family, or organization that knows you exist is after you. After your magic. The world knows things about you that you can't even conceive of right now. Your potential. Your power. Everyone wants it, and they will do absolutely anything to get it. Each of them will kill anyone who stands in their way. His eye dilates, and he pauses briefly to make his next words hit home. *They'll start wars for you.*

Uh huh. Sure. Isaac just finished telling me all the same things.

"So, let me guess. Your home is the only place on Earth that's safe for me." I roll my eyes.

No, it's not.

I pause, looking him over in confusion, once more ensnared by those golden eyes of his.

Most of all, I'm floored by his honesty. Given my upbringing, I'm not really used to it.

My home isn't safe for you, he continues. *Not even close. The people in my family would use you, manipulate you, hurt you. I won't allow it.* He sighs, pausing a moment. *If you were some hapless human, I perhaps wouldn't care. But you're not. You're a warrior, and you deserve better.*

"You don't even know me." I don't understand this dragon. I don't get why he's here, why he's helping me, or why he even cares.

I've been watching you, and you have continued to impress me. Surprise me. Confuse me.

I shake my head. "That's not possible."

Since you left the ritual pit, I've only lost track of you twice. He stares me down, his intense expression riveting me to the grass.

"You're lying," I say, not wanting to believe him. Not wanting to think about what it would mean if he's telling the truth.

Oh, am I? I hear one of those odd dragon-laughs escape him, and it grates on my nerves that he could be so cocky right now given the gravity of what he's claiming. *After the swarm, you went back to a house on the edge of town and were nearly intercepted by Mason Greene of the Vaer.*

The red dragon's piercing golden eyes dare me to interrupt. He's daring me to prove him wrong.

I don't. Because, to my utter horror, he's not.

He continues. *You proved yourself as a truly impressive warrior by thwarting Mason before I even had a chance to help. What's more, you found shelter in that shed, recovered somewhat, and formed a new plan. You were tenacious and unyielding, even though you were clearly sleep deprived and on the run. You never stopped.* He sighs, relaxing, an expression of pride briefly crossing his face. *Not once.*

My eyes go wide, and the icy shock of all he knows splinters through me. Despite my training, despite my skills, I can't hide my surprise. "This... you can't know any of this."

You then went back to Mason's house, much to my bafflement and horror. He glares at me, smoke billowing through his nose as he seems to relive the moment. *Yet again, you got out alive, without my help, and impressed me once more even though it was foolhardy of you to—*

"I don't need a commentary," I interrupt, narrowing my eyes in anger despite the gravity of the situation. "Prove you're telling the truth. Tell me what else you saw."

He snorts in irritation, his body brimming with energy and power that would intimidate anyone else. But I'm used to it, used to watching dominant people throw their weight around.

None of this shit fazes *me.*

Fine, he says, grumbling. *You met an acquaintance in a seedy tavern at the edge of town, where this idiot found you yet again.* The red dragon glances briefly toward Tucker, who suddenly wrinkles his brow in confusion, realizing he's being mentioned in some way.

I roll my eyes. "Don't be rude."

I've only lost you twice. The red dragon presses his head possessively into my hand, as if it will keep me from escaping again. *Once when you left town in that stolen sedan, and then again when you disappeared into the Vaer compound today. Aside from that, nothing you've done has escaped me.* His eyes narrow. *Nothing.*

The weight of his confession tunnels through me like a bullet, and for a moment, I can't breathe.

Not even Tucker could keep track of me that well. And what concerns me even more is that I could never tell I was being followed by the red dragon.

Not even *once.*

"Who are you?" I ask, my voice quiet as I lean away, not sure I should be near this dragon any more.

I've fought dragons my whole life, but he's the first I consider to be truly dangerous.

I am not like the others, he says. *I'm seen when I want to be seen. I am obeyed, but I obey no one.*

"That's not an answer."

And you won't get one. A shot of hot air blows through his nostrils in defiance. *That's not my point. Do I really need to continue? Do you want me to outline every step you've made? Because I will. I can.*

"No," I say begrudgingly.

His breathing is rough and ragged, clearly frustrated, clearly at a loss for words. *I know your every step, woman. I've followed your every movement, but I don't understand any of these choices you're making. You're not safe out here, not safe around the Vaer, and yet you won't leave them the hell alone!*

I lift my chin defiantly. "And why should I tell you anything? You're just like the rest of them, as far as I'm concerned." I nod toward where the Palarne soldiers stood moments prior. "Whatever is going on within me, whatever this magic is, you want it as much as any of them do."

I did. He glances at the ground, and I'm surprised to see a flicker of shame in his eye. *But no, not anymore.*

"I don't believe you," I admit, tensing my shoulders, ready to jump out of his reach the moment this conversation turns sour. Because at this point, I'm convinced it will.

He seems to sense my desire to inch away, and he leans into me even more. *You did something no one else has ever done, and you managed to do it twice. You are the only one in my entire life who has ever managed to escape me, Rory. For that, you have my respect, and I look out for those who I respect.*

I freeze. He knows my name.

I don't understand you, he continues, grumbling. *You're a fighter. A warrior. You're sharp and talented, capable of killing even if you prefer not to. You're kind, yet also a brutally efficient assassin. What are you? Who trained you? The more I watch you fight, the more I watch you win, the more—*

He groans, as if he isn't sure how to finish his statement. He pulls away, and to my surprise, I don't want him to. I want—no, *need*—him to finish his thought.

He doesn't.

When he presses his nose once more into my hand, he's all business. *What have you been experiencing, Rory? Tell me everything. I've seen the magic, but I can't tell if you're wielding it or it's wielding you.*

God, where do I even start?

I shift through the memories, wondering if I should share any of this, wondering if he's even someone I can trust. I don't want to trust anyone, much less him, but my concerns over this wild magic bubble to the surface. The seedy bar. The middle school. The Knights. The Andusk dragons. The surges of power boiling through me, taking over, erupting at the worst possible times and never when I need them.

In the end, I just shake my head.

He growls softly, the sound almost tender, almost soothing. *It'll be okay, Rory.*

I lift one eyebrow in confusion, and it takes a moment to understand what he means.

He just read *my* mind.

Yes, he confirms. *In the connection, you must be careful of what you share.*

"Oh, *hell* no." I pull my hand away, entirely done with this. My heart skips beats, wondering if he knows I'm a Spectre, if *Isaac* knows.

This is bad. So very, very bad.

The red dragon stops me with his wing, drawing me closer, pulling me near his face as he lowers his head toward me. I wrestle against him, but he's too strong. Before I know it, he presses his forehead against mine, pinning me between his skull and his wing.

It's almost intimate. I'm surrounded by him, engulfed in him, with very little of the world around me filtering through. It's just us. The connection between us opens again, and I feel a surge of possessiveness bleed from him.

I need you to be safe. I need you to master this magic before it destroys you. Jace and the dojo can help you, but not if you get caught out here. You're running out of time, Rory.

"Let me go," I demand, wriggling in his grip. It doesn't seem to faze him. He doesn't even have to move or adjust his grip to keep me completely immobile.

He's too strong.

At the edge of my vision, I see Tucker lift the stun gun off the ground and aim it at the red dragon's neck. His expression is grim. Tense. Ready for war, all trace of humor and joy gone.

For a moment, Tucker and I share a tense gaze, and we both know he's not going to shoot.

He's bluffing—if he shoots, I would also get a full blast of enough electricity to knock out a full-grown dragon.

It could kill me.

I have to talk my way out of this, and I have to choose both my words and thoughts very carefully.

"Do you know what I am?" I ask the red dragon, careful to lock away the truth in my mind, to bury it deep and not let the answers float to the surface.

You mean this magic? The dragon vessel?

"No. What I was before."

The red dragon tilts his head in confusion. A clear answer.

No.

I nod, trying not to process it until we break the connection. "First off, I'm a human. Second, you have no idea who trained me or who I work for. You don't know my thoughts on dragons, or how I feel about all of you. You know I'm a warrior, that I have advanced skills and a knack for killing people. Why do you think it's a smart idea to send a human into a dragon's den?"

You're not human. Not anymore. He snorts impatiently, the hot air running down my thighs, igniting a strange and magnetic sensation deep in my core that I try not to acknowledge.

I hold his glare, daring him to continue, daring him to tell me more.

You aren't a dragon, either, he says. *You're in between, beholden to neither, hunted by both. Dragons don't like each other, but we do honor the embassies.*

"Whoa, wait." My eyebrows shoot up in surprise. "This dojo is an embassy?"

The red dragon gently nods. *It's called the dojo to remind the world of its military power and might. The embassies are safe, except for any owned by the Vaer.*

A low growl builds in his throat as he casts a brief look of disgust toward the Vaer compound.

I try not to think about what I know about embassies, trying my best not to let my hard-won knowledge and training bubble to the surface. I don't want to share too much through the connection, but this new information is deeply important.

It's not some random dojo. It's an embassy, and that changes *everything*.

He seems to pick up on the shifting emotion within me, tilting his head slightly in curiosity, but he plows ahead nonetheless. *You aren't human or dragon, but you absolutely are magical. You have power that can destroy dozens, maybe even hundreds or thousands in a single blow. I saw what you did at the human school. Don't tell me you aren't concerned about having such feral abilities.*

I glare off into the trees, unwilling to let him know how right he really is.

You can't learn to tame that power by yourself, Rory. His voice echoes in my mind, powerful and assertive. *You seem far too comfortable with isolation, with doing things on your own, but wherever you come from and whatever life you're used to, it's gone. These are different times, and like it or not, you are a different person.*

"Don't lecture me," I snap.

It's not a lecture. It's the truth. You absolutely must go to Jace. He can help you. Thunderbirds like him understand magic like yours in a way not even I ever could. He can train you. He is the master of the dojo, and not even the Vaer are stupid enough to defy him.

I hesitate. I don't want to admit he's right. I don't want to go to a dragon den. I don't want to step into the light after a lifetime in the darkness.

But I have to.

If I don't, this wild magic could take over. If I don't, the Vaer could catch up to me. If I don't...

I grimace, trying desperately to keep my thoughts to myself, to prevent anything sensitive from rushing to the surface for him to see.

"Let go of me so I can think," I command him.

To my surprise, he obliges me. With the connection broken, I finally feel safe enough to let my mind wander, to fully explore my options.

Every moment that passes means Zurie is closer to death. When there's nothing left to beat out of her, the Vaer will slice her throat.

More importantly, every moment I spend chasing down Jace leaves Irena vulnerable. She was getting sicker when I left her in that safehouse, and now Mason has her. I have no idea if she's even still alive.

I rub my face in frustration. I have no allies except for Levi and Tucker, who I don't entirely trust yet. No options. No leads. Wandering around in the forests isn't going to get me any closer to saving either Zurie or Irena.

But a dragon embassy…

Now this is truly an opportunity, and I impulsively stand up straighter as my mind works over this new possibility. I don't know a ton about dragon embassies, but I do know they operate differently than human ones. They're neutral zones, yes, but in the Spectre circles we heard rumors they were also used for gathering intel. This dojo could be a spying hub, a prime chance for me to scour sensitive files not available to me otherwise. Files on the Vaer. On Mason. Hell, perhaps even on Zurie.

This could be an in, the lead I've been looking for.

"I'll go," I say softly, nodding to assure myself I'm making the right decision.

The red dragon sighs in relief and, without another word, takes to the skies. I know in my heart I'll see him again, but I'm not certain that's a good thing.

After the red dragon leaves, Levi snaps at the air in annoyance, never taking his eyes off those red and gold scales.

The threat gone, Tucker drops the stun gun and

races to me, holding my arms as he looks me over. "Are you okay? Where are we going? What did he say?"

"I'm fine." I watch the sky, eyeing the red dragon as he becomes nothing more than a silhouette against the clouds. "I'm going to a dragon embassy."

"No. Nope. Bad idea." Tucker shakes his head, his grip tightening around my arms almost in desperation. "Rory, you can't. You're clearly specially trained. I know you're not an idiot, but I don't know if you know the dragon world. I *do,* okay? They're not going to take care of you. They're going to use you until there's nothing left."

"And how do you know all that?" I glare at him, daring him to answer.

I agree with pretty much everything he said. It's all the same things I've heard over my life, and it's interesting to me how many similarities there are between what the two of us know.

It makes me wonder.

It makes me once more doubt this man I'm starting to begrudgingly enjoy.

He can't possibly be a Spectre... can he?

Tucker hesitates, at a loss for words, gaping as he stares at me in earnest. By the way his eyes widen, it's clear he wants to say so much, to spill everything to me.

I wait.

After a tense moment, he sighs and leans his forehead against mine in a movement so very similar to the red dragon's possessive grip. He holds me close, and out of exhaustion and curiosity, I allow it.

"I really hate being around all these dragons," Tucker says with a weak laugh. "So uncomfortable."

Levi snorts, likely not altogether pleased with Tucker's company, either.

"You don't *have* to be around them." I pull back until I can see his face, until I'm once more captured by those green eyes that snare me. "No one's making you stay."

For a brief moment, he looks hurt. It doesn't last long, and he instantly dons that goofy grin of his, as if all of this is one big joke. "What, and let you have all the fun?"

But in that moment of flickering emotion, I saw the truth. This humor, this smile, it's just a mask.

He doesn't *want* to leave.

And when the alternative is walking into a dragon's nest, I continue to wonder *why*.

CHAPTER TWENTY

Out of options, I drive through the night toward the dojo.

With every mile that passes on the long trip, I rub my face, grumbling to myself, swinging back and forth on whether or not this is a good idea.

On the plus side, it's an embassy. I can get intel. I have enough voids to conquer a place like that, though it would likely deplete my remaining supply. It's my one remaining lead when it comes to gathering information on Zurie and Irena. Even if the dragons don't have news on either of them, specifically, they'll be tracking the Vaer.

No one likes the Vaer. And in this cutthroat world, we have to monitor our enemies closely. It's pretty much a guarantee that, somewhere in the embassy, there's information that can help me rescue the two Spectres I care about most.

I just have to find it.

I briefly look at Tucker, who's lightly snoring in the passenger seat, the chair reclined and his feet resting on the dash.

I chuckle. I can't help it. He's too relaxed around me. Too at ease. For whatever reason, he really trusts me.

It's trust I don't deserve.

My smile falls, and I return my attention out the front windshield. Zurie would tell me he's an enemy, too. That he needs to not only be monitored but thrown over a cliff. She would have already killed him, probably the second time he surfaced.

To a Spectre, everyone outside of the organization is a potential threat.

But deep down, I'm not so sure.

Leaning against the headrest and tilting my neck to get a good stretch, I return to my internal debate about the embassy, determined to tackle one problem at a time.

Mentally, I check off all the cons of this plan. I'm not even sure where to *start*.

Dragons. In a dragon den. Controlled by dragons, funded by dragons, all deemed "safe" by what is essentially a pinkie promise not to kill anyone.

My grip on the wheel tightens. Damn this. Damn all of this.

I hate being cornered.

It takes a few moments and several deep breaths, but I finally clear my head. Logically, I'm not cornered—I'm just low on options. I am, however, a fighter, and nothing cages me for long.

Nothing holds me back.

Nothing stops me.

In the darkness, a shadowy silhouette crosses the moon above, stealing my attention away from the patchwork road illuminated by my headlights. My heart skips a beat before I recognize the brilliant blue scales of my ice dragon.

My ice dragon.

It was such an instinctive thought, so possessive and already comfortable. I shake my head, my life becoming too surreal to even process anymore.

Levi dips across the sky, slowly tracing back and forth above the street as he follows us. I knew this would happen, that he would come, and I'm surprised at how grateful I am to have his company.

I'm also nervous. He's an inadvertent beacon signaling my location to anyone curious enough to investigate.

Good God, how I miss my life of staying in the shadows, of remaining unseen. I don't like walking out in the open. It's vulnerable. It's weakness. It means I lose the element of surprise, and I never realized until now how much I relied on that in the past.

With yet another steadying breath, my heart begins to settle. I can handle this.

I survived a lifetime in the Spectres. I'm third in command to the highest-ranking assassin in the organization, trained by the best to hunt and kill. I have lived a life of darkness and stealth, and absolutely nothing in this world can stop me from achieving what I set out to do.

Time to adapt and overcome. Whatever I find in the embassy, it will only fuel me onward.

I am Rory Quinn. Be it dragons or Spectres, kings or traitors, I fear *nothing*.

CHAPTER TWENTY-ONE

The moment we pass into embassy territory, the sky swarms with dragons.

I guess nuance and subtlety isn't really the vibe they're going for here.

Dragons perch in the trees, watching us as the truck speeds down the flawless asphalt road, and dozens more fly overhead. Except for the swarm above the ritual pit, I've never seen this many dragons in all my life.

My grip tightens around the steering wheel as I ready for war. At this point, it's reflex when I see a dragon. I can't help it.

Two snow-white ice dragons take up position slightly behind us, a rear guard of sorts as we race down the thin street.

Escorts.

Either they want to make sure we get there all right —or, more likely, they want to make sure we don't leave.

My jaw tenses, shoulders aching as I carefully monitor every wing beat, every movement, every twitch of a head or tail within my sight. Between the trees and the sky, I'm kept quite busy.

There are easily eighty fire dragons and thirty ice dragons so far. Probably more hidden in the trees. The Fairfax family are known as the only ones with thunderbirds, but I haven't seen any yet.

Since they're incredibly rare, I may not.

Beside me, Tucker yawns and finally opens his eyes. As his gaze flits across the trees, he sucks in a sharp breath. "Shit, is this a dream?"

"Afraid not." I scoff. If only.

He scans the skies, his fingers tapping nervously on his knee. "Still sure this is a good idea?"

"Nope," I admit, watching a blood-red fire dragon weave back and forth across the road ahead of us. "Never really was, to be honest."

"The Fairfax family is supposed to be fun though, right?" Tucker shrugs, clearly trying to play down the danger. "They host those dumb adrenaline competitions and own sports teams in every country."

"They also have one of the greatest military powers in the dragonlands," I point out, gesturing to the horde flying above us. "Don't underestimate them, Tucker."

"Sure," he says anxiously, running his thick fingers through his hair. "Whatever you say, boss." He leans back against his seat and looks out the window, shoulders a little hunched, his hands coiling into fists.

Oh.

Oh, wow.

It takes a moment to realize he probably wasn't trying to reassure *me* that things would be okay. I probably won't be killed on sight. Except perhaps with the Vaer, I'll be fine because I'm wanted. I have magic they desperately need. They probably won't hurt me.

But Tucker? He's an accessory. Short of ethical obligation, dragons have no reason to keep him alive.

"I won't let them hurt you," I add, clearing my throat because these warm-fuzzy moments make me feel weird. "You're going to be okay."

He smiles at me and, briefly, relaxes. It's one of those flickering moments that's gone in a flash, but yet again, I see a bit of the man behind the goofball mask. That's gratitude on his face and, if I'm not mistaken, a hint of surprise.

Seconds later, though, he's back to the same old adorable twit I've been fending off from the start.

"Damn right, Rory. You won't let them hurt me because I'm too pretty." He points at his rugged jaw line. "Can you imagine a scar across this canvas? The angels will weep, woman."

I shake my head, unable to suppress my laughter. "You're such an idiot."

"You love it." He leans back, clearly calmer now, and sets his hands behind his head. He looks like he's headed to the beach, not into a dragon den.

I may never understand Tucker Chase, and I'm kind of okay with that.

Around the next bend, the forest ends at a cliff, and we finally see the embassy. It looms in the air, a slew of black stone towers cutting through the clear blue sky. A huge chasm digs into the ground between our road and the embassy, and I hate to think of how far down the ravine goes. It would be a long fall with lots of screaming.

Mist rolls along the road as we drive, and I wonder how high up we really are. Since there's no barrier between the road and the cliff, I keep close attention on the wheel even as I marvel at the building. I don't want to test my luck and accidentally veer off the asphalt.

The embassy looks for all the world like a castle. The massive building sits on the edge of the opposite cliff, with a long stone bridge serving as the only access. A waterfall roars over the edge, a thundering reminder of how deep the ravine goes. Grass and small trees cling to the sheer rock wherever possible, and I'm in awe.

I didn't know dragons could create something so

beautiful. I thought they were all fire and smoke and blood.

This is one case where I happen to enjoy being wrong. A small smile creeps across my face, and to my surprise, I'm eager to go inside. I feel like a kid, and all I want to do is explore.

"Whoa," Tucker says, dropping his guard for a moment as he stares at the massive building. "That's an *embassy?*"

"Apparently," I mutter, not entirely convinced. "I guess they evicted a king to get it?"

"Evicted, or murdered?"

My smile falls, and I don't answer him. Dragons get away with so much in this world, and so much of the truth is swept under the rug. People disappear all the time. Companies mysteriously change owners, and wars sometimes end without any clear winner. It often feels like so much of our lives are ruled by people we can't even see, and we humans may never get the answers to questions like Tucker's.

A gate blocks my way to the bridge, so I slow down. The truck rumbles up to the gate and, surprisingly, it opens before I can even come to a complete stop. The metal bars raise, giving us easy access to the bridge.

"No turning back," I say with a deep breath.

Tucker shrugs. "I mean, we technically *could—*"

I accelerate before he can finish, not really in the

mood for banter. As I drive over the ancient stone, I try not to look over the edge.

Rule 12 of the Spectres—always know when and how to escape.

I am breaking that rule so badly right now that Zurie would slap me *hard* if she knew about this.

There aren't many exits in this situation, and if the dragons were to attack right now, I would be utterly screwed. I search the skies, grateful to find Levi still close on our tail. His head shifts around, no doubt keeping an eye on the dragons swarming around him, equally as tense as me.

The second gate into the castle courtyard opens, the two mighty wooden doors swinging aside to let me through. I let out a tense breath as we finally leave the bridge.

This is it.

The moment of truth.

The gates open to reveal a massive courtyard large enough for a full army to stand in. It's empty, with only a wide staircase against the far wall leading to a set of large black doors at the base of the castle. Along the walls are several other smaller doors, and I absently wonder how many passageways this castle really has.

Once inside, I park. Before getting out, though, I scan the courtyard for dangers. The black stone from the towers continues to the ground, layering the square in a breathtakingly dark layer of marble. The longer I sit in the truck, however, the more dragons begin to land on the walls overlooking the courtyard.

It isn't long before the walls around the courtyard are covered with dragons, red and orange and white and blue. Their tails drape over the edge as they all sit perfectly still, all of them staring at the truck, at *me*. Every tower—every *surface*—has a dragon on it, all quietly waiting and curiously watching.

Spectres always make the first move, so here goes nothing.

I take a deep breath and slide out of the driver's seat, my boots thumping on the hard, black stone. Levi lands beside me, the ground shaking briefly from the force, and I square my shoulders as I prepare myself for whatever comes next.

It's do or die time.

"I'm looking for Jace," I say loudly, eyeing as many of the dragons as I can. I take a few cautious steps forward as Tucker hops out of the truck.

A low rumble in Levi's throat concerns me, and it doesn't take long to figure out what has him on edge.

Across the courtyard, the massive double doors at the top of the wide staircase are opening, and I wonder if I'll finally get to meet this Jace character who's supposed to be so helpful.

The man who walks into the sunlight, I admit, is a bit disappointing. He wears a long black jacket with a high collar. The buttons are all undone, and the white shirt beneath his coat is crisp and bright, as though he's never seen dirt in his life. His long brown beard is like a bush around his face. There's a slight wrinkle to his nose, like he smells something foul.

I frown. I can't help myself. This can't possibly be who we were sent to find.

"Welcome to the Fairfax Embassy, young lady," he says, taking the stairs at a leisurely pace. "It's an honor to have you in our humble dojo." He pauses at the bottom of the steps and bows his head slightly in welcome.

"Thanks," I say flatly, never one to appreciate formalities or fanfare.

Tucker elbows me none too gently in the side and lifts an eyebrow, gesturing subtly toward the guy at the bottom of the stairs.

Keep talking, his expression says.

I sigh. This should be fun.

"I didn't realize you're so welcoming to humans," I admit.

"To most, no, we're not. But you're not a normal human, are you?" The stranger smirks, his eyes roving my body, no doubt drinking in the way my skin glows.

"I guess not," I admit, and I wonder how many of these dragons sitting on the walls know what I really am. "I'm here because I was told Jace could help me." I look around the walls, suspecting some kind of trick. This man can't be Jace. "Where is he?"

The stranger chuckles and gestures smugly to himself. "What makes you think I'm not Jace?"

"You don't want me to answer that," I confess.

Beside me, Tucker sighs deeply and rubs his face in frustration.

"Well, it's the truth," I mutter quietly to the weapons expert next to me.

"So, *this* is how I die," Tucker says softly, rolling his eyes.

"Hush, you." I return my attention to the man at the stairs, who is no longer smugly grinning.

The stranger gives me a brief once-over, and I recognize the expression slowly dawning across his face.

Internal debate.

He's weighing two options, and by the way the cogs seem to be turning in his brain, it's clear at least one of those options does not bode well for me.

I lift my chin, catching his attention, and cross my arms in defiance. I whip out my murderous expression, the one I reserve for assholes I'm about to rip to shreds. The look I use to threaten thugs who are stupid enough to corner me in an alley.

I fucking dare you, my face says.

He seems to get the hint, and he clears his throat briefly. With that, whatever thought had crossed his mind disappears.

For now. It'll be back.

It always comes back.

"Who are you?" I ask, nodding to him apathetically, never once revealing the anxiety swimming in my gut at being surrounded by so many dragons. By having so many of them look at me with hunger.

They know there's something different about me. From the way most of them tilt their heads in slight confusion or curiosity, however, I suspect most don't know what it is.

Best to keep it that way.

The stranger hesitates, lips pursed a bit in annoyance. "My name is Guy Durand, second in command here at the dojo. Jace is... *occupied.*"

"Is he, now?" My eyebrow lifts in mild surprise.

Oh, fabulous. At first, I was convinced this was some kind of test, some way to gauge my interest and ability. But now, I'm starting to think Jace is dead in a ditch somewhere.

My fingers ache to hold the gun in the holster on my belt. To my right, Tucker shifts his weight, and in my periphery, I see his hands casually rest against his hips—near the pockets loaded with handguns and throwing knives and who knows what the hell else. To my left, another slow rumble builds in Levi's throat.

If I have to fight my way out of this, I'm going to tear that red dragon a new asshole the next time I see him.

"Can you *fetch* him?" I ask, a bit more derisively than I intended. "This is kind of important."

"He'll be along soon, I promise," Guy says with a nod of his head. Slowly, he begins to walk closer, feigning calm as he nears. I see it in the way he holds his head, his hands, his shoulders—he's on edge, ready to spring, ready to snare me in whatever trap he's concocted.

But I know how to deal with his kind. This isn't the time for subtlety.

Brazenly, I rest my right hand on the butt of my gun and tilt my head, my lips a tense, thin line as I stare him down. Daring him to move. Daring him to do the stupid thing he's thinking about doing.

Rigid and calm and quiet, I merely watch him.

I don't need to say a word for him to get my message loud and clear.

He stops walking.

Good boy.

Guy's smile fades, and with it goes his welcoming demeanor. "If you come to the dojo looking for help, there are rules you must follow. You're human, so you don't know any better, and we'll forgive you this one mistake. But I'm afraid we don't allow second chances or do-overs here. You understand?"

"I understand that you're *stalling*." I narrow my eyes, fed up with the games. "And I want to know why."

"I'm not *stalling*," he says the word with disgust. "I'm

protecting the dragons of this dojo and of the Fairfax family by making sure you understand what it means for you to be here. What your obligations are." He scans my body again, with a hint of envy in his eyes that he's barely containing. "Everyone who walks through those gates is under our care and must obey the hierarchy of this dojo. You may be coveted out there, woman, but in here you're to treat me with *respect.*"

Oh, great. He's one of *those* guys.

He has no inherent authority, no natural leadership ability, so he hides behind rules and hierarchies.

Pathetic.

I tilt my head, studying him as he continues his little rant, imagining all the ways I'd kill him in a fight. Judging by his body shape, his dragon form is probably slightly larger than average, but not by much. From the steel blue color of his eyes, I'm guessing he's an ice dragon. Dangerous, deadly, but well within the realm of what I can handle.

If it were one-on-one, he'd be an easy mark. And given his posture, he likely favors his left side, which would make him easy to predict in a battle.

But then—oh. That's not good.

I see a glimmer in his eye as he's speaking, something oddly familiar to me. Something unsettling. It digs deep into me, setting off alarms left and right as I try to place it.

The word comes to me in a disturbing rush, and I grit my teeth in loathing.

Leverage.

That's it.

Diesel looks at Irena like this every time we see him. He wants her as his woman, and he wants her *bad*. He wants her to be his and only his, even though our organization has never condoned monogamy. He just wants to own her. She won't admit it, probably because there's so little we can do to avoid him, and she brushes it off any time I bring up my concerns. But I know the truth. He'll do anything to have her, and though she and I despise him with a mutual passion, crippling or deadly "accidents" seem to happen to the men she brings into her bed.

And whenever he comes to Zurie's place, Diesel looks at Irena, and sometimes even me, like Guy is looking at me know. Always looking for a new weakness. Always searching for a new way to break us, should the need arise.

Here and now, Guy *is* stalling, but not to spring some impressive trap. He's looking for anything that gives him control over me, using the time to study me and the way I move, the way I hold myself. He's looking for a weak knee, or a limp, or the slightest tremor in my lip to signal that the topic is uncomfortable, a possible trigger.

This asshole is cold-reading me. He's looking for

vulnerabilities, and there's only one reason to do that in a supposed neutral zone.

He knows who I am. He knows *what* I am. And if he's looking for leverage against me, he plans to *use* it.

Disgusted, my grip slides to the gun at my side. It'll be a cold day in hell before I let *that* happen.

CHAPTER TWENTY-TWO

Guy Durand doesn't know the danger he's in.

And if he keeps using this arrogant tone with me, he's going to get one hell of an ass-whooping.

"You're new to this world," Guy says, droning on. "So, I understand if you're unclear on how things work. Let me clarify. You don't get to come in here and make demands of me. Quite the opposite, in fact. I need to make sure you're safe to be around. I need you to understand the gravity of the situation you're in."

I eye the dragons along the wall before deciding what to say next. I'm tempted to call him out on his own flaws, of course, but this isn't the time or place. I'm tempted to tell him how much he bores me, but that would be only for my own amusement and would likely not end well for us.

Time to swallow my pride and play his bluff.

"I promise you that the longer you stall, the fewer of my weaknesses you'll find." I smirk, daring him to defend himself. "You're not even that good at it, honestly."

He stutters for a moment. "I don't know what—"

"If you're going to cold-read me, you need to at least be subtle about it."

"I'm not—"

"You are. You're just doing it badly." I give him a once-over, not bothering to hide my disdain. "Now, listen closely. You're going to take me to Jace. Immediately. Or we leave." I gesture over my shoulder with my thumb. "What'll it be, Mr. Durand? Are you done bull-shitting, or is it like breathing for you?"

Tucker laughs quietly at my side. On the walls, several of the dragons snicker as well.

Oh, good. They hate this man, too.

Guy sputters for a moment, clearly thrown off guard. "Fine. But first, we have rules. While you are an exception, no humans may enter the dojo. He must leave." He points at Tucker. "And before you can continue, you must order your dragon friend to shift to human form." Guy looks at Levi and mocks my tone. "*Immediately.*"

"Nope." I shake my head, unfazed, arms still crossed.

"No—what do you mean, *nope?*" Guy's brow

furrows in anger. "I am acting commander, and all within these walls must obey me!"

I suppress the deep, *deep* desire to roll my eyes. He's obviously new at this. "By 'nope,' I mean no, Tucker will not be leaving, and Levi does not have to shift." I shrug. "Or, if you prefer, we can all three leave together. But, no, I will not stay without both of them."

Tucker leans toward me, whispering. "Aw, babe, I'm flattered. Guess I'm too pretty to let out of your sight, huh?"

"Don't push your luck," I whisper back, never breaking eye contact with Guy.

There's a tense standoff between me and Guy. In the silence, I lean the heel of my palm against the gun at my side, my fingers itching for a fight. Calves flexed, shoulders braced, I already have a plan.

The truck is shit cover. It'll be blown to bits in seconds, but none of the dragons will expect the sheer volume of explosives Tucker has stashed in the back. Any fire to that baby and the truck is an instant bomb. First goal will be to get away from the truck and to something vaguely resembling cover. I eye a doorway to the left, just out of reach of where I think the blast will hit. Good. After that, we'll need to get out of the castle, but we don't have to use the bridge. My gaze shifts briefly to Levi, and he catches my eye. A terse nod later, and we're on the same page.

Poor Tucker. He's not going to like this.

"Marvelous, wow." Someone starts clapping from up on the walls of the embassy, and I scan the walls again in search of whoever is applauding us.

A man ducks out from behind one of the dragons tightly packed along the walls. He sits on the edge, his legs draped over the side, nothing between him and the four-story fall to the courtyard but his own balance. From this distance, I can't see much of his face, but his broad shoulders, strong physique, and dirty blond hair would leave lesser women weak at the knees.

"I am truly impressed," he says, laughing, his voice carrying through the quiet courtyard. The applause slowly fades as the dragons around him inch away, giving him space and an audience with me. He smiles and, to my surprise, jumps off the edge and into the courtyard.

"What the—" Tucker sucks in a breath, clearly horrified.

In their human forms, any dragon would still be badly hurt from a fall like that. Even a shifter's body can be severely damaged, though it takes more to hurt them than a normal human.

Any dragon, of course, except thunderbirds. And I have a theory on who this newcomer is.

Instead of breaking his legs on the black stone, instead of writhing in agony as his body shatters, the blond stranger lands lightly on his feet. He's entirely unfazed, walking toward us as though he jumped a fence instead of leaping off the side of a four-story wall.

He tilts his head and scans my body, though I note his eyes aren't drawn to my chest or hips. He's looking instead at the strategic locations—the gun, the knife hilt sticking out of my boot, the scars on my biceps from my training years.

In one fluid movement, he lifts his chin and looks at me. I open my mouth to ask him what kind of game he's playing, but the words die in my mouth when our eyes meet.

With that subtle motion—just our meeting gazes—I feel something hit me in the chest. Hard. It knocks the breath out of me, and for a moment, I think I'm shot.

Dazed, a little delirious, I absently brush my fingers along the skin between my breasts, but I'm fine. No blood. No pain. Just—whatever this strange sensation is that's slowly eating away at me.

He feels it, too. As we watch each other, he hesitates, and it looks for all the world like he's trying his best to stay collected. To say something, anything at all. His smirk falters, and the world around me dissolves into nothing.

It's like time stopped, trapping us here, trapping me in those stormy gray eyes. He's a solid ten feet away, and yet even being this close to him is kicking up a flurry of desire and an innate craving within me that I'm actively trying to ignore.

I'm an assassin, damn it. I don't indulge sensations like this. Romance, affection, vulnerability—it's beaten out of us when we're young.

But whatever just hit me, whatever is going on now, it's different.

I'm powerless against it. I can't ignore *this*.

No matter how hard I try.

"You're Jace," I manage to say.

In my heart, I just know.

He nods.

It's just him and me, and it's getting harder to breathe. I don't understand this pull, this drive to be near him, for him to be *in* me. I want to hold him until time stops and we're nothing but ash.

It's primal.

It's raw.

It doesn't make any damn sense.

But my body doesn't care. Whatever's happening, whatever he just did to me, I have absolutely no control over it.

Seeing him is like coming home. Like finding my place in the world. Like losing myself in an ocean and never wanting to come up for breath.

There's a crackle in the air between us, a blistering burst of energy, and I feel like the world around us could be burning and neither of us would care. If people are talking, I can't hear them. I can't feel, can't sense, can't understand anything but this strange connection.

Us.

"Rory," Tucker says beside me, voice tense and concerned, so muffled and distant that I can barely hear him. "What's wrong?" He gently shakes me, his strong fingers wrapping around my arm, and the movement snaps me from whatever enchantment Jace put on me.

And just like that, the pull toward Jace fades. It isn't gone but thank goodness it softens. I can breathe again. *Think* again.

I narrow my eyes in suspicion, wondering if I should confront the thunderbird and make him tell me what that was, but I don't bother. I wouldn't trust his answer, anyway. Not yet.

The spell seems to have broken for him as well. The shifter takes a step back and stands a bit taller, a guarded expression now on his face. Though he briefly looks at Levi and Tucker, his eyes never leave me for long.

My head feels light. My cheeks flush with a twinge of nausea, but I fight it. I'm not sure what just happened, but something in my gut tells me it's irreversible.

Jace—he's unique. And I need to know what the *hell* he just did to me.

Like a match in a gas tank, my inner fire returns

with full fury. I ball my hands into fists, lifting my chin in challenge as I watch the master of the dragon dojo.

I'm getting some damn answers, even if I have to burn this beautiful place to the ground.

Jace opens his mouth to speak but hesitates. It's brief, almost unnoticeable, but it's clear he's choosing his next words wisely.

Smart man.

"Welcome to the dojo," he says with a bow. A real one. A regal one. One that hints at a lifetime of class and sophistication. Yet again those stormy eyes capture me, and I have to look away to prevent myself from diving into them once more.

"I'm Jace Goodwin, master of the dragon dojo. And you are…?"

"Seriously considering leaving." I glare at him to drive my point home.

His smile falters, replaced for a moment with concern, but it barely lasts long enough to register. In a flash, that cocky smirk of his comes back. "You wouldn't have come here if you had anywhere else to go."

Touché. Time for a new approach, then.

"Don't make me regret coming here, Jace," I say quietly, my voice dripping with the unspoken warning I'm giving him. I'm not trying to challenge him in front of his people. I don't want him to get prideful. I just want to make a point.

Because when I regret a decision, I usually have to kill a *lot* of people to fix things.

"You won't," he says softly. Tenderly. It's gentle and soothing, and his tone catches me off guard. Judging from the broad shoulders and thin scars on his muscled forearms, he's a seasoned fighter. He's a thunderbird, a shifter brimming with magic and power. From the way he moves, it's clear he's not afraid of spilling a little blood—or a lot of it.

This man is a killer. If Zurie ordered me to kill him, I would think she had sent me on a suicide mission.

And yet, when he looks at me—and only when he looks at me—I see a softer side of him that doesn't make sense.

In any other situation, I would leave. This is too much, too new, too raw. But I'm in deep, and he's right. I have nowhere else to go.

I gesture to Levi and Tucker. "My friends stay."

"Friend! That's cute, honey." Tucker laughs like I told some kind of adorable little joke and leans one elbow on my shoulder. "I'm her boyfriend, actually. She's really shy about it, but—"

"Tucker, I will break your damn arm," I mutter.

"Right, of course, babe." The weapons master removes his elbow, only to slide his hand possessively around my waist instead. "She has such a way with words, doesn't she?"

"Oh, my God," I mutter quietly to myself, pinching the bridge of my nose.

"It's fine," Jace says, though the smirk is gone. His voice is tense and dark, with a deadly edge to it. He watches Tucker like a hunter watches prey from afar, judging its strength, trying to figure out how to best kill it.

Oh, fantastic. This will go well.

"Are we staying, boss?" Tucker's grip tightens around my waist, and I realize then what he was doing —positioning himself to throw me in the car if he needed to, to get the hell out of here if things went south.

Ah.

I'll forgive him, then. This time.

"We're staying," I say with a tense glance toward Jace.

The dojo master lets out a small breath, and it's odd to me how in tune with him I am. How I can sense the subtle changes in his mood, in his body.

I shake my head, trying to get rid of this damned pull. Thunderbirds are magical, but I've never heard of them doing anything like this. Their power is restrained to balls of energy and light, to destroying entire buildings with a pulse of magic.

No, whatever he did to me just now, it's different from anything I've ever heard of. Before I leave this place, I need to know what he did... and how to undo it.

I can't be beholden to a dragon.

"All right, then." Tucker stretches, and several joints in his arms and back crack with the motion. "Since that's settled, what is there to eat? Any takeout nearby? I could go for a burger. Maybe some teriyaki. What are you in the mood for, pumpkin?"

Instead of an answer, I just sigh warily.

Tucker casually grabs a few bags from the backseat, swings one over his shoulder, winks at me, and heads toward the front door as if he's moving into a dorm. It's a long walk to the stairs, though, and as I watch Tucker retreat into the dragon den, I notice Guy. The second in command still stands on the stairs, arms crossed, glaring at me as though he wishes he could kill with a look.

I find it hard to believe such a pathetic man could ever be second in command. It seems I have another little mystery to explore while I'm here.

Though Guy can't seem to look away from me, Jace is now watching Levi warily. He frowns, eyes scanning the blue dragon's wings and neck. "He's feral."

The dragons along the wall growl, their collective snarls beginning to shake the ground beneath my feet. Their claws scrape against the stone, agitated and on edge, their bodies tensing at their master's observation.

A few spread their wings, all of them sneering at Levi, preparing to attack.

Levi bares his teeth, scanning the other dragons, a guttural growl ripping through him as he prepares to defend himself.

I step between Levi and Jace, making my stance on the topic clear. "He's safe."

"He's *feral*." Jace reaches for my arm to drag me out of the way.

But I'm faster.

"He is, yes." I step backward toward Levi, never breaking eye contact with Jace. "But he won't hurt any of you, as long as you don't hurt *him*." After a few more steps, my back bumps gently against Levi's chest, and I look up to see the blue dragon tilt his massive head just enough to look down at me.

The truth is, he won't hurt them as long as they don't hurt *me*. It's a fact I don't think I should divulge just yet.

Jace takes a tentative step toward me. He looks mortified, like Levi could snap at any moment and he's desperate to pull me to safety. "I know he seems safe now, but I promise he isn't. You don't know much about our kind, yet, but this one is very dangerous. All feral dragons are."

He's expecting me to be terrified, so I bite my lip to keep from laughing right in his face.

Oh, how adorable.

Jace thinks I'm just some human girl who doesn't know the first thing about who they are or what they're like.

Poor man. If he's going to be as helpful as the red dragon claims, he'd better be a fast learner.

With a genuine look of deep concern, Jace reaches toward me with one hand, gesturing for me to come closer. "I need you to come here."

"Levi, will you please lay down?" I pat the dragon's neck, and he obliges me, shooting me an irritated look over the tip of his wing as he lounges beside me.

Jace, to his credit, looks down at Levi in confusion.

Levi is no pet. He's a man trapped in a dragon's body, and I respect him as such. To ask him to do tricks like some dog at a show hurts my heart, but it's the only thing I can do right now to save his life.

Jace doesn't seem convinced yet, so I gesture toward the truck bed and the bags of weapons stored there. "Levi, do you mind helping Tucker with a few more of those bags, please?"

Levi huffs and stands, flicking me with his ear in annoyance as he passes. From the grumpy way he brushes past me, I can almost hear him saying, *I'm not your errand boy.*

But I made my point to Jace. That's all I needed.

"There's still human left in him, Jace." I set one hand on my hip as I watch the blue dragon shuffle toward the castle. "He's not dangerous to anyone as long as they don't do something stupid."

Above us, the dragons still growl, every head slowly moving in time with Levi's steps. They're still tense and ready to spring into action against a feral dragon in their midst, so I need Jace to restrain them.

Back arched, hands clenched at his sides, Jace glares after Levi for several moments. He looks seconds away from giving a kill order, and my confidence begins to crack. For a moment, I worry. I worry that I put Levi in danger by bringing him here. I worry I made a mistake.

I worry that I'm going to have to kill a diplomat in order to keep Levi safe.

"Astonishing," Jace says, still staring after Levi as the dragon carries four painfully heavy bags in his strong jaws as if they're empty.

And with that, my worry dissolves into thin air. Thank goodness.

"I still don't trust him," Jace says, looking at me over his shoulder. "And neither should you."

I groan. "We just—did we not *just* go over this?"

"Feral dragons always snap," he says with an apologetic expression. "Sooner or later, they *always* do. He's unique, yes, but you can't get comfortable around him."

"Jace, seriously—"

"Please," Jace adds softly. It's that same tender tone as before, and once more I'm caught off-guard that someone this strong, someone who is clearly such an adept fighter could be so gentle, even for a second.

With a frown, I rest my hands on my hips and shake my head. I'm not promising Jace anything, not yet.

Not until I'm sure the red dragon didn't make a mistake by sending us here.

"So, what's the catch?" I ask, changing the subject.

"The catch?"

"Don't play dumb with me." I narrow my eyes. "You know what I am, right? You know who's after me? The risks of keeping me here?"

Jace nods. "I know quite a lot about you, Rory."

For a moment, I can't speak. A jolt of dread shoots through me, and I'm rooted in place.

Damn it all.

Not again.

My jaw tenses, and I fight the active impulse to reach for my gun. "How do you know my name?"

His expression softens, a strange blend of possessiveness and concern. "A lot of people know your name now."

I shake my head, trying desperately to hide my deep-set irritation and frustration.

I miss my darkness. My secrets. They were safe.

But now, they're gone. To survive, I need to stay focused and keep my guard up, but being around him corrodes me.

"What's the catch, then?" I ask again. "I was sent

here because you can help me train, and I assume that's not a free service. If I stay here, what do you want in return? I don't write blank checks."

Surprisingly, the edge of his mouth curves into a small smile. Nothing diabolical. Nothing cocky. It's charming, if anything. Endearing. A little proud, even, like he wasn't expecting me to have so much fire.

And once more I'm drawn to those gray eyes of his, lost in the storm brewing in his soul.

I forcibly look away to break the spell before it starts again. I don't know why he makes my body ache, or what he did to me. My body has never betrayed me like this, not once, not until the magic fused with me. Now that I have the power of dragons in my veins, my blood suddenly runs hot. I'm lost in lust and desire so easily, lately. In Tucker's goofy charm. In Levi's brooding possessiveness. And now, in Jace's spell-binding gaze.

They're distracting, and they all arrived in my life at a time when I can't afford to lose focus.

"There's no price, Rory," Jace says affectionately. He walks toward me, his hands outstretched, and takes my fingers in his. The sensation of his warm skin against mine ignites that deep-set longing in me, setting me ablaze, driving me mad with need for him.

I lift my fingers to avoid the sensation, doing every-thing in my power to fight this spell. Though my body aches at there being any space between us at all, I refuse to allow this.

I am a fighter. A warrior.

Not a love-struck schoolgirl.

I lift my chin in defiance only to find his face mere inches away. The drive to lean into him, to throw my arms around his neck… it's overpowering, but I resist.

"There's always a price," I say quietly, determined not to be the one who looks away first this time. Determined to override the power those storm clouds have over me.

He smirks and brushes a knuckle over my cheek. It's intimate, something I imagine lovers do, and a blistering bolt of warmth shoots through my skin where he touches me.

I want to grab his muscular arms and shake him until his head rattles. I want to demand that he tell me what spell he put me under, but I refrain. I can't let him know how much he's getting to me, how deeply he's already burrowed under my skin.

"I'm going to enjoy training you, Rory." He laughs and gestures to the open doors at the top of the steps. "Shall we?"

With no witty comeback on the tip of my tongue, I indulge him and head for the doors. With every step, I'm careful not to let him slip into my blind spot, always angling my body just so in an effort to keep an eye on him and the dozens of dragons along the walls.

And just like that, I become a refugee, taking asylum in a dragon embassy. Jace walks beside me, and even when I'm not looking at him, I feel his powerful presence. He feels like safety. Like home. Like nostalgia and summer all blended into one.

It doesn't make any damn *sense*.

I've always dreamed of freedom, but never in my life did I imagine the world without Zurie would look anything like *this*.

CHAPTER TWENTY-THREE

As I walk through the dragon embassy's halls, I can't resist the temptation to look for its weaknesses. For ways out. For possible secure locations and sensitive intelligence centers.

It's habit.

Besides, usually if I were being escorted through a dragon's den, I would be in chains and looking for an escape. Zurie and Irena would be outside somewhere, casing the building, preparing their attack.

Surprisingly, the black stone doesn't continue inside. It's light and airy, with white walls and plenty of windows to let in the stunning sunlight outside. The massive hall could easily allow ten people through shoulder to shoulder, and again, I'm left wondering if this massive fortress was, in fact, originally built to house an army.

Dozens of corridors and doorways pepper the walls, and the place begins to feel like a labyrinth. I keep tabs on our path, quietly taking notes on where we go, determined to learn the layout as quickly as possible.

Up ahead, Levi tucks his wings in close, ducking as he nearly army-crawls his way through the hall. Tucker leads, though it's pretty obvious he has no idea where he's going.

Jace walks beside me, his steps in time with mine, his strong body a little too close for comfort. My stomach twists at how near he is, how easy it would be to brush my hand against his. Warmth runs down my thighs as my imagination temporarily runs away with me, imagining what his hand would feel like at my waist, on my thigh, between my legs—

Get a grip! I resist the impulse to smack myself out of it, instead biting my lip to distract my thoughts.

But I can't help peeking.

The master of this dojo stands a good foot taller than me, his broad shoulders toned and muscled in a way that betrays his storied fighting experience. Pale scars, just a shade or two lighter than his skin, cover his forearms, and I wonder how many more cover the six pack abs I can see through his thin white shirt.

For a dragon to have wounds like that, he must have survived some bloody battles. The best fighters usually have the most interesting scars.

He knows how to take a hit, clearly, and from his confident gait and his thick fingers, I figure he knows how to give one, too. My eyes trace the curves of his muscle, up his arms and to his pecs, to his thick neck and the sharp jawline covered in delightfully tempting stubble.

His gaze shifts towards me, catching me staring at him, and he smirks as I quickly look away.

Before long, we end up at a balcony overlooking a second courtyard. The black marble continues throughout the square, and several sloped roofs along the walls offer shelter from the elements.

Jace nods to the courtyard. "I figure your feral friend can stay here, since he won't fit inside."

Levi grumbles, a thin trail of icy mist billowing out of his nose as he slowly tilts his head toward Jace.

"Well, what were you sleeping on *before*?" I lift one eyebrow, daring the blue dragon to continue complaining. "It has to be a hell of a lot better than sleeping in an open forest."

Levi's attention shifts to me, ensnaring me again in that ice blue gaze, and he presses his nose against my forehead. Fleeting, frantic images dance through his head, none of them long enough for me to process, and a growing sense of unease builds within me as the feral dragon tries to speak.

A blistering sensation of suspicion bleeds through from him, consuming me, overpowering my own emotions for a moment as he finally finds the words. *I do not trust this one, Rory.*

"Yeah, I know," I say softly, rubbing my hand along his jawline. "It'll be okay."

With a brief glance toward Jace, who's watching our exchange with a slight frown, I remember the red dragon's comment about being able to read my thoughts, too.

Hmm. Let's try using this to our advantage for once.

Keep your guard up, I think to Levi, wondering if he can hear me.

And you, Rory. A soft growl rumbles through his body, and I can feel the vibration in my fingers. It's possessive and tender. Comforting.

I smile. *I will. Look for any rooms with possible intel, okay? Let me know what you find.*

Levi's eyes narrow slightly in suspicion. *Stay out of trouble. These are not forgiving dragons.*

"Will it suffice?" Jace interjects. He looks annoyed, and the way his jaw tenses makes me think he knows we're having a quiet conversation—one he doesn't want us to have in private. He crosses his arms impatiently, and his pecs bulge with the movement. As his muscles pull against his shirt, I'm once more distracted by his rock-hard body.

"Yes, it's fine." I clear my throat, trying to stay focused. "Thank you."

Levi takes off, and a gust of air from his wings cuts through my hair as he glides down to the courtyard below. Tucker stands a short distance away, on the other side of where Levi was moments before, leaning his elbows against the railing as he looks over the edge.

"So, it's a dragon stable, basically?" the weapons expert asks.

Jace grimaces, casting his attention between Levi and Tucker. Instead of answering, he gives Tucker a once-over, those strong arms still crossed and intimidating. "And how do you two know Rory?"

"Long story," I answer before Tucker can.

My voice seems to cast a spell on Jace, and I don't quite understand why. One moment, he's glaring at Tucker; the next, he's looking at me, his expression softer, his shoulders relaxed.

Huh. It's clear I'm not the only one affected by whatever this connection is.

For a moment, no one speaks, and Jace looks at me expectantly. "Care to share it with the class?"

"Nope." I smirk and gesture back toward the castle. "Shall we?"

Tucker laughs, walking ahead of us, taking the hint before Jace catches on. To his credit, Jace eventually chuckles, shaking his head. With a nod to the door, he obliges. "Follow me."

Much to my surprise, we actually get a tour of the embassy. We see the kitchens, the barracks, a few training halls, and even an armory. All the while, I'm left baffled that the master of a dragon embassy would share details like this with two humans he doesn't even know.

I pore through the reasons why he would do such a thing, and the only motivation that makes sense is actually quite simple.

He wants me to trust him. More than that, though, he wants me to *stay*.

Not happening.

Most surprising of all is when he leads us past a room with two guards posted out front. They salute Jace as we pass, and he nods in respect. Behind them, wires run along the wall and through a small hole at the top of the doorframe, a key sign that this room isn't just some dusty old treasury. It has something worth far more than gold or jewels.

It has *intel*.

I allow Jace to lead us away, careful to keep track of our movements so that I can find my way back here.

But as we walk, Jace keeps close. He's never more than five feet away, and I feel his presence melting me. When he speaks to Tucker, he looks annoyed, bristling with testosterone and authority. But when he looks at me, he softens. His whole body relaxes, right to his eyes, and for however long it lasts, he just seems... happy.

It's freaking me out.

Jace leads us up a flight of stairs, and as we round the curved steps, he gently places his fingers on the small of my back. It's a quick motion, gone in a flash, but a blaze of heat burns through my body beneath his fingertips.

As we climb the gently curving stairs, Tucker breaks the long silence. "Who's that Guy character?"

"Guy is a blowhard," Jace says with a groan, "but he's earned his spot as my second. I apologize for his greeting. He's fairly new and still figuring out how life in an embassy works. I knew he would be insufferable, but I didn't think he would be that bad."

"He sure likes rules," I say, not bothering to hide my disdain.

Jace frowns. "He is right, though. Our rules are deeply ingrained in the embassy's existence." The thunderbird pauses, that intense gaze driving home how serious this is. "Our rules matter, Rory."

"No loud music after ten?" Tucker asks, jogging up the steps ahead of us.

I sigh. "Can you be serious for two minutes?"

"Nah." Tucker shrugs.

"The rules," Jace interjects with a shake of his head, "are simple. No killing." He looks briefly at my gun and tilts his head knowingly. The subtle motion betrays so much—he knows I *can* use it and that I'm probably not opposed to using it, either.

"Fine." I purse my lips in annoyance.

"We don't use titles or last names here, either."
Jace's fingers return to the small of my back, and for
a moment, I forget how to breathe as the uncontrolled rush of heat and desire burns beneath his
touch.

"You told me your last name," I point out with a
frown. "So did Guy."

Jace chuckles. "Yes, because the acting commander
is the highest authority of the dojo. We get certain
privileges." He winks.

"But he's not acting commander. You are."

With a grin, Jace rubs the stubble along his jawline.
"For the test, I allowed him to pretend he was."

The test. I knew it.

"Care to explain what you were looking for in your
little test?" I give him a sidelong glance, lifting one
eyebrow in curiosity, daring him to tell me what he
learned.

It'll tell me how he thinks. How he processes
information.

He really shouldn't tell me anything.

Given the way he hesitates, I figure he's thinking
the same thing I am. He's probably tempted to give me
a curt nope, just like I did on the balcony, just to get
under my skin.

For whatever reason, he doesn't.

He nods toward my gun. "I learned that you're not
afraid to arm yourself, and that is at least a bonus.

Though I wonder how well you could hold up against a dragon."

I stifle a laugh. To his credit, so does Tucker, though the normally agile man does trip on a step, bumping into the wall as he quietly snickers.

"I learned you aren't as scared as you should be," Jace continues with a furrowed look of concern. "In fact, I don't think you're scared at *all,* and that worries me considering who's after you."

"And who's after me?"

"Everyone." His stormy eyes snare me again, driving home the point with an intense stare. "*Everyone,* Rory. Everyone I've ever fought. Everyone I've ever been allies with. Everyone I've ever monitored."

Oh, good. He doesn't know it, but he just confirmed there's intelligence gathering happening in this building.

"*Everyone,*" he continues, oblivious to the impact of sharing that little nugget of information with me. "Dragons and humans alike are hunting you down, yet you drive into my dojo with a human and a feral dragon, asking me to train you and telling me you don't write blank checks." He laughs, running his hand through his hair as he pauses to relive the moment. "You're insane, and I am too for how much I love it."

A small smile pulls at the corners of my mouth, and I look away to hide how much I enjoyed that little compliment.

Oblivious to my reaction, Jace sighs and rubs his jaw. "But that's why you're safe here. One thing you have to understand about the dragon embassies—the hierarchy of the diplomats matters. It's a way of life for dragons. Outside my walls, you may have wealth and power, but in here only the dojo's chain of command exists. Even the Fairfax Boss cannot be addressed by her title within these walls."

Huh. I chew on that for a moment, wondering why they've implemented such a system, but I suppose it makes sense. This is a neutral zone, and it doesn't make much sense to allow foreign ruler to throw his or her weight around here.

I absently rub my neck as we continue to climb the stairs. "Guy said you don't allow humans here. Who *do* you allow? Why do shifters come here?"

"Good question." Jace smiles warmly, a hint of pride in his eye, and I wonder if this is all a façade. He's so easily agitated by anyone who isn't me—it just doesn't seem like his softer side could be real.

And yet, there's something very clearly going on between us.

Something foreign.

Something distinctly *dragonish*. I feel it deep in my core, in the blistering orb of power the dragon gods shoved into me what feels like eons ago.

Maybe he has no control over this, either.

"We accept shifters from every family except the

Vaer." His nose wrinkles in disgust. Good, at least we agree on that much. "Shifters come here seeking asylum from their families if they do something to anger their Bosses. Some come here to train under me, to learn the advanced flying and fighting methods. Others come to escape laws and forced marriages in their own homes." Jace frowns deeply, eyes glossing over as we walk up the steps. "We are a haven, and as long as a shifter is on our land, he or she is safe. Attacking us is an act of war, one few know how to win."

At that not-so-subtle comment, I study his face. He watches me, equally curious, and we continue our climb in silence. His eyes are so much older than the rest of him, and I feel like he's seen horrible things. Maybe *done* horrible things.

This is a man who is unafraid of blood. Of war. Of death.

In fact, I suspect there's very little he fears.

I chew the inside of my lip, lost in thought as I return my attention to the staircase. He's being so gentle, almost doting, but I can't let my guard down. I have to remember who he is and what he's capable of doing to me the second I'm no longer useful.

I'm still a Spectre, and he's still a dragon. A young one at that, maybe twenty-five, just a few years older than me. And yet he has command over a lethal army.

Dragon titles and hierarchies don't work the same

way humans' do, but he is essentially the General of the Fairfax family's army.

There's a lot to Jace Goodwin I don't know. I can't underestimate him or the tricks he might be playing on me. Sure, this is supposed to be a neutral zone, but the rules tend to change when something valuable is at stake. Namely, my magic.

Namely, *me.*

Anything and everything I hear, see, and feel in this place could be a trick. I'll need to be extra careful. Extra cunning. Extra ruthless.

"My *God,* are we at the top yet?" Tucker huffs, impatient and out of breath as he climbs the stairs. "Do you have any elevators? Jesus."

Instead of answering, Jace glares at the back of Tucker's head with a deep frown, equal parts annoyed and disappointed.

A few minutes later, we finally round the last curve and reach an open doorframe. The landing beyond is bright and airy, its white walls and tall ceiling filled with sunlight. A floor-to-ceiling window to the left lets in the brilliant day outside. Seven doors line the far wall, all of them inlaid with gold and gemstones that glitter in the sun.

"Damn. The king's chambers, I assume?" Tucker asks with a nod to the door.

"Suites specially designed for our guests." Jace smiles and looks at me. "And any *friends* they might bring along," he adds dryly, looking back at Tucker, his smile fading.

"*Boyfriend.*" Tucker corrects with a ridiculous grin, lifting his pointer finger for emphasis.

I sigh, rubbing my eyes in frustration, not even bothering to correct him anymore. "Shut up, Tucker."

"Sure thing, honey bun." He winks at me and walks toward the nearest door, whistling in awe as he peeks his head in. "This is amazing!"

"Only the best," Jace says softly, and I look up to find him watching me.

Tucker disappears into his room, evidently confident I can handle myself, and I open a door a few down from his. I peek in, momentarily gob-smacked as I stare blankly at the opulent room inside.

Between the ornate crystal chandelier, the elegant white and gold furniture, and the massive marble fireplace that could roast a cow, I almost don't know where to look.

I can feel Jace behind me, and I'm careful to keep him in my periphery as I walk inside. My boots sink into the plush white carpet as I trace my fingers over the gold wallpaper.

My wonder doesn't last, and moments later, my training kicks in. I scan the ceilings for cameras, mind churning as I scope out locations for possible microphones to be hidden.

I can't be too careful. Not here, not with Jace. No matter how safe the red dragon thinks it is.

Behind me, I feel Jace move closer. It's more than seeing him in my periphery. It's as though I can feel the air around him shift, sense his body moving closer, anticipate the steps he takes before he takes them. It comes and goes, fluid and fuzzy, completely undefined and utterly confusing. But it's an undeniable connection, one unlike anything I've ever experienced.

Even though my body *craves* him, I don't like it one bit.

"It's beautiful. Thank you." I turn and, as expected, I find Jace inches away, his nose nearly touching mine.

He doesn't answer. He doesn't need to. Instead, he lifts his finger to my chin, the rough texture of his skin almost tantalizing. I hold his gaze, daring him to make the next move.

For the time being, I allow him to touch me. I want to see what he's going to do.

Warmth spirals from his touch, snaking across my cheek, across my lips, into my head. It's electric. His finger traces slowly up my face, toward my ear, until his palm presses gently against my jaw.

I resist the impulse to close my eyes and lean into him, to *give* into him. I try to ignore the way my stomach flutters, the way my body intuitively aches to sink into him.

"Explain." I stare him down, none too gently, shattering the tender moment quite intentionally.

He seems to snap out of a daze, blinking a few times in confusion as he looks down at me. "What do you mean?"

"So, we're going to play this game?" I sigh in disappointment. "You can't get away with playing dumb, Jace. I know you aren't."

What did you do to me, shifter? I want to shake him until answers fall out of his ears if that's what it takes.

But I refrain.

He backs away, releasing me, and my skin feels painfully cold without his touch. It's uncomfortable, and my heart skitters for a moment, flooded with the desire to pull him back into my arms.

No, damn it all.

I need my body to work with me, not betray me.

"I'm sure you've been dealing with a lot," he finally says, giving me space. "There are certain things about you we need to discuss, things you need to know, but we don't have to do it now." He gestures to the beautiful room around me. "Enjoy yourself. Relax. You're safe. We'll start training when you're ready."

With that, he leaves. No goodbye, no final glance backward, nothing. When the door clicks shut behind him, I'm left in a quiet room, surrounded by opulence I'm only used to seeing in the homes Zurie orders me to break into.

I cross my arms, a little uncomfortable in the vast space, and distract myself by opening every door in the hunt for secret entrances or locked access. Instead, I find a beautiful bedroom with an almost endless view of the forests and mountains beyond the embassy. A closet large enough for a small family to move into. A bathroom with a two-person tub and a rain shower. Hell, even the *toilet* has its own room.

Good God, whoever built this suite knew how to *live*.

I could get used to this, but I shouldn't. There's no telling how long I'll actually be here. The thought rips through my heart, and I grit my teeth through the pain.

Jace Goodwin cast some kind of curse on me to make my body crave him like this. Thunderbirds aren't well documented, and they possess abilities the rest of the world doesn't understand. Whatever magic this is, it's real, and if I don't rein it in, it might be the death of me.

I can't get comfortable here, no matter how much I crave Jace, no matter how real and raw and primal this thirst for him seems to be.

Right now, I'm at war with the world. No one can be trusted.

My mission remains.

Save Zurie.

Save Irena.

Save my magic.

And that last one—that's for me, not the Spectres. Diesel helped me, likely because he knows how useful I'll be if I survive, but the rest see the world in black and white.

Protect all Spectres. Kill all dragons.

I may well have to fight them to keep this, but it's worth all the blood I might have to spill.

With an agonized groan, I sit on the plush sofa by the massive fireplace, lost in thought.

I would go to the ends of the earth to save my sister. There's no doubt in my mind she'll love me in the end and accept me for what I am, even if I have dragonish bits to me.

But Zurie…

I'm not sure what Zurie will do. Whatever she decides, the Spectres will obey. She is the Ghost, after all, and to defy her is death.

Right now, she's close to death herself. If she's gone and Irena is ill, that technically leaves me as the Ghost. I doubt the Spectres would honor that, though, and Diesel would take over.

My options are quite simple—rescue her and take my chances or let her die and allow Diesel to take command.

I sigh and set my head in my hands. It's an easy choice to make, but it could still backfire dramatically.

My mentor might not like my new magic, but she raised me. She's no mother, but she's the closest I've ever come to having one. I've spent my life at her side, listening to her every command, and even now rule number one echoes in my head.

Obey the Ghost.

Zurie is the only one who can help me rescue and heal Irena. I can't just let her die.

Still, convincing her I'm an ally and not a threat won't be easy.

I stare at my palms, more certain than ever that I will not give this up. Zurie will demand it, claiming it's a curse that will unravel the Spectres from the inside out, but I can prove her wrong.

And once this is over, Zurie won't be my master anymore. Because whatever I am, it's not something she can contain or control.

I'm certain of that. I just don't know how well she'll take it.

CHAPTER TWENTY-FOUR

I wait until nightfall to implement the first phase of my plan to steal information from Jace's embassy.

Well, not *steal*. Borrow. Peruse, even. He still gets to keep a copy.

It's strange. Though he's left, I still feel him faintly. I can sense him moving through the castle, a vague shadow somewhere behind me and below me, though I wouldn't trust this in a tricky situation.

I try to ignore it. To tune him out. Him and his spell, whatever he did to me.

This embassy poses a delightful challenge: to sneak through its walls when (a) the dragons can all feel me, at least in some sense, when I pass; (b) Jace has some kind of super-connection to me that might give away my location effortlessly; and (c) I'm likely being monitored at all times, as I am a highly-wanted stranger in their midst.

Let the fun begin.

The hallway outside my door has one camera, poised in a corner at the far end of the corridor. I count my remaining voids, sifting through the pack around my abdomen, and I should have enough for a few more missions. After that, however, I'm going to need to resupply. Or just learn to live without them.

I briefly entertain texting Diesel, but I swore to myself I wouldn't. I'm a Spectre, damn it, and we pride ourselves on natural ability. I don't need tech to do my job.

With a frown, I sigh and slip the voids back into the bag, along with a few other pieces of tech I'm saving for later. Sure, I don't *need* this stuff, but it sure does make things easier.

As I crack open the door to the hallway, a thin ray of moonlight peeks through the utter darkness. I cautiously peer around the corner, gauging the distance, seeing where I'll need to aim.

Time to play.

In a flash, I kneel and shoot. The void hits exactly where it's supposed to, and with a small spark, the camera's tiny red light turns off. Even if someone had been watching, they wouldn't have seen me move.

I dart into the hallway, recounting all of the cameras I noticed along the way to the intel room we passed by earlier. Three, plus a possible fourth depending on whether or not I need to take a side route.

I steal through the shadows, pressing myself against doorframes and slipping into dark hallways as guards pass through the hall. Each wears a simple tunic that reminds me of a martial arts robe, their yellow and black uniforms stark and sleek. Each of the men and women who passes by walks calmly, relaxed or sometimes even animated as they talk to each other.

Interesting. They're not patrols—just students going from one class to another, one room to another, living a normal life. Well, as normal as one can be in a dragon dojo.

From their toned arms to the strong, solid backs, however, I can clearly tell they're fighters. A few have deep scars along their biceps or forearms, some even across the face, and I know better than to treat these dragon shifters as harmless students.

They're deadly—all of them—and they can all sense me to some degree.

It's difficult and time consuming to sneak through the three stories of the castle between my room and the information center, but I'm patient. Step by step, breathless pause by breathless pause, I inch my way closer.

Finally close and no one the wiser, I calmly peek out from a dark side hallway to see two guards still stationed outside of the door. One of them plays on his phone, while the other lazily scans the far end of the corridor.

Night duty. They look tired, bored, and a bit hungry.

Good. Distracted guards work in my favor.

I pause, studying the duo, and realize the second guard isn't keeping watch on the room at all. From his slouched posture and the way he leans lazily against the wall behind him, he's just keeping watch for his friend.

In the five minutes I stand there, watching them, he never even looks my way. It seems like they just don't want to get in trouble for slacking on the job.

If Jace and I become allies, I'm going to have to talk to him about his night guards and their lax attention spans. For now, it works in my favor, and I'll keep mum.

Time for phase two—actually getting in the damn room.

Con—I can't go in the front door.

Pro—they won't pay very close attention to what's going on inside. That leaves me a beautiful opportunity to slip in through a window that I sincerely hope is there.

I return back down the hallway and jog to the window at the end. It's an antiqued style, with two glass doors and a simple latch to keep them closed. I'm tempted to just throw them open and get on with it, but after all my years of learning things the hard way, I know better.

Yet again, I have to sit and wait.

To watch. To study.

Two dragons fly past, nothing but blurs of darkness in the night, each keeping watch on the exterior and perimeter. There could also be cameras out of my line of sight, but with this many dragons keeping watch, I doubt they'd waste the manpower to monitor the outside walls.

As I watch the guards fly by, I time their patrols. I'll have a five-minute gap to make my move, and though it's not ideal, it's all I get.

If it's too easy, it's no fun.

Time to go.

Once the second dragon passes, my countdown begins. I unlatch the windowpanes and swing them open. A gust of cool night air brushes past my face, and I smile, drinking in the starry sky.

There's something magical about this place. If it weren't taken over by dragons, I would love to live here forever.

Though the moonlit glow across the forest below is enchanting, I focus on the castle walls. Windows pepper the black stone, light shining through some of them, but one is dark. Judging by the distance, I think this is the one I want.

Score.

Going by the dry stone, I figure it hasn't rained lately. Good. That will give me better grip.

The ground below is thankfully not the open chasm. Though a mist rolls through the trees beneath me, the canopy will break my fall and not my back if I do lose my hold on the uneven stones of the castle walls.

I can live with that worst-case scenario.

Slow and steady, with the countdown timer going in my head, I swing out onto the wall. I carefully close the window behind me, not letting it latch, careful to make it look closed even though it's unlocked and ready to let me back in as soon as all this is over.

Bit by bit, I inch my way across the bare stone. A gust shoots up my shirt, chilling me, and I suppress a shudder as my hair kicks around my face.

Four minutes left.

Focus.

One wrong step means a quick plummet and a lot of pain. I won't die, but it'll still hurt like hell.

Breath steady, hands tightly gripping the loose stones, I finally make my way to the window that, by my calculations, should lead into the intel room.

Two minutes left.

Careful to keep my grip with my left hand, my body pressed against the cold black stone, I test the window, seeing if they left it unlocked.

They didn't. Okay, fine. Plan B it is.

One minute.

I tenderly reach into my pocket for one of my knives. It takes a moment of prying, but I eventually work the latch free. As yet another gust of ice-cold wind blasts me, the windows swing open.

Ten seconds.

Not letting myself pause to savor the small victory, I jump into the room and latch them closed behind me. I duck, taking cover in case there are any live cameras in here.

Moments later, a dragon's silhouette tears by the window. I hold my breath, listening for a roar, for some hint of discovery.

It's silent.

Slowly, I let out the breath I was holding. The party isn't over yet. Time to get to work.

With very little light to guide me, I do a quick scan of the room. Ten rows of desks covered in monitors fills the massive space, and an enormous television covers most of the far wall. All of the screens are off, the only light streaming in from the small frosted window embedded in the door to the hallway.

This isn't just a data gathering hub. It's a full-blown command center.

"Whoa," I mutter under my breath, in awe. Jace doesn't mess around, and I have incredible respect for that.

I scan the walls and find two active cameras. It's always a risk to dive blind into a new area, and in this case, I had no choice. I aim and fire, nailing both cameras with voids, and the little red lights go out.

Much to my disappointment, there aren't many exits or decent places to hide in case of emergency—likely by design. The window, obviously, is my best route out of here, but that's not good for a sudden escape. It puts me in a vulnerable position to slide along the sheer castle wall, so I'll have to resort to hide and seek if someone barges in while I'm snooping. Several desks are deep enough to offer decent cover, with drawers and backs that create a small cave to hide in. It's not great, but it'll do.

With a brief glance to the door, I see a silhouette briefly pass by the opaque window into the hallway. I tense, eyes darting to the nearest desk, but no one comes inside.

Behind me, a row of five desks with sleek and shiny computers sit on an elevated platform, and I assume these are the important ones.

Not willing to waste even a second, I sit at the helm of this massive command center and reach into the pack strapped around my abdomen for one of the finest pieces of Spectre tech, a device Zurie has reminded me to no end costs a small fortune—and my life, should I ever lose it.

An exaggeration, perhaps, but it drives the point home.

I slip the override mechanism out of my pack and examine it briefly in the light to ensure it hasn't been damaged. Thankfully, it's still good—the small, silver rectangle still has the pincer-like spikes at the end, curved slightly at the tips, perfect for piercing cables. The voids are one-time use, but this baby can be used again and again as long as it's not dented. And in my line of work, I've dented quite a few of these overly sensitive little things.

I find a data port on the computer and plug in the override. Instantly, the screen flashes blue, and my eyes dart again toward the exit. I half-expect someone to barge in after seeing lights flash in a supposedly empty room, but to my delight, their shadows don't even move.

The screen flashes green, then white. Seconds later, the desktop appears, signaling that the magical little machine bypassed security and granted me access to the system.

No time to celebrate, though. I scan through the files, bringing up programs I've never seen in my life and skimming them as quickly as I can for information on the Spectres or the Vaer. It's difficult to navigate someone else's system while simultaneously keeping a lookout, and I find my attention easily stolen as the guards' shadows fidget and shift.

So far, I'm not finding anything, and it's pissing me off.

I scour file after file, lost in my search, looking for answers. But then, deep in my soul, I feel something shift.

It's alarming. I pause, listening to it, searching for the root cause.

Jace.

The sensation I've tried to subdue, to stuff deep down and ignore, surfaces with a vengeance. It's stronger than before, almost as strong as when—

My eyes widen. Almost as strong as when he was right next me.

Outside, the guards' shadows straighten, jumping to attention.

Shit.

I tug the override device out of the data port, and the screen instantly powers off. Pulling it out without a clean disconnect is terrible for the tech. I might have just broken it or even left a trace of my visit in the machine, but I don't have a better option right now.

Outside, several men talk in hushed tones.

I dart toward the nearest desk-cave as the doorknob turns. The desk is roomy, wide enough for me to lay down, but it's too open. If he turns on the lights, I'm screwed.

The door opens.

I roll, keeping my head low, and slip into the

cramped space between the thick wooden desk and the wall. I crouch, shoved between the desk and some cables. Out of instinct, I silently draw the dagger in my boot, my fingers tightening around the heavy metal hilt.

The lights flicker on.

I close my eyes, grateful I made the call to pick a different spot.

Heavy boots thud against the floor. Toward me. Toward my hiding spot. I grit my teeth, feeling for Jace as he nears, both loving and hating the way I can sense his movements.

But they're fuzzy. Hazy. If I didn't know he was walking toward me, I would have thought he was at least four rooms over. I can feel him, but only faintly.

And as I wait, knife drawn, I hope he can't sense exactly where I am, either.

The chair I was just sitting in rolls across the floor, followed by the tapping of fingers on a keyboard. Jace mutters under his breath, and though I try, I can't make out what he's saying.

The thunderbird sighs, and once more, those boots thud against the floor. I wait, half-expecting to be found, not sure what will happen next.

I *hate* not knowing, especially this close to danger.

"I knew it," Jace says with a groan. "I *knew* he was trouble." The dojo master storms from the room, the lights shutting off as the door slams behind him. I hear him shout muffled orders, but for the moment, I'm in the clear.

I let out a slow breath, careful to be quiet, careful not to make a noise just in case this is a trick, but I can't resist the surge of relief that floods me. I sheathe the dagger and peek around the corner of the desk to find the room once more empty.

Briefly, I look at the computer, wondering if it's worth the risk to dive in once again. In the hallway, Jace continues to yell muffled commands at the soldiers, and several shadows flit by the door.

Nope. Not worth it. They could return at any moment to assess the damage, and hiding behind a desk is hardly suitable cover for a long-term stakeout. I'll have to come back later—once I'm certain Jace is suitably distracted.

Rule twelve. Time to make my exit.

I sneak toward the window, staying low, always keeping an eye on the door for sudden movements. I watch outside, splitting my attention between the skies and the entrance, half-waiting to be caught.

As I watch for the dragon scouts, checking to see if the rotation has possibly changed since Jace might have sounded an alarm, my mind wanders back to his comment.

I knew he was trouble.

He.

Not she. Not *me*.

Jace thinks someone else came here tonight, and while that might work in my favor, I suspect I already know the man at the top of Jace's shitlist.

Tucker.

Outside, the second dragon guard passes by, making the same rounds as before. Good, that means Jace hasn't sounded an alarm yet, and that's my cue to leave.

Frustrated and furious that I didn't get my intel, I slip out into the night.

CHAPTER TWENTY-FIVE

With Jace on the warpath, I need to make sure Tucker doesn't die tonight.

The hurried trip back to our suites is uneventful, with only a few students still out this late in the otherwise vacant and dark hallways. Still, every step is a risk, and I *absolutely* cannot be caught on the stairs.

The stairs are a weak point in my silent sneaking—they're a bottleneck, and while the curve of the stairwell makes it a sorry spot for a camera, I would still be screwed if someone caught me racing up them in the middle of the night.

As I get to the stairs, I hesitate at the bottom and feel for Jace's presence. I sense him somewhere in the distance, and I grimace as the sensation proves utterly useless.

What good is it to feel him if I can't even tell *exactly* where he is?

Not willing to waste a moment, I charge up the stairwell. If Jace really is going after Tucker, he could run up here at any moment—or already be on the landing.

As with so many things in my life, it's a risk to be on these stairs right now. In an instant, I could be discovered sneaking about in an embassy, and that would *not* bode well for me.

As I race up the spiral staircase, I keep an eye out for someone ahead of me. Straining my ears, I listen for conversations or the thunder of boots along the stone.

So far, silence.

Thank goodness.

When I reach the landing, I peek around the corner to confirm I'm alone. Thankfully, I am, and the long corridor is still and quiet, as if I never left.

The coast is clear. For now.

Without missing a beat, I press my ear against Tucker's door. The cool wood is hard and smooth against the side of my face, and I instinctively press my fingers against the doorframe as I listen.

Silence.

I frown. That's not a good sign.

Careful not to make a sound, I gently twist the knob and peer inside to find Tucker's suite empty. The doors are all open, except for the double French doors that lead to the bedroom. Sheer white curtains cover the glass, blocking my view.

Briefly, I scan the room for cameras or signs of a struggle. Everything is neat and orderly, without even a couch pillow out of place. He has much the same décor as I do, though his room is white and navy blue instead of white and gold like mine.

I duck inside and shut the door behind me, not really willing to believe the space could be empty.

It just doesn't feel right.

It concerns me that Tucker's not here, and I wonder if I'm perhaps too late. If Jace already dragged Tucker out of bed and threw him into some dungeon.

Gently, I lean against the elegant French doors that lead to the bedroom. Their ornate silver handles curl at the end, and I rest my fingers against one of them as I listen for sounds of life. Breathing. Snoring. The shuffle of skin beneath sheets.

Silence.

I grit my teeth, concerned, a fluttery part of me wondering if my actions tonight are going to get Tucker killed.

Behind me, the thump of boots on the landing catches my attention. I dart into the bedroom and close the door behind me, careful to leave it cracked so that I can hear and see what goes on if someone walks into the suite.

The bedroom is elaborate in design but lacks much

furniture beyond the bed and end tables. Without a more elegant option, I roll under the gap between the floor and the bed, disappearing into the shadows.

Delicately, I shift and shimmy until I'm on my stomach, looking out at the living room through the tiny crack left in the French doors.

The main door slams open, hitting the wall *hard*, and a ripple shoots through the floor beneath me from the sheer force.

The first thing I see is the cluster of soldiers in their crisp yellow and black uniforms standing in the hall. Seconds later, Jace pushes someone into the room—a blur of dark clothes and cargo pants.

Tucker.

I let out a small sigh of relief. Good. At least he's not dead. Yet.

Jace stands on the threshold, glaring at the man he just shoved into the living room. Without a word, he slams the door behind him.

Yet again, the entire suite trembles beneath his anger.

"You're going to wake Rory," Tucker says in a chiding tone from somewhere in the living room.

"Don't even *start* with me," Jace says with a dark rumble to his voice. "You're going to give me answers."

From somewhere else in the living room, Tucker scoffs. "Answers? To what? How is going to the garden against the rules?"

"Seeing as we don't *have* gardens, you and I both know damn well that's not where you were going."

"I'm going to have to stop you there." Tucker chuckles, like this is all some big joke. "I'm sensing a little hostility."

Jace tilts his head, his frown deepening, his thick neck and broad shoulders reminding me of a cage fighter sizing up an opponent.

"Where is this coming from?" Tucker asks. "Rory told you to play nice."

"Rory isn't here." Jace's voice drops an octave, and a murderous expression flashes across his face.

I reach for the knife in my boot, wondering if Jace is going to make me use it. If he's going to make me hurt him.

Deep down, I hope not. With whatever spell he put on me, I don't even know if I *can*.

Tucker just laughs. "She's, like, two doors down. Talk too loudly and she'll hear you."

"I've seen men like you before," Jace says casually, taking two menacing steps, his hatred focused on the man I still can't see. Jace disappears from view, but I can still hear him. "Your kind always work for someone dangerous, and you always die young. I don't know who you work for, but I guarantee I'll find out. And when I do, Rory won't even *want* to save you."

"Personally, I've never been fond of listening to a boss," Tucker says, walking into view. He bumps the

French doors as he passes, opening them, allowing me to see more of the room. He stands at an angle, half of his face visible, with his hands on his hips in a relaxed manner. "Except my girlfriend, of course."

I roll my eyes, wishing he could stop being an idiot for two seconds and see the danger of this situation.

"*Enough!*" Jace's voice echoes through the room, and it penetrates even Tucker's ridiculous charm. The weapons expert's smile fades briefly, and I see a flickering look of concern as Jace once more walks into my line of sight. "You don't know who she is. *What* she is, or what's going on. She's under my protection, and I will look after her at any cost."

I frown, watching Jace, the way his body is stiff with rage, the way anger and dominance roll off of him, daring Tucker to disagree.

Dragons are possessive, sure, but this goes beyond anything I've seen before. After all, he's not just saying I'm under *his* protection—by attacking him, a person would really be attacking the entire Fairfax army.

For me.

There's something else at play, here. Has to be. Something more than me and him, something more than this enchantment that connects us.

Maybe even something more important than the ancient and coveted magic blistering through my veins.

"Tell me why you're with her," Jace demands. "Now."

"Oh, sure. For starters, she's a firecracker." Tucker laughs, crossing his arms as he sighs wistfully. "She's gorgeous, of course, but I like her tenacity the most. Nothing can stop that woman."

"God, how I wish I could hit you." The floorboards creak as Jace takes a few looming steps toward Tucker.

"Can't touch a visitor, huh?" Tucker laughs. "Thank goodness for those pesky dragon laws, I guess."

"Give me a straight answer," Jace demands, ignoring the jibe. "You've been following her, haven't you? What do you want with her?"

"Oh, you know, the white picket fence, the dog, the works." Tucker shrugs. "Maybe kids, but that's up to her."

"That's *enough!*" Jace shoves Tucker against the wall, and suddenly I can see both of their faces quite clearly.

Jace's hand is pressed against Tucker's chest, pinning him to the wallpaper, and Tucker's smile disappears in an instant. The two stare each other down, glaring, daring the other to make the next move.

"I'm going to find out what you and your bosses want from her," Jace says in a gruff voice. "And when I do, she will see you for the lying sack of shit you are. Understand?"

To his credit, Tucker doesn't answer this time. He simply glares at the thunderbird, shoulders tensed, ready to throw a punch if the situation calls for it.

My grip tightens around the blade in my boot. At

least he's finally waking up to the danger of the situation.

"Good," Jace says, taking Tucker's silence as confirmation. "Tell me what you were looking for tonight," he demands. "*Now.*"

An expression of utter confusion crosses Tucker's face. "I legitimately have no idea what you're talking about."

"Damn it." Jace reaches for Tucker, like he's going to strangle him, but stops. With a brief glance in the direction of my room, he lets out a frustrated sigh. "The next time you try to comb through my system, I'm going to catch you. And not even Rory will be able to stop me from giving you what you deserve."

"What—systems? Is that a come-on?" Tucker tilts his head slightly in bewilderment. "Is confusing the hell out of your prey some new interrogation tactic? Because I kind of like it."

Jace shakes his head in disdain. "How does she put up with you?"

"I'm pretty." Tucker shrugs, grinning like an idiot.

Jace's grip tightens on Tucker's collar. They're staring each other down, neither giving up an inch. Jace looks deadly serious, ready to slit throats, and Tucker's obnoxious smirk isn't helping.

"Tell me how you found her," Jace commands. "Tell me how she came to trust you, of all people. A human with too many guns, and a suspiciously large number of dragon killers."

I mean, I *don't* trust him. Not really.

But Jace's comment drives home a more concerning point—they must have confiscated and searched his truck. That means all of Tucker's weapons, all of his toys, are locked away in some vault. Even worse, that means we have no vehicle for an escape should the need arise.

"Speaking of," Tucker says with an annoyed tone. "I want my guns back. I've named them all, so I'm a little sentimental." He pauses. "Don't tell the others, but Betty is my favorite."

Jace's voice is nearly a growl. I can virtually feel his anger vibrating in my own chest. "When I'm convinced you aren't a danger to Rory, perhaps you'll get them."

"If I were a danger to her, she would already be dead," Tucker says in a surprisingly deadly tone.

It's like night and day—a total switch from his usual jovial personality. I raise my eyebrows in surprise, unaware until now that he could even sound this dangerous, much less look threatening enough to follow through.

Jace isn't too fond of this little development, either. His grip on Tucker's shirt tightens, pressing harder against Tucker's shoulder, no doubt sending sharp pains down his back. If Tucker feels them, though, he doesn't flinch.

"If I wanted to hurt her, she would be in a ditch." Tucker frowns, eyes locked on the dojo master, not giving up an inch. "She wouldn't have made it this far, and I wouldn't have let her come here in the first place."

"*Let* her." Jace snorts derisively, as if the very idea of Tucker controlling me is a joke with a terrible punch line.

"You saw my weapons," Tucker nods toward the window, no doubt referring to his truck. "You think those are for show? She's here because I want her to be safe, to—"

"Don't lie." Jace laughs, the sound rough and humorless. "You could be monitoring her and waiting until she's not useful anymore before you act. You could be gathering intel. You could be trying to lead her into a trap, and she's simply eluded your efforts thus far. There are so many ways you could still be a threat, and I won't let you near her."

"Excuse me?" Tucker lifts one eyebrow in challenge. "I'd like to see you try to stop me."

"Gladly." In one fluid motion, Jace grabs Tucker's neck and pins his pretty head against the wall. He cocks his arm to punch Tucker in the face, and the dojo master looks like he'll gut Tucker at any second.

Everything I've discovered about Jace says he's a warrior unafraid to kill should the need arise, and he will *absolutely* see this through. His eyes narrow, focused on his prey. Jaw tense, the veins along his neck pulse between the thick muscle and hot skin.

Tucker doesn't give an inch, though. He glares back, the dark hair along his square jawline a sharp contrast to his cool skin. At his side, his hand hovers on one of the many pockets in his cargo pants, no doubt waiting for the right moment to draw his weapon and dig it into Jace's body.

They're going to kill each other.

I can't let this happen.

I tense, wondering if I should intervene, what the consequences would be if I darted out into the fray now. Wondering if I would have to explain my trip to the intel center, or if I could avoid the truth.

"I don't trust you," Jace says quietly, voice tense and low. "And I won't allow her to be alone with you."

Tucker laughs, though absolutely no humor reaches his eyes as he continues to glare at the powerful dragon shifter pinning him to the wall. "Good luck controlling that woman."

Despite the danger of the situation, I smirk. At least someone has been paying attention.

Jace releases his hold on Tucker and, after a few more moments of an intense faceoff, storms out of the room.

When the door slams behind the thunderbird, Tucker's entire demeanor shifts. It's like he takes off the badass mask and lets his real emotions shine through. His shoulders relax, and he lets out a long breath as he anxiously runs his hand through his hair.

"Damn it all," he mutters under his breath.

Hmm. This is actually a prime opportunity for me to see what Tucker's like when he thinks I'm not around.

Instead of revealing myself, I wait.

I watch.

"You're in deep, dude," he says to himself, rubbing his jaw absently. "Real deep."

He begins to pace the living room, slipping in and out of my view, mumbling incoherently to himself. I catch bits and pieces, but it doesn't make sense without context. He seems to be seamlessly shifting between thinking and talking.

"…and if you're not careful, she's going to… ugh. But I can't… Damn it. I wish this was just easy." He sighs, his back to me, both hands in his hair as he stares at the far wall.

Well, since he's not making any sense, I think it's time to proceed with the original reason I broke in.

As he continues brooding with his back to me, I roll out from under the bed and slip silently to the door-frame, opening the French doors without so much as a breath to give me away. Casually, I lean against the wall, arms crossed, looking relaxed and for all the world like I've been here for hours, just waiting.

He sighs and turns around. As his gaze lands on me,

he flinches, his eyes going momentarily wide as I catch him off guard.

Hand on his chest, he leans over for a moment to catch his breath and ease his racing heart.

"Jesus, woman," he says. "You scared the shit out of me."

"Flatterer." I smirk.

"Did you—where the hell did you come from?"

"What did you do to piss Jace off?" I ask with a nod toward the door, ignoring his question.

He should know better than to think I would answer.

"Ah, well…" Tucker sets his hands on his hips, and he seems to inwardly debate telling me. "He might have caught me trying to sneak around the compound." Tucker grimaces. "Just a little."

I chuckle. "Talking a midnight stroll through the gardens they don't have?"

Tucker crosses his arms, clearly baffled. "Seriously, were you here the whole time?"

"You need to be careful," I say, ignoring him again, my smile fading, imploring him with my expression to be serious for a second. "Jace has it out for you."

"Yeah, no kidding." Tucker gives me a once-over and grins. "He's just jealous I scored such a hot chick."

"You're such an idiot." I shake my head at him, but I can't stifle the laughter in time.

"Rory," he says softly, his smile fading slightly. "Why

are we here? I mean really, what is it you want from this place? Because that guy..." Tucker stares at the door, after Jace, and it's easy enough to fill in the blanks of what he's thinking.

"Training," I lie, examining my palms for added effect. "This magic is too much sometimes. I need to control it."

"Uh huh," he says with a disbelieving frown, clearly seeing through it.

"I'll talk to Jace tomorrow," I continue, as if I can't tell he's trying to goad me. "I don't want to waste any time."

That part, at least, is true. Though it's not the main reason I'm here, getting some instruction on taming the wild magic will benefit me. It will also let me get to know Jace a bit more, and perhaps learn his schedule.

The next time I break into the command center needs to be the last. I have to go when Jace is distracted and I have the best odds of getting at least fifteen uninterrupted minutes to hunt through the files.

"You did something, didn't you?" Tucker nods toward the door. "Something he's blaming me for?"

Hmm. Smart man.

I bite my lip, wondering how much I should tell him. What might backfire. "Just be careful," I repeat. "I'll look out for you, but I need you to watch your back."

Tucker swaggers up to me, a playful grin on his

face, testing my boundaries as he brings his nose inches from mine. His lips are tantalizingly close, and a flash of heat burns between my thighs as my traitorous body reacts to him. He knows better than to touch me, but he comes so close that it's hard to resist the sexual charm dripping off of him.

"You want to do a bit of looking out for me now, Rory?" he asks, his voice low and gravely, teasing me with the desire he knows I feel. "I'm not feeling well. Want to play doctor?"

I lean in, my mouth almost touching his ear. "Try harder," I whisper.

With that, I leave. For the first time, I turn my back to him completely—because if I look at him again, it might corrode the last of my willpower, and I might not be able to resist him *or* Jace anymore.

CHAPTER TWENTY-SIX

I don't get much sleep. I can't. All I can think about is Jace, this dojo, the secrets this building must hold.

The traps in my room make it safe—well, safe enough to sleep, anyway: the knife jammed into the doorframe, which will alert me to any late night visitors; the wedges shoved into the window panes to block them shut; the way I've already memorized the creaks and groans of each floorboard, so I'll know where to aim in the dark should someone be stupid enough to break in some other way.

Rule 87 of the Spectres—always have a failsafe.

I can live with mild exhaustion, though, and after about four hours of hit-or-miss sleep, I'm up when the sun's first light breaks through the window behind my headboard.

The morning blurs by, uneventful enough, and before I know it, I'm standing outside in a large, open-air arena a short distance from the main building, the tall stone walls blocking my view of all but the highest spires of the castle. The ground beneath my feet is more of the black cobblestone, which will mean a hard landing if I'm thrown off balance during whatever training Jace has in mind.

It isn't long before the cast iron gates at the far end creak open, and Jace enters.

I can't help but think of last night. Of the threatening and menacing man who shoved Tucker against a wall, interrogating someone he genuinely thinks is going to hurt me.

It's flattering, really. Misguided, perhaps, but flattering. And I must admit Jace has a point.

I *want* to trust Tucker, but deep down, I don't. I can't. I keep waiting for the *gotcha* moment, the second he drops the mask and exposes the truth.

He has no reason to follow me. No reason to want to be near me. Everything I've learned tells me Jace is right—that, any time now, Tucker is going to betray me.

But deep down, it's hard not to like the adorable idiot anyway.

"Good morning, Rory," Jace says as he walks toward me. He smiles briefly, his gray eyes softening as he nears, and I hate the way my body aches for him. The warm pull urges me to throw my arms around his neck, to dive into his lips, to give in to whatever he asks.

When I find out what the hell he did to me, I'm going to beat him over the head with whatever device he used to ensnare me like this.

A gust of wind tears through the arena as a familiar blue dragon sails overhead. He lands on the wall, tucking in his wings at his side as he prepares to watch.

"You need to leave," Jace says with a frown toward Levi. "Given the highly sensitive nature of her magic, you can't watch."

Levi snorts in defiance, an icy mist trailing from his nose as he stares Jace down.

"I don't repeat myself." Jace's eyes narrow in warning, his tone taking the same dangerous and gravelly edge as last night with Tucker, and I realize I need to intervene.

"Let him," I say softly, gently setting my hand against Jace's shoulder.

The motion disarms him, like I knew it would, but it also sets me on edge. The dojo master tilts his head toward me, his expression softening once more, and his jaw tenses. I can see him fighting something inwardly, probably balancing asserting his dominance as the undisputed leader here with keeping me happy.

In the end, my happiness seems to win. Begrudgingly so.

"You shouldn't let anyone see this power yet," he says softly, closing the distance between us. He doesn't touch me, doesn't reach for me, but the motion is still so intimate I'm tempted to step away. Being near him kicks up such raw vulnerability in me that I feel like I need to keep a gap between us, to never let him get too close.

The air between us crackles with energy, and I try my best to ignore it.

"Hey, babe!" Tucker shouts from behind me, and I look over to find him sitting up on the wall next to Levi.

The great blue dragon rolls his eyes and scoots a hair to the left, adding some distance between him and the weapons expert.

Tucker bites into a pear and lounges on top of the wall, somehow making a thin perch of stone look comfortable.

Jace just sighs in frustration. "Are they going to follow you everywhere?"

"Yeah, probably," I say quietly, simultaneously annoyed and a little grateful.

Just a *little*.

"Fine. For you." Jace crosses his arms and looks me over briefly. "Show me what you can do."

"With magic specifically, or…" I gesture to my body, subtly referencing my lifetime of Spectres training, because he sure as *hell* isn't going to see any of *that*.

"Whatever you're willing to share," he says with a shrug.

I frown, completely unsure of how to approach his relaxed attitude. Any other mentor would have already demanded things of me, established dominance, asserted the clear hierarchy between us to remind me of my place in their world.

But not him. He's so gentle. Understanding. Patient. It's a stark contrast to the fury he unleashed on Tucker, and I wonder if this is how it's always going to be—or if this is all a show.

When it comes to a gentle and kind teacher, though, I don't quite know what to do. Compassion isn't exactly part of the Spectres curriculum.

"I don't control it," I admit, hating the idea of sharing my lack of control over the wild magic burning through me. "It just kind of happens."

He doesn't miss a beat. "When?"

"I think it happens when I'm threatened." I grimace, thinking of the Andusk dragons attacking me on the exposed stretch of road. "When I have no other options."

"Emotional response." Jace nods and rubs the stubble along his jaw, lost momentarily in thought. "Your magic takes over in self-preservation, protecting you in an otherwise deadly situation."

"If you call that protecting me," I say with a huff. I

nearly disfigured the red dragon, after all. Thank goodness that shifter is *fast*.

Jace begins to slowly circle me, his arms crossed, his
eyes roving my body as he speaks. "I'm going to run
some tests to see the depth of your power and abilities.
This is going to unlock some deep magic, and it might
be frightening. But remember, I'm here, and I won't let
anything happen to you."

It's sweet and all, but I suppress an eye roll. It's not
his fault he doesn't know what I'm capable of doing.
I'm withholding it from him on purpose.

Let him underestimate me. That usually works out
in my benefit.

He walks behind me, and I turn my body toward
him out of habit, to keep him in my peripheral vision.
He smirks, noticing the motion, and I pause.

"Who trained you?" he asks, his attention shifting
between my shoulders, my posture, my stance. "You
move like a seasoned fighter."

I don't answer. I just lift my chin slightly in defiance, making it clear this isn't something we're going
to discuss.

He's so damn perceptive. I have to be careful.

"Okay, that's fine." He shrugs and walks behind me
again. Though I turn impulsively once more, his hand
on my back stops me. A bolt of heat shoots down my
spine and between my thighs. I tense instinctively,

resisting the impulse to grab my gun as his palm settles into the space between my shoulder blades.

The knuckles of his other hand brush against my shirt, trailing slowly toward the small of my back, kicking up flurries of desire and sparks of heat beneath his touch. I fight the enchantment as best I can, resisting his power to sway my traitorous body, and try my best to keep my mind clear.

"Relax," he says softly, his mouth inches from my ear. "What do you feel?"

I'm about to punch him in the nose for all these come-ons when I feel a flurry of something else— something stronger than this attraction toward him. It's like a cyclone, small at first but gradually building, stirring the depths of my soul.

It's like *fire*.

I gasp in surprise as the torrent builds beneath his touch. As it grows, I find myself struggling to breathe.

"Just feel through it," he says softly again. "Raise your hands. Aim toward that target." With masterful control, he gently tilts my body toward a circular red and white target set up in the far corner, away from Levi and Tucker. "Whatever flows through you, let it out. Don't hold back."

I fight against the idea of sharing it all, of showing him what I can do, but I *chose* to be here. I can't learn to control this power on my own—I don't know anything about dragon magic, and he knows infinitely more than me.

My training warns me that he could use this against me, that this might end badly, that this might make everything worse.

But right now, I don't have much of a choice: show him and finally learn to control this magic; or hide it, and let it continue to control *me*.

Fingers straining beneath the growing cyclone of power and fire in my soul, I lift my hands and aim.

The magic burns within me, stronger with every passing second. Overtaking me. Consuming me. Burning away the last shreds of resistance as a flood of heat rips through my palms.

My world flashes white, all color momentarily draining from my vision, and I release the power pent up in my body.

A thick funnel of blinding light tears toward the target, obliterating everything in its path. The beam glimmers in the sunlight, iridescent and beautiful, sparkling with trails of gold and blue energy. It's as wide as I am tall, a massive funnel of beautiful light and devastating destruction that spins and tears through the land around me.

It burns through the wood and fabric of the target, through the stone behind it, soaring into the sky beyond.

As the magic leaves me, I feel suddenly weak. Spots

dance along my vision, and I teeter. Jace's hands are instantly at my waist, holding me upright, and I impulsively lean my body against him for fear of falling over completely.

Dazed, a little delirious, I tilt my head back against his solid chest, craning my neck so I can look at him, only to find him gaping at the obliterated wall.

"Sorry." I clear my throat, but it's so *dry*. "Didn't mean to, you know…"

"That's impossible," Jace says quietly, his voice a whisper, his eyes still wide and disbelieving as he stares at what was once the northern corner of his practice arena. "To have that level… and so young… with no experience… but…"

It takes a moment for him to snap out of it, and I use that time to study his face. I've studied dozens of liars and charlatans in my life, but the shock on his face is real.

Jace has never seen magic like this. Like mine.

I'm not entirely sure if that's a good thing or not.

"Holy shit!" Tucker laughs incredulously from his perch on the wall, pumping his fist into the air. "Babe, that was amazing!"

Levi roars in victory, wings spread, and nods to me in congratulations.

I smile. They're so ridiculous, but I kind of love it.

As I slowly regain my strength, I stand on my own again and face my instructor. I cross my arms, wondering if coming here was a mistake. "Can you still train me?"

"Absolutely." Jace's voice is so certain, excited almost, and a broad grin slowly crosses his lips. "Without question. I'll simply need to do a bit more research to ensure you're able to dig into the deepest recesses of your potential. *Wow.*" He runs his hands through his hair, staring again at the damaged wall as a block falls and shatters on the ground. "I'll need to find the old texts, maybe the ancient scrolls, as well. And then... just *wow.*" He grins, watching me, those gray eyes bright with excitement. "We may need to find a new practice arena, though. I don't want everyone to see what you can do."

"Do they know?" I nod toward the wall, wondering how many of his soldiers are watching from a distance as we speak.

Jace shakes his head. "Only Guy, and he's bound by a formal command to keep his mouth shut."

Hmm. I relax a little, but I also don't quite believe it. In a place this big, people talk.

"That said," Jace adds, arms crossed as he turns his full attention toward me again. "I can't keep your secret forever. Sooner or later, the wrong people will spread rumors, and the other families will find out that you're here. It's inevitable. I can only delay it and buy you some time to train, to get stronger before they demand to meet you."

"Why would I care what they demand of me?" I chuckle. "It's not like I have to obey any of them."

"No, but you still need to be diplomatic." Jace narrows his eyes a bit, as if he's a tad surprised by my reaction. "Unless you want to live in the shadows, you're going to run into them. You need to know how to play their game."

I frown, not answering. I rather *like* my shadows, thanks.

"Rory," he says tenderly, holding my shoulders, the warmth of his touch blistering through me, activating all the double-crossing bits of my body that want him so badly. "You can't run from them."

I match his gaze, never one to back down from a challenge, but yet again I keep silent. He knows them—but he doesn't know me.

However, he does bring up a valid point, one I need to address. "Helping me is dangerous. Why are you taking such a risk, Jace?"

The question seems to catch him off guard, and though he opens his mouth to answer, he quickly closes it again. His jaw tenses, his body stiffens, and I can see him inwardly wrestling with something he's not sure he should share.

"I can't trust you if you aren't honest with me," I say, fully aware of my own hypocrisy.

"I know." He nods and sighs, his grip on my shoulders tightening, bringing me a little closer. "I'll tell you everything in time."

Red flag.

I briefly glance at Tucker, and we share a tense moment of concern. Between his hatred for Tucker and the risks I face staying in one place too long, we might not be able to be here much longer.

Though everything in my body wants to be close to Jace, to trust him, I have no logical reason to do so.

"Have you heard of Ashgrave?" Jace asks, head tilted in curiosity.

I lift one confused eyebrow. "Is that a spell or something?"

"Not quite." He laughs, his face lighting up with the sound, and I can't help but think he looks even more handsome when he smiles.

Damn it, Rory, snap out of it!

"It's a legend," he says, gesturing toward the mountains beyond the embassy. "It's the castle of the three dragon gods, a place of magic and the birthplace of your power. No one knows if it still exists, or if it was ever anything more than a rumor." He sighs, rubbing his neck, eyes glossing over as he debates something. "If it exists, it would be the safest place for you."

I frown, unconvinced. It would probably be nothing more than a few walls, easily scalable and just as flammable.

"I'll cash in some old favors," Jace says, eyes snapping toward me. "See what I can find out."

I pause for a moment, shocked at the offer. "Thank you," I say genuinely, surprised he would cash in favors for me.

Perhaps dragon favors aren't as hard-won as a Spectre's, but my best guess is that they're actually even more rarely granted. For him to use something so valuable to get me information, well...

I don't really know what to say. Besides Irena, no one has ever done something that selfless for me before.

The promise also raises a curious thought—Jace must be so much more than he seems. He's young, yet already a battle-hardened General with some apparently high-ranking connections.

And that's when I wonder about the enchantment. The way I can feel him, the way my traitorous body aches for him—this can't go on unchecked.

I have to know.

"Jace," I say softly, wondering if he'll tell me the truth.

He watches me, waiting, his eyebrows pinched in slight concern, as though he knows this isn't going to be a fun question to answer.

"What was *that*?" a man outside the arena asks, interrupting me.

I snap my mouth closed, glaring at the gate, wanting

to strangle the moron whose obnoxiously loud footsteps are now racing toward us.

Seconds later, Guy runs up to the gate and leans on the wrought iron bars, huffing and a little out of breath. He gapes at the obliterated wall and turns to Jace, an incredulous smile on his face. "Was that the *girl?*"

I grimace. *The girl.* Ugh, the gall of this one. If there weren't any witnesses, I would smack some sense into him.

Unfortunately, I have to let that little quip go.

For now.

Jace, on the other hand, is not as forgiving.

His mood shifts instantly. Though he was gentle and tender seconds ago, he's now possessive, his back arched, his broad shoulders more imposing than before. His grip on my shoulders pinches me briefly as he maneuvers me back, almost entirely out of Guy's view. "Leave."

"But the wall—"

"*Immediately!*" Jace's voice echoes through the arena, cementing him as the unquestionable authority, and I peer around his thick body to see Guy flinch at the command. He stands a bit straighter and scowls, glaring at Jace briefly before he leaves without another word.

Tucker points toward Guy's retreating form. "You know, I really hate that guy."

Up on the wall, Levi snorts in agreement.

"Don't speak ill of my second in command," Jace says curtly, not even bothering to look up at Tucker.

I lean toward Jace, whispering. "He is kind of an asshole, though."

A tiny chuckle escapes the dojo master, and he briefly looks me over with those stormy gray eyes. "Yeah, he is," Jace whispers back.

"So, why is he your second?" I know it's prodding, and perhaps even irrelevant, but I'm curious. Supposedly useless information can sometimes turn out to make all the difference.

Jace sighs and looks down at me, a small smile playing at the corners of his mouth. "Dragons live and die by honor and law. The good ones do, anyway, and his assignment to this post was one I simply had to allow."

Hmm. I frown, looking after Guy even though he's long gone, and wonder just how much of dragon culture I don't know. They aren't overly fond of sharing it with the world, after all, and what I've learned thus far was all hard-won.

Jace leans in, his fingertips resting against my chin, and I resist the impulse to break his wrist for getting too close. I allow his touch, looking up at him as his face hovers mere inches from mine.

"You have natural ability, Rory." His eyes scan my features. "I see it in the way you move, and this test just confirms what I already suspected—there's a lot I can teach you. It's still early, and though you're not a thunderbird, your magic is similar. And, just like a young thunderbird, your magic is getting used to your body. There's not a ton I can do yet, but as you and the magic connect with each other, I will be able to teach you more and more." He pauses, letting out a small sigh. "I hope you stay long enough for me to show you all of it."

Ah. The catch.

I want to doubt him, to assume he's making things up to keep me in one place for longer. But the earnest expression on his face, the way his eyes search mine, *pleading* almost, I just know—he's telling the truth.

This won't be an easy fix. Though I could learn a new weapon in hours and master it in days, I won't be able to check this off the list that easy.

Damn it.

I brush my fingers against his wrist, and crackles of heat and desire burn through my arm. If nothing else, I'll stay as long as I can—both to learn what can be taught about my magic, and to figure out just what Jace Goodwin has done to make my body ache for him this way.

But Irena is more important. The moment I can save her, I'm gone—and not even Jace can stop me.

CHAPTER TWENTY-SEVEN

"Sir!" someone yells from beyond the walls. "Sir, it's urgent!"

Jace groans and releases his gentle touch on my chin. "Come in."

I briefly glance up to the wall to find Tucker and Levi both scowling at Jace. Their expressions look almost jealous, and a thin trail of icy mist coils from Levi's nostrils. When they see me looking at them, though, they snap out of it, both occupying themselves by glancing over the walls at things I can't see.

I frown, wondering what's gotten into them.

A soldier in a black and yellow uniform stops just beyond the gate, breathless, and salutes. "A shifter just crossed the border solo. He's headed here now."

Back straightening slightly, Jace frowns and briefly

glances toward me. In that moment, it seems like we share the same thought.

Have I already been discovered?

If so, he needs to have a chat with his people about keeping secrets.

Jace sets his hand on the small of my back and ushers me toward the gate as he continues prodding the soldier for more info. "Who is it?"

"We're not sure, sir. No one recognizes him yet, but we can guess the family he's from."

The soldier lifts his eyebrows, frowning, and it seems to be some silent clue. Even though I miss the deeper meaning of the exchange, Jace shakes his head in frustration. "Damn it."

"What?" I subtly shift as I walk, doing my best to avoid his touch so that I can focus instead of losing myself in the sparks his fingers send through me. "Who is it?"

"Let's not get riled up until we know for sure." Jace jogs off, so I nod a quick farewell to Levi and Tucker as I follow him and the soldier.

We race up a flight of stairs, weaving through hallways as we bolt toward a high balcony at the front of the embassy. It overlooks the courtyard and gives us a decent view of the long and winding road leading up to the bridge.

As Jace leans against the stone railing, shoulders tense, his glare focused on the road, I wonder if this is where he stood as I drove up.

Seconds later, a flashy red sports car speeds along the road, the top down as the convertible races toward the gate. I can't see much from this distance, just a man with broad shoulders and dark hair, one arm casually resting over the empty passenger seat as he effortlessly steers the car at breakneck speed.

"Damn it," Jace says, smacking his fist against the rock. It crumbles beneath his hand, nothing but pebbles and dust, and I'm left wondering just how much of my magic is indeed similar to his.

Quite a few walls now have been crushed to pebbles under my fist since I discovered this dragon magic, and it seems thunderbirds possess similar power and strength even in their human forms.

Good to know.

Four white ice dragons trail the car in perfect formation, and I find it odd that this newcomer has twice the guard I did. "Who is this, Jace?"

Leaning his hands against the stone railing, Jace turns his head toward me, and I finally see the deep-set anger on his face. His jaw is tensed, his shoulders arched, and he looks like he wants to break more than a little stone wall. "He's a threat." Jace turns his attention toward the solider standing beside us. "Add more point guards. He doesn't get to turn around."

"Yes, sir."

"Wait, this guy is trouble, but you don't want him

leaving?" I quirk an eyebrow, incredulous. "Wouldn't that be a good thing?"

"It's the law." Jace stands to his full height, attention once more on the red sports car as it races toward us. "We stand guard so no one can retreat once they approach the embassy. If someone crosses onto our grounds, they must come in unless they're forbidden." He cusses under his breath. "And damn it all, I wish I could forbid this one."

"Because…" I gesture with my hand, trying to get him to stop being so damn cryptic.

"Stay up here." Jace ignores the prodding and points at the balcony to emphasize his point. "Stay out of sight." He pauses briefly in front of me, radiating authority and anger, but his gaze relaxes ever so slightly when he looks at me. He brushes his knuckle against my chin, gentle and doting, before storming off into the castle without another word.

I stand there for a moment out of surprise more than obedience. It's almost adorable that he thinks I'm going to obey.

Now, time to get a better view. I peer over the edge, but this balcony won't work. I'll see nothing but hair from this angle.

I duck back inside and jog through a few of the hallways, hoping I don't miss my chance to see who this mystery man is. Within minutes, I reach a window that overlooks a small section of roof about five stories up and has a perfect view of the courtyard.

Since I'm not *really* sneaking around, I don't bother looking for cameras, scouts, or students. They can report this back to Jace if they want.

I throw open the window and climb onto the roof as the red car tears across the bridge. The driver narrowly avoids the still-opening doors, the car almost too fast for the gate. As the dojo master reaches the bottom of the stairs, the car screeches to a stop mere inches from Jace's feet.

Jace, to his credit, doesn't flinch.

Privately, I wonder who would win in that situation, Jace or the car. Based on his solid frame and innate thunderbird power, my guess is Jace would be fine and that the car would be nothing but twisted scrap metal.

Jace crosses his arms and stares down at the convertible, a haze of white smoke still wafting from the tires as the driver steps out. Without so much as a word said between them, the driver lifts his arms in surrender and places them on the back of his head, tilting his body toward me.

I finally see his face, and his gaze shifts almost knowingly toward mine.

He has a thick build, standing almost as tall as Jace, but with broader shoulders and a barrel chest. Jace is a fighter, lean and muscled, but this newcomer is like an armored *tank*. His brown hair and beard contrast with a square jaw and a thick neck. He radiates calm authority, walking with a confident swagger.

Though he doesn't smile or sneer, I can tell he's used to being in control. In fact, I have a sneaking suspicion he's fully in control even at this moment. That expression—he knows what's about to happen, and he's playing it to his advantage.

Deep within me, a twinge of knowing stirs to life, and something about those dark eyes feels safe. It's a sense of familiarity. Nostalgia, almost.

As he's led inside the front doors to the embassy, I'm left wondering… is this the red dragon?

It has to be.

I dart back inside and race down the stairs, doing my best to catch up to them without being seen. I manage to find them as Jace leads the newcomer down a flight of steps toward a heavily guarded set of double doors, and I curse silently under my breath as they disappear into a hallway I've never seen before.

Hidden in a side corridor, I stakeout the four guards blocking my way. They barely move, and I notice a slight difference to these soldiers than the rest. They stand straighter, their backs arched, their form more confident than most guards I've seen.

Begrudgingly, I figure these are probably some of Jace's elite soldiers—the best of the best, sent to guard the most secure part of the embassy.

And if the command center with all that incredible tech and monitoring software only had two lax guards to guard it, I wonder what delightful little treasures could be down *here.*

For now, I want to know only one thing—who the hell this new guy is.

If this guy is the red dragon, I need him to confess it to me. Otherwise, he could play me. I won't show my cards—not unless I have to.

But one little nugget makes me doubt myself. If that *is* the red dragon, why would he send me to train with Jace, of all people—a man who clearly hates him?

It doesn't quite add up, and that sets my nerves on fire. There are more players on the board than I can see, more people after me than I know. Every move could be my last, and I have to be more careful than ever.

Starting with this stranger, I'll get the answers I need... and not a soul is going to stand in my way.

CHAPTER TWENTY-EIGHT

If I can't follow Jace and the mysterious newcomer, I may as well use this as my chance to break into the command center. The more I think about this plan, the more I like it—especially since it seems like Jace is going to be occupied for a while.

From the way he was glaring at the new guy, Jace is probably going to have a *lot* to say to him.

This is my chance.

I don't love the idea of a midday break-in, since it's likely bustling with people and puts me at a higher risk of discovery. I've dealt with this before, though, and there's always a fire alarm or some sort of distraction that can empty even the most secure room.

Besides, it wouldn't be fun if it was easy.

Casually, I make my way through the halls, acting for all the world like I have nowhere in particular to be and nothing pressing on my mind. I try not to look at the cameras as I blatantly walk past them, building my alibi in case things go south and I need evidence of me being far away from the location in question.

I take the south halls one by one, slowly meandering toward the command center, strategically walking through the corridors I know have cameras on my way to those I know *don't* have any surveillance. It's a long and winding route, but daylight break-ins require much more patience than those done at night.

Without my shadows, I have to be far more clever to go unseen.

My sensitive ears, always attuned to my environment, pick up the shuffle of someone pacing across the thin strip of carpet inlaid into the center of the black stone floor.

I slow, straining to hear more, wondering who else would be back here in these remote hallways—and more importantly, what they might be up to. Though I can't see anyone yet, a familiar voice trails around the corner.

As I near, I can finally hear more than mumbles and grunts of annoyance.

"… just an ass, and I'll *kill* him," a man says, still out of sight.

Breathlessly, I stop dead in my tracks, not wanting to turn the corner. I know that voice.

Guy Durand.

This alarms me for two reasons. One, as Jace was so careful to drive home to me, killing in the embassy is illegal. And two, the people of the dojo get along fairly well—as far as outright death threats, I can only think of a handful of people who are less than admired within these walls. Guy probably has a beef with one of *my* men, and he'll die in his sleep before I let him come close to touching them.

For a distracting moment, I pause, wondering when I got so protective. Wondering when I started calling Tucker and Levi *mine*. But I kind of like it, and I'm not going to stop now.

Guy's feet brush against the carpet once more, the footsteps getting louder.

He's coming my way.

Per my training, my impulse is to hide. It's easier to gather information when no one knows I'm there. But this corridor is sparse, with only two doors and no available hiding spots.

I quickly brush my fingers along the door handles, testing them.

Locked.

No time to break in, either.

Oh, fun. Time for the offense, then.

I stand in the middle of the hallway, one hand on my hip, a taut frown on my lips and my chin slightly lifted as I wait for him to round the corner. Eyes trained on where his head will be in a few seconds, I want to watch him flinch when he sees me.

He rounds the corner and, much to my delight, nearly jumps out of his skin when he finds me standing in the middle of the hallway.

"Lost?" I ask, a bored challenge in my tone, daring him to tell me the truth—or better yet, try to get away with a lie.

I'm not fond of torture, but I think I would have a lot of fun breaking Guy Durand's spirit.

Guy looks me over, and as his eyes hesitate on my chest, his hands ball into fists. I can see him restraining himself, debating something inwardly once again. Whatever thought crossed his mind when we first met resurfaces, and he proves me right—no matter how men like him try to shove it down and act nonchalant, that look, that *lust*, always comes back.

"You shouldn't be back here." His voice is deep and quiet, as if he's trying to sound intimate or seduce me, and I resist the impulse to laugh in his face.

"Jace said I have free reign," I lie, shrugging casually. "I assume that means I can come to this part of the embassy."

At the dojo master's name, Guy frowns, all pretense gone. The anger I heard earlier in his voice returns now to his face, and he quickly closes the gap between us.

Ah, I guess he quickly realized he doesn't intimidate

me. Now, he's going to go for a more aggressive approach.

Idiot.

"Don't get too comfortable, *princess*," Guy says through clenched teeth. He grabs my arms, his fingers digging into my skin. He shakes me a little, just a bit, just enough to rattle most women.

But he doesn't rattle *me.*

For the moment, I allow this, however obnoxious and insulting it may be. The shifters here don't know what I'm capable of, yet, and I want to prolong their ignorance as much as possible.

Besides, I want to see what this little asshole is capable of.

His grip tightens around my biceps, but I flex my muscles in response, and my newfound strength, courtesy of the dragon magic in my veins, keeps me rooted in place even as he tries to pull me toward him.

Clearly annoyed, he looks me over briefly before getting in my face. "Jace won't be master here long, and when I'm in charge, you won't be in that cushy suite anymore."

Ah.

There it is.

Guy doesn't want to kill Levi or Tucker—he wants to kill *Jace.*

Though I don't know the dojo master well, a

protective surge of rage bubbles through me at the very idea of Guy going anywhere near him.

In the split seconds that follow his threat, I debate my options. My first inclination is to drive my dagger through his heart, twist, and plunge it deeper—the only sure way to kill a dragon shifter in human form, short of a headshot. It would be effortless. Instantaneous. Within seconds, the threat would be neutralized, and I could probably find a sufficient way to dispose of his body.

He would simply disappear.

But then I wouldn't have any proof, and judging by the cameras, I would be the last one in the area. I would become the prime suspect in his disappearance and murder.

It would put Jace in a precarious position—trusting the word of the killer. However fond of me he is, I'm sure it would violate scores of rules and laws. I might even have to leave, all before I have my intel or training.

I have only one other option.

As Guy's grip tightens around my arms, I lean in, tilting my head slightly to expose my neck and draw his eye. Like the easy prey he is, his gaze shifts, following the curve of my neck and landing at the thin line of cleavage visible at my chest.

I lean toward his ear, my lips inches away from him, teasing him with the allure of what it would be like to be inside of me. "If you touch him," I whisper with a deadly little smile, "I'll slit your throat while you sleep."

At first, he pales, and I relish the look of fleeting terror on his face. With a grimace, he releases me and puts some space between us.

Slowly, warily, he begins to walk around me, and I quite enjoy the fact he's strategically keeping himself out of reach.

Short of pinning him to the wall, I can't stop him—so I simply watch, a deadly serious glint to my eye, daring him to be so stupid as to challenge Jace for mastery of the dojo.

Once he's safely past me, Guy pauses. "I know you weren't a normal human girl before you became the vessel." He looks me over with a hint of disdain. "I know someone dangerous trained you, that we probably shouldn't allow you here except in chains." He flexes his hands anxiously at his sides, his eyes roving my body, that subtle glint of lust coming back. "And once Jace isn't here to protect you, I'm going to enjoy beating the truth out of you."

Relaxed, as if he hadn't just threatened me, I set my hands on my hips and smirk. "I guess we'll see."

He scoffs and continues down the hallway, though I notice he isn't stupid enough to turn his whole back to me. He keeps his head tilted, always watching me in his periphery, until he turns the next corner.

As soon as he's gone, my smile fades.

I have to choose.

Either I warn Jace of the impending danger, or I use this as a prime distraction. With their master challenged, not a single dragon will remain at his post.

This could be the absolute best chance I have to break into the command center without interruptions. Maybe the *only* chance.

Torn between the two, I groan and pace the hallway, internally debating.

No.

I can't.

I can't leave Jace unprepared for the tornado headed his way.

Fueled by anger and nerves, I bolt toward where I last saw Jace. I tell myself it's because the outcome affects me so directly. I tell myself this takes precedence over my information gathering because, if Guy wins, everything I'm here to do is in jeopardy.

It's what I tell myself, but it's not what I believe.

Truth is, enchantment or no, my very soul aches at the thought of Jace getting hurt. The thought of him dead on the black stone of his own dojo shoots horrified flurries of grief through me.

And as I race to warn him, I wonder just how much of the Spectre beliefs and way of life remain in me—and how much the ancient dragon magic has taken over.

CHAPTER TWENTY-NINE

"JACE!" I hear Guy roar, his voice bellowing through the window from outside.

It's coming from the courtyard.

Shit.

I'm too late.

I tear down the last flight of steps between me and the main hallway, running at full speed toward the open double doors that lead out onto the square. Behind me, I hear others running as well, all drawn to the commotion.

"What's happening?" Tucker asks, suddenly beside me.

"Nothing good," I admit.

Crap. I'm already adopting Jace's stupid habits. He's the king of saying cryptic shit during critical moments.

We reach the door and funnel into the courtyard to

find Jace and Guy standing in the middle of the black stone square. Though Jace watches his opponent with a frown, Guy huffs and stretches, his shirt already off and balled into his hand as he circles the dojo master.

"I challenge you for your title," Guy shouts, throwing his shirt on the ground. "For everything you own and everything you love."

Jace briefly glances toward me, his dead-serious expression unwavering, and I don't like the implication he just made.

"You don't want to do this," Jace says simply, returning his attention to his second in command. The dojo master crosses his arms, merely watching his opponent as the other shifter circles him.

Though Guy is fuming, clearly pumping himself up for the fight, Jace hardly moves. He looks bored, as if hasn't registered the threat currently circling him.

"Oh, I definitely do." Guy laughs, the sound harsh and grating. He's already bristling with energy and testosterone, and as I watch, his form begins to shimmer.

He's about to shift.

A rush of wind cuts through the air, and before I can even look toward its source, the ground shakes as Levi lands beside me. He spreads his wing, placing it protectively over me, glaring at the battle slowly forming in the square.

I expect that to annoy Jace, but he doesn't seem to

notice. He's now entirely focused on his rival. "Failure means death or banishment," he says, a hard edge to his voice. "If you lose, you will never return here or to any Fairfax lands. You will be disowned and dishonored. You will be forgotten and dead to us."

"I know the law, damn it!" Guy shouts. "Accept my challenge and fight me!"

Briefly, Jace looks at the ground and shakes his head in disappointment, as if he saw this coming, and I wonder if I should have taken this opportunity to sneak into the command center after all. He doesn't look fazed, though I wonder if that's part of his battle strategy.

It's part of ours, after all.

Rule 23 of the Spectres—never let the opponent see your doubt.

Though I seriously wonder if Jace even has doubts. If he can even *feel* fear.

However calm he may be, I'm far from relaxed. This fight has direct consequences for me.

I set the palm of my hand on my gun, my attention squarely on Guy. There are no more opportunities to be discreet. If, by some miracle, he wins this challenge, I won't have the time to kill him quietly in the night. He'll act swiftly, and I would be in chains before I could escape or hide. He would use Levi and perhaps even Tucker, if he can catch the man, as leverage to make me obey.

Leverage—it's the main reason Spectres remain isolated. Loving someone else, being loyal to *anyone*, leaves us vulnerable.

In that instant, I make up my mind. If Guy somehow wins, he still won't leave this courtyard alive.

The embassy is my last lead. My last chance to save Irena. Some asshat on a power trip won't threaten that.

Or *me*.

"I accept your challenge." Jace is calm. Quiet. The unquestionable leader facing a difficult choice. "And I accept the burden of sentencing you when you lose."

I smirk, impressed. Damn, that was a good way to undercut Guy's confidence.

In answer, Guy roars, the furious screech of his dragon escaping his human mouth as he shifts. His skin turns snow white as the ice dragon within him takes over, dozens of spikes growing along the massive beast's head. His beard becomes a host of silver scales along his angled jaw, and he digs his claws into the black stone as if it's butter. With another ear-splitting roar, he signals the start of the fight.

Guy charges before Jace can even shift, and I wonder if that's legal. No one in the gathered crowd reacts, though, so it must be fine. Everyone is stone silent as they watch, no doubt rooting for the same man.

As the white dragon charges him, Jace rolls out of the way, nothing but a blur. Guy swipes at him with his spiked tail, but Jace leaps over the razor-sharp tips and rolls effortlessly to his feet.

Whoa.

I lift my eyebrows in surprise, astonished Jace could be so nimble even in human form. There's so much to thunderbirds I don't know, but I figure even they need to shift to beat another dragon in a duel.

Unfazed, Guy fires a blast of ice at Jace. Yet again, Jace rolls out of the way just in time, mere *seconds* before the ice shards shatter against the wall. Some of the ice is thick enough to pierce the stone, sticking out of the barricade like spears.

I wince. That would've hurt.

Guy shoots blast after blast of ice at his opponent, but Jace never stays in the same place for more than a second. He rolls and dives, light on his feet, and I realize after a moment that this is all just a show.

He's *toying* with Guy. Proving he's the better fighter. Provoking the unchecked ego that motivates and controls Guy Durand.

This is all just his way of pissing off his opponent, taunting him, driving home how Guy is such a weak fighter that Jace doesn't even need to be in dragon form to stand a chance.

Furious, Guy roars at Jace, the grating screech echoing off the mountains, almost loud and shrill enough to break glass.

I grin.

Aw, somebody's *mad*.

His expression grim and serious, Jace charges the ice dragon. I wonder what the hell he's doing until he shifts—midstride, his body shimmers and blurs. Too quick to see, he morphs into something massive, something dark, something brimming with blue light.

One second, he's human and blurry; the next, he's a massive black dragon barreling into Guy's side.

As Jace digs his claws into Guy's hide, pinning the ice dragon to the ground, he stretches his wings as wide as they'll go, emphasizing his size. It's an intimidation tactic, reminding Guy of the sheer power and ability he's up against.

But for me, it sparks a memory.

His dark skin reminds me of midnight, of shadows and silence. Two sharp horns protrude down the center of his forehead, one between his eyes and the smaller one closer to his snout. The veins in his wings glow blue, as do the spines along his back, and as he opens his mouth, I see a brilliant blue light burning within him.

My lips part in shock, and for a moment, I can't breathe.

It's the thunderbird from the swarm.

"It can't be," I say softly, not really hearing myself speak.

Jace followed me along the forest as I ran from the horde.

Jace tried to pick me up in his claws and carry me off, just like all the rest.

The one who saw me, *sensed* me in the woods… it was *Jace.*

A piece of me splinters. Betrayed yet again, I debate leaving. I debate stealing back Tucker's truck and barreling through the gate, swearing to shoot the red dragon in the leg next time I see him for suggesting I come here.

But these two dueling dragons block my only exit, and for the moment, I'm trapped.

Guy slips out of Jace's grip, blood oozing down his side, the red ooze staining his perfectly white hide as he once more circles the dojo master. Jace snarls, a growl rumbling in his throat, so powerful it shakes the castle behind me. I feel it resonate in my chest, barreling into me, surging through all of us as Jace begins to demonstrate his full power.

They charge each other, the two of them coiling, teeth and claws gnashing at wings and hide alike. Light and dark, the two fight in a flurry of fangs and blood, driving each other into the ground time and time again, cracking the black stone with each other's skulls.

The two of them snap at each other's necks, their sturdy jaws chomping at the air with each missed attack. Blow after blow, they roar into the sky with each attack that lands.

It's brutal.

Even growing up with the Spectres, I've never seen anything this grisly. Puddles of blood become small ponds as they roll and gnash at each other.

It doesn't take long for the tide to turn.

Jace digs his claws into Guy's back and flips him over, pinning him wings-down against the stone beneath them. Guy flails, snapping at the air, the sharp click of his jaw a menacing hint at what he so desperately wants to do to Jace's neck.

As the black scales along his face glint in the sun, Jace digs his teeth into Guy's underbelly.

It's a fight-ending blow.

The ice dragon screams in pain. It's agonizing to hear, and I can't help but cringe as it trails on seemingly forever. Beside me, several of the younger dragon shifters flinch, the sharp intake of breath from those nearest to me a clear indicator of how much that must hurt.

Noted. That might come in handy later.

Blood pours out of the wound, staining the ice dragon's bruised body, and Guy just flails harder. He wrestles free of Jace's grip, but it's clear the dojo master is done playing.

It's time to end their little dance.

With just two beats of his incredible wings, he soars over Guy and dives. The tackle is hard and fast, propelling the ice dragon into the ground. The world shakes as they hit the black stone, a crater left in their wake, so deep I can't even see the white dragon.

I hear his pained roars, the screams. I can even see the occasional frantic flick of his tail or the tip of his wing, but it's clear.

This is over.

Jace stands in the crater, pinning Guy to the ground, and the blue light in his mouth gets brighter. He aims into the pit, out of my sight, and I wonder if I'll be able to see a thunderbird's magic for the first time.

The students near me gasp, but the more weathered faces of the soldiers are stoic and calm. They've seen their master fight—they've seen his destructive power.

From their expressions, it's clear they all believe the same thing I do: Guy Durand was an idiot to challenge Jace.

If Jace hears his students gasp in horror, he doesn't care. His magic builds and grows. It's a sure-thing, and he can't possibly miss from this close. He opens his mouth, about to unleash the destructive power of his innate magic on the white dragon beneath him.

I doubt it really takes this long. He's giving Guy a chance to surrender.

That's a mistake.

Do it, I think. *Do it now.*

Finally, a defeated groan escapes from the white

dragon, and he goes still. No more snarling. No more snapping.

He surrendered.

Don't let him go, I silently plead, wishing Jace could hear me. *Don't let him live.*

Jace won. Clearly. But Guy isn't going to stop just because of banishment. I've run into men like him before, and they don't stop until they're dead. They're driven by a singular purpose, a thirst to conquer and tame others to make themselves feel big.

Guy wants what Jace has, and he won't stop until he either owns or destroys it. He wants the dojo. He wants vast power.

He wants *me*.

Once more, I rest my palm on my gun, willing to finish this even if Jace won't.

Victorious, Jace roars into the sky, his opponent still pinned to the bottom of the crater. The students and soldiers around us cheer, pumping their fists, no doubt as grateful as I am for the outcome.

Jace tilts his head toward me, his body heaving, the scrapes along his body still bleeding. Those magnificent eyes glow brilliantly blue as he stares at me, *into* me, deep into my soul.

Just as it did when we first met, I feel the world fading away. The cheers, the noise, they start to dissolve, muffled by whatever enchantment he put on me.

I shake my head, snapping myself out of it. He has a lot of explaining to do, and he won't get away with this any longer.

Never one to celebrate very openly, I cross my arms and nod my congratulations to him for the victory.

Now kill him, I demand, wishing he could hear me.

Jace looks down at his conquered rival and, much to my dismay, steps aside. The white dragon quickly climbs out of the hole, keeping low to the ground, his spirit apparently broken. His head bobs along the shattered black stone courtyard, awaiting his fate.

But even as he cowers, even as he plays the role of the wounded loser, he eyes Jace's neck. His jaw tenses. Those claws slowly dig into the ground, gaining traction, waiting for the chance to strike.

That *coward.*

Jace circles the white dragon, calm and quiet, his gaze shifting between Guy and the crowd. I figure this is the moment of judgment. He steps on Guy's neck, pinning the white dragon to the ground once more, and a growl escapes the loser's throat.

What follows happens almost too quickly to see.

Guy rolls out of Jace's grip and lunges at his neck, cheating during what should have otherwise been the moment of judgment. I draw my gun, running purely on instinct, the barrel aimed for Guy's forehead as he goes for the kill. Jace barely reels back in time, lifting his head fractions of a second before the white dragon can rip a chunk out of his neck.

My finger presses against the trigger, but before I can fire, Levi's nose hits my hand hard.

It throws off my aim.

The gun fires, but the bullet burrows into the black stone at my feet, and Guy bolts into the air, free.

I glare daggers at Levi's piercing blue eyes.

My ice dragon growls, the soft rumble in his throat a tender warning. With the scales of his nose pressed against the exposed skin on my wrist, a sense of dread begins to seep from him into me. His thoughts echo through our connection, rough and unclear, but a single word comes through.

Don't.

I scoff. *I can't let Guy live when—*

A pang of danger interrupts me, rough and raw. The thoughts echo again as he tries to speak. For a moment, I'm tugged into the recesses of his mind, and the courtyard briefly fades. All I see is swirling darkness, with the silhouettes of dragons charging through the mist.

Whatever this memory is, it's buzzing with dread.

You would have cost him the fight. Levi's voice echoes through the fuzzy memory.

And just like that, I'm back in the black stone courtyard, surrounded by shifters, with Levi's face blocking most of my view. The ice dragon's pleading expression shifts, and a foreboding flurry of anger and sadness seeps into me through our connection.

I groan in frustration. *But—*

Dragon law is different. The anger intensifies, and I almost pull away as his emotions overtake me. *The fight does not end until judgment is passed.* Levi snorts in annoyance. *Jace was cocky and moved too slow.*

I return my attention toward the crater to find Jace staring at me. His glowing eyes zero in on me, intense as ever. I'm not sure if he's going to attack or not.

The entire dojo stares at me, the weight of their attention worsened because Guy isn't lying dead on the courtyard ground. I could deal with the attention if I had at least done what I set out to do.

Begrudgingly, I sheath the gun, cursing dragon custom and laws. They have so damn *many*.

Besides, I didn't see Jace pass judgment, and yet Guy fled. Even now, the coward tears through the sky, already a blip over the forests as he bolts toward the horizon.

Two red dragons shoot out from the ravine below the bridge and tail him, no doubt ensuring he makes it to the edge of the embassy lands and never returns.

In his own way, Guy still controlled the match. He escaped, knowing he couldn't win, but his wounded ego won't let him stop. He'll nurse this grudge to the end of time, until either he or Jace is dead.

He'll be back, Levi. I glare at the blue dragon, furious

he threw off my shot, my blood nearly boiling in my rage. *I was protecting us.*

I know. Levi sighs and breaks the connection, removing his wing and tucking it against his side as he returns his attention to the courtyard.

To the thunderbird stalking toward us.

Now, I have a much different danger before me— the thunderbird who tried to steal me away in the swarm. As he nears, I wonder if I need to draw my gun again.

I square my shoulders, facing down the most powerful dragon I've ever seen as his mouth and veins glow with unbridled magic.

He and I have some unfinished business—an issue I intend to address right *now.*

CHAPTER THIRTY

The thunderbird approaches me and Levi, his glowing eyes intense and unwavering. I can't tell if he's angry—covered in all this blood, even a smile would come across as threatening.

To my left, Levi tenses, a guttural growl building in his throat as he finally senses the threat I've felt from the moment I saw Jace shift.

My fingers itch to draw my gun, but I wait.

Midstride, Jace shifts back to human form, never missing a step as he seamlessly becomes a man again.

A very *naked* man.

Despite the danger and risk, I can feel an embarrassed rush of heat burn along my neck and cheeks. Though I try to keep my eyes on his face, I can't help but notice he is *hung*.

Modesty for a naked body is a human custom—

shifters could not care less about seeing each other's asses. No one else seems fazed by their naked boss, and I suspect everyone here has seen everyone else's exposed figure at some point or other during shift changes or form drills.

They're used to it, but I am most certainly not.

As Jace nears, the familiar, fluttery ache for him swirls within me yet again. The bolts of heat down my thighs. The subtle pull at my navel, urging me to walk toward him, to touch him as soon as possible. My eyes trace the curve of his rock-hard body, the muscle, the abs. The sweat along his neck. The blood from the fight. The way the muscles at his hips angle in a tantalizing V shape toward his hardening cock.

He's brimming with testosterone. Adrenaline. Strength. And yet again, I feel the uncontrolled flash of hunger for him burn through me.

Focus, woman, I chide myself. *It's just a trick.*

It has to be.

Wordlessly, he grabs my wrist, his hot skin on mine igniting the depths of this rampant and otherworldly need for him.

I twist in his grip, expertly breaking his hold on me as the entire dojo watches. "What the hell do you—"

"Come with me," he says. It isn't a command, but it's not a request, either—it's somewhere in between, a blend of the two, an assertion of dominance stirred together with an intense desire to talk in private.

Hesitantly, I scan his face, the embarrassed heat creeping up my neck again as I try so hard not to look down. "Only if you put on pants."

"Fine." He grabs my wrist again, and this time I allow it.

Silently, he leads me through the halls and up a staircase to a wing of the castle I haven't explored yet. All the while, he moves with urgency, his grip strong but soothing, never yanking me anywhere even though he never once looks back.

We end up at an ornate set of double doors that he kicks open. Inside is an elaborate living room the size of a small house, complete with statues and a fire pit at its center. It's more elaborate than any mansion I've broken into, and for a moment I'm lost in awe of its beauty.

The doors slam behind me, and before I can so much as react, he pins me against the wall. Breathlessly, his body tense and covered in sweat, he grabs my waist and kisses me.

There's no request.

No pause.

Just *hunger.*

His lips press breathlessly against mine, nibbling gently with each kiss. It's passionate. Rough. Carnal.

His fingers tighten around my waist, pressing my hips against his, stealing away every last inch of personal space. The wall is flat and cool against my back, a sharp contrast to his sizzling skin and curved muscle as he sandwiches me between his hard body and the wallpaper.

And for one inexplicable moment, my traitorous body wins.

Mind numb, lips buzzing, body aching, I give in.

My body moves on its own, my lips just as hungry for his, my hands exploring his muscle as he subtly rocks his hips against mine.

And my *God*, it feels amazing.

There's suddenly a sharp realization that the only thing between him and me is the thin fabric of my pants, and I debate ripping them off. In my hazy, primal state, I need to be closer to him. I need to wrap my legs around him. I need to—

Between my legs, his thick cock gets hard. It brushes against my entrance, reminding me again of the thin layer of fabric that separates us.

That snaps me out of my daze.

In one fluid movement, I twist his arm and pin him against the wall to my left. With my enhanced strength, I twist it further, yanking his arm behind his back as I hold him in place.

"What the *hell* are you doing?" I snap, twisting his wrist a bit more for emphasis.

Nothing breaks. He's fine. I just want to drive home a point to him—no one pins me against walls unless I *ask* them to.

He laughs, breathless, his cheek pressing against the wallpaper as he looks at me over his shoulder. "You never cease to amaze me, Rory."

"Explain yourself." As I hold him in place, I once more become aware of our skin touching. My body had a taste of him, and now it wants more.

I groan in annoyance as more sparks of need and lust shoot up my arm, the throbbing ache for him warming the space between my thighs.

I hate feeling so out of control of my body. My mind buzzes again, and it takes everything in my power not to give in to him once again.

"Sorry." He grins, still catching his breath. "I got carried away. Fights always do that to me."

I clench my teeth, aggravated, just looking for a fight. "You go off, pinning girls to walls after every duel?"

"Just the ones who want it," he says with a flirty grin. "None of my students, of course. But every now and then, when the opportunity arises, I'll have fun with a visitor." He catches my eye and smirks. "You're not jealous, are you?"

For some reason, *that* makes me angriest. Not his smarmy come-on, but the fleeting image of him ripping off another girl's shirt as she wraps her legs around his waist. Before I can stop myself, I imagine them grinding against each other, her moaning as he thrusts into her, giving her the pleasure my body so desperately wants.

Furious, horny, and confused as all hell, I blush and let him go. I pace, trying to cool off as I shake the mental image. I shouldn't care if he's had sex with other women, and yet...

For some reason, I do.

"What the *hell* did you do to me?" I ask, not willing to look at him.

"I didn't do anything, Rory."

I shoot him an annoyed glare, only to find him still *very* naked, with his arms crossed and his raging erection drawing my eye. My cheeks flush yet again, and I stare at the ceiling to avoid gaping like an idiot at his gorgeous body. "Would you *please* put on some damn pants?"

He groans in disappointment and stalks toward a set of cabinets built into the nearby wall, tugging out a loose pair of trousers. Watching me with a mischievous little smirk, he takes his sweet time pulling them on.

I shake my head and cross my arms, entirely fed up with him. With us. With whatever the hell is going on. I want answers, and I'm not waiting one more second to get them.

"You were at the swarm." My voice drips with accusation and anger, and when I finally glare at him again, he's shirtless but at least he's wearing trousers. The hard angles of his muscles tease my eye lower, drawing me to his perfect abs and the erection barely hidden by the taut fabric of his pants.

Good God, it's so hard to think around him.

He sighs. "Yeah, I figured you would recognize me once I shifted." He rubs the back of his head absently, biting his lip in a dangerously seductive way. "From your perspective, you probably didn't understand what was going on. It probably looked pretty bad."

"That's because it *was* pretty bad." I frown, refusing to go near him for fear of my body taking over again. "You tried to fly off with me in your claws like I was livestock."

"Okay, for starters, that's a little racist. Stealing livestock is a gross stereotype we don't appreciate." He waggles a finger at me.

I roll my eyes. "Oh, don't even start."

"Second, I tried to *save* you," he continues softly, hands on his hips, a teasing smile on his face. "You're in the middle of a dragon swarm, and you think I'm going to just stop and have a chat?"

"Yeah, actually," I counter.

That's what the red dragon did.

Jace chuckles and rubs his jaw. "Rory, come on. You *must* have felt it."

"Felt *what*? I am so sick of your cryptic—"

"The connection." His smile fades, and the serious but somber expression that replaces it disarms me. "The call."

"The—what the hell are you even—"

But then, I remember.

The thunderbird's head tilts towards me, as if he senses me. As if he knows where I am.

Across the expanse, our eyes meet.

And it hits me. A thundering jolt shooting through me like a bullet. It shakes me, rattling my bones, and I tightly grip a nearby tree to catch my balance.

"I…" I'm not even sure what to say. What this is.

"And when you drove through those gates," he nods toward the window, toward what I assume is the now-destroyed courtyard. "You felt it again. Stronger. For some reason, it's always stronger in human form." He laughs, eyes glazing over briefly as he loses himself in some memory. "I saw you, and Rory, I felt it too."

With that, his complete attention returns to me. He takes slow and steady steps, closing the gap between us, looking for all the world like he's worried I'll panic and bolt.

That's not my style.

When he reaches me, the sexy stubble along his jaw drawing my eye, he sets his warm hands on my waist. It's disarming, and with his touch, spirals of warmth and comfort coil into my hips.

He pulls me closer, testing my limits, testing the boundaries of my self-control as the oh-so-foreign need for his touch snakes through me.

"You know what this is," he says softly in my ear.

I really don't, but one thing is clear—the enchantment I thought he put on me is not within his control. Whatever our connection is, neither of us has any power over it.

The fact is our connection binds us, even if I don't understand it.

"You want me," he says, his voice deep and seductive, daring me to disagree. "Stop fighting it."

My body sure does, but at least I have a *bit* of self-control left.

I can't give him what he wants. Dragons are possessive. They don't share.

Spectres, however—we don't have just one partner. I've never seen monogamous couples except on television, and after a lifetime growing up with that, monogamy just doesn't make any sense to me. I have no intention of giving myself over to just one man.

We're not supposed to love at all, but we do, in our own way. It's the unspoken agreement among the Spectres—every Spectre has his or her favorites, people they would do something for even without owing them a favor.

As my body aches for him, I remember the way Jace ordered me to stay on the balcony, the way he just expected me to obey him. He wants someone he can control, but I won't just wait in someone's tower, safe and protected. It's not who I am.

And that's who Jace wants me to be.

As his hands slowly rove my body, up my waist and around to my back, I can feel his possessive grip tighten around me.

It drives me *wild*. Once more, I have to fight the primal urge to throw my arms around his neck and forget the world.

With one hand, he tilts my chin upward, until our lips are once more inches apart.

"Give in," he demands, those stormy eyes snaring me like they always do.

But I'm stronger than this.

And I never give in.

"No," I say simply, my breathy answer not quite as intimidating as I had intended. My voice shakes with barely contained desire and lust.

That was definitely not what he wanted to hear.

His gaze drifts down to my lips. With a deep sigh, he releases me, my body suddenly cold as he lets go. My instinct is to grab his hand and pull him close, kissing him deeply until I can chase away his disappointment, but I stuff the treasonous desire deep down.

"I'm going to go work out, then." He rubs his neck and, without looking back, leaves me alone in his room.

Yet again, he baffles me. I can't fathom why he would trust me so unconditionally. I'm a stranger, and yet he's left me alone in what can only be his private suite.

Instinctively, I look around, tempted to rifle through whatever he may have in here, but my heart isn't in it.

It just feels... wrong. Like a breach of the trust he shouldn't have in me.

As I leave, I rationalize away the morals keeping me from digging through his things. After all, he's probably not going to keep files about Zurie and the Vaer lying out on his couch.

But deep down, I know the truth—Jace is slowly becoming one of my men, one of the few people in my life I would kill to protect.

And though this all apparently makes sense to him, I don't understand our connection at *all*.

CHAPTER THIRTY-ONE

I may have resisted the impulse to raid Jace's bedroom for intel, but that doesn't mean I'm going to play nice from now on.

With the dojo master distracted and the rest of the castle abuzz at Guy's banishment, I have a chance to finally sneak in to those forbidden hallways beneath the castle that are usually so well-guarded.

It doesn't look like I'll be able to sneak in a window this time, though. Secure facilities usually require access cards and are fitted with other modern tech to keep out the curious and unclassified.

Like me.

I don't have a ton of time, since even Jace can only work out for so long, but I still can't rush. Rushing means a higher chance of making mistakes, and I can't afford even one.

First things first—a disguise.

This will help me blend in as I make my way through areas of the embassy I'm not yet familiar with.

In the bowels of the castle, I sneak into the laundry room and steal myself a clean school uniform. My skin may glow with the magic of dragons, but the long-sleeve version of their outfit will cover enough of my body to make me less obvious on camera. I also rifle through their dryers until I find a hoodie with the dojo's emblem on the chest—this will partially hide my face.

It won't be foolproof, but it will get me farther than my regular clothes would.

Changed, with my effects stashed in the highest empty shelf in the laundry room, I slip out and find my way to the busier areas of the bustling dojo.

The courtyard is packed, the low hum of conversation between guards and students alike rolling over the stones as they clean and repair the courtyard. Everyone works together in a carefully orchestrated assembly line, and I figure repairing damaged stone is probably a routine event for dragon shifters.

As I jog down the stairs to join them, only a handful look my way and pass me over just as quickly. Good. Ordinarily, they would have all paused as I walked out to join them—the stranger in their midst, the one they're not sure they should trust—but for the first time since getting my new magic, I blend in.

Mostly.

Now, to find an elite guard to trail—and whose access card I can steal. This won't be easy, but it's my best bet to get down to the forbidden halls.

With Irena sick and the Vaer torturing Zurie, I just don't have the luxury of time.

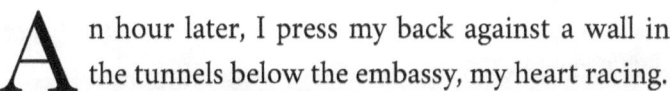

An hour later, I press my back against a wall in the tunnels below the embassy, my heart racing.

A cluster of guards trot past my hiding spot, and I hold my breath as they pass. I don't want to kill any of Jace's soldiers, but I don't mind breaking a few bones.

Dragons heal quickly. They would be fine.

After a few too many close calls on the way down, I'm on edge. Ears strained, I wait for the next guard to nearly find me, to sense me, but this stretch of the complex is thankfully vacant.

The coast finally clear, I do my best to walk with purpose, as if I belong here, chin lowered so that the cameras can't see my face under the hoodie. I don't exactly fit in, but with the dojo uniform, I stand a better chance of being overlooked.

Each door in this hallway has a window beside it, and I quickly scan each one as I pass. Two empty conference rooms. Four empty interrogation rooms. One broom closet.

Damn, I'm striking out.

The corridor ends, and I carefully peek around the corner to confirm I'm alone. At the far end, a camera is trained on the hallway, and I begrudgingly walk toward it.

It's not really a matter of *if* I get caught; it's just a matter of how much I learn before I do. By now, Jace must know I have secrets—he'll probably expect something like this. As long as he doesn't catch me doing something illegal, I should be fine. I may not get much freedom afterward, and he'll probably watch me more closely, but I won't be punished for it, either.

Probably.

Reward comes down to the risks we take, after all.

As I pass the dark windows, I notice the rooms in this hall are different. They have bunks. Chairs. Lamps. And most curiously of all, mirrors—most likely two-way mirrors to observe their prisoners.

It seems as though whomever is unlucky enough to spend time down here ends up staying for a while.

Considering the reception he got, the red dragon has got to be *somewhere* down here.

Through the windows beside the doors, I check the rooms one by one.

Empty.

Empty.

Empty.

Jackpot!

I pause at a window with a lone light on in the corner and, sure enough, a familiar man reclines in the cot against the far wall. A large two-way mirror takes up most of the wall to my left.

Now, to come up with a plan.

It would be foolish to simply open the door and start asking questions, as someone that big could possibly overpower even me, so I decide to have a little fun first.

The door next to his—the one that probably leads to the observation room—is locked with an access panel. Briefly, I press my ear against it, but I don't hear anyone inside. Not a sure thing, of course, as these could be reinforced doors that muffle sound, but it's a risk I'm going to have to take.

I swipe the access card I stole from one of the guards, tentatively looking up and down the empty hallway as the panel debates whether or not to let me in.

It flashes green.

I open it, fully prepared to find people inside, debating my options if I do, but thankfully the observation room is empty.

As the door closes behind me, I get to work. On my way here, I walked down the hall for about five minutes, which means there's a high chance I was noticed. A lone unidentified soldier entering a secure observation room is *probably* going to set off some alarm bells for the folks monitoring security.

Since I don't have much time, I make good use of the minutes I have left.

Through the two-way mirror, the stranger lounges on his miserable-looking cot as if it's a hammock on a tropical island, one arm draped over his eyes to block out the light. He's even bulkier up close, pretty much nothing but six feet of solid muscle, and I wonder if he's a body builder or just naturally endowed.

I blush a bit at my choice of words, especially considering the show Jace just gave me.

A large panel covered with buttons and screens fills up most of the room, with a small gap between it and the mirror just wide enough to walk through.

I lean my hands on the panel, scanning the buttons until I find a com that will let me talk to him.

"Are you enjoying your nap?" I ask into the microphone, a hint of amusement to my voice.

He stiffens as I speak, though to his credit he otherwise hides his surprise well. "Yes, thanks."

His voice is deep and resonant, and I confess I'm a little disappointed. He doesn't sound like the red dragon at all, though it's hard to know if a dragon's thoughts and his voice sound similar.

Their eyes and skin change when they shift. Why wouldn't their voices change, too?

I frown, frustrated. I was raised by dragon assassins,

dang it, and yet there's so much even the Spectres don't know about them. I wish I had come into this situation better prepared, but I have to do the best with what I have.

I skip the pleasantries. "Who are you?"

Instead of answering, he sits up and gets comfortable, one elbow resting on his knee as his eyes scan the mirror. "Show yourself."

"No. Answer me."

He grins and shakes his head. "I have all day. You don't."

I frown. Just as I suspected, this is a man used to being in control. He knows the rules and regulations. He knows the routine, he knows protocol, who has access and who doesn't. He knows damn well I'm not supposed to be here, and he knows I'm on a tight timeline.

My advantage disappears in an instant, so I decide to play ball. After all, I'm free, and I'll probably be fine even if I'm caught. *He's* the one locked in a cage.

Briefly, I scan the panel until I find a button that disables the mirror glaze, allowing him to see into the observation room.

When the dark sheen on the mirror fades away, his eyes settle on me, dark and intense. He stands and takes his time approaching the mirror.

As I get a better look at him, I'm momentarily distracted. He walks with a calm and confident gate, so sure of himself, of his place in the world. His confidence is intoxicating, his broad shoulders and square jaw giving him the intimidating look of a king. I'm fairly certain he doesn't have an ounce of fat on his body, though his black shirt and long pants hide most of him. My eyes trace the lines of his biceps, down to his thick forearms and fingers, and I'm left wondering what kind of magic he can work with those.

Briefly, I squeeze my eyes shut to shake these filthy thoughts from my mind. Sexually frustrated and driven to the brink, I'm obviously still recovering from my earlier brush with Jace.

When I open my eyes, he smirks. His dark eyes are hard and confident. Familiar. There's that intense gaze again, same as those golden eyes that have stared me down so many times before.

He's the red dragon. I just *know* it.

Never one to be intimidated, I casually lean against the control panel. "Why are you down here if everyone's equal in an embassy?"

His just shakes his head, wagging his finger, as though telling me I'm asking questions he can't answer.

This infuriating bastard isn't going to tell me *anything*.

I cross my arms, studying him, debating the ways I can crack his shell. I try to think of what he might want, but I just don't know enough about this guy yet.

"I'm glad you're safe," he finally says.

Oh, awesome. Another cryptic dragon. Just what I needed.

"How are you feeling?" He gestures to his cell. "Are they treating you better than me?"

"Just admit it," I say, shaking my head in frustration.

"Admit what?" He smirks again, and damn it all I wish I could smack him around a little bit.

He's so *infuriating.*

The stranger laughs. "You're cute when you're mad."

Livid, I smack my fist against the panel, and the metal edge dents beneath my hand. "Damn it, you tell me right now if—"

The door to the hallway opens, and I sigh in disappointment as Jace enters. His beautiful, muscled torso distracts me briefly, the sweat and dried blood from his fight still there, but his stern expression drives home just how he feels about my little misadventure into the deepest parts of his embassy.

"What are you doing?" he asks, his voice quiet. Accusatory.

I meet his gaze, chin raised, not backing down and not answering. He knows damn well what I'm doing.

"She's getting answers," the stranger responds for me.

"Shut up." I shoot a brief glare at the man in the cell.

"On that, at least we agree, Rory." In just a few steps, Jace is beside me, his strong arms reaching past as he flips off the microphone and two-way visibility. This close, he's pushing my body to its limit, torturing me with his warm skin and hard muscle, and I wonder what he's going to do.

Assuming he wouldn't punish me was a calculated guess—but I could absolutely be wrong. This is his dojo, after all, and he alone enforces the very strict laws of his people.

On the other side of the mirror, the stranger tenses, his eyes absently searching the mirror as he apparently loses sight of us both. "Don't you dare *touch* her, Jace."

That only pisses Jace off more.

He grabs my arm, and though I could slip out of the thunderbird's grip, it would be a bit of a moot exercise. This is a small room, and he's between me and the door. His touch is thrilling, even through the fabric of the hoodie, and my traitorous body reactively leans in to him.

A blend of desire and anger dances over his face as he no doubt fights his own body's reaction to me. Anger eventually wins, though, and he frowns down at me. "Why is a dragon like Drew so protective over you?"

Ah. So, this guy's name is Drew.

I look briefly at the stranger, who pounds his massive fist against the wall. A small crack appears in the glass beneath his hand.

"Wait," Jace leans back a bit, starting to piece things together. "You don't know him, do you?"

"No," I confess.

It's at least partially true.

Jace rubs his jaw, releasing me, and I cross my arms instinctively as I feel a surge of cold in his absence. He stares at Drew for a moment as the other man gets progressively angrier, and the dojo master seems to make up his mind about something.

"I want you to see what we're up against, Rory," Jace says softly, looking at me, driving the point home. "I can't legally keep him contained any more—but you can't trust this man. He says he's been protecting you, but you just proved to me he's a liar. He and his kind—their entire family just *lie*, Rory. Always. They lie and cheat and kill. They'll do *anything* to get ahead, *anything* to take control. Remember that, no matter what else he says."

I nod, more to keep Jace happy than anything else. While I appreciate his experience in this world, I make those decisions for myself.

Without another word, Jace taps a few buttons on the panel. Drew's door buzzes, as does ours, and it's clear both have just been unlocked.

In seconds, Drew shoves into the hallway and yanks open the entrance to the observation room. Frowning, hands balled into fists, glaring at Jace, Drew walks in with such a commanding presence that he seems to outrank even the dojo master. His broad shoulders fill the doorway, and even though

Jace is a bit taller, Drew looks like a gladiator in comparison.

He briefly shifts his attention toward me, and a flash of relief crosses his face. "Are you all right?"

I cross my arms, sick of the games. "Tell me who you are and why you care."

That disarms him, and he lets out a frustrated huff. He pauses, mouth open to answer, but no words come out.

"He's *unwelcome*," Jace answers instead.

The full force of Drew's glare shifts toward the dojo master, and in the ensuing silence the two simply stare each other down.

Drew and Jace clearly hate each other, and I'm not sure if that's a can of worms I want to get into right now.

But it does make me doubt my theory and intuition. If this *is* the red dragon, why would he send me to train with Jace, a man he so clearly despises? It's not even just a petty conflict—from the way their shoulders tense, from the slight tremor in their hands, I can tell they're barely holding back from throwing punches.

This is *hatred*.

"You have no idea what I've done to keep her safe," Drew says, voice tense.

Jace laughs derisively. "You mean by not kidnapping her in the swarm? She was too fast for you. For all of us."

I quirk an eyebrow in curiosity, wondering if this little dispute of theirs will actually get me some useful information after all.

"Did you pause to think about *why?*" Drew sneers. "How she could outrun *me?*"

"Oh, stuff your ego back up your ass." Jace rolls his eyes.

Drew takes a step toward me, lifting his hand as if asking me to take it, even though he never once takes his eyes off the dojo master. "Unless we make some changes, she won't be safe here for long, Jace. You *know* that."

"She's safer here than with *you.*"

Hands on my hips, I start to wonder if dragons are always this possessive, or if I'm just special.

Yay me.

Drew raises his voice, clearly pissed. "If you would just put your grudge aside for a *second* and hear me out—"

"*Grudge?*" Jace stands straighter, disgust and outrage clearly blistering through him. Electricity crackles across his body in his anger, and I stifle a gasp of surprise.

I didn't know thunderbirds could do that, and *damn.* That's impressive. For him to access magic in human form—it makes me wonder what other little secrets Jace is keeping from me.

"You think this is some petty *grudge?*" Jace is now

consumed by his rage, never taking his eyes off Drew. Small arcs of lightning dance across his arms and torso.

And that's my cue...

As the two men bicker, I slowly creep toward the door. This is beyond me, now, and quickly heading into the territory of petty bickering I don't care about.

"Yes!" Drew shouts. "You won't listen to reason, won't—"

"You know damn well why I hate you. Why I hate *all* of you."

With my back to the door, I wait for a proper distraction so that I can leave without them realizing I'm gone.

Back and forth, their dispute rages on. They don't even see me, don't even look at me as they follow this tangent about a grudge, but I don't have the context for any of it to make sense.

Carefully, I prop open the door just a hair. Then a bit farther. Bit by bit, I slowly get ready for the right moment—I just need a loud noise to cover the sound of the door closing behind me.

A few minutes later, they're still consumed in their argument, and, sure enough, Jace gets pissed off again. Electricity crackles over his skin, and this time one of the arcs hits the wall. A loud crack thunders through the small room, and the light flickers. Fast and quiet, I dip into the hallway, the door shutting in time with the boom.

And just like that, I'm free.

Though I'm tempted to continue exploring the tunnels below the embassy, I've seen at least a third of it so far—they're all cells or meeting rooms, and any intelligence centers would be crawling with guards and people. I wouldn't get very far, at least not when sneaking solo through such a heavily guarded area.

It's best to call it a day. I can hunt for more intel later tonight.

Fuming at the lack of answers even after all this time, I slip into routine habit as I pause at each corner, scanning the next hall for exits. I need to find Zurie, not stand around while two grown men bicker. I need to heal Irena, not hang out in an embassy.

I need to master my magic, sure, but the clock is ticking... and with each day, this place feels less and less safe.

CHAPTER THIRTY-TWO

Tonight, I'm getting answers, come hell or dragon fire.

Jace, to his credit, has not been by to apologize for earlier. I'm a little surprised, I confess, since I figured I would get chewed out for disappearing into a classified section of his building. But maybe his embarrassment from his little spat with Drew is enough to wipe the slate clean.

Or maybe the poor fool is waiting for *me* to apologize. I don't know.

My gear packed into the thin pouch hidden under my shirt, I tug on the last of my black clothes. The dark suit covers virtually all of my skin so that I can better blend into the night, and after my last few experiences, I suspect I'll need all the help I can get.

As I finish up, I wrap a scarf loosely around my

neck. I'll need this to hide my face in the event Jace hid cameras I somehow miss tonight. He strikes me as an overly cautious man, someone prone to adding more security if what he has fails, and I fully expect something will go wrong.

If it does, I'll just have to be clever.

As I finish with the scarf, I absently wonder who it belongs to. Hopefully, the dojo owns all of this, and I didn't just steal half of someone's wardrobe from the laundry room.

Ready for my mission, I lift my hood to cover my hair, and I open the door to leave. Tense and ready to disappear into the shadows, I press my back against the wall and peek out into the hall.

Instead of the empty corridor I was expecting, Tucker leans casually against the doorframe, lazily cleaning under his nails with his pocket knife. "Hey, babe."

I sigh. The unshakeable Tucker Chase lives up to his reputation yet again.

"Nice outfit." He scans my body, lingering ever-so-briefly on my hips and chest.

I lift his chin with my finger in a less than subtle reminder of where my eyes are. It's meant to be assertive, but a rush of desire bleeds down my arm as I touch him.

His green eyes disarm me as he leans against the doorframe, the dark stubble on his jaw tantalizing, just begging me to rub my thumb across it. As the burst of desire bubbles through me, I wonder if other dragons are always this horny, or if the god-magic just did something nefarious to *me*.

Tucker shifts, blocking the exit entirely with his body as he faces me. "What mischief are you getting into tonight, honey?"

"Some breaking and entering," I say with a carefree shrug. "Maybe some petty theft." After his spat with Jace, it's a guarantee that Tucker won't breathe a word of this to anyone. It's not like a human weapons expert has many allies in a dragon den.

Just me.

"That sounds delightful." He claps his hands together gleefully and nods toward the stairs. "Shall we begin, my darling?"

I laugh. "You don't get to come."

"Of course I do." He weaves his hand through my arm as if I'm the gentleman of the relationship, leading him to a dance. "What are we stealing?"

Chuckling, I shake my head. "I mean it. You can't come, Tucker."

His smile fades. "You got caught earlier," he says, serious and somber as he scans my face. "Down in the tunnels below the embassy, Jace found you. He's not going to be forgiving if he catches you again. Let me help you this time. You only get so many chances with a dragon, Rory." He pauses, letting the words sink in. "Don't push your luck."

My smile fades at the memory of Jace's expression as he entered the observation room. "How did you hear about that?"

"You're not the only one up to mischief, sweetheart." Tucker winks.

I roll my eyes at the new pet name, but I can't stifle a grin. "And just what have *you* been up to?"

"Nope." He clicks his tongue playfully. "Healthy relationships have secrets, dear. We each get to live our own lives."

"Uh huh."

He's just ridiculous. Adorable, but ridiculous. I don't even know what to say half the time.

"C'mon," he gestures toward the stairwell. "I'll keep lookout, and you don't even have to tell me what you're looking for."

For a moment, I hesitate. I like him, sure, but I don't *trust* him. There's too much about this man I don't know, too much unexplained about his past and skills.

And on top of everything else, he's clearly been sneaking about the embassy as well, on the hunt for who knows what.

It's alarming on multiple levels. I could make a quilt out of all those red flags.

But he has a point. A lookout would make things much easier.

Ugh.

Fine.

"You can come, but there's a catch," I say, crossing my arms. "Are you scared of heights?"

"Heights?" He raises one curious eyebrow. "Why do you ask?"

I laugh and toss him an extra scarf I found in the laundry room. "Oh, you'll see."

Tucker isn't scared of heights, but he has made it quite clear—*repeatedly*—that he doesn't like them, either.

"I mean, that's one *hell* of a fall," he continues, refusing to shut up as we scale the dark castle, inching toward the command center window as the countdown to discovery ticks in my head.

One minute, twenty seconds.

Good, we're moving faster than I thought we would. I knew he would slow me down, but I thought it would be worse.

"Hush," I say, digging my knife into the window to unlock it, the action already familiar and routine. It pops open, and I lift the scarf around my neck to hide all but my eyes. With a quiet gesture toward Tucker, I instruct him to do the same.

I don't bother to wait and confirm he understood, though. No time.

I kick open the window and roll as I dive across the floor. To my surprise, the room is dark and quiet. I had honestly expected an ambush, or guards to be in the room.

Something, *anything,* other than silence.

With a quick scan, I count four cameras this time. As expected, my loops have been removed from the cameras, and I suspect Jace now has someone monitoring them at all times.

Gun drawn, attachment already in place, I fire off my voids. One by one, they hit the camera cables and spark, disabling the little red lights as they set the cameras on loop.

Jace is smart, though. I suspect he won't rely just on the cameras—he'll have a few traps to catch the perpetrator this time, and I can't be too careful.

Never taking a moment to relax, I press myself against a nearby wall and watch the door, running through options on what I can do if someone heard me. I need to be ready to act, with a plan in place in case someone enters while I'm here.

I *really* don't want to kill anyone.

Four guards—these more alert than the last two—stand at attention in the hall, their silhouettes visible through the frosted panes in the door.

Tucker casually slips in through the window, and

honestly, I'm a little appalled. Considering his skill with weapons, he must have training, but he moves like there isn't a time limit.

"Go *slower*, will you?" I whisper sarcastically, sheathing my gun as I walk toward him, scanning the floor for traps or alarms.

"Not all of us have the speed of the dragon gods, dear," he quips, lowering the scarf to reveal his gorgeous face.

"What are you doing?" I whisper incredulously through my own scarf. "Put that back on!"

He glances up at the cameras. "Didn't you just do something to—"

"There could be others."

With an indulgent shrug, he returns the scarf to his face. I frown, none too impressed with his lax attitude, but I have to remember not everyone is a Spectre. Not everyone was raised with the discipline and laws that govern my life.

Lucky bastards.

He slowly walks around the room, his eyes on the computers and cabinets instead of the floor. I notice a little red light near the ground, and I grab his jacket, tugging him backward seconds before he steps in front of a red laser alarm beam inches from the floor.

We share a brief look of nervous relief, and he seems to take this little lesson to heart.

"I'll let you lead, then." He lets out a slow puff of air, and I silently wonder if bringing him was a mistake.

At least he's paying attention now.

I maneuver around the laser triggers and chairs until I'm on the top platform again, and I once more pull out the override from my hidden pack. Tucker's gaze hovers on the bag under my shirt, and I quickly hide it again.

Having a lookout is fine, but I don't like how many of my secrets he's discovering on this little adventure.

"What's that?" he asks quietly, nodding to the silver device in my hand.

"Keep watch, please," I say, ignoring his question.

As he leans against the wall, eyeing the door, I place the override in a data port in the computer, holding my breath as I wait for the glorious welcome screen.

That's the trouble with advanced tech like this—it breaks so easily. Every use is a gamble, and I never know if it's going to work or not.

Thankfully, the override bypasses the security systems, and I'm in the clear. I get to work as Tucker leans against the wall, his attention split between me and the door.

I bring up a few of the dojo's proprietary programs, scanning through them as I look for one that might contain something useful to me. A few have audio recordings, but with no headphones nearby, I don't want to risk listening to anything. I continue my search, trying to find the right keywords to bring up what I need.

Jace has a lot of intel to comb through. This man watches *everything*.

I have incredible respect for that.

Vaer safehouses.

Vaer security protocols.

Estates owned by Vaer Boss Kinsley.

Oh, my. As tempting as all of these are, I really have to focus. Narrowing down the search terms is harder than I anticipated due to the sheer volume of information available to comb through.

Tucker glances at my fingers as they race across the keyboard. "Aren't you worried about leaving fingerprints behind?"

"Not really," I admit.

They were burned off before I was allowed to go on any missions, since Spectres leave no trace.

For a moment, there's silence, and I assume Tucker is once more watching the door. But when I look up a moment later out of habit, I see him staring at me in bewilderment.

"Who *are* you?" he asks, altogether serious, his jovial humor gone.

I frown, a little annoyed that he's still asking this question.

He leans his palms against the desk, his back entirely to the door, shirking his *one* job. With a deep frown, he studies my face, those gorgeous eyes shifting across my features as he struggles to find words. He seems to be fighting something internally that he isn't sharing.

"I mean," he finally asks, "are you a Knight?"

I laugh. They *wish*.

"Fine," he says, clearly frustrated. "Then who trained you?" Though his tone is more baffled than demanding, he just won't stop. "I mean, the way you move, this tech, it's unlike anything—"

"Tucker," I interrupt, shooting him an impatient glare. "If you think I'm going to spill secrets to you because we're in a high-stress situation and could be caught any moment, you're sorely mistaken." While I watch him, looking for signs of weakness in his resolve, my fingers continue to fly across the keyboard. My brain is working on autopilot as the red *"No Results"* warning continues to flash in my periphery with each of the more-specific search terms.

I hold his gaze, his dazzling eyes searching my face until he finally gives in. "All right." He holds up his hands in surrender. "All right, you win, Rory."

"Explain," I say absently, returning my attention to the computer.

"You win," he repeats softly, not explaining himself at all.

"Like, is there a prize?" I ask, a little distracted, not

bothering to mask my sarcasm as I hunt for data. "A cookie bouquet, maybe?"

Tucker chuckles, shaking his head as he rubs his jaw in mild irritation. "I think I've found the one person on Earth more stubborn than me."

I laugh.

Yep.

"It's just…" He shakes his head, and I briefly watch him as he struggles internally. It's like he doesn't know if he should share it or isn't sure how to word what he wants to say.

My smile fades as I watch him, wondering what he's fighting.

"Can I say something mushy?" he asks, looking at me, his little smirk back on his face.

"You're going to say it anyway, so…" I shrug.

He smiles, nodding. "You know me so well."

I grin. "I'm perceptive."

"I don't know you at all," he says, rubbing the back of his head as he speaks in hushed tones. "I don't know where you grew up, or who your parents are. I don't even know your last name. But when I'm with you, I just…" He sighs, looking down at the floor, a hand in his hair as he reluctantly finishes his sentence. "I feel like I'm home."

My fingers pause, and for a moment, I lose track of what I was doing. It's such a surprising thing to hear that I don't quite know what to say or how to react.

He looks at me, his emerald eyes soft and serious, and I'm utterly disarmed.

"Is this some magical power you have?" he asks seriously, staring at me with a bit of accusation, like I've bewitched him. "To make people love you? Worship you? Do anything for you?"

"What—no, Tucker. No." I shake my head, dumbfounded and completely unsure of where he's going with this.

He sighs, rubbing his eyes angrily, one hand on his hips as he struggles to find words. "You make me..." He groans in frustration. "I just... Even though I don't know you, can't trust you, can't even begin to guess who you really are..." He pauses and looks me dead in the eye. "I want to do right by you."

I watch him, equal parts confused and flattered and alarmed, entirely at a loss for words. I've never had anyone say things like this to me.

I've never been adored. I've never been wanted or loved.

All of this is just so... foreign. I don't know what to do. How to respond. How to feel about any of this.

"You don't have to say anything." He shrugs and crosses his arms, looking again at the door. "It's probably better if you don't, actually."

"Tucker..."

"Don't." He holds up a hand, releasing me of any

obligation to speak, and meanders toward a row of file cabinets.

At a loss for what else to do, I begin typing again, my fingers moving a bit slower than before as I try to figure out what he means.

I feel like I'm home.

I keep coming up with questions to ask him, ways to prod into his confession, but nothing feels right. Nothing *sounds* right.

And before long, the moment is lost.

Absently, Tucker rifles through the odd file cabinet, no doubt just trying to occupy himself, suddenly consumed with his job to keep watch. He doesn't monitor me anymore, even as I feel myself continue to search for something else to say.

The screen flashes briefly, and it takes me a moment to realize it's returned a result for my latest search.

I scroll through the notes on recent Vaer movements, and my heart skips a beat as I finally find an answer.

Finally.

Originating from the city where I was mercilessly thrown into a pit, the Vaer had four stealth convoys leave in the dead of night within two hours of the event. The report chronicles the entire migration, tracking everything right down to the number of trucks and cargo planes used to transport whatever they were trying to so quietly move.

Bingo.

Irena and Zurie were in one of these convoys. They had to be.

I scan through the documents, memorizing the relevant location data as quickly as I can, using the tried-and-true memorization techniques Zurie drilled into me during my training.

A Spectre doesn't exactly have the luxury of waiting on a printer, and even if there's time, there should never be a paper trail.

Horrific childhood aside, I smile, grateful I finally found a lead. A *real* lead.

Zurie and Irena are at one of these four locations, though I note with a bit of disdain that each bunker is in one of the four corners of the lower forty-eight— Oregon, Arizona, Maine, and Florida. They're about as far from each other as possible without crossing an ocean or a country's border.

It's no guarantee, of course, but it's a start. The question is, which one do I hit first?

"Rory, look at this," Tucker says.

"Kinda busy." I continue typing furiously at the keyboard, seeing if I can dig deeper into the manifests or inventory to get a clue on which one has my sister.

"It's about you."

That catches my attention, and I look up to find him waving a manila folder, of all things.

I furrow my brow in curiosity. "What is it?"

Careful to sidestep the motion sensors, he hands it over. Sure enough, my full name is written on the tab.

"Damn it," I say under my breath.

"Rory Quinn." Tucker leans against the desk, looking at me like a lovesick fool, his goofy demeanor back. "Pretty name, babe."

I sigh and shake my head, leafing through the pages of my file, most of it thankfully labeled as "unknown." I look for any information about what I am, about the vessel or my magic, but a bulk of the file is redacted, the black lines rendering it mostly useless.

"Damn it." I lean back in the chair. "He must have the classified copy somewhere else." I bite my lip, deep in thought, wondering if Jace has just recently tightened security or if maybe the un-redacted version was here last time, too.

"So far, it's quite a read," Tucker says, deftly tugging it from my fingers before I can stop him. "Tactical abilities," he reads off the paper. "Adept fighter, clearly trained by an unknown organization or individual. Suspected ties to American military, likely through blood relations or CIA."

I suppress a laugh. Talk about speculation and wild guesses.

Tucker turns a page. "Current location, Western Dojo Embassy of Fairfax. Status, mate-guarded."

"Mate-guarded?" I tilt my head in confusion. "What does that mean?"

"I have no idea," Tucker says with a shrug. He flips another page, leafing through the information. "Identifiable by the golden glow of her skin and tattoos of illuminated gold chains." He pauses, looking at the words as if he read them wrong. "What the hell?"

Reluctantly, I lift my sleeve, exposing the soft glow of my skin and the otherworldly tattoos that snake up my arms. He knew about the glowing, of course, but it seems he never got the chance to see the golden chains fused to my body.

"Hot *damn*," Tucker says, eyebrows shooting up his brow. His voice softens, a little tender now as the surprise penetrates his mask. "Who did that to you, babe?"

"Whatever is in the bottom of that pit," I say, pausing, lost in thought for a moment. "So, I have no freaking idea, Tucker."

I stare vacantly at the screen, sifting through the memories of what happened that night, trying to make sense of all this. My eyes glaze over, the search bar just a blurry line in my vision as I briefly wonder what information Jace has on me.

The printed file may be partially redacted, but perhaps the system isn't.

I type my name.

The screen flashes red. *No Results.*

Damn.

He scrubbed all mention of me from the database. Whatever I am, whatever he knows about me, he's not sharing.

"You're going to be okay, Rory." Tucker kneels beside me, leaning in, his expression gentle and comforting as he sets a hand on my shoulder. He smiles, everything about his demeanor warm and kind. "I know it doesn't seem like that's possible, but it's true."

If it were anyone else, I would brush off their hand and make a joke, probably lie and say something about how none of this bothers me.

But the gentle weight of his hand on my shoulder soothes me.

With that one, simple touch, this tender and doting reassurance, I feel kind of... *safe.*

Except for Irena, I've never felt safe with anyone before.

"Thanks, Tucker," I say with a grateful little smile.

Without a word, he takes my hand and kisses the heel of my palm. The subtle gesture shoots through me, up my arm, into my chest, and it feels like he just kissed every inch of me.

The warm sensation of his lips on my skin is alarmingly intimate. His mouth lingers, and his eyes dart upward, snaring me once more, daring me to tell him to stop.

I don't.

"I'll put this away." He stands and carefully makes his way back to the filing cabinet, avoiding the traps along the floor. "Did you find everything you were burgling for, dear?"

"I… uh…" My mind is momentarily numb from his touch, and it takes a second before I can get my thoughts in order again. "Yeah, all I can find."

There's nothing else. No hints on which convoy had Irena or Zurie, no inclination of which base to hit first. I'll just have to scope them out one by one, and considering how far apart they are, that *sucks*.

But at least I know where to go. The people I need to save are in one of those four bases. No other large-scale movements have been detected going to or from these locations, and all signs point to the Vaer holding my sister and mentor hostage in one of these places.

I'm so close to finding them, I can almost taste victory. As I stand to leave, however, the lingering sensation of Tucker's lips on my hand reminds me of all the ways my mission has changed. Of all the ways *I've* changed.

And Zurie isn't going to like *any* of it.

CHAPTER THIRTY-THREE

As the sun rises on another day in the dragon den, I sit on the roof of the tallest tower. Frigid wind cuts through my hair, snapping it away from my face as my cheeks burn red from the cold.

Ribbons of pink and gold cut across the horizon, drenching the clouds with vibrant color as the world slowly wakes up.

The forest around the dojo seems to stretch on forever, and even from this vantage point, I don't see an end to it. Mountains slice through the canopy like glaciers, with only a smattering of breaks in the tree line to imply there are, in fact, some roads besides the main entry into the compound.

This place is a tactical dream—isolated on an island cliff surrounded by an endless drop into an abyss. The forests make it hard for anyone to approach except on foot or by air, giving the embassy the advantage either way. It's great for those living here, and terrible for anyone who either wants to escape or attack.

I let out a frustrated huff of air. Getting off this rock is going to be a nightmare.

Jace isn't just going to let me leave. The possessive way he touches me, his habit of talking like it's us versus the world—no, I'm not getting out of here with his blessing. He likely wants me to remain here forever.

I'll have to carve my own way out.

As a chilly gust tears past me, I scan the embassy walls far below, looking for weaknesses. Six dragons stand guard, and each turns his head toward me as my gaze passes him. They're still as statues, red and blue and orange monuments of grit and muscle, and I look away with a frustrated sigh.

Nope. Won't be easy.

Screw this. I need a break.

Rubbing my eyes, feeling the bite of exhaustion from another night of poor sleep, I make my way across the slanted roof of the spire. Being here has completely ruined my routine, and I can no longer consider myself nocturnal. At this point, I'm mostly just tired.

As I dart across the shingles, I make my way back toward the window I used to get up here. Getting back into the building is easy enough—with a little swing and a dive, I'm through the opening and trotting down the stairs.

Mind racing with ideas of how to spend my time, I figure I'll go see Levi. I haven't gotten to be around him much since we got here, and I think it's time we talk about the way he blocked my clear shot to Guy's head.

I grumble, still a little resentful Guy Durand got away.

That's going to cost us. Silently fuming, I run my hand through my hair at the thought of that sleazy bastard.

In my periphery, I notice movement. Instinctively, I pause and press my back against the wall to remain unseen.

Across the hallway, Tucker briefly looks around the empty corridor, dressed in all black. Face grim and serious, he checks both directions of the hallway a second time and hugs the wall, like he doesn't want to be seen.

Oh, how interesting.

"You're not the only one up to mischief, sweetheart." Tucker said earlier.

It seems I might get to see this for myself. I wait, wondering what kind of trouble he's getting himself into now.

Without a word, he pulls on the wall sconce. It

rotates on a hinge, and a hidden door in the black stone slides open with the barest whisper of a sound. He darts inside, and the yellow beam of a flashlight cuts through the darkness as he disappears into the secret passage.

My, my. It seems he's been up to mischief after all.

The door slides shut not long after he ducks inside. I dart over to it, running my fingers along the wall to find the crease. It's almost perfectly seamless, and I marvel at the ingenious design of whoever installed it.

I wait, watching the hallway to make sure no one sees me, either. I want to give him just enough of a head start to not hear me.

No cameras monitor this section of the castle, which I assume is intentional—though I doubt the builders expected anyone unclassified to discover the passage. I count off the seconds in my head and, when I'm sure he's likely far enough ahead, I also pull the sconce.

The wall opens for me just as it did for him, and I slip into the dark tunnel. Eyes closed, I listen, preparing for an attack out of habit more than anything.

Nothing. No breath. No metal clink of a gun or dagger against the stone. Except—*there.*

In the distance, the scuffle of boots over the bare floor.

Light on my feet, I follow the noise, never making a

sound, never giving my position away. It takes a few minutes, but I eventually catch sight of the yellow beam of light around a corner. It's easy to recognize his lean silhouette against the flashlight's beam.

I follow, silent and curious as he leads me through the tunnel. The minutes turn into an hour, and I eventually wonder where the *hell* this man is going.

The passage goes on forever, and I always let him keep a good distance ahead. The walls get progressively damper as we take staircase after staircase. From my count, we've already descended past every known level of the compound, at least those I'm familiar with.

Gradually, the oppressive darkness begins to lighten, and I assume we're coming to the end of the tunnel. Sure enough, a brilliant light cuts around the next bend, blinding me for a moment as my eyes adjust.

Daylight.

Strange enough, the tunnel simply ends without a gate or bars to block it. The black stone turns to a jagged cave's edge, implying it was carved as seamlessly as possible into the mountain, probably when the embassy was built.

A secret escape tunnel. Interesting. It seems I've found my way out after all.

Without missing a beat, Tucker jogs out into the bright forest. As the light cuts through the trees above him, he flicks off his flashlight and stows it in one of his many pockets.

He found a way out. And he didn't even *tell* me. Jerk.

I frown, feeling a little betrayed. This would have been useful information, and I had to stalk him to get it.

Pisses me off a little, to be frank.

I follow him into the woods, light on my feet, using the trees as cover and constantly scouring the skies for lookouts or dragon scouts flying overhead. It seems foolhardy to run so blatantly through the forest like he is, and I wonder if he knows something I don't.

Hmm.

We jog for a good ten miles until we reach a massive black wall. Clearly, a dojo border, but Tucker ducks easily through a discreet hole in the stone. It's subtle, hidden by some strategic underbrush and overgrowth.

It seems Jace has quite a vulnerability on his hands. After I don't need this exit anymore, I'll have to tell him about it.

Huh.

As I duck through the hole, careful to remain unseen, I muse over how natural that strange thought felt—resolving to let a dragon know about an unmonitored entry point.

I shake my head. These men of mine are slowly corroding my defenses.

As Tucker runs through the woods, my mood shifts. My curiosity is dissolving with each stride, quickly replaced with growing suspicion. Every step feels like a betrayal, a lie uncovered, and I get the feeling I'm not going to like whatever I discover at the end of this little adventure he's having.

He jumps up on a log and looks back at the castle, though I duck behind a tree before he can see me. He doesn't look at my hiding spot, thankfully, but he does seem to be watching something through gaps in the trees. I chance a look back to find nothing but the canopy. Wherever we are, the embassy is out of sight, and I wonder what he sees.

Apparently satisfied, he continues along a roughly worn trail that becomes clearer as we go along. As I peek ahead through the thinning trees, it becomes clear the route he's taking leads to a clearing.

The low hum of men talking in the distance catches my attention, and this is where I have to make a choice —continue to follow, in case he branches away from the clearing, or monitor the newcomers.

I wait for Tucker's next move before I make my choice.

He slows, takes a steadying breath, and walks into the clearing without his trademark grin. From the bits I catch of his face, he looks grim and somber.

It's bizarre to see this expression on his face—it's almost like he's an entirely different person.

I carefully maneuver myself onto a high branch overlooking the clearing. My hiding spot is covered in thick leaves, and I peek through the small gaps to get a good view of the meadow.

Two jeeps covered with high-caliber anti-dragon guns sit under thick overhanging branches, hidden from the skies. Four men lean against the hood of the closest one, talking in hushed tones while they relax.

They each wear black tactical uniforms with a white emblem on the chest. I frown, squinting as I try to see more detail, and it only takes a moment before I recognize the shield and swords logo of the Knights.

Oh, *shit.*

The freaking *Knights* are here, barely ten miles from the dojo. From Levi. From Jace.

From *me.*

If Tucker's here to take them out—if he's trying to be a hero, then—

"Gentlemen," Tucker says with a casual nod to them.

"About damn time, boy," one of the men says, his bald head glinting momentarily in the sun as he spits into the grass. "Slow as hell, like always."

Tucker rolls his eyes. "Good to see you too, Moose."

For a moment, I just gape at the clearing as the

horrible truth crashes through me, breaking me, shattering my heart.

Tucker is a Knight.

This whole time, he's been lying to me.

Using me.

Playing me.

All at once, I feel a thundering sorrow rip through me. It's devastating. Catastrophic. Heart-wrenching. It overwhelms me, and every good moment I've had with this man flashes before my eyes.

Worse than that, though, is the truth of what I have to do.

He's going to make me kill him.

A traitor in my midst can't be allowed to live, and yet...

It's *Tucker*.

This is all too much to process. The pain, the betrayal... it's more than I can bear.

The sadness becomes anger.

Becomes *rage*.

In my fury, I grit my teeth so hard they hurt, my hand tightening around the nearest branch until pins and needles shoot through my arm.

Another of the four men, a blond with a messy mop of hair, sheaths a dagger. "You need to answer your damn phone, kid."

"Sorry, Ma." Tucker crosses his arms, frowning with annoyance.

"No reports," the bald man says angrily. "No updates. No answers. You're supposed to tail the girl, not have a vacation."

"It's a little hard to take calls from you in a dragon den," Tucker snaps. "It's not like I can just excuse myself to the girl's room and have a chat whenever you feel like calling. Do you *know* how many cameras they have in there?"

The bald man frowns deeply. "Your *report,* Captain."

I didn't think it was possible, but my heart shatters *more.* He isn't just another no-name recruit or some grunt on the ground.

He's a high-ranking official within the Knights. He has clout. He's dedicated himself to them enough to have status.

Fuming, my hand turning red from the unbreakable grip on the tree, I'm nearly blinded with rage.

I've never felt so played.

The branch shifts quietly beneath my hand, and I open my palm to find a thin crack through the wood. A few more minutes, and it would have splintered entirely, sending the entire thing crashing to the ground.

With a few slow, quiet breaths, I try to calm myself down. I can't let my anger get me caught.

"What's there to report?" Tucker shrugs. "I've told you everything about her already. I don't know why you insisted on this meeting."

"The *magic*," the blond says, gesturing vaguely in the direction of the castle. "What else did you discover? Can she control it yet? Is she human or dragon? Can we extract it from her? Weaponize it? You haven't given us *anything* we can use. The General wants answers. He needs to know if she's useful or not."

My throat stings. My eyes burn. I'm not used to feeling this much, this deeply, this *horrible*.

"She's not," Tucker says curtly, all of his humor gone. "Honestly, I don't even think this is the girl we should be tailing."

The blond scoffs. "What do you mean?"

Tucker shakes his head, clearly annoyed. "I *mean* this is all a waste of time. There's nothing special about her."

Without so much as a breath, I draw my dagger from my boot. These men have tactical weapons and probably loads of smaller ones stored in their vehicles, so I'll need to take them out one by one, probably as they drive away. And Tucker—

Suddenly, it's hard to breathe. It's hard for me to plan how I would kill Tucker. I try to imagine each scenario, but in each one, I can't follow through, not even in my imagination.

Knife in my palm, I pause and weigh my options, trying my hardest to think rationally, but I can barely focus. Now and then, the overpowering sadness cuts through my bitter rage, blurring the two together.

These emotions have compromised me, making this so much harder than it should be. If Zurie were here, she would slap me to snap me out of it.

If Irena were here, though, she would hold me. We would cry a little, get some clarity, stuff the feelings deep down, and kick some ass.

I draw a shaky breath, trying to calm myself enough to do what must be done.

"What else have you discovered about her magic?" the bald man asks.

"She doesn't *have* magic," Tucker answers with a deep frown.

I hesitate, momentarily deflated. My sadness, my anger, it all momentarily dissolves into a hazy blend of confusion and concern as I try to figure out what he means.

The blond eyes Tucker suspiciously. "You told us she had some kind of powers when you found her at the bar."

Tucker shrugs. "I must have misinterpreted the situation. She's not showing any signs of ability."

I hesitate, my grip tightening on the knife in my palm. I'm so damn *confused*. I showed him my magic just yesterday. Hell, I destroyed a whole corner of Jace's training arena—and Tucker cheered me on for it.

The blond man scoffs. "Then how do you explain the reports from Jones and Morris? The dead soldiers?

Why did Anderson, of all people, defect after his run-in with her?"

It takes a second to understand what he's talking about, but it quickly becomes clear. The middle school. The three Knights who survived. They must have reported the event to their superiors—but wow, a run-in with me made a Knight quit.

Despite the severity of this situation, I smile a little. I'm actually pretty proud of that.

"I don't deny their run-in happened," Tucker says with a wave of his hand. "Obviously *something* blew through the school building. But between then and now, I think we tailed the wrong girl. Lost the original one, somehow. A doppelganger, maybe, or a well-placed decoy." He gestures over his shoulder, in the general direction of the embassy. "This one hasn't done anything unusual. Not one thing, guys. No magic. No glowing. *Nothing.*"

He looks pissed, glowering at them like this is all their fault, and I'm left speechless.

Tucker just... *lied.*

Brow furrowed in bewilderment, I lean forward, scanning the forest, wondering if this is all staged. If I'm somehow missing something.

I'm not.

These five are the only ones here, and Tucker definitely just told the four of them he's never seen me use magic. But I very obviously have, several times, right in front of him.

He's trying to make them believe I'm not the vessel. That I'm not the one they want.

For whatever reason, Tucker is covering for me.

I frown, not quite believing this little turn of events, not entirely certain of what he's trying to do.

A flash of anger crosses his face, and he glares daggers at the bald man. "You gave me a bad lead, Moose, and you *know* how much the General hates wasted time."

The bald man stands a bit taller, clearly insecure and a little afraid at the implied threat. He quickly shifts to the defensive. "All reports stated—"

"Shut it!" Tucker's command is swift and brutal.

None of the men smirk anymore. They watch Tucker, holding their breath, all of them nervous now. The bald man's face pales a little, and I wonder just how much of an asshole the General must be.

"We had her back at the incident site," Tucker snaps, his voice tense and authoritative. "The *real* one. We had clear visual of her from the start. So, if this one in the embassy isn't her, it's *your* ass, Moose."

"Sir, I swear—"

"Get back to HQ and get me every damn file on this woman you can find!" Tucker snaps, pointing off into the distance. "I want to know if I'm wasting my time. I don't give a shit if you think it's useless information, get it to me, and do it immediately!"

"Yes, Sir!" The four men weakly salute, and I'm baffled that someone as young as Tucker could have these four grown men nearly pissing themselves.

But it was a very convincing show.

Obviously, Tucker has some sway with the General —that's the only reason I can think of that these men would cower so completely at the mere mention of their commander.

And once again, I swing from surprise to the blurry combination of anger and sadness. He may have lied to them, but that doesn't mean Tucker is on my side. He could be biding his time until he can strike against me, or perhaps these grunts just aren't important enough to know what's really going on.

The lie didn't absolve him. It just postponed judgment.

I slide the dagger back into my boot.

The men jump in their vehicles and drive off, kicking up dirt and leaving Tucker alone in the clearing as the dust settles.

When they're gone, he relaxes his shoulders and lets out a nervous breath. His tense, angry expression fades instantly, and he's once more the anxious guy I saw in his bedroom after Jace interrogated him.

The mask is off—and he's on edge.

Completely confused, I lean back against the tree, unsure of what to do.

The fact is, Tucker could have given me away so many times by now. He's had what almost no one else has—access to me in vulnerable moments, where he could have overpowered even me, provided he had enough men to help him.

I'm good, but I'm not infallible.

For whatever reason, he hasn't acted on the opportunities he was given to hand me over to his General.

And I need to know *why*.

CHAPTER THIRTY-FOUR

I follow Tucker back to his room, silent as a ghost, never once letting him know I've seen everything.

He doesn't notice me. He doesn't sense me, though that could be partially from how distracted he is. I occasionally catch sight of his face as we slip through the hallways and corridors, and his eyes are glazed over for most of the trip back.

He's lost in thought. Debating. Concerned.

About what? I wonder.

Tucker trots up the stairwell to our rooms and, to my surprise, goes straight to my door. I frown, wondering if he's going to break in, if I'm going to have to beat him senseless after all, but he just lifts his hand to knock.

His fist hovers over the door, and for a moment, he just stands there in silence.

In the end, he doesn't follow through.

Eventually, without ever knocking, he sighs in disappointment and walks to his room instead. Once the door shuts behind him, I steal to the entrance and wait with my ear pressed to the door, listening to him grumbling to himself as he heads for his bedroom.

Apparently, he's going to get some sleep. It makes sense, as I'm fairly certain he's been up all night.

Briefly, I glance at the camera monitoring our hallway, delighted to find that my void is still there.

Good.

I try the knob, but it's locked. No matter. Ever prepared, I slide the lock picking kit out of the slim pack I always keep buckled around my abdomen, beneath my shirt. After a few minutes of fiddling with the knob, I let myself into his room.

The splatter of water hitting tile catches my attention, the sound muffled a bit by his half-open bedroom door, and I quietly shut myself in his suite. He's still mumbling to himself, so I wander closer, pressing my back against the living room wall nearest him so I can listen from a safe distance.

"...what are you going to do, man?" he asks himself with a groan. A torrent of water hits the shower floor as he moves under the stream. "She's badass, but she can't take them all on. No one can." He sighs. "You really screwed up. You're in deep. Damn it," he says quietly. "But she's... *Rory*. She's smart and sexy and deadly. You just *can't*."

A brief smile plays at my lips. I instinctively wonder if he's just saying that because he knows I'm listening, but it's impossible. He hasn't hesitated, hasn't shifted uncomfortably, hasn't given any indication at all that he's sensed me during this entire mission.

"No," he says to himself, resolute this time. "You started this, Tucker, and you've got to finish it."

I'm left debating just what that means.

This goes on for several minutes, and as he slips between thinking and mumbling to himself, I'm left to pick up the pieces of what he's internally debating.

Fact is, the Knights are at war. With dragons, and therefore with me. They're coming for me, but it's still unclear which army Tucker plans to fight for.

I think it's high time I find out.

The water shuts off, and the thump of his feet on the floor marks his path to the bed. He passes by the half-open door, and his silhouette through the sheer curtains reaches for the handle. I tense, slipping farther along the wall and fully out of view just in case.

His finger pushes against the door, which shuts abruptly.

Moments later, the light inside disappears with the swish of curtains shutting. The muffled rustle of covers over skin catches my attention, and he sighs deeply.

I give him ten minutes to fall asleep. When his

breath evens, I inch closer and gently turn the handle on one of the French doors between us. It opens, allowing me to silently enter.

A thin ray of light cuts through a gap in the curtains, hitting the floor and giving me just enough visibility to creep easily toward him. He lays on his back, the covers down to his waist as he lays there shirtless. His wet hair leaves streaks of water across the pillow as he fidgets in his sleep.

Slowly and with great care, I straddle him, one leg on either side of his torso to give myself the upper hand if we fight. My thighs brush against his naked abdomen, the warmth of his skin seeping through the fabric.

Though I would normally flush with desire, especially since the dragon magic seems to have boiled my blood with lust, I'm able to contain it this time.

This is different. This is life or death.

I draw the knife from my boot, never making a sound, my shoulder tilted backward to hide the blade in case he wakes up.

With a quiet little breath, I prepare myself for what has to be done.

It's time to get the truth.

My hand covers his mouth, clamping down on his jaw, and he startles awake. He grabs my wrist, his green eyes wide with shock, his other hand already reaching for the gun I suspect is hidden under his pillow.

But when he sees me, he pauses. His shoulders relax, and though he watches me with concern, he instantly stops fighting.

He might regret that choice.

With my hand still over his mouth, I decide to show just a few of my cards. Enough to get him talking.

"You don't get to keep secrets anymore, Tucker Chase." My voice is deadly and low, edged with a threat I am fully prepared to carry out. "You are going to tell me the truth, and if you lie or withhold anything from me, I'll send the Knights a clear message as to the kind of woman they're dealing with. Do you understand?"

The look of shame that crosses his face—it's heart-breaking. And though I remain stoic, trying to appear emotionless and calm, my gut twists with sorrow.

His brows tilt upward, and those captivating eyes of his dance across my face, as if he's trying to find the words to apologize.

There aren't any.

"I'm going to let you speak," I say quietly. "And when you do, start at the beginning. No jokes. No bull-shit. Just the truth."

Tucker nods, his fingers still wrapped tenderly around my wrist. His grip is soft and warm, almost inviting, and I ignore the ripples of longing that snake through me at his touch.

I slowly release him, fully prepared to throat-punch him if he moves too quickly or goes for the gun.

He doesn't.

"How did you find out?" A hint of sadness taints his voice.

I don't answer. Hopefully my dead-serious glare is enough of a reply.

With a sigh, he lifts himself onto his elbows and briefly scans my body, the way I'm straddling him, and he must see the danger. He knows one of my hands is out of view for a reason, and that should scare him.

If it does, he isn't showing it.

He sighs deeply. "You know, I've been trained for a moment like this."

"I assumed as much," I confess.

"The training was all about seduction and how to get out alive if you fall for it." He laughs, scratching his head absently, staring at the floor. "Disarm. Kill. Disappear. Leave no trace and show no mercy."

"The Knights' motto," I say bitterly.

He looks at me, intense and tortured. "It's not *my* motto."

I don't move. I simply stare him down and wait for him to continue.

Tucker looks off toward the bathroom, eyes glossing over briefly as his nose wrinkles with disgust. "It was never my choice. I grew up in the Knights. I was never allowed to have my own thoughts, or to disagree, or to want out."

My deep frown softens—just a little, since this is still an interrogation—and I can't help but feel for him.

It sounds like the Spectres and Knights may not be that different after all.

"You know why I'm a master gunsmith at twenty-five?" He gestures wildly, animated and angry as his confession continues. It seems as though I turned the faucet on, and now the truth is spilling out of him. "My father, that's why. I've lived my whole life under his thumb, at his command, doing horrible things because I have no other choice." Tucker rubs his face and falls against his pillow, staring up at the ceiling.

"Your father is the General," I say quietly.

Tucker groans, squeezing his eyes shut. "Yes."

With a small sigh, my shoulders relax a little as I process this new development.

I know enough about the General to be wary. The guy used to be a career American military man before his connections to the Knights were leaked and he was dishonorably discharged. Disgraced, he disappeared from the public eye—and though most people don't know it, he changed his name and took control of the Knights. It was a bloody coup, and since he took over, no one dares oppose him. I've never met him, but Zurie mentions him on occasion. They've loaned each other soldiers before, and he owes her a few favors. They're not exactly friends, but they're as close to it as possible in my line of work.

Not good.

"And what do you think about dragons, Tucker?" I watch him with a neutral expression, never showing a single emotion, never letting anything through.

"Some of them are assholes." He points briefly toward the door. "I'm not too fond of that Jace guy, to be honest. But as a whole?" He shrugs. "They're just people with a weird mutation, in my opinion. I've seen plenty of dragons do good in the world." He runs a hand through his hair absently. "I mean, the Fairfax and Darrington families have stepped in loads of times during natural disasters when local governments either couldn't or *wouldn't* help people. *Humans*, Rory. Dragons took care of us when they didn't have to. Hell, look at the Palarnes!"

"Yes, it was so kind of them to not kidnap me," I say dryly.

Tucker shrugs again. "Eh, okay, maybe we have lower expectations for dragons. I don't know. I'm no philosopher, but I know the hatred my dad feels for them has to stem from something else. Fear, maybe. It's definitely not founded in logic. Do I trust a dragon with my life? No. But do I want to kill them all? Hell no."

Interesting. I scan his face, looking for the usual tells of a liar, but there aren't any. He's being completely truthful. No masks, no lies.

Just Tucker. The *real* Tucker.

"I'm hot," he says without a hint of humor. "Not trying to be arrogant, just saying it how it is. I mean, you know." He gestures to me. "You know what it's like, and I'm sure you use your beauty to your advantage all the time."

While I appreciate the compliment, it's going to take more than that to break through *this* barrier.

He rubs his neck. "Anyway, being pretty means I get away with shit others can't. I learned how to charm people so I could weasel out of murder missions, assassinations, that kind of thing. But it wasn't enough to get me out of all of them."

With a raw and wounded sigh, he pinches the bridge of his nose and pauses, like he needs a moment. I wonder what he's reliving. I'm tempted to comfort him, even though I'm not great at it, but I can't let my guard down. Not yet. Instead, I just let him speak.

"I know what they think of me." He points out toward the forest. "The commanders think of me as the lazy son who was given his rank out of nepotism, and honestly, I don't care. I would rather they didn't trust me with missions at all. I want to be kicked out and would have quit by now if it didn't mean treason and a death sentence."

"Anderson defected," I point out, recalling his earlier conversation with the bald man in the clearing.

Instead of replying, Tucker just groans in disappointment. "Ah. That's how you found out."

I narrow my eyes, silently warning him not to derail the conversation.

"Anderson is dead, Rory," Tucker says softly, looking up at me with a wounded expression. "He's been dead since the day after your incident at the school. He missed a rendezvous, and my father found his house empty. His wife and kid fled with him to Mexico, thinking my dad couldn't follow them there. They were wrong."

My stomach twists, suddenly quite sure I don't want to hear the end of this story, but I have to. I force myself to remain silent and still.

"Rory," Tucker says softly. "My father hunted Anderson down and killed his *entire family*. He posted the killshot photos in HQ as a *warning*."

"Jesus," I mutter under my breath, my mask broken as I'm unable to stifle the surge of disgust and horror. "That's monstrous."

"That's my father." Tucker's nose wrinkles in revulsion. "He could have pardoned Anderson, *would* have in any other situation but desertion. Dad ordered the hit, and—" Tucker's voice breaks, and he looks away as his eyes water. "It doesn't matter who you are, not to him. Anderson was one of my father's closest friends, Rory. Basically, my uncle. They grew up together. My father ordered the hit on his own *goddaughter* to punish his *best friend*."

I grimace, momentarily lost in my revulsion. It

takes me a moment to see where Tucker is going with this.

"So, he would kill you," I finish for him. "If you left the Knights, your dad wouldn't care that you're his son."

"I don't think so." Tucker shakes his head. "I mean, is there a chance? Yes, a slim one. I'm the best shot in the Knights, except for a few ex-military guys. He would consider it wasted talent to kill me, and he would reprogram me into obedience."

I frown. "What do you mean?"

"Let's just put it this way, Rory—I think with some of the drugs my dad has in those labs of his, he could make a bear think it's a bunny." Tucker sighs. "If he doesn't kill me, it would still be a fate worse than death to have him break my spirit. Since leaving the military, he's lost every last shred of decency he had. And when he set his sights on *you...*"

Tucker's hand slides up my thigh, his fingers wrapping possessively around my leg as he stares at me in dismay. "I have orders to bring you in, Rory, to hand you over to him and walk away. They won't tell me what they want with you, but I've seen what they do to the enemy in that place. To women in particular." His grip tightens protectively around my leg, and he clenches in jaw in his anger. "I won't let him touch you."

With that simple motion, one thing becomes

painfully clear—whatever he feels for me isn't just friendship.

It's devotion.

I frown. "But you told them to get all the files on me—"

"To find out what they know," Tucker interrupts, looking at me with such raw intensity it leaves me momentarily breathless. "To look after you, to see what goose chase I can send them on to lead them away from you." He sighs and looks at the floor. "What goose chase they can send *me* on. If I can lead them away from you, I will."

Behind me, my grip on the knife loosens.

"You were never supposed to know any of this, Rory," he says softly. "You're too damn smart, you know that? This threat was supposed to just disappear. *I* was supposed to disappear, even if I don't want to." He adjusts himself, sitting upright and sliding his legs out from under me, until we're sitting together on the bed.

I don't protest, though I'm still on edge. "How did you get assigned to tail me in the first place?"

"I was the only qualified official near the incident site when it all went down," he says with a shrug. "At least, the only one they thought could get anywhere near you. I'm a decent tracker and have charmed my way into plenty of women's pants. The guys figured that was the best way to get you to trust us."

I frown, a flash of irrational jealousy flaring within me before I can squelch it.

He doesn't seem to notice. "When I first found you in that forest, speeding away in that jeep, I admit I was a little smitten." He grins, staring off for a moment, lost in the memory. "I figured I could have overpowered you, taken you in pretty easily, but you were so full of fire that I procrastinated. I kept coming up with excuses why I couldn't bring you in yet. Truth is I just didn't want to. The more time I spent with you, the more I liked you. The jeep, the mansion, the bar…" He sighs. "And then, when I found you in the road…"

Ah. After the Andusk attack.

"I just couldn't," he finishes with a weak shrug. "I guess I can't hide this anymore, so I'll just stop trying." He snares me in his gaze, and my heart flutters as he sets a hand on my ankle. "There's something about you, Rory. I fall for you harder every time I see you. You're more of a family than my father has ever been."

His gaze is so intense, so raw, so heartfelt that I can't hold it. I look away, using the moment to subtly slide the knife back in my boot.

Tucker gently holds my chin and turns my head until I can't help but meet his gaze again. "When you came back after your hit on the Vaer compound, things shifted for me. I couldn't do this anymore. I couldn't lie to myself, so I started lying to my superiors. I started ignoring calls. I started missing reports and meetings. I got written up so many times my dad had to start calling me to get answers." He pauses, his thumb brushing against my cheek. "And when we faced off with the Palarnes and that red dragon, I just snapped." His jaw tenses, and he shakes his head as the emotions roll through him again. "Rory, I thought I was going to lose you, and I just broke. I was ready to kill that red dragon. I *would* have killed him if he hadn't been holding you so close. But it wasn't for the Knights. It wasn't because my mission was to hand you over. It was because I'm mad about you. That was the moment I realized I would do anything for you."

I gently run my fingers along the curves of his hand as he holds my chin, running my fingertips along his knuckles, unsure of how to feel. I've never had anyone confess things like this to me, these raw emotions, this devotion.

For a moment, Zurie's voice rings through my head, and I simply don't feel worthy.

But the way he looks at me—it makes me want to be worthy.

"What do they know about me, Tucker?" I ask softly. "The Knights? Your father?"

He sighs in shame and breaks eye contact. "In the beginning, I told them the truth," he admits with a mortified grimace. "They know about the magic beam at the bar. They know you have enhanced strength and that your skin glows. They know you have some kind of advanced weapons training, but after that, the lies started. I told them you have night terrors and an overpowering fear of spiders." He shrugs lamely. "I was just trying to come up with something stupid, don't hate me. Whatever they try, I want it to fail."

I chuckle. "Spiders are actually pretty cool."

"Yeah, they really are." He smiles, but as our eyes meet again, it slowly fades. "Rory, I don't expect you to forgive me. I don't deserve it. But if you do, just know I'll follow you to hell and back if that's where you want to go."

I scan his face. He's said his piece, shared all there is to share. It seems this is the time for judgment.

Right now, I have to choose between two impossible choices—either I, a Spectre, trust a Knight; or I kill this man I adore.

The conflict between my two choices kicks up old anxieties, the kind that live deep within and wait for the perfect moment to take over.

Either I honor the ruthless training that's kept me alive thus far... or I give myself over entirely to this new future I'm carving for myself.

There's no in-between. No middle ground. No compromise.

And I have to choose *now*.

CHAPTER THIRTY-FIVE

As I watch the beautiful man in front of me bare his soul, my mind buzzes while I try to figure out what I should do.

At this point, Zurie would kill him. She doesn't suffer traitors, not even those she *suspects* of double-crossing her.

But damn it all, I'm not Zurie.

I care about the truth, and I care about loyalty.

I care about *Tucker*.

"What will you do now?" I ask.

"Stay here," he says simply. "Stay with you."

"And the Knights?"

He nods, frowning. "I need to make sure you're safe, and that means stringing my connections along for as long as I can. I can use my reports to buy you time and weave in so many lies they won't know what's true."

"And when your father won't wait any longer?" I tilt my head, never taking my eyes off of the weapons master. "When the General demands you hand me over, and there's no way out?"

He looks me in the eye, deadly serious, without a hint of remorse. "I'll defect."

Treason against the Knights. In other words, he's willing to die for me.

I debate my options. Part of me wonders if I've trapped him here, given him no choice but to tell me what I want to hear.

The doubt is there, and I need to know for sure.

Begrudgingly, I sigh. "Tucker, look. I can give you an out. If you want to escape, I'll give you a day's head start to get back to—"

"Let me rephrase," he interrupts. "They think I'm loyal, and they would take me back if I ran off right now. But I won't. Consider me defected, and we'll play them for as long as we can."

I search his eyes, making sure he means it, that there's no doubt in his mind this is really what he wants to do. He watches me intently, earnest and open, simply waiting for my final word.

In that moment, everything becomes crystal clear. He means it. Everything he's said is true.

"What's the verdict, boss?" he asks softly, watching me with a hint of dread. "What are you going to do?"

For a moment, I simply sit there, watching a high-ranking Knight bare his soul to me. He sits there in nothing but his boxers, his pecs and abs drawing my eye in the tense silence. The flurry of emotions within me rocks back and forth between unease and desire, between commitment to trusting someone new and loyalty to my old way of life.

Whatever I do next, there's no going back.

My lips part, and for a moment I hesitate. His eyes drift to my mouth, and he doesn't bother to restrain his desire. He stiffens, muscles tensing, and waits for the verdict.

"I'm going to trust you," I say quietly.

He smiles, slowly at first, almost disbelieving. It becomes a wide grin, and he lets out a grateful sigh as he impulsively grabs my face and kisses me.

The sensation is like blissful fire along my lips, and even though I wasn't expecting it, I love it. A twinge of joy burrows into me as his hand wraps around my waist, his hot skin a welcoming comfort.

"Sorry." He pauses, a little breathless, breaking the kiss. "I got carried away."

"Don't be." I wrap my arms around his neck and pull him into me, continuing where we left off.

It's not just a kiss. Not for me, anyway.

I let down my guard. I stop listening to the room, stop preparing in case someone slips out of the shadows to kill me. I simply enjoy myself, enjoy Tucker, and lose myself in his touch.

For the first time in my life, I give in completely.

And I kiss him. Fiercely.

Before he can say a word, before he can even react, I weave my hands through his hair. He doesn't miss a beat. His fingers explore my back, holding me tightly against his hard body, like he's afraid this is all a dream.

The kiss deepens, rough and primal. My hands on his shoulders, I shove him against the headboard, my knees on either side of him as I lean in. His mouth explores mine, insatiable and ravenous.

A switch is flipped in me, and I love every sensation. His skin. His hands. His lips on my neck.

I indulge all of it.

Tucker expertly navigates his way into my pants, sliding his hand between my skin and the fabric. Seconds later, I feel his fingers against my opening, and I gasp into him, arching impulsively as his fingertip slides between my sensitive folds.

He doesn't give me an inch. His mouth presses hard against mine as his fingers rub against me, teasing me, inching their way toward a part of me I rarely explore.

But this angle doesn't give him much leverage, and he stops just short of where I want him to go. He adjusts and lays down again, maneuvering me until I straddle him once more.

With my legs spread, knees pressed against the

mattress, I now feel his erection press against my thigh through his boxers. He reaches back into my pants, but I playfully bat his hand away.

Ready to give him some of his own medicine, I nudge the fabric of his boxers aside and undo the buttons constraining his cock. I slide my hand through the opening and tenderly brush my fingers along his thick shaft, silently delighted with his size.

That apparently pushes him over the edge.

Quick as lightning, he grabs my waist and flips me onto my back. My world spins. As I lay sideways on the bed, my instinct to always maintain the upper hand takes over.

I tuck my leg around his and roll, trapping him beneath me, breaking the kiss as I stare down at him with impulsive fury and fire. Adrenaline surges through me, the itch to fight temporarily killing the moment.

He watches me, breathless and smiling, as I pin him against his mattress.

"Oh, sorry." I release him, laughing. "Force of habit."

He chuckles and rolls me onto my back more gently this time. "I'll try not to throw you around. Don't want you to break my neck, now."

"Definitely not." I laugh.

"So, are you, uh…" He watches my face, toying with his words. "Are you on birth control?"

I nod. Zurie made me get an IUD just in case, since it's tough to go on missions while pregnant.

"You're clean?" I ask, running my gaze over his beautiful body, thinking of all the other women in the world who are equally dazzled by his gorgeous looks. It's hard not to think of all the women who have spread their legs for him, begging him to screw their brains out.

"Yep. Tested last month, actually." He trails kisses down my neck, shooting sparks through me with every brush of his lips across my skin.

"Tucker, if you…" I pause because I don't quite know how to say it. I told him I trust him, but an old and familiar flicker of doubt bursts through me. It's hard to shake.

He pauses, looking up at me tenderly. He seems to understand, and with one more playful kiss on my nose, he gives me a warm smile. "I will never lie to you, Rory. Ever. About anything."

And he means it. His calm and sincere expression melts me, tearing down the last wall of distrust I had built between us. I relax, running my finger along the stubble of his jaw as I smile back at him.

He must sense the shift in me because his eyes take on a mischievous glint. He grins, running his hands down my stomach without ever breaking eye contact. With agile fingers, he unbuttons my pants and pulls them down my legs even though my panties and shoes are still on.

I laugh. "I think you're doing this out of order, babe."

His grin widens, and he looks genuinely excited. "You just called me babe."

"Well, yeah," I say with a sheepish shrug. "It felt right."

"Just for that, you get a prize."

"What kind of—*oh*!"

His lips press against my entrance, with only my panties to separate him from me. As he pauses his kisses to drag his nose along the skin of my inner thigh, I can't fight the rush of heat that creeps up my neck.

Seconds later, he slides my panties down as well, and I'm exposed before him.

It's strange, having my shirt and pants still technically on while his mouth teases my entrance. I blush, the entire thing surreal, but I figure this is his way of taking a bit of control.

The moment his tongue finds my clit, however, the world around me melts, and I no longer care.

He's a freaking *master*.

With his hands firmly on my hips, his thumbs in the grooves of my thighs, he pins me mercilessly to the bed. Tucker explores me with hungry abandon, like he's wanted to do this for ages. All of his desire, all of his lust and sexual drive has been pent up all this time, and he's finally unleashing it.

On *me*.

His tongue dances across my entrance, slipping in and out, his kisses peppered along every sensitive inch of me.

It's divine.

It's *heaven*.

And he's not even *in* me yet.

As if he read my thoughts, he slides two fingers into me, his lips trained on my clit as he brings me close to an orgasm. His fingers work their magic inside of me, moving gently against me in a "come hither" motion that drives me wild.

I arch my back, adoring this, loving every minute of his masterful kisses.

"Oh, you don't get to cum yet, darling," he says, his hot breath against my entrance as he pauses. "There's more I want to do to you first."

"Don't stop," I command, but he isn't listening.

He straddles me, his knees on either side of my waist, his cock aching to break free from his boxers. He grabs my hands and pulls me upright, our lips meeting again as he tugs off my shirt. It flies across the room, and I don't even care where it lands.

With a brief look of confusion breaking through the lust, he pauses, his eyes on my chest. I look down to see my thin tech bag strapped around my abdomen, nestled beneath my bra.

"Oh, right." I unhook them both and gently set them on the floor even though my body aches with lust and desire for him. I may be horny as hell, but I can't let any of this tech break. I may never resupply, and it's probably all I'll ever get.

"Good idea. Let's get some teamwork going." Tucker tugs off his boxers, and I'm momentarily dazzled by his massive cock. As the underwear comes off, the thick shaft bounces once, already hard as a rock.

Thirsty for him, I gleefully bite my lip as I stare at his dick.

He doesn't let me enjoy the view for long.

In seconds, he's yanking off my shoes. His grip is rough, and I lose my balance, laughing as I fall once more on my back.

The knife in my boot clatters to the floor, and he pauses at the racket it makes. He clicks his tongue in disappointment, lifting the dagger by the blade and raising an eyebrow at me in mock disappointment. "My darling, I'm hurt."

"Oh, please." I roll my eyes and grab his pillow, revealing the gun hidden beneath it. I nod toward my legs to hurry him along. "Now, I believe you were in the middle of something?"

"So bossy." He grins and tosses the knife over his shoulder.

As it slides across the ground, I wink. "You love it."

"I really do." With that, my pants and underthings are tugged off, flying over his shoulder as well.

I lay on the bed, one leg propped as his eyes rove over me, drinking me in. I take the chance to do the same, studying his handsome face, solid chest, and strong arms.

Tucker Chase is all muscle and jokes, here to save the day with his gorgeous cock.

We simply admire each other for a moment, and for once I don't try to ignore the swell of adoration I feel for him.

The trust. The safety. It's all so new, and I kind of love it.

I kind of love... *him.*

With a dashing smirk, he grabs my hips and tugs me roughly toward him. His grip controls me, tilting my entrance upward as he presses his tip between my legs. I gasp in pleasure and arch my back, the sensation of his dick against me almost too much to bear.

With his cock teasing me, refusing to enter even though I desperately want him to, he leans over me. Oh so slowly, he leans his head toward mine until his hard body presses against my chest. His mouth to my ear, I can feel his breath along my neck as he nibbles. It just heightens every other sensation, and shivers of ecstasy ripple through me.

He's such a tease.

His tight grip on my hips pulls me slowly toward his dick. The tip pushes past my entrance, toying with me as the first inch of his cock slides in. I moan again with the joy of it all, aching for him to continue.

"Out there, you're a badass warrior." His voice is rough and gravelly, dripping with lust. "Out there, you're a goddamn queen." He kisses my jaw. "But when I'm in you, you're *mine*."

With that, he shoves himself into me as deep as he can go.

I gasp, a wicked little smile on my lips as he finally gives me what I want. Arching my back, I take it all, spreading my legs farther apart so I can take in every glorious inch of him.

My fingers grip the sheets, my nails digging into the fabric as he fills me. I sigh with pleasure, lost in him, barely able to think straight as his thick cock stretches me to the limit.

Once inside, he pauses to let me savor it, pumping his hips ever so slightly to stimulate my clit.

"Holy *shit*," is all I can say.

This is *amazing*.

Blips and ripples of ecstasy flicker through me like shooting stars as he teases me. I gasp again, eyes fluttering shut as the rational part of my brain shuts off.

This sensation, the way his cock slowly teases in and out of me, the subtle strokes—it's primal. Carnal.

And I *love* it.

I angle my hips upward and spread my legs as far apart as they'll go. I want him to have it all. I give him everything, letting him have me entirely and savoring every minute of it.

His hard abs press against my stomach. He leans one hand on the mattress for balance, but the other remains on my hips, controlling my body as he takes over.

My thighs hot against his, I wrap my ankles around his calves. It gives me a bit of leverage as I grind back, lost in the bliss of the moment.

Lost in *Tucker*.

"You feel *incredible*," he moans.

Though I agree, it feels so good I can't even put words together.

He slowly pulls out of me, the movement sending ripples of sensual pleasure throughout me. I shiver with delight as he tortures me, taking his sweet time, in no rush at all.

When the tip of his cock slides out, he hovers at my entrance, rubbing his tip lightly against my folds as he torments me.

"You fucking *tease*," I say, throwing my head back as he pins one of my thighs to the mattress.

"You like it," he says, voice gravelly and seductive.

"I really do," I confess, grabbing his wrists, wishing he would just take me already.

He plunges in yet again, and I gasp once more in ecstasy. He rubs his pelvis against my clit as he finishes the thrust, one beautiful and fluid motion that shoots ribbons of bliss clear down to my toes.

"Oh, God," I sigh, slurring a bit.

This man has stamina.

I moan, my grip tightening around his wrists, wanting—no, *needing* him to continue.

He pulls out again, but this time he doesn't hesitate. He bucks into me, grunting from the force, a sexy smile on his face as he watches me quiver beneath him.

In his bed, with my legs spread beneath him, I allow him to have full control. He thrusts into me again and again, dominating me with every powerful stroke as he rides me to a climax. His cock pushes me to the edge, and I don't know if we've been screwing for minutes or hours at this point.

Deep within my body, a surge of pleasure rips through me. It starts at the tip of his dick and radiates clear through my veins.

It's bliss.

Heaven.

As I cum *hard* on his dick, I tighten my legs around him, squeezing my thighs against his washboard body as I moan.

His hands slide along my back as I arch into the

orgasm. He never stops, riding me through it, taking it further than I thought was possible. Ripples of joy pulse through me, hard and fast, to the point where the only thing I can feel is his warm and soothing touch on my skin.

When the overpowering sensation slowly begins to fade, I relax. My chest rises and falls as I desperately try to catch my breath, my brain still trying to form coherent thoughts.

Tucker continues to pump into me, harder now, and it nearly drives me to a second orgasm.

He abruptly sighs, his eyes fluttering closed, his grip on my body tight as ever. A hot rush flows into me, filling me as he continues to thrust deep inside. He finally slows, falling into me, setting his head on my chest as his cock slides out.

We lay there together, breathless and blissed out. As the minutes pass, our breath begins to slow. Tenderly, I run my fingers through his messy hair. His warm hands wrap around my side, his thumb pressing into the base of my breast as he holds me close. He kisses my cleavage, and I chuckle.

"Pervert," I mutter, grinning.

Without missing a beat, he peppers kisses up my neck. "I'm a *romantic* pervert, thank you *very* much."

I laugh, grateful to have my ridiculous Tucker back after coming so close to losing him forever.

He rolls off of me, laying on his side, leaning his

head on one hand as he looks me over. He rubs his thumb along my jaw and over my lip, his doting gaze soft and sweet, and I smile at him.

"Thanks for not killing me," he says with another stupid grin.

Smiling, I shake my head and close my eyes. "You're such an idiot."

"Yeah, but I'm cute." He kisses me, his lips warm and soft against mine.

I roll into him, pressing my head against his hard chest, loving the way his arms wrap around me and hold me close.

He cradles my head with his hand, and for the first time in my life, I feel truly safe.

"The whole Knights army is going to come after you," he says softly, the humor draining from his voice. "All of them. Every asset, every weapon, every plane."

"I know." I kiss his chest and snuggle closer to him, not caring enough to let it ruin the moment. I'm grateful to have him at my side through it all, and that's what matters most.

We lay there in silence, listening to each other breathe. It's nice to forget my obligations for a bit. To relax. To work off steam and then simply sleep, in the arms of someone I can trust.

I never want this to end.

He runs a hand through my hair, startling me awake.

Strange. I look up at the window to see the sun brighter, the light along the floor now in a different place.

Whoa. I was actually asleep.

It's hard to believe I dozed off in front of him. I thought there would be a period where I had to get used to being around him, to letting my guard down, but this just feels natural.

"You snore." He chuckles.

I smack his chest playfully, grinning as I return to snuggling against him. "*You're* one to talk."

"Nah, it's cute." He runs his fingertip along my arm, like he can't quite believe I'm real. As if he can't believe this—*us*—happened. "For the record," he adds softly, "I know I can't keep a woman like you to myself, even if I want to."

I smirk. Smart man.

He shrugs. "But if you ever want to bring another woman to bed with us…"

I laugh. "You're so ridiculous."

"Eh, had to try." He kisses my forehead. "All that said, I'm still going to be jealous when Jace touches you, though."

I chuckle. "Well, just don't challenge him for ownership of the dojo."

"God, no. Shit." Tucker laughs. "Sorry, babe, but I like life too much."

Still grinning, I press my forehead against his warm

chest, listening to his heartbeat. Naked and alone, we simply lie there together, joyfully wrapped around each other.

It's not like me to trust anyone, but these are odd times, and I'm not the girl I used to be.

Hell, I'm not even sure I'm really a Spectre anymore —and, strangely, I'm okay with that.

CHAPTER THIRTY-SIX

The day floats by as I lie in Tucker's arms, lazy and carefree. Before I know it, the sun is halfway across the sky. We've been drifting in and out of sleep all day, catching up on life, talking about everything and nothing.

Tucker still doesn't know I'm a Spectre, but I dance around it. I tell him things here and there, hint at my past without giving anything significant away. It's for his safety as much as mine that he never knows.

But the world hasn't stopped spinning, and I still have a sister to save.

As I finish dressing, I look back to find him still sound asleep. He wraps his arm around the pillow I put in my place, snuggling with it. I'm tempted to climb back between the sheets to join him.

With a sigh, I slip my dagger back into my boot and leave.

Before Tucker's adventure out into the forests began, I had been on my way to check on Levi—so I head there now. I need to make sure he's okay.

It's a simple route, and I'm looking out over the balcony in a matter of minutes. Levi sits on the far wall, perched like a giant blue cat with wings as he stares off into the distance.

I pause, admiring the sleek curve of his body, the long and powerful neck that arches regally as he scans the horizon. His tail twitches ever so slightly, the tip dragging back and forth along the stone ground.

Majestic. Commanding. Dangerous.

The perfect combination.

I lean against the balcony, wondering if I should even bring up my annoyance with the way he interfered in my hit on Guy, or just leave it.

Probably just leave it.

"Hey, big guy." I trot down the stairs toward him, looking up at the giant ice dragon as his beautiful blue head twists abruptly toward me.

A happy growl escapes him, and he jumps onto the black stone ground. His claws scrape against the cobblestones, and in seconds, he's pressing his great big head against my torso.

Rory. The word echoes in my mind as ribbons of joy and gratitude swim through our connection.

Touching his scales feels like getting an instant gateway to his mind. I feel everything, sense everything, instantly know exactly what's going through his head. It's intimate and beautiful, and I'm honored he trusts me so deeply.

And as the surge of joy seeps from him into my core, I smile. It's a gift to have someone as powerful as him excited to see me. I affectionately scratch behind his ear.

He shoves me playfully with his nose, a hint of annoyance flashing through our mind link. *I'm not a dog.*

I laugh. *Sorry.*

He leans into me again, and this time, another feeling rips through the connection, blurring with the joy and gratitude—possessiveness. It's not dominant or aggressive—in a strange way, it feels happy. Secure. Comfortable.

I'm not sure how I feel about that, and I absently pat his forehead while I try to dissect this strange new emotion of his. Even with the blurry mind connection, he can sometimes be so damn hard to read.

His voice echoes through my head again, but I can't make out any clear words this time. He inhales deeply, and the mood seems to instantly shift. The emotions through the connection change direction, like winds shifting in a blizzard.

The joy becomes suspicion. The gratitude becomes jealousy.

Levi presses his nose against my hip, then my thigh, and I can see where this is going.

"Stop it." I playfully smack his neck as he gets a little too close to my crotch.

An aggravated little moan, almost like an angry whimper, escapes his throat. He sits upright, wings tucked tight against his body, and he gives me an accusatory look.

I cross my arms, a small smile still on my face. "Don't judge me."

He hesitates briefly before setting his nose against my cheek. *Tucker,* his voice says through our connection, his voice resonating through my mind, a hint of jealousy as he says the weapons master's name.

"I don't belong to anyone, buddy," I say curtly, pointing a stern finger at him to drive my point home.

A low rumble builds in his throat, soft and pouty, and he breaks away again. The connection gone, he lays down on the ground with his head tilted away from me.

"Oh, you're going to pout now?" I shrug in annoyance. "Really?"

He grumbles incoherently, briefly tilting his head back to me, lest I otherwise not understand any of his dragonish gibberish.

"Real mature, Levi."

He mumbles again, this time mocking my tone.

I know he's mad, but I don't play this kind of game. Besides, his nonsense just makes me smile. I cover my hand to stifle my laughter, trying not to make him angrier, kind of grateful he's looking away.

"Levi—" I set my hands on my hips, waiting for him to stop this garbage. When he doesn't, I set a reassuring hand on his side, but he just grumbles again and inches out of my reach.

I can't help it. This time I laugh out loud.

He turns to face me this time, his pouty eyes sweet and wounded. I just grin and gesture for him to come to me.

With a massive sigh and a brief look at the ground, he seems to be debating what to do. In the end, our connection wins. He gets up and walks toward me, pressing his head into my torso again.

As my hands wrap around his massive head, our link opens once more. This time, a flood of love rushes through. It's gentle and kind, appreciative, filling me with the sort of happiness I thought only children could have.

We sit there for a moment, not speaking, not moving, just enjoying the sensation of being together.

Two men yelling shatters the moment.

In unison, Levi and I turn our attention to one of the windows on the third floor above us, a little to the right. The wall curves, and through an open pane, I hear two familiar voices.

Jace and Drew.

In unison, Levi and I groan in annoyance.

I frown. "I better go make sure they don't kill each other."

Levi lifts his front claw and tilts his head, as if to say *is that really so important?*

I laugh. "Stay out of trouble, big guy."

The ice dragon huffs and gently brushes his nose across my cheek in what I assume is the dragon version of a kiss. With two powerful strokes of his wings, he leaps into the sky. A gust of wind from his wings cuts through my hair, whipping it around my face as he soars overhead. I watch him loop and arch through the sky, a little envious of his freedom.

It must be wonderful to fly.

Above me, Jace's voice cuts through the courtyard again, sharp and angry. I still can't understand what they're saying. I need to get up there, maybe listen in on their conversation in case they share something useful, but there's no way to do it from the inside. This section of the castle has been either guarded or locked every time I've checked, so there's no way I'll get into that room unseen.

Ah, well. Guess it's time for a climb.

At this point, I'm used to climbing the rough black

stones of the castle's outer walls. After a brief look around to make sure I'm alone, I start the ascent.

Since it's only three floors up, I'm at the window in minutes. Inside is a dark office with nothing more than a simple desk and chair. A few loose papers litter the surface, the corners lifting gently in the subtle breeze filtering in from outside.

The deep rumble of Drew's voice rolls through the crack in the door that I assume leads to a living area or hallway.

I slip in through the window and peek outside to see if I've been spotted, but one of the orange dragons is making his rounds at the far end of the castle. His head tilts toward the ground, and he hasn't increased speed.

It looks like I'm in the clear.

Quietly, I shut the window and creep through the study toward the door. I briefly pause at the desk, scanning the papers in case there's something useful on them, but the scrawled handwriting has symbols and letters I don't recognize. It's either shorthand or another language altogether, and this isn't useful to me right now.

"I don't have much respect for liars," Jace says curtly, interrupting something Drew had been saying. "Or murderers, for that matter."

"She wasn't *supposed* to know, damn it!" Drew shouts. "That was the whole damn point!"

"Why? She doesn't know who you are. *What* you are," Jace adds with disdain. "You had no reason to hide your identity from her."

"I have plenty of reasons," Drew says, his deep voice taking on a threatening tone. "It's just that none are any of your business."

"This is my dojo, and she is my mate. So yes, it's my business!"

I frown. Mate?

Briefly, I recall odd phrase written on my file back in the command center.

Mate-guarded.

My back pressed firmly against the wall, I lean toward the door, eager for some answers.

It annoys me to no end that Drew seems to talk more to *Jace* than to *me*.

"I sent Rory here so she could be protected!" Heavy feet begin to pace along the carpet in the next room over, and I assume that's Drew. "I didn't send her here for your hermit ass to get a girlfriend!"

Jace groans in disgust. "You're acting like a child. You know the mate bond isn't something we thunderbirds control."

"I never would have sent her here if I'd known you connected with *her*." Drew is seething, and I detect a possessive twinge to his voice. There's a hint—just a little bit—of sadness. Of loss.

Absently, I drag my fingertip across my lips, lost in

thought, wondering what would make a shifter like Drew feel loss. And it somehow involves me, no less.

"You would *dare* keep a thunderbird's mate from him?" Jace's voice takes on a deadly edge.

I can feel the tension in the room sizzle. Any moment now, a fight will break out. Blows will hit. Lips will bleed. And I'll never get my answers.

No longer caring about keeping quiet, I open the door and casually lean against the doorframe. Even though I'm annoyed, even though frustration buzzes through me, I have to pretend none of this bothers me in the slightest. If I don't bluff, I won't get anywhere. They have to think I have the upper hand—even when I don't.

Game face on.

Arms crossed, I tilt my head and smile mischievously at the two shifters. They're glaring at each other, and for a moment, they don't see me. It's just the three of us in a small sitting room, with a modest fireplace and sofa against the far wall. The white and red tones of the room seem more subdued than my or Tucker's rooms, so I assume this is where they keep the less-welcome guests.

Namely, Drew.

"Rory," Jace says in surprise, the first to see me. His voice softens, gentle now, and the rage on his face quickly dissolves.

Drew looks over his shoulder shortly after, and

both men relax. They step away from each other, hands no longer balled into fists, and I'm confident I timed my entry just right.

I wait for one of them to have the balls to speak first, to explain what they had been discussing, but neither do.

When I'm sick of the silence, I shake my head. "Really? You're not going to explain yourselves?"

Drew chuckles, a hint of pride in his eye. "I've never had *anyone* demand that I explain myself."

"Get used to it," Jace mutters, his smile briefly fading.

And just like that, they're glaring daggers at each other again, as if Jace speaking reminded them both that the other still exists.

"Explain," I interrupt. "Tell me what mate-guarded means."

Jace's head whips around, and he looks at me with a hint of suspicion. "Where did you hear that term?"

I shake my head. He's not the one asking questions here.

Drew sighs, crossing his arms as he looks at me. "I can't believe he hasn't told you, Rory—"

"It's not the time," Jace interrupts.

Drew wrinkles his nose in disdain. "She deserves to know—"

"Don't even try," Jace demands curtly, glaring at Drew.

"She's not something to be coddled, Jace!" Drew snaps, his voice shifting abruptly from the calm and relaxed tone he used with me.

"And *she* is right freaking *here*," I say tersely, entirely done with the bullshit.

They both shift their gazes again toward me, and both of their mouths close. The slight frown on both men's faces just pisses me off even more.

Drew walks toward me, and as he nears, Jace stiffens as if Drew's defying a direct order.

At this point, I know who this man really is—at least how he relates to me.

Without a doubt, Drew is the red dragon. And, for whatever reason, he sent me here to train with someone he hates. But this man certainly likes to keep his secrets, and I suspect he's not confessing who he is out of some misguided decision probably meant to "keep me safe."

Ugh.

"Admit it," I command, daring him to lie to me again. Daring him to play games.

Drew hesitates, mouth opening as he briefly fumbles with his words. He finally sighs. "I'm the dragon who has been helping you."

God, freaking *finally*.

I nod, as I know this much already. "Why?"

This time, Drew doesn't answer. He simply watches me with an obnoxiously stoic expression on his face, refusing yet again to give me what should otherwise be simple answers.

Fine.

I turn to Jace, giving him a chance to step up where Drew failed. "What does mate-guarded mean?"

"If you don't tell her, I will." Drew glares at the dojo master and crosses his arms, his thick biceps looking even bigger as they press against his solid pecs.

Jace scowls. "I know you're aren't used to obeying others, but this is *my* dojo. You don't make demands of me, and you don't defy *my* demands of *you*."

I roll my eyes. "Have your pissing contest later, ladies!"

"Rory, look," Jace says with a sigh. He opens his mouth to say more, but in the end, he just rubs his face, as if this is a complicated subject he isn't quite sure how to get into.

Three loud knocks on the door behind Jace catch our attention, and the dojo master just groans in annoyance.

"Come in," Drew says.

The door swings open, and a breathless soldier in a black and yellow dojo uniform sticks his head inside. When his eyes land on Jace, he lets out a sigh of relief. "Oh, good. Jace, we have an emergency."

"What *now?*" the dojo master asks, beyond aggravated at this point.

"A forbidden visitor at the gate," the guard says, his

eyebrows lifting in pleading concern, as if he's trying not to say too much in front of those of us who aren't supposed to know.

For a moment, no one says anything. I'm not quite sure what to think. Jace and I look at each other with concern, and I'm left wondering if this is going to happen every time he gets a visitor.

The concern.

The shock.

The question of whether or not this is it. The moment I'm discovered.

"Come with me," Jace says to me, offering his hand.

I'm a little torn. On one hand, he's a little too comfortable ordering me around. On the other, I *really* want to know who this is.

In the end, I walk toward the guard, ignoring Jace's gesture.

The guard leads us toward the front of the embassy, with Drew hot on our heels. I'm careful to keep him in my periphery, but he certainly gives me a run for my money. He seems to prefer my blind spot, easily stepping out of my sight every chance he gets. I finally look over my shoulder at one point, only to find him smirking at me.

The bastard was testing me, damn it.

We round the next corner and quickly make our way toward a small balcony that overlooks the front doors. As Jace pushes them open to allow in the sound from outside, he stops abruptly and steps in front of me, blocking my view of the square. All I can see are the dozens of dragons lined along the walls on either side and the students filling the courtyard, their uniforms like a crisp ocean of black and yellow fabric. Every head is trained on the front gate.

There are even more out here than there were to greet me. Whoever this is, the entire dojo is on high alert.

"I know she's here!" a familiar man's voice echoes through the square.

Wait.

I know that voice.

"Mason," I seethe through clenched teeth.

In my peripheral vision, Drew looks at me in surprise. His shoulders tense, and he's suddenly wary not of the visitor, but of *me*.

As all wise men *should* be.

CHAPTER THIRTY-SEVEN

M ason Greene is here.
Looking for *me*.

As we stand in the small parlor that leads to the balcony overlooking the square, I debate what I should do.

Arguably, this could be a bluff. He could be going on a best guess that would mean bad things for me if I play into his hands.

But it seems doubtful.

With the sheer number of people here, I can guarantee someone has talked. Someone has given me away —even unintentionally, as the strange newcomer in their midst.

However, my suspicions lie squarely with Guy Durand.

I don't have proof, of course, but there's that

bubbling intuition again. It would make sense, and at this point, I doubt Mason is bluffing.

"What did I miss?" Tucker asks from behind me. I briefly look over my shoulder as he jogs cheerily into the room. He glances at Drew, nodding a hello with a bit of trademark carefree candor, but Drew barely acknowledges his presence.

Though I'm grateful to see him, I huff in a barely veiled attempt to suppress the rising tide of hatred and loathing that's surging within me. "You didn't miss anything because I'm about to have a *chat* with this jackass out there."

Jace turns toward me, his broad shoulders and lean frame blocking my view of the square. "I forbid it."

Behind me, I hear Tucker's sharp intake of breath.

Tucker knows what Jace doesn't—no one orders me around, and *no one* forbids me to do *anything*.

I, however, merely square my shoulders. The master of the dojo may control the lives of those who dwell here, but he's a fool if he thinks he has any control over me. "You can't stop this, Jace."

"Like hell I can't." He takes a menacing step toward me, and though he radiates control and dominance, I see the flicker of dread break through his calm.

Either he's worried about what will happen to me if Mason discovers me here, or he's worried I'll hate him for standing in my way.

I ball my hand into a fist. "I'm giving you one

chance to back down." I gesture to Drew, Tucker, and the guard whose name I don't know. "It's only the five of us here. No one else has to know."

"This is not a debate."

He's right. It's not.

I'm going out there.

Mason is my best bet of getting to Irena and Zurie. I have four leads on opposite ends of the country, and he can narrow down my search.

I will *not* miss this chance, and not even Jace will stand in my way.

"Come out to play, Rory!" Mason shouts into the courtyard.

Nearby, Levi soars over the square and lands on a free section of the wall. The dragons on either side of him shift ever so slightly away, as if becoming feral is a disease they can catch.

Assholes.

Apparently, I'm surrounded by those right now.

"Jace, I don't want to fight you in your embassy, but I *will*." I lock eyes with the thunderbird, trying to convey just how desperately I need to get past him.

"Uh, Rory, babe," Tucker says quietly. "We agreed not to do that."

"Hush," I shoot him a warning glare.

I'm not in the mood.

"I'm going to ignore that challenge," Jace's eyes narrow. "Instead, care to explain to me why a Vaer *Lord* is here asking for you by name?" His voice is low and tense, demanding an answer.

I frown, less impressed by the minute. "I'm grateful for the risks you've taken by keeping me here, Jace, but I don't owe you my life story."

It's clear this isn't going anywhere.

"I've come alone, promise!" Mason shouts, a hint of boredom in his tone. "Any day now, woman. I just want to talk."

"Is he really alone?" I ask the guard who brought us here.

For a moment, the guard hesitates, his attention shifting between me and Jace. "Yes," the soldier eventually says. "There are two Vaer convoy trucks to the south with a few soldiers in each, but they're seven miles away. They couldn't get here in time to be useful to him, and we wildly outnumber them. We would destroy them before they got close, so we assume they're just transportation for Mason."

"Fair assumption." I nod, rubbing my chin as my mind races with what he could want.

He's forbidden to be here, and yet he came. I can't fathom why he would risk it just to talk.

Unless…

I stiffen, my jaw clenching as my mind goes to the worst-case scenario. Unless this is it. This is his last chance to draw me out into the open, to tempt me with the only things I want.

My sister and mentor.

"Jace," I say quietly. Tensely. "He already knows I'm here. This isn't some elaborate ruse. Guy knows what I am, and he was banished. You *should* have killed him."

The dojo master answers me with a withering glare, but those don't work on me.

"Fine. I'm done asking permission." I turn to leave.

In my periphery, Jace reaches for my wrist. He moves blindingly fast. So fast, in fact, that my training overrides my rational thought.

Time slows.

Driven by instinct, I shift my weight and cock my arm to throw a punch.

Jace adjusts instantly, ready to match my blow.

I'm furious. Seething. Bristling with rage and frustration, knowing that this may very well be the last chance I ever have to save Irena. My sister. My family. The emotions blur within me, kicking up my fight or flight response.

Deep within my core, my rage stokes the embers of my new magic.

A flash of heat shoots up my arm, hot and quick. To my surprise, a blistering bolt of white light spirals down my arm toward my fist.

As if in response, arcs of lightning shoot down his.

Our fists hit with a shattering boom, and a crack of blinding light cuts through the parlor. My body surges with the energy of my magic as it once more comes to the surface.

As quick as it came, the light of our blow fades. Jace and I stare at each other in disbelief, frowning and furious.

My magic races over my skin, up and down my arms, over my torso. Little blurs of white light dancing in time with my anger.

Arcs of lightning continue to race across his body. It looks like he's just waiting, prepared and ready to go again if I have the nerve to throw another punch.

A hush settles over the room as Jace and I square off. We each breathe heavily, waiting for the other to act, debating what to do next.

I'm something he feels he needs to protect, to store away in a tower like gold.

And he's in my *way*.

The last few times my magic has come to the surface, it fizzled as soon as it appeared. But this time, it continues to burn and bubble, easily within reach, and I wonder how long this will last.

Probably not long.

Jace shakes his hand out, and the lightning disappears from his arm. "I'm going down there. You're *not*."

Without another word, he leaves the room and gestures for Drew to join him, likely so I'm not left alone with him. The unnamed soldier leaves as well, briefing Jace on something as they walk. The door clicks behind them, and the slide of a deadbolt locks me and Tucker in the room.

Tucker chuckles and gestures toward the door. "It's adorable they think that'll work."

"At least *you* get me." I peer through the glass of the balcony's double doors as a gust of wind slowly widens the crack between them.

Mason stands at the open gates, his hands on his head as he stares into the crowd. He stands on the bridge, and I'm quite certain even one step across the threshold into the square would mean a bloody violation of dragon law.

In my palms, my magic aches to break free. It was brought to the surface to defend me, and barely any escaped in my little spat with Jace. It pushes against my skin, and I grit my teeth as I try to rein it in.

This situation is dangerous enough without the risk of a massive blast of magic destroying half of Jace's dojo. He's being an ass, but I still like this place enough not to reduce it to rubble.

The double doors of the main entrance right below me hit the wall as they're thrown open, and Jace trots down to the bottom step. He stops, arms crossed, glaring at Mason.

"You aren't welcome here, Mason," the blond shifter says with a murderous expression. "And you don't get to make demands."

It's cute that Jace thinks he's protecting me, but

right now he's just making this more difficult than it needs to be.

I scan the castle's outside walls, looking for a way down. I'm only two stories up. Barely anything. And with my magic still bubbling at the surface, I have a delightful little idea.

Oh, this is going to be *fun*.

If I act before Jace can say I'm not here, I can make anything I do look like his idea. He can't tell me to stop without admitting to his entire audience that I'm outright defying him—something that seems to matter a great deal in this place.

So, I hatch a devious little plan.

Zurie once taught me that a dramatic entrance can make the difference between winning and losing a fight—if I can shred my opponent's confidence, I can win before I even have to land a blow.

Considering all that's at stake in this situation, I would say it calls for a little flair.

I throw open the balcony doors and hop easily onto the stone railing separating me from a short drop. A few of the soldiers look my way, but I'm not going to stop here.

With my magic buzzing through my hands, I jump.

My enhanced strength takes me to the center of the courtyard, and I aim my hands at the ground. The magic in my palms aches to break free, and I finally let a little of it go. It's damn near impossible to control, but I manage to release a short burst of white light. Just enough to soften my momentum.

The magic blows a small crater in the black stone, and I land easily. Shoulders back, a deadly serious expression on my face, I stand and glare at Mason Greene.

The man who stole my sister from me.

"Lovely." He claps, chuckling a little as he looks me over. "My darling beauty still lives!"

I grimace, wrinkling my nose in disgust. As much as I want to break his legs, I know a better way to put him in his place.

As the magic tears at my body, almost too much to bear, I aim my palm in his direction. Though his gaze drops to my fingers, I don't think he realizes the danger he's in.

With a little smirk, I release the last of the magic burning within me. It rips free, and a thick blast of deadly white light sails toward him.

His stupid sneer disappears as the beam flies toward him. I aimed just close enough for him to get the hint—but not kill him. As the white beam barrels toward him, he rolls aside. The magic sizzles through the air, barely missing him, and he looks at me like I'm crazy.

Good. I have his attention.

"Start talking." I walk toward him, slow and steady,

never once betraying my rage. My loathing. How much I want to break his scrawny neck.

To my delight, all the pretense and cocky sneers are gone. I guess nearly dying has a sobering effect on people like him.

Mason looks at me with blurred hatred and fear, taking an unconscious step back as I near him. "I know what you're up to, Rory."

I close the gap between us, walking steadily until the thin line between the bridge and courtyard is the only thing separating us. I pause, not entirely sure what the ramifications are if I leave the dojo limits.

"You think making friends will help you?" Mason lowers his voice and gestures to the dragons around us, lowering his voice to a grating whisper. "You think any of *them* are going to help you get Irena or Zurie back once they know what you are?"

"When I said, 'start talking,' I meant say something useful." I give him a once-over. "You're just wasting air."

"You don't scare me," he sneers. "If you kill me, it'll give the entire world an excuse to come after you." At that, his smile broadens. "Your little warning shot was cute, but you know better than to kill on dojo grounds. Doing that would mean you're fair game."

"That's quite a risky gamble when the bet is your life." I lift my chin, careful to bury my rage beneath a blank expression. I can't let him know that he gets to me. "You infected my sister. You tortured my mentor.

You left me in a pit to die." I tilt my head, narrowing my eyes at the bastard. "Are you sure I don't hate you enough to risk all that?"

He takes a wary step back, suddenly realizing how close to death he really is.

I nod to the other side of the bridge. "How fast can you run, little man? Think you can make it out of here before I fire? Or did you want to tell me something useful for a change?"

Even though my magic has once more faded, I lift my hand again, aiming for his heart.

I love a good bluff.

"Zurie is in the Oregon base," Mason says, taking several wary steps back. "Irena is in Florida. You're smart enough to know the coordinates. Pick one to save, bitch, because you don't get to save both."

With that, he bolts toward the end of the bridge. His form shimmers as he flees, and his dragon bursts through, ripping his clothes to shreds. His thick horns spiral around the sharp angles of his face. As he takes to the sky, I simply watch. His dark red dragon is the color of dying embers, and the underside of his scales glow orange as he bolts into the clouds.

It's a shame such a gorgeous dragon is stuck with such a coward.

I lower my hand, my rage sizzling as the jackass disappears. I can feel Jace's withering gaze on my back, but I don't care. I got what I needed.

And now I really do have to choose.

I was hoping I could somehow save them both, but for the moment, there's only a chance to save one.

Do I save Irena and lose the mentor who trained us both, or do I save Zurie and trust in her experience to rescue Irena before Mason kills my sister out of spite?

These are the kinds of choices Zurie makes, not me. I've never had either of their lives in my hands before, and flickers of doubt burn within me as I struggle to weigh the pros and cons.

Fact is, I don't have the luxury of following Zurie's lead anymore. It's time for me to step up.

And as much as it leaves my stomach in knots, I'm pretty sure I already know exactly what I have to do.

CHAPTER THIRTY-EIGHT

I sit with my arms crossed and my legs perched on the table of Jace's war room, staring at the wall as he paces beside me. We're shut away in a room in his private suite, designed for sensitive discussions and confidential conversations, but I'm pretty sure he just wants to yell at me. I can feel the rage rolling off of him like steam, but I've never been one to nurture a man's ego.

I have shit to *do.*

Without a word, Jace pulls on my chair. My feet hit the floor. In one deft motion, he spins me until I'm suddenly facing him. He leans a hand on either side of me as he brings his face inches from mine.

Before I met him, I would have broken the nose of any man who dared to do this to me.

But now...

Deep within me, I feel a now-familiar tug in my chest. My entire body aches for him, driving me closer, tempting me toward his lips.

Though my eyes dart toward his mouth, I shove the temptation deep down.

"You can't do that again, Rory." His voice reverberates through him like thunder, and as his forearms brush my shoulders, I can feel the vibration resonate through me as well.

It's not a threat, but it's not doting, either.

"Rory, what am I going to *do* with you?" He sighs in deep frustration and leans his forehead against mine.

His touch is electric.

It burns through me, and before I can help it, my eyes flutter blissfully shut. My lips instinctively part, and my traitorous body leans into him before I can stop it.

He inhales deeply, his nose pressing against mine as he gives in to a sensation I'm barely controlling. His skin is hot, soothing and smooth. My mind wanders to lip-biting places, and my impulsive desire is to wrap my legs around his waist.

Good gracious, this dragon magic makes my blood boil with lust. Or maybe it's Jace. It's hard to tell.

I try to snap myself out of it. I try to break free, but before I can, he runs one hand through my hair.

His warm palm slowly works its way through my loose curls, never pulling, each moment a temptation.

He rests the flat of his palm against my jaw, his powerful fingers gently pressing into my skin. He tilts my chin upward, and I don't fight him as our lips meet.

The last time he kissed me, it was rough and primal, like he couldn't take me fast enough.

But this time, his touch is warm and gentle. I didn't know he could hold me this tenderly, or that his mouth knew anything but ravenous, sexual hunger.

He holds me suspended, each masterful movement of his lips leaving me breathless. As he leans into me, deepening the kiss, my soul flutters for him. For his power, for his strength, for everything he is.

My world buzzes, and I lose track of time.

He eventually breaks the kiss, and my lips feel cold as he sets his forehead once more against mine. My body *misses* him, even though he's right here. It aches for him. Drives me toward him in a way I never knew was possible.

It's surreal to think I could ever feel this way for a dragon, that my body would ever crave a shifter's touch like this. It's not just desire.

It's *need*.

But somehow, this is real. I can't deny it—I can only try to understand what's happening and regain control.

"You can't defy me like that," he says gently, breaking the spell.

Ugh.

He can't even have a sweet moment—he has to assert himself at any opportunity.

My anger momentarily overrides my body's desire for him. No longer ensnared by his touch, I frown. "You can't order me around like that."

He groans. "Rory, this is serious. You don't know this world, and—"

"You don't know *anything* about me," I snap. "You don't know what I can do. You don't know what I've done, or how much of your world I understand. Stop assuming I'm weak."

This catches his attention, and a blurry mix of confusion and concern crosses his face. "Explain."

"I'm not some damsel, Jace." I stand, pushing the chair backward.

He doesn't give an inch, but neither do I. The chair topples over behind me, and we stand mere breaths apart. He squares his shoulders like he's digging in for a long argument, but I'm just not interested in having one.

I press my finger into his chest to drive home my point. "I'm not going to sit obediently in some tower while you order me around and shield me from the world."

He frowns. "You still haven't explained anything."

"And I'm not going to." I glare at him, the urgency of my impending rescue taking precedence over his need to control me.

He lifts his chin defiantly. "Then I will continue to treat you as though you know nothing about dragon culture."

"And you will continue to be frustrated as I ignore your commands." I cross my arms.

"Damn it, woman." He begins to pace again, his anger returning. "What you did out there—that wasn't just reckless. It was possible suicide! We don't know for sure that Mason had your location. We don't—"

"Guy Durand knows what I am." I train my glare on the thunderbird, not really asking.

Jace lets out a brief sigh of frustration. "He had a vague idea, yes."

"Guy had the audacity to challenge you in your own dojo."

"Yes," Jace says again, eyes narrowing in suspicion as he entertains my train of thought.

"And Guy was allowed to live after your duel."

"Rory, if you have some sort of point to make, just do it."

Huh.

Fine.

I set my hands on my hips. "Right before the duel, Guy threatened me. He said once you were dead, I wouldn't get the comforts I—."

"He *threatened* you?" Jace bristles, looking like he's ready to hunt Guy down and finish what he started.

I frown. "It's fine. I knew he would lose."

Despite his anger, a brief but prideful smile pulls at the edges of Jace's mouth. "I'm glad you think so highly of me."

"You're still an ass." I can't suppress a grin. Though I want to grimace or roll my eyes in annoyance, Jace just gets to me in ways no one else does.

He sighs, rubbing the back of his neck. "Yeah, I can be."

"Look," I say, trying to refocus the conversation. "I don't know who forced you to give him the role as your second, but he played you all. He never had any intentions of obeying you. He just wanted your spot."

"I *know*, Rory." Jace rubs his face. "I've been in the process of outing him, of documenting his transgressions. He has contacts in another family, which is treason for a man who ranked as high as he did." Jace pinches the bridge of his nose in frustration. "We suspected he had connections to the Vaer."

My mouth drops open, and for the first time in ages, I'm dumbfounded. "And you let him remain at his post?"

"We had no proof!" Jace gestures to the door, most likely in the vague direction of the command center. "He's a coward, but he's a sneaky little bastard. He covered every track, deleted every communication—"

"And that's why you were concerned when Mason showed up." I close my eyes as it all starts to make sense. "You thought he was perhaps there on Guy's behalf, and you were trying to milk more information out of him."

Jace snorts in annoyance. "Yes, until *you* barged in and ruined everything."

"I didn't ruin a damn thing, and you know it." I give the shifter a curt once-over. "He was here to talk to me *because* Guy told him I'm here."

"You had no way of—"

"I've faced Mason twice before and *won*, Jace." I smack my hand on the table for emphasis. "He and I have unfinished business, and he had something I needed. My business with him is my own."

Business I intend to finish, once and for all.

"And that is?" Jace crosses his arms, lifting one eyebrow in expectation.

"Complicated." I set my hands on my hips, unwilling to betray any more than that.

Mason is an asshole, but he's right about one thing —once these dragons learn what I am, they will probably want to rip me to shreds.

Mate-protected or no.

"So that's it." Jace runs his hands through his hair, pacing as he shakes his head in frustration. "You're not going to tell me anything. You expect me to just trust you and do what you say."

"It's what you're asking of *me*," I point out.

He sighs, shutting his eyes as he tries to calm down. "Touché."

"If we're done, I need some air." I head for the door, mind already racing ahead to where I can secure a vehicle for the long trip ahead of me.

"Wait." He gently grabs my arm, pulling me to him.

I let him, mostly because my anger is slowly fizzling out. My treacherous body longs for him again. As ribbons of desire snake through me from his touch, I resist the impulse to lean into his hard chest. It takes everything in me not to throw my arms around his neck and kiss him deeply.

Instead, I simply look at him expectantly, waiting to hear whatever it is he wants to say.

"To answer your question earlier, mate-guarded means my dragon has chosen you." He sighs, not looking at me, though his thumb tenderly rubs across my wrist. "It means my dragon has imprinted on you in a way that will never happen again to anyone else. It means we're connected, for better or worse, always."

He looks at me then, those stormy gray eyes snaring me as the weight of what he's saying hits me.

The blow to the chest when I saw him in the court-yard. The way my body aches for him. This is all dragon-magic.

"You *did* put some kind of spell—"

"No, no." He laughs. Though I should be furious, I'm once more distracted by his dashing smile. "It's just something that happens to us. To thunderbirds. Fire and ice dragons don't have the powerful pull to find a mate like we do. We can't help it. I can't control it. It just… happens."

I frown, still skeptical, though the reality of what he's saying is slowly dawning on me. "So, being your mate means—"

"Well, it means…" He rubs his jaw, trying to find the words. "Look, a dragon is tied to his human self in ways that are deep and primal. What I want, he wants. And vice versa."

"Okay," I say hesitantly, waiting for him to get to the point.

"So," he continues, "being my mate means he wants you and only you. Nothing else will make him—and therefore me—happy. It means I want you. Only you. Forever. No one else will ever come close, and no one else will be good enough for my dragon."

Oh.

Oh, no.

"That's… a lot to process," I confess.

"Which is why I didn't want to tell you," he says. "Well, at least not until we got to know each other better."

"You mean like when you dragged me into your room while you were stark naked?"

"Yeah, about that…" He chuckles, a devious little grin on his face. "I got carried away. That's the other part of our bond. We're being called to complete the connection, so to speak, and it's driving us both crazy.

It's driving me mad, anyway." He shrugs. "We're not fully connected until we, you know…"

"Fuck."

He rolls his eyes. "That's not quite how I would have put it."

Uh huh.

Wait a minute…

A flash of anger burns hot within me. "So, you were trying to have sex with me, never explaining the ramifications of what that would actually do?"

"I got carried away." He sets his hands on my shoulders, his stormy gaze snaring me. "I'm sorry."

Briefly, my anger softens, and all I can do is study his striking face in surprise. I've never heard Jace apologize before. It's not really something I thought he even did.

Still, it's not enough to cool my brewing rage.

Jace stutters for a moment, clearly flustered. "Look, you don't have to forgive me right now." He gently squeezes my shoulders and reluctantly releases me. "With everything that's happening, it's hard to just find time to get to know each other. But we will."

He smiles warmly, and oddly enough, that's what melts my anger. His relaxed shoulders. The hint of hope and joy on his face. The assumption that he and I are going to be okay—eventually. That we'll fall in love. That I'll eventually stop fighting him—fighting *this*—and just give in.

But this poor, sexy dragon shifter has no idea who I am. *What* I am.

It leaves me speechless, and all I can think is that I don't want to hurt him. If the mate-bond is as powerful as he says, I'm fairly certain I'm destined to devastate him. Maybe break him.

I can't—I *won't*—do that. Not to Jace.

I sigh. Damn, I really am going soft.

"It's okay," he says softly, though his smile fades. "There's no rush to this. None." He lifts his hands, laughing a little. "I mean, I knew I wouldn't mate with a weak-willed woman, but good lord I wasn't expecting someone with *your* fire." He laughs harder and takes a few steps around the table, putting some space between us.

I nod. I just don't know what to say.

"Rory, I know Mason said something to you at the gate." Jace pauses, training his gray eyes on me. "It's becoming increasingly clear to me that you know more about dragons than you're letting on, and worse, you're more willing to risk your life than you should be."

I cross my arms, wondering if he has a point.

"Whatever you do, don't bite." Jace leans against the wall, his hands in his pockets as he watches me. "Don't take the bait, because that's what this is. Don't fall into his trap. Because if you die—"

His voice breaks, and he looks at the ground. In the

silence that follows, I'm left to use my imagination to fill the gaps in what he's telling me.

The mate-bond seems stronger than I thought. I wonder what my death would do to him. If he would break.

The thought is so foreign—that anyone but Irena would care if I die. That anyone but her would even notice.

"Don't go," he says softly.

It sounds *almost* like a request, perhaps as close to one as Jace can get.

My heart twists, and my body urges me to hold him. The drive to give in to him, to this, to *us* is overpowering, the strongest it's ever been. As I stand by the door, I feel like I'm fighting hurricane winds just to remain still, instead of staggering to him and inhaling his warm, woody scent.

But the drive to save Irena is stronger.

Without a word, I turn the knob on the door. As it opens, I once more fight the urge to stay. Grimacing, I push forward.

Because if Irena dies, I will never forgive myself.

Never.

CHAPTER THIRTY-NINE

As I steal through the hallways toward Tucker's room, I can't shake the image of Jace's wounded expression when I left.

To everyone else, he's a hardened master who accepts nothing less than perfection. Nothing less than order. Nothing less than absolute obedience.

But toward me, he softens. His unshakeable resolve weakens. He's tender and, in his own weird way, doting.

It's strange to think I have that kind of influence over someone—especially on a powerful man like Jace.

The sun casts shadows across the hallway at the top of the stairwell that leads to my room. Tucker's door is unlocked, and I let myself in. Deep in the suite, muffled by a few closed doors, droplets of water hit the shower floor. I weave my way toward the bedroom to find the covers just as I left them earlier, right down to the decoy pillow I gave a sleeping Tucker to snuggle. I smile and head for the bathroom, and a plume of steam rolls past me as I peek inside.

The warm fog from a hot shower soothes my face as I silently let myself in. It's fine—I'll just wait for him to finish.

More out of habit than anything else, I sit on the counter without making a sound. No footsteps, not even a rustle of fabric as I get comfortable. Absently, I tap my finger against my jaw as my mind races over my conversation with Jace.

I bite my lip in an effort to distract myself. I really can't think about him. Not right now. I need to focus.

My choice is clear—I have to save Zurie first.

An agonizing pang rips through my chest, but this is the way it has to be.

Irena is, and always *will* be, my top priority. My big sister has saved my ass more times than I can count, and I would give up anything to save her life.

But a good warrior has humility—and I can admit I'm out of my league.

Except perhaps for Mason, Zurie is the *only* one who knows what happened to make Irena sick. Zurie is the *only* one who knows what the antidote is. Even if I found a way to storm the compound solo and get Irena out, I wouldn't have the first clue of how to wake her up. Hell, she might even die on me. I know basic first aid, but Irena needs serious medical help and monitoring.

Of the people I can trust with Irena's life, only Zurie knows how to bring Irena back.

My intuition screams for me to go to Irena first, but even if I did, I really don't think I could keep her alive long enough to find the antidote and revive her. The Vaer are most likely keeping her alive as bait, if nothing else, and they won't kill her after I save Zurie. They still want to have leverage on me, and they wouldn't dispose of the only thing they have left that I want.

It's a dangerous bet—and I hate to bet with Irena's life—but I believe they will keep her alive even if I rescue Zurie first.

They need me, and therefore, they need her. Alive.

I grimace. I hate taking this risk. It breaks my heart, but I have to put my emotions aside. Right now, logic has to win.

But as I debate how to rescue my mentor, I begin to have second thoughts.

Before, this was easy. Find mentor. Save sister. Everything goes back to the way it was.

I lift my hands, studying my fingers, feeling the faint pulse of the magic l deep within me.

Now, it will *never* go back to the way it was. Not with this ancient power I possess. I'm the dragon vessel, something between human and shifter, given this sacred magic by supposed gods. I'm something else, something *other*, and I'm no fool.

Zurie will never let me keep this. Not if I want to remain a Spectre. Not if I want to stay alive.

It won't matter that she raised me. It won't matter that she's known me since before I can remember. She has never treated me like a daughter, and I see no reason for her to start now.

I frown and lean my head back against the mirror, staring at the steam as it shifts and swirls above me.

My childhood was brutal, my training cruel. But I have to confess, there were moments of something beautiful.

Moments where Zurie helped me to stand after a devastating fall. Moments where she smiled at me—and only me—with pride. Moments where she squeezed my shoulder while I was holding back tears, never looking at me—but with the gesture, I knew she was there. That I wasn't alone.

Over the years, she was adamant I never call her Mother. But in the lonely moments, in those times when there's a flicker of something more than the mission between us, I can't help but hope.

Zurie won't like what I am, now. But she might still like me enough to look the other way.

Lost in my torturous thoughts, I rub my face as the thick humidity starts to bead on my skin.

Emotions. Feelings. Ugh. This isn't working.

For me to make a rational choice, I need to do what I always do—weigh my options.

Option one: hide what I am from Zurie. Hide my magic.

This is barely worth considering. With the rumors spreading, with my identity leaked by that asshat Mason, there's no way to hide this from her. Even if that weren't the case, however, I can't control my magic—one wrong move, one difficult fight, and I could betray everything.

Nope. Strike. Next.

Option two: tell Zurie I'm the dragon vessel.

I grimace at the mere thought, but I need to at least consider this. I have to explore every alternative and weigh the risks.

Zurie will tell me that I am a disgrace. Dragons are the enemy, and an obedient Spectre destroys anything connected to a dragon in any way. She will demand I pour my efforts either into finding a way to give up the magic or to kill myself to be rid of it.

I refuse to do either.

My heart skips beats at the thought of defying a direct order. In all my years, I've never flat-out disobeyed my mentor before.

Not once.

To do so breaks rule number one.

Even if I can give up the magic, it would be foolish to do so. My power is immense and growing every day.

If Zurie sees reason, she and I can become allies. Only she has the power to pardon me from the other Spectres, to allow me to honorably leave an organization that punishes desertion with death. Even if the other Spectres don't accept me for what I am now, they would have to obey Zurie.

I shake my head, frowning. It just seems like such a fantasy.

Option three: leave my mentor to die.

Instantly, my throat stings at the thought. All those moments through my life, all those lessons she taught me, all the times I hoped I could one day think of her as family.

But I have to see this through.

If Zurie dies without me or Irena around to take over for her, Diesel is the next in line. My nose wrinkles with disgust. He would try to use me, and when that fails, he'll order hits on me and everyone I love. Everyone I've spoken to. Everyone who's helped me.

Even though he wants Irena, I think he would want power more. He would definitely have her killed, too.

That man can't be reasoned with.

Beyond a life of Diesel as the Ghost, a deep part of me rebels at the image of Zurie lying dead in a dragon cell. The thought of me being the only thing between her death and survival is almost too much to bear. Forget that she's the Ghost—without her, I might not have lived this long at all. She's awful in many ways, but I still owe her a great deal.

Zurie is cruel. She raised me to kill, molded me and Irena into assassins, but she also instilled in us a deep sense of loyalty and honor from a young age.

That loyalty burns within me, and it's impossible to ignore.

She will never say it, but Zurie is more than my mentor. She's the closest thing I will ever have to a mother. Irena and I are true family, our bond unbreakable and stronger than anything on earth, but Zurie's connection to us is close.

And because of that bond, I hope I can make her see reason.

I grimace. These options all suck. If I save her, she could come after me with a vengeance. If I let her die, I will always wonder—if I had tried, would things have been different?

The Spectres will come after me regardless of whether or not Zurie leads the attack. That's irrelevant. Yes, she knows me better than the others, knows my weaknesses, knows my ability and limits. But I suspect there's a backup, a docket somewhere that lists those for every Spectre, lest the Ghost die.

I suspect that somewhere in the organization, someone else knows all of my weaknesses, too.

Hmm.

Briefly, I toy with a wicked and sinful little thought.

If I could save Irena, and if Zurie were left to die, Irena would become the Ghost by matter of hierarchy. While she hasn't been initiated formally, this is a gray area. No one would challenge Irena, except perhaps for Diesel, and he would lose. With Irena as the Ghost, I would be safe. Though I'm not sure what Zurie will do, I know Irena better than anyone. My sister would never come after me, no matter what I am. She would demand they leave me be and kill anyone who defies her.

But that would mean letting Zurie die, and yet again, my heart twists with guilt.

I still don't know how to bring Irena back without Zurie, so my plan hasn't changed. I still have to rescue Zurie first.

Ugh.

If this is going to work, I have to be careful. My one chance is to appeal not to the brutal assassin who trained me, but to the woman deep within Zurie—the woman who raised me, who watched me grow, who I believe loves me in her own, fractured way.

There's a high chance this could all backfire, but I must convince her I'm not a threat to the Spectres. If she's willing to listen, I won't have to fight off assassins for the rest of my life.

I sigh. This is either going to work brilliantly or fail miserably.

But I must at least *try*.

One thing, however, is abundantly clear: I am no longer a Spectre. To remain one, I would have to give up my magic—something I wouldn't do even if I knew how.

My life as a Spectre was one of survival. Of the day-to-day. Of near-mindless obedience.

As the dragon vessel, my life is one of power. I don't just survive anymore—I thrive.

But no one is allowed to leave the Spectres.

As much as I hate it, I'm finally clear on what I need to do.

The question burning in my soul is simple. When I rescue Zurie, will I be able to convince her I'm an ally? Or am I about to rescue the deadliest enemy I could ask for?

The shower water shuts off and, seconds later, the curtain pulls aside to reveal a very naked Tucker.

He flinches when he sees me and sets a hand on his heart. Once the brief surprise fades, he throws his head back as he laughs. "Damn it, woman, will you stop *doing* that?"

"Probably not." I shrug. "Listen. I need to rescue a friend who doesn't like dragons, but this place is too big for me to hit solo. You down for a little adventure?"

For a moment, Tucker just looks at me, grinning. "Did hell freeze over, or did you really ask me for help?"

Even though I'm not in the mood for banter, I

chuckle. I'm pretty sure he could even make me laugh in a firefight. "So, is that a yes, or—"

"Duh."

I nod. Good. As a human, Tucker won't be at risk around Zurie. She won't like having a Knight around, but she would put up with it if he saves her.

Tucker grabs a towel but never bothers to cover his thick cock, which hardens as my eyes naturally drift toward it. I grin, shaking my head, and he lifts his eyebrows expectantly. "See something you like?"

"Maybe." I hop off the sink and walk into the bedroom, just to tease him.

He follows shortly after. I let him wrap his semi-dry arms around me as he gently glides his nose along my neck. His lips pepper kisses along my skin, and I briefly smile at the indulgent delight of his touch.

His hard cock presses between my thighs, trying to pry them apart. Despite everything on my mind, I'm tempted to throw him on the bed, to ride him and take back the control I let him have earlier.

But right now, I need to focus. I'll need that energy and adrenaline in the upcoming fight, so I shouldn't use it now.

He lands a last kiss on my cheek. "I know I'm distractingly pretty, so I'll get dressed."

I grin, shaking my head. "You're ridiculous."

He trots into the closet, and for a moment, I hear the

rustling of fabric. Instead of coming out with clothes, however, he brings out two long-range sniper rifles. "Is it going to be a 'hide in the bushes' kind of assault, dear, or are we going for a 'stab you in the face' vibe?"

I laugh, trying not to let my eyes wander over his beautifully naked body. "Definitely a 'stab you in the face' vibe."

"Roger." He walks back into the closet, and I hear the metallic clink of gun metal. "I'm still bringing the sniper rifle."

"That's fine," I say with a chuckle. "You do you, babe."

"Don't ever stop calling me that!" he shouts from the closet. "Ever, you here?"

Instead of answering, I smile to myself and lean against the wall as I wait. "Where did you get those guns?"

"Borrowed them from Jace." Tucker leans against the doorframe and tosses me a pistol.

I chuckle as I catch it and check the clip. Should have known.

As Tucker walks back into the closet, the mood begins to shift. The air between us feels a little heavier. A bit somber. Serious.

We're both preparing for war.

I have to admit, it's nice to know I won't be going in alone. I used to dream of solo missions—of freedom—

but it's a comfort to know someone has my back. To know every angle is covered.

Levi, Jace, and Drew won't like any of this, of course. Jace wants to lock me in a tower, but Levi and Drew would probably want to help. I just can't allow it. I can't allow them anywhere near Zurie because she will try to kill them before I can get so much as a word in.

If she sees a dragon, she shoots. There's never mercy. There's never a moment to debate the choice. I don't even think she feels anything anymore when she pulls the trigger. Except maybe recoil.

She just goes for the kill, and if she sets her sights on my men, I'll have to break rule number one.

I sigh, once again wondering when I got so gooey that I would feel this devoted to dragons, some of whom have been nothing but annoyingly sexy jerks.

But if I'm being honest, I kind of love it.

CHAPTER FORTY

I once more sit on the roof of the tallest spire, watching the sun set on the horizon. The possible escape routes out of this place are few and far between, and it looks like we'll have to use Tucker's tunnel to get out.

Since the Knights know about that route—at least part of it—I don't love the idea. However, given the sheer limitations of this unscalable fortress, it's the best one we have.

I try to ignore the stares of the dragons manning the walls. Some don't even pretend to keep to their posts, and nearly every dragon head is turned toward me. They sit on the walls, blue and red islands among the black stone, their intense gazes trained on my face.

And I wonder.

I wonder if they finally know what I am. Where the

magic bubbling through me comes from. I wonder what it means if they do. Jace won't let them hurt me, but I wonder what these dragons might try when he's distracted.

Poor souls. I dare them to try.

Movement by the window up onto my patch of roof catches my attention, and I tilt my head enough to see who's about to join me. Two strong hands grip the edge, and seconds later, Drew pulls himself effortlessly onto the dark shingles.

He doesn't look at me. His strides are slow and smooth, utterly at home two hundred feet in the air. Without a word, he sits beside me, propping a knee and leaning an elbow on it casually. He scans the horizon without ever acknowledging my existence.

Below, every one of the guards goes back to his or her post. Suddenly, they're involved in their surveillance and forget I'm here.

All because of Drew.

"You're certainly feared," I say casually, pretending I'm bored instead of morbidly curious.

"I wouldn't say that." He shrugs, still scanning the sky.

"Then what *would* you say?"

He briefly looks at me, that obnoxious smirk playing at the corners of his mouth.

Ugh.

Yet again, he's not going to tell me anything. He's

hot, he's strong, and there are a million tantalizing secrets floating around that gorgeous head of his, but this isn't going to fly with me.

"You want me to trust you, right?" I lift one eyebrow inquisitively.

He shrugs. "It would be nice, yes."

"It's not going to happen if you keep this up. I mean, come on—if you don't tell me anything, I have no reason to trust you."

"Not true." He shakes his head gently, then leans his chin into the crook of his elbow as he watches the sunset.

"Is that so?" I rub my eyes. Jesus, no one gets under my skin like this guy.

"I let you go at the swarm." His piercing eyes shift toward me, the only bit of him that moves. He looks like a predator, stoic and still, radiating power and calm.

"I *escaped* the swarm," I say stubbornly.

He tilts his head, a slightly annoyed expression on his face.

Yeah, fine. In that one moment, yes, he had me pinned. And in that one moment, yes, he let me go. It still doesn't count.

I cross my arms, refusing to indulge him.

"Okay, fine." He raises one eyebrow. "When the Andusk attacked, I saved you."

"I had it covered. If anything, you nearly got a bullet to the brain."

He laughs. "Damn, you're stubborn. Can't you give me any credit?"

"Nope." I smirk.

"Fine, then. When the Palarnes—"

"I don't know what you said to them, but you didn't save me. He was trying to convince me to go back with him, and I know enough about them to understand their moral fiber. He wouldn't have tried to take me."

I lean my hands on the black tiles, reclining on the roof as red ribbons of light snake through the clouds along the horizon. There's a moment of silence before I check on him in my periphery, only to find him watching me with silent curiosity.

But I have some questions of my own.

"Why did you want me to come here?" I tilt my chin downward, giving him a withering glare. "The *real* reason."

He sighs, still watching me silently, and it seems like he's not going to answer.

Again.

I groan, annoyed, and stand. Enough of this. I have a mentor to save and a sister to rescue. I can't wait around all day for this enigma to finally speak more than five words to me.

As I pass him, he reaches toward me so quickly I

can't move in time. It's too fast. Too sudden even for my instincts to kick in.

For someone to get the jump on me like that is deeply alarming. Instead of grabbing me, however, he gently brushes his fingers along my wrist.

I watch him, confused and curious. As his hand touches my skin, sparks of delight dance up my arm. My knees go momentarily weak, and I stop mid-stride to keep from falling. My heart skitters in my chest, and I hate the way my body reacts to these men.

To these dragons.

But only a few of them. My blood runs hot, but at least my traitorous body is picky.

"What?" I say abruptly, trying to use exasperation to mask the effect his touch has on me.

"At first, all I wanted was your power," he says softly, his voice gentle. There's a hint of sadness, of remorse, and that alone catches my attention.

We study each other's faces for a moment, neither of us wanting to speak next. His obnoxious smirk is gone, replaced with a gentle smile. It's almost... affectionate. On a man as dominant and commandeering as Drew, it's surreal to see such a gentle expression.

And he's looking at *me*.

"I wanted to use you," he confesses, standing. He gives me space, his broad shoulders blocking my view of the sunset as he towers over me, all muscle and power.

"You and everyone else," I say, crossing my arms, trying to hide my disappointment.

"But the longer I watched you..." He sighs, rubbing the back of his neck as he tries to form words. "I respect you, Rory. Nothing stops you. Nothing slows you down. Nothing deters you. You're the most tenacious woman I've ever met, and I admire that. Watching you fight, seeing you move—it changed things for me."

He looks at me, his expression softening. His shoulders relax, and I see in his face something more than what he's saying. There's a gentle pleading, there. Something unspoken, something he doesn't dare say, at least not yet.

His eyes drop to my lips, and I notice the almost imperceptible way he leans toward me, like he wants to do more than just look.

I remember his conversation with Jace, the way he was so possessive over me. Over what he wanted for me, what he hoped Jace could do for me. But most importantly, how he never would have sent me here if he'd known Jace's dragon had claimed me as its mate.

The loss in his voice. The pain.

Drew wants me. He wants more than he's willing to admit.

But I'm not an idiot. I question how much I can trust this man. He's clearly influential. Feared. Powerful. He understands far more than he lets on, and I know without a doubt that I will never unravel all of Drew's secrets.

He could still just want to use me. And even if he doesn't, I'm not a one-man kind of girl. I may not be a Spectre anymore, but that doesn't change the fact I was raised with them. That's my normal. My culture. A Spectre doesn't take just one partner, and it's pretty clear dragons don't like to share.

"Rory," he says soothingly. Tenderly. His deep voice rolls over me, sending a delightful little shiver down my spine.

A flash of heat burns between my thighs, and my treasonous body briefly aches for his thick fingers to brush aside my underwear and search for my entrance. I quickly suppress the image, astonished at how hot the dragon magic makes me burn.

Makes me *ache*.

He closes the gap between us, not touching me, just watching. When his solid, rock-hard chest is merely inches away, I can feel the heat radiating from him. He reminds me of a sauna, of sweat and skin.

He lifts a hand toward a lock of hair covering part of my face, but he hesitates. Briefly, he watches me, likely to see what I'll do.

I wait.

Drew gently tucks the lock of hair behind my ear, and his warm thumb brushes my cheek. A flurry of desire swirls through me at his touch, but I never let it show on my face.

None of these dragons can know what they do to me.

"I know Mason tempted you with something," Drew says quietly. "My best guess is he probably gave you information you've been after for a while, but you can't go for it. The Vaer can't be trusted. They're liars, they're cheats, and they will scam you. Guaranteed."

I resist the impulse to roll my eyes. He and Jace can't seem to get enough of ordering me around.

"Look," Drew says with a sigh. "I get it. You don't know me yet. You don't trust me, but you need to know this. The Vaer want you. Bad. They will do anything, kill anyone, destroy everything between them and you. They're on a warpath. I don't know what you did to piss them off, but you're all they talk about anymore."

Hmm. How interesting.

Apparently, Drew monitors Vaer communications —just like Jace, he must have access to advanced surveillance tech. In which case, he must be even more influential than I thought.

His eyes rove over my face, and he takes one more step toward me, his hard body finally pressing against mine as he looks down at me. "Who are you going after, Rory?"

I lift my chin to meet his gaze, entirely unfazed by

how much he seems to know. At this point, I'm no longer surprised.

He knows the Vaer have at least one person I care about.

He just doesn't know who she is, or what we did to piss them off.

And he doesn't *get* to know.

We simply sit in the silence that follows. Anyone else would have filled the quiet with chatter, but not him. Drew isn't afraid of a lull.

Neither am I.

He nods, apparently understanding I won't give him anything, and smiles. "I know a woman like you can't be forced into anything, Rory. I respect that."

"Thanks." I set my hands on my hips, wondering what other little secrets I'll learn about Drew today.

He runs his fingers along my hair again, this time trailing his fingertips along my neck. His caress is pleasant and soothing, igniting flashes of warmth along the route his fingers take across my skin.

Bit by bit, I lose control of the mask I use to hide the effect he has on me. My cocky little smile begins to fade, and I simply watch him, a little breathless.

"Whoever she is," he says quietly, "this woman you're saving? I suspect she's equally as talented as you. If you go, I suggest you find a place for her far from here—and that you return alone."

Ah.

I sigh and look toward the courtyard, doing the first thing I can think of to break the magnetic pull his gaze has on me.

He's so damn perceptive. Right now, he's dancing around the fact that I'm part of an organization the other dragons here won't like. He has to know at this point that I have special training, and I wonder if he's pieced it together yet.

Judging by the fact that he's not killing me, I suspect he hasn't. He probably doesn't want to act until he knows for sure.

He presses his warm palm against my neck, wrapping his thick fingers around the back of my head, and my mind swims in the pleasure of his touch. "Whatever you really are, Rory, you have my respect."

My heart skips a beat at the implication, and I wonder if this is a trap.

I don't answer. I simply study his face, waiting for him to continue. Wishing I could believe him. Wishing there was any dragon alive who could really accept me that unconditionally.

"And, whatever you are," he continues, "I won't let you get hurt. Neither will Jace. We may hate each other, but we won't let our disagreements get in the way of keeping you alive."

He gently kisses my forehead, his warm lips sending a flurry of desire through me, and leaves. He doesn't look back as he returns through the window, disappearing from the roof.

I run my fingers over my forehead, over the lingering tingle of his kiss. I'm not sure what to make of him. He's overbearing and dominant, and yet has this hint of something softer, of someone who's gentle and kind.

Logically, I don't want to trust anyone, but in my heart, there's the flicker of intuition. I think he might actually be telling the truth. I squeeze my eyes shut, trying to suppress the hope.

As amazing as that would be, I don't want to get too optimistic. That's burned me before—and gotten more than one Spectre killed.

CHAPTER FORTY-ONE

I have one last thing to do before we go, and I really —*really*—don't want to do it.

I steal into the small courtyard at the back of the embassy to find my ice dragon still keeping watch. He sits on his perch, on the edge of the wall, the tip of his tail sweeping along the ground as he watches the skies.

His ear flicks toward me as I race down the stairs, somehow picking up on my movement even as I dash silently through the growing night.

Clever dragon.

His head pivots toward me, and a happy growl escapes him. As he did earlier, he leaps off the wall and meets me as I reach the final step. With his forehead pressed against my body, he hums softly in welcome.

I run my fingers over his scales, and as our connection opens, a surge of delight funnels from him. He murmurs happily, and I melt a little in the swirling warmth of his emotions. No one but him is ever this happy to see me, and it brings me immense joy.

It's also why I'm here.

I'm going to be gone for a little bit, I tell him, deciding to rip off the band-aid. *But I need you to stay here.*

He snorts in anger, and a thin plume of icy mist escapes his nose. The delight blurs with frustration and suspicion, and I feel him tug on my mind through the connection.

I resist. I need to stay focused, and if anyone can sway me at this point, it's Levi. I can't give in.

Stay here, I tell him. *Stay out of trouble. I'll be back. This is the safest place for you.*

I hope.

I've been over this in my head again and again, but it's the only option that makes sense. Jace won't let anything happen to anyone I care about—and he knows I care about Levi. Anyone else, *anywhere* else, would kill Levi instantly for being feral.

Staying here is his one shot at survival.

He snarls, his lip curling as the sound rumbles through him. His body reverberates, and the powerful vibration tunnels through my chest.

"Don't give me that," I snap at him, smacking him on the neck.

He presses his forehead against my body so hard that I stagger backward into the castle wall, thrown momentarily off balance. I once more feel the tug at my mind as he tries to take me deeper into the connection.

This time, he wins.

The world around me fades to darkness as he pulls me under. Images flash through my mind too fast to process, too quick to even see. Emotions swirl within me—love and anger, lust and possessiveness. Desire. Joy. And just a hint of fear.

Rory. His voice echoes through my mind.

All at once, the blurring images stop, and I'm facing the man I saw in the mirror when I first met the ice dragon in an abandoned field.

Levi—his human self, the part of him that's locked away within the dragon before me.

He holds either side of my face, those piercing blue eyes staring into me, penetrating every shield and defense I have. He looks into me, knowing more, seeing everything, all without saying a word.

My heart hurts, looking at him. It hurts to feel so raw, to have someone look into me and see everything. I tense, trying to push away, but he only holds me tighter.

You're safe with me. Not out there.

My thoughts bubble to the surface, and with a connection this raw, this intense, I don't know if I can hold them back.

I try, but the most painful thought slips through.

Zurie will kill you, and I can't let that happen. It would destroy me.

His expression shifts, his eyes widening slightly in surprise, and I wonder how much of the truth he saw. If he knows who Zurie is. What I am.

In a rush, the embassy returns, and I fall to my knees. I suck in deep breaths, and my chest aches. Hand on my heart, I struggle to regain my composure.

I'm not used to feeling or allowing emotions more than a fleeting moment or two before shoving them away. Levi, however, seems to make me feel in ways no one else can.

I love it and hate it in equal measure.

The ice dragon sighs and lays down, his massive head at my feet, looking at me with pleading eyes. His expression says everything his thoughts would have —*don't go.*

"I have to," I say softly.

He lets out a sad little moan and nips at my boot, untying the lace with a sharp tug of his teeth. Despite the thundering ache still lingering in my chest, I chuckle. It'll take more than that to make me stay.

He nudges my boot softly with his nose and shuts his eyes. I kneel, gently rubbing my hand along his face.

I lose track of how long I'm there, patting him, soothing him. Eventually, his breathing slows and evens out. It reminds me of when we first met, when he curled around me and slept by the dying embers of a fire.

But I know him well enough by now. He's probably faking. Even if he really is sleeping, he'll know when I leave—and not even I will be able to hear if he follows.

I sigh and stand, jogging back into the embassy to my rendezvous point with Tucker. Deep down, all I can do is hope my ice dragon won't do anything foolish— either while I'm gone, or by following me.

Because if he follows me, I don't see how he could possibly survive.

CHAPTER FORTY-TWO

Asphalt blurs past the headlights of the car I stole just outside of the embassy's land. Tucker has his window down, and the wind whips through my hair as we speed down a sideroad toward the coordinates I stole—er, *borrowed*—from Jace's command center.

Tucker's been staring at me for the last ten minutes, and I'm just pretending not to notice. I have enough on my plate right now as it is.

He finally sighs, rubbing his forehead as he decides how to word what he wants to say.

Tense and a little concerned about what lies ahead of us, my grip tightens on the wheel. "Do we *really* need to talk about this now, or can it wait?"

"Now." His voice is deep and tense. Certain. Confident.

Damn.

I sigh. "Fine."

"Rory, I would follow you anywhere." He rubs his jaw. "I would follow you to hell and trust we wouldn't go unless we had a good reason, but this joyride of yours is different. I see it in the way you tense every time we talk about the mission. I see it in your face every time you drift off into thought. We're going to a different kind of hell, but you don't know what the outcome is going to be—and that concerns me."

My jaw tenses, and for a little while, I don't answer. It's probably annoying to him, but I just don't know what to say.

"You trust me," he eventually says.

I look over to find him watching me intently. It's an observation, not a question.

I nod.

"You want me," he adds.

Again, not a question.

I nod once more.

In my periphery, I see him recline against the seat, a blurred expression of contentment and frustration. Happiness that I want and trust him, but disappointment that I won't answer what should ideally be a simple and straightforward question.

But worst of all, I see him holding back. I study his face, and he looks like he's restraining a monologue's worth of confessions. He has so much he wants to say, and for whatever reason, he doesn't feel like he can tell me any of it.

That's what breaks me.

That's what makes me want to tell him everything— the thought that if I don't, *he* might lose faith in *me.*

I briefly shut my eyes to steel myself for what I'm about to do. What I'm about to confess. The severity of everything I'm about to share—and how he might react.

When I'm ready, I keep my eyes on the road and just dive in.

"We're going to rescue my mentor," I say softly, my grip tightening again on the wheel. "She's... brutal. Unforgiving. Not entirely fond of Knights, but she doesn't hate them either."

"And..." He lifts one eyebrow, daring me to stop talking.

"*And,*" I say, a hint of annoyance creeping through my nerves. I sigh, the anger dissolving as quickly as it came. "And I'm a Spectre. We're going to save the Ghost."

I brace myself.

Here it comes.

The anger. The betrayal. The moment I might lose him entirely. Because even though the Knights respect the Spectres, they don't always love us... and not all of them admire the Ghost.

Tucker stammers, his brain moving too fast for his

mouth to keep up. "You're a—and she's—that means you're—*Jesus* fucking *Christ*, Rory!"

I swallow hard, preparing myself for the worst.

"The Ghost." Tucker pales, rubbing the stubble along his jaw as he looks out the window. "And—well, damn, that makes you the second in command?"

"Third," I correct.

Irena is second.

"Oh, my god." Tucker runs his hand through his thick hair and looks everywhere but me as he processes this.

For a while, the whistle of the wind through the open window is all I hear. The road cuts through the forests beyond the embassy, and the quiet is beginning to unnerve me.

But I won't speak first. He needs time to fully process this, and I won't rush him.

"I knew you were something special," Tucker finally says. "I knew you were something else, maybe even connected to the Spectres, but that felt like a fantasy. I figured, no way—no one but my dad knows any of the Spectres for real. And you…" He laughs. "Holy shit. I never imagined for a second that you studied under the Ghost."

I look straight ahead, not wanting to see his face when I ask my next question. "Are you mad?"

"Mad?" His voice sounds incredulous. "No, Rory. It's just a lot to take in."

I look at him, then, to find him watching me with a tender expression, like he hadn't realized I was nervous until this moment.

"Do you still want to do this?" I ask.

He sighs and leans back into his seat. "The Ghost really is brutal. She and my father have worked together, and even he thinks she takes things too far."

I nod. It's true. She sometimes can. I never really saw it before my time away from her, but looking back, it's obvious.

Funny how a bit of distance can give me so much clarity.

Tucker shrugs. "I mean, I'm pretty sure this is a death sentence, but goddamn I love your sense of adventure."

Despite my anxiety, I laugh.

"Seriously, though. If she's your mentor…" Tucker leans his head back, staring at the ceiling for a bit. "I mean, I'll do anything for you, Rory."

I smile. I can't help it. "Thanks."

He grins. "'Thanks?' That's it? I declare my love for you, my willingness to ride into hell at your side, and all I get is a 'thanks?'"

I laugh, my nerves finally melting because of the wonderfully ridiculous man beside me. "Yep."

"No respect." He grins and closes his eyes, relaxing into his chair. "No respect at all."

As we drive through the night, I sneak the occasional peek at Tucker. He's calm, now. He got what he needed, and I realize with a content little smile that I did, too.

I trust him. I truly do.

And that breaks about forty Spectre rules.

CHAPTER FORTY-THREE

I lay on my stomach with Tucker at my side, eyeing the Vaer compound where Mason claims Zurie is being held.

It's a full army base with four security checkpoints and enough barbed wire fencing to protect against the apocalypse. The four-story building sprawls across a massive compound, with watch towers every hundred feet and a roving spotlight on the central guard tower in the middle of it all.

Seven dragons pace along the roof of the building. As they pass each other, they nip and snarl, growling and spreading their wings in challenge. Each tiff lasts only a few seconds, but it's clear even the *Vaer* hate each other.

This is the bait Mason laid for me, and he's learned by now that I don't bite unless there's something good on the line. I'm confident she's here. The question isn't *if* I'll find her here—it's how in the hell I'll get in, much less *out.*

"This is intense," I mutter, scanning the compound.

"Yeah, no kidding." Tucker peeks through the scope on his sniper rifle, taking in details I'm missing. "This place is crawling with shifters."

I tap my finger on my chin, lost in thought, a few ideas formulating in my head about how to get in.

The rumble of truck engines nearby catches my attention, followed by the hum of thick tires over asphalt. A small convoy of three Humvees races toward the first check point. The gates open long before the vehicles enter, and they don't even stop to do an ID check.

I scoff. Talk about horrible security. I expected more stringent protocols in a place like this.

"That must be someone important," Tucker says with a sneer. "What kind of security checkpoint doesn't do an ID check? They didn't even stop."

"Someone important, or they're further setting up the bait." I sigh. "They *want* me in there, Tucker. They just don't want me to *leave.*"

"Good point." He peeks through his scope again, angling the gun over the walls of the fortress. "What kind of traps do you think are waiting?"

"All of them."

He laughs. "Oh, good. Thanks for narrowing that down for me, babe."

I shake my head. "Just be ready for anything. We don't know if—"

My body hums in warning. Before I can process what might be the matter, a massive blue dragon's head is on the other side of me, inches away and resting calmly on the grass.

The next three seconds happen entirely on impulse. I twist my body away from him, grabbing my knife and angling it for the dragon's one soft spot in the skull by the ears, ready to drive it clear into the shifter's brain.

The only thing that stops me are a pair of familiar, piercing blue eyes.

"Levi, *damn it.*" I lay my face in the ground, the adrenaline still pumping through me.

My blood goes cold at how close I came to killing my ice dragon. My Levi.

"Jesus," Tucker says, returning his pistol to the holster at his side. Apparently, I'm not the only one who was taken completely off guard.

Levi snorts in a terse welcome, his intense gaze now trained on the fortress.

"Go back to the embassy!" I order, my voice as quiet as I can keep it despite my boiling anger. "Right *now!*"

He flicks his ear at me in annoyance, which only pisses me off more.

Before I can say anything, he presses his nose

against the back of my hand. As our connection opens, a swirling fog of anger rushes through.

His anger.

It's an overprotective surge, a sense of defending what's his, of doing what's right no matter the cost.

It would be noble if it weren't a suicide mission.

I'm helping you do this, he says, his voice thundering through my mind. *Whether you like it or not.*

You absolutely won't!

A confusing blend of defiance and curiosity rush through the connection from him. *Why?*

The truth springs immediately to mind, and I once more try to hide as much of it from him as I can.

Zurie. Her hatred of dragons. Her rigid rules.

He snorts in aggravation, icy mist swirling from his nose. *Why would you save someone so cruel?*

I sigh, biting my lip as I fight for the words to answer him. I break the connection, leaning on my elbows as I stare out at the compound once more.

But Levi isn't having it.

He presses his nose against the side of my face, forcefully reopening the connection.

Why? he presses.

I groan in annoyance and close my eyes, summoning the good memories I have of Zurie. Of the fleeting moments of affection. Of my loyalty to my mentor. Of my desire to at least try. Of what it would mean for me—and more importantly for the sister I love—if I fail.

Without Zurie, my odds of saving Irena drop to almost nil.

Levi simply watches me, drinking in my thoughts. He's still, and eventually, he sighs.

A surge of pride flows through our connection. *The people you love and protect are mine to love and protect as well.*

No. You need to—

I'm not leaving. His eyes narrow, daring me to try.

I groan. This ruins so much. Puts him in danger. Compromises the mission. I should cancel it entirely, but he'll just come next time, too—and I may not get another chance. *Fine. If you see Zurie, do not engage. Leave. Immediately.*

He snorts and breaks the connection, returning his attention to the compound, and I can't tell if that was agreement or refusal.

"We've got movement," Tucker says, interrupting our discussion.

Another convoy tears down the road, this one twice the size of the last. The gates come immediately up, but this time I recognize the passenger in the first car.

Mason.

"That's him, car one," I say to Tucker.

Tucker trains his scope on the vehicle. "Yep, that's our asshole."

I grit my teeth, trying to stifle my hatred. I need to focus, and emotions will only cloud my judgment.

The trucks pull up to a loading bay just past the final fence, and Mason shouts several orders I can't make out. His voice carries over the compound, loud but garbled as he runs inside.

"Something's happening," Tucker says, squinting as he peers through the scope.

"Details?" I wish we had binoculars, but it is what it is.

"None yet. Everyone's excited about something. Think they know we're here?"

"Nope. We would have visitors if they did."

Tucker shrugs. "Well, *something* is happening in there."

My heart stutters at the thought of Zurie escaping on her own. The idea that maybe she's racing through the compound, while Mason tries desperately to keep his bait in place.

"We need to get in there." I point toward the open bay door as another six soldiers charge by on foot. My eyes shift toward a door beneath the loading bay, accessible by a short flight of stairs, and I get a much better idea. "Actually, let's go in below."

"What—below?" Tucker lifts his brow in confusion.

"It looks like there's a maintenance tunnel down there." I point to it. "Those aren't patrolled as often as regular halls. It's our best bet."

"If you say so, Boss." Tucker sounds a little doubtful, but I know what I'm doing. Hell, I've done this before.

The rumble of another convoy catches my attention—our ride, if only Levi weren't with us. One way or another, Mason is going to regret making this easy for me.

"We need a distraction," I say absently, wondering how we can get as deep into the compound as possible without being seen. Something to draw their attention to the wrong side of the compound.

I run my hand through my hair as I debate my options, and only then do I notice Levi is missing.

My heart skips a beat, and I scan the forests behind us, cursing that damned dragon and his impossible stealth.

"Where in the hell did he—"

On the other side of the compound, an ear-splitting roar cuts through the night. Every shifter on the roof looks toward it, alert.

Levi tears out of the forests, unleashing a torrent of ice spikes at his unsuspecting prey. Several dragons are instantly speared through the heart and collapse, falling to the ground as their comrades race toward Levi. He unleashes another stream of ice, and it freezes an entire fire dragon solid. The shifter falls to the ground and shatters into a hundred pieces.

He's taking on the entire compound—alone. My

heart nearly seizes in my chest, and for a moment, I simply freeze with alarm.

"Well, you wanted a distraction." Tucker quickly stands, keeping his head low as he nods toward Levi. "That'll work."

As the convoy approaches, I don't even have time to process the full depths of my rage. If Levi gets himself killed, I'll never forgive him—or myself.

The onslaught has only just begun, and everything is already screwed to hell.

Oh, this will go *great.*

CHAPTER FORTY-FOUR

As a war amongst dragons wages outside, I press my back against the cold wall of the compound to catch my breath. Tucker pauses beside me, completely in sync, every step fluid with mine.

It's weird to lead, instead of follow. To give the commands.

I kind of like it.

The dark maintenance tunnel stretches on before me, lit only by the occasional uncovered light bulb every twenty feet or so. I've taken out a few of the cameras, using three of my precious few remaining voids, but this rescue is worth it.

I hope.

Hooked on my belt is a pair of walkie talkies I snagged on the way in. The panicked chatter of the

Vaer guards buzzes through the devices, the volume lowered to a soft hum. I dial down the volume a bit more, worried we'll be heard, even though this tunnel seems mostly deserted.

I listen for signs of Levi's onslaught, worried for my ice dragon, hoping he doesn't get himself killed. So far, he's holding a fair fight. The longer he goes and the more terrified they sound, the more confident I am in letting him take care of this.

After all, my focus needs to be on what *I* have to do.

Unfortunately, I have to turn this off. With a frown, I fiddle with both of the walkie talkies and tune them to a different frequency.

I have a plan, but I'm honestly not sure how well this is going to work. It's a best-of-the-worst situation.

Briefly, I wonder if Zurie ever has doubts like this. As she leads me or Irena through a mission, I wonder if she ever runs into dead ends. If she ever secretly fails and simply bluffs her way through the rough spots, never letting on how lost she really is.

Before this whole mess started, the very idea would have been laughable. But the more time I spend on my own, the more I begin to suspect that's exactly what she does. Bluff. Guess. Roll with the punches.

Tucker taps his knuckle against the back of my hand, and I tilt my body toward him with a curious twist of my eyebrow. It's a silent question from me to him—*what's wrong?*

He nods toward the walkie talkies with a confused expression, and I just smile.

You'll see, I silently mouth to him.

To his credit, Tucker shrugs. With a hint of a smile, he gestures for me to continue our expedition into the Vaer compound.

It's nice to be trusted.

As we sneak through the maintenance tunnel, I pause at every door and peek through the thin stretch of foggy glass at the top. I'm looking for a space with something specific—something I can use to my advantage, something I can use against the Vaer to keep them from shifting on me.

I can handle one shifted dragon by himself, but more than that is a death wish.

Kitchens. Nope. Might have knives, practically useless otherwise.

Boiler room. Eh. Not enough space, no real military advantage unless I want to take out the whole building, which I don't. Yet.

Garage. Hmm. The tanks and assorted motorbikes mean this might be useful later, but for now it's too visible. I pause, briefly considering this location anyway, but a horde of ten Vaer guards drive in on another convoy, and I decide against using this place to draw out Mason.

Because that's what I have to do—bring him to me.

Unless Zurie escaped—which I'm starting to doubt,

judging by the lack of panic on most of the faces I've come across so far—she's going to be locked away in quite possibly the most secure location on the facility.

That means I have to make Mason bring her to me, or better yet, bluff him into telling me where she is.

I'm on his turf, and the only way to catch him off guard is to take control of a small piece of it. To lure him out and let him think he's won.

I pause at the next door, peeking through another cloudy window to find a strange room full of what looks like storage crates. Tucker takes watch behind me, scanning the hall to give me the space to investigate.

Crates pile along the walls and in the middle of the room, towering in the massive space and creating a maze of possible passageways. I crane my neck as I look through the small pane of glass, only to find a catwalk three stories up. The elevated metal path curves along the edge of the room and, through the thin scope of the window, it seems like this massive chamber goes on for ages.

With all the crates, this must be a warehouse of some kind. Briefly, I wonder if the Vaer use this place to store their smuggled goods.

Considering the sheer number of passageways that cut through the space, this is prime territory for my little game of cat and mouse.

The question is—what's in all these crates?

I peek in to find two cameras, one trained on the door and the other on one of the paths that cut through the boxes. I'm sure there's loads more, but for now, these are the only two I need to worry about.

These cameras scan the space, moving back and forth to cover more ground. The lens on the nearest one slowly begins to rotate away. I pause, watching their movements, and I find the one moment where neither of them are looking at the door—my one chance.

I wait, using a stolen access card to crack open the door ever so slightly to give myself an advantage and save myself time. I have to get this *just* right, or I lose the element of surprise.

Hand on the knob, I count the seconds, keeping my breath steady as I wait for my moment.

Now.

I throw open the door, roll into the room, and fire two shots. The voids hit, and the little red lights shut off. The cameras go still, effectively dead, and I let out a slow breath.

Tucker laughs and shuts the door behind us. "I have to say, that is the coolest party trick ever."

I chuckle.

Curious, I lift the lid on the nearest crate. I'm thinking perhaps these are exotic sculptures or something equally expensive, maybe gold and artwork they're smuggling through on the way to black market buyers.

But I'm wrong.

Oh, so delightfully wrong.

Inside the crate are guns. AK-47s, all stacked neatly in the box, waiting for their day to shine.

I peek into the next box to find a *shitload* of guns this time. Assault rifles.

I smile. *Oh, Mason. You have no idea the gift you just gave me.*

"What's the plan, Boss?" Tucker peeks over my shoulder. "Oh, presents!"

I nod. "Exactly. Grab everything you want out of here and scope for more cameras, but stay out of sight." I pat the pouch beneath my shirt, briefly counting another dozen or so voids. "I have enough to get us out of here. Probably."

"What a vote of confidence." He laughs. "I love it."

I look up at the catwalk, and my plan begins to finally weave itself together. "Tucker, can you get up there?"

"Yeah," he says hesitantly, watching me with a wary expression. "Why?"

"I need you to spot me." I look him dead in the eye. "I'm going to draw Mason in here, and when I do, he's going to unleash hell on this place. He's going to use that catwalk to try to smoke me out, and I need you to do everything in your power to keep that from happening. If anyone goes up there, I need you to take them out."

"That's risky, babe." He shakes his head, scanning the catwalk, no doubt hesitant about the sheer amount of ground he'll need to cover. "This place is huge. I mean, look at that." He points up at the catwalk, his finger following the length of the room and then around the corner. "This place goes on forever."

"Which is why we'll be contained to a single space." I peek around a crate and scan my options. Eventually, I find one. I nod to an alcove at the far end of our row, where the boxes stack highest and there's the least visibility between the crates. "Down there, I'll have more cover."

"Rory," he says softly, hooking his sniper rifle over his shoulder so he can gently grab my shoulders. "Babe, I know the Ghost is a big freaking deal, but you can't use yourself as bait. You're—" His voice catches, and he briefly looks away. "You're worth more."

I can't help it. I smile. I lean in and brush my lips against his, grateful for this ridiculous goofball who wouldn't leave me alone.

The one who made me let down my guard. The one I can trust.

"It's going to be fine, Tucker." I take a deep breath and stow my gun in the holster at my waist. "I'm not bait—I'm just playing his game. Only, I'm going to do it better."

"I trust you, Half Pint." He winks, and I playfully roll my eyes.

"Get some guns, hop up there, and keep watch." I nod to the catwalk and lift the lid on the nearest crate, looking for a few fun weapons of my own.

"It's hot when you're bossy." He smacks my ass, and I suppress a gasp of surprise. When I wheel around, he's already jogging away, laughing.

I shake my head. What an adorable idiot.

The next few crates are pretty basic—mostly assault rifles of some kind. Decent, but not quite right for what I need. I need something with a blow-faces-off kind of power as a backup in case this all goes to hell.

The next crate has two rocket launchers in it. My eyebrows shoot up.

Huh. One of these will work.

I grab it and a few pistols from another create, grateful for my enhanced dragon strength now that I'm loaded down with so much weaponry.

It doesn't feel like enough, though. I feel like I need something else, and through this little adventure of mine, I've learned to listen to that voice.

That intuition. That warning that something else is headed my way, and I need to be prepared.

I keep scanning the crates, careful to keep an eye out for the catwalk and any possible cameras. Eventually, I find a crate that's long and thin, and I pause briefly out of confusion before lifting the cover.

I've never seen a gun shaped like this, but I might as well have a look.

Instead of a gun, however, an elegant sword lays on a bed of straw, with jewels glistening in the hilt. Elegant wisps of silver weave around the handle, beautiful but functional enough to protect the hand of whoever wields it. The blade is thick and wide, as long as I am tall.

I lift the magnificent sword, and something about it feels so right. It's perfectly balanced, so well designed that it feels like an extension of my arm.

Yeah, I want this. I try to tell myself it's in case I face a dragon—once they shift, guns aren't very useful. I'll either need a massive explosive or a blade of some kind. But in reality, I just think it's pretty.

I rifle through the case to find a sheath. With one this long, it has to go on my back—not ideal. It'll be clunky, but I don't really care at this point. The black sheath is inlaid with golden swirls, and I almost feel like this should be on a wall. It's too pretty to use.

Yep. This is mine now.

I carry my spoils off toward the isolated section of the warehouse—the rocket launcher, the walkie talkies, a few extra pistols, a boatload of ammo, and the sword.

With each step, I iron out the details of my plan.

Lure Mason to me.

Take him on a little road trip through the maze.

Get him talking.

Kill him.

Sure. Easy.

I sigh and begin my setup, trying to ignore the little sliver of doubt that's slowly creeping up my spine.

CHAPTER FORTY-FIVE

"Oh, Mason," I say in a sing-song voice through the walkie talkie. The device hovers by my mouth as I stand in the shadows of the warehouse with my back pressed against a crate. "Come out and play with me!"

I peek through the gaps between a few of the crates nearest me to check on the other walkie talkie, which is hidden behind a stack of boxes on the other side of the strategic alcove I chose.

The decoy.

I rigged the setup to prevent any loud bursts of static or beeps to give away that it's a walkie talkie—it's important that he think he's following my voice to my real location.

That's the plan, anyway. I'll draw him toward the decoy while stalking him through the maze.

Ideally. If things go perfectly.

And if they don't, well, my new toys are hidden within an empty crate nearby, ready at a moment's notice.

"Mason!" I shout into my walkie talkie. The other one blasts my voice at the highest possible volume.

I left a few of the cameras working, so they'll hear me. He'll come. And hopefully, he'll fall right into my trap.

With any luck, this little decoy of mine will work just long enough for me to get what I need out of him.

A door slams. Carefully, I climb the sturdy crates and peek through a few gaps between the boxes to find a metal staircase leading from the floor to a second-story door.

And there he is.

Mason pauses at the top of the stairs, scanning the boxes. He wears a bulletproof vest and carries an intimidating pistol while ten soldiers in all-black tactical suits flank him, armed to the teeth and awaiting his command.

I grit my teeth, reining in my temper with every ounce of my self-control.

"I thought you would never come, my darling!" he shouts into the warehouse. "Miss me?"

"Very much." I say into my walkie talkie. My voice blasts nearby from the decoy speaker.

Silently, Mason signals to the soldiers behind him. I

suspect there are far more coming, likely already heading up in the catwalk to scope out the warehouse from above, but it seems like a bulk of his warriors are dealing with Levi. Mason probably also has a large group set aside to monitor Zurie. He can't have the Ghost escaping, after all.

And as important as I may be to them, he's no high-ranking official. He won't have much of the Vaer army at his disposal. That's good news for me.

His army is divided, and that works in my favor.

"Where's Zurie?" I ask. Might as well get to the point.

Mason shrugs. "Comfortable."

"Oh, good," I say sarcastically. "I was worried she wouldn't have her usual tea times."

"But the question is where are *you*?" Mason cocks the gun at his side, pointing it toward the ground as he scans the paths. Interesting—I assumed they wanted me alive, but he looks fully ready to shoot me. His soldiers fan out, their loaded rifles guiding them through the maze.

He's isolated, now, but this isn't a good shot. I need to get him closer to me.

One of his soldiers walks below, and my moment comes. I don't like killing—but these people wouldn't hesitate to hurt me, Tucker, or Levi. I can't show mercy, except perhaps to ensure they don't feel pain.

With the silencer already attached to my gun, I

shoot him in the back of the head. The muffled pop is barely audible. The shifter falls without a word, but his gun clatters to the ground.

Mason pauses and scans the boxes near me, but it's clear he can't tell what direction the racket came from.

Good. He's not as familiar with this location as I thought he would be. I guess he has his grunts handle the warehouse maintenance.

As Mason turns down one of the routes through the boxes, starting to walk away from me, I shift gears. After dropping silently to the floor, I run a short distance across the warehouse and swipe the decoy walkie talkie, moving it to a new location—just to mess with him.

Moments later, I climb a different set of boxes to monitor the guards as they patrol my maze. One happens upon the old location of the decoy walkie talkie, hovering and scanning the area more closely than he has the others, and I suspect he's convinced I was there moments before.

Well, he's not wrong.

As they continue to patrol, I decide to take a page out of Drew's playbook. "If you're not going to talk, Mason, I'll just leave."

Mason flinches at the sound of my voice, his gun twisting to face the general direction of the decoy walkie talkie. A brief expression of panic crosses his face, but he quickly sneers to hide it. "Well, we can't have that, can we? What do you want to talk about?"

"Zurie." My voice is angrier than I intended. I take a moment to regain my composure. "And Irena."

Mason laughs. "You made your choice, woman. Zurie or Irena—you chose Zurie. Why do you care about your sister?"

"Oh, shove it, you idiot," I snap, calling his bluff. "You won't let her die. I'm valuable to you, and she's valuable to me. Only a moron would kill her. You're stupid, but you're not *that* stupid."

He scowls, and I grin.

Rory, one. Mason, zero.

"She's going to die anyway." He's seething, trying to gain the upper hand again. "Our little cocktail will see to that."

Oh.

Oh, *shit*.

"She's not sick with a natural disease," I say quietly, piecing it together. "You *created* a virus and exposed her to it." My voice is calm, matter-of-fact, even though my gut is churning at the realization. Twisting. My head is spinning. I want to puke, but I force myself to persevere. "You injected her with a handcrafted bioweapon."

A vile little grin spreads over Mason's face. "You're smart *and* pretty."

I grimace, squeezing my eyes shut as rage boils

within me. I grit my teeth, trying to keep the hatred at bay. Warmth flashes through me, coiling to my fingers as the magic threatens to break free.

No.

I have to maintain control.

I'm in a warehouse filled to the brim with weapons and gunpowder. If my magic lets loose in here, it will set off a chain reaction. If I lose control of my power in this place, we *all* die.

Me. Tucker. Everyone.

I can't let that happen.

Beneath me, another of his guards passes by, never bothering to look up. I take him out, and he falls without a word.

Above me, I hear a quick gasp and the rustle of fabric on metal. Gentle and familiar footsteps retreat across the catwalk, and I'm grateful I can rely on Tucker.

He has my back, and I can absolutely handle this.

Mason snakes through the walkways toward my decoy, drawing slowly closer. With a few more silenced shots, I pick off his soldiers, letting Mason sit in silence, letting him wonder if I've left.

It's down to him and just three others on the warehouse floor. I can see him getting more impatient, more anxious, more and more worried he's lost me. I move the decoy again, since I still haven't gotten the info I need.

"I have the antidote," Mason shouts into the ware-house. "Only I have it. If you turn yourself in, I'll give it to Irena."

I snort. "Bullshit."

"Hey, had to try." He shrugs, grinning again now that he knows I haven't left.

However, he now also realizes he has to keep talking if he wants to track my voice. I'm not going to give anything away—this is my only advantage, and I'm not letting the tides shift out of my favor.

"The antidote does exist, though," Mason says, still prowling. "I guess you could call it a proprietary blend. You won't get it elsewhere, Rory—just us. No one else even knows it exists."

That little confession tells me so much more than he realizes.

The Vaer are secretly testing a bio-weapon that has the ability to take out even strong, healthy humans like Irena. There's no telling what they want to use it for, what scale they want to use these on, or who they want to sell them to.

For all I know, this could be their attempt to eradi-cate humans from the planet. The implications are endless—and deadly.

"Zurie tried to steal it." Mason turns a corner and frowns, his eyes scanning the empty path where he probably thought he would find me. He's getting closer, but he's still not close enough. He grumbles under his breath, but eventually, he keeps talking. "I figured she and Irena could get a taste, since they wanted it so badly. Irena got hit with most of it, since Zurie broke the needle before we could inject her whole dose. Don't worry, though, I had to give Zurie the antidote before I could get any more info out of her. She's fine—you'll see her soon."

The deeper meaning behind what he's saying hits me like a fist to the face, and for a moment, I can't breathe.

Zurie was sick, too.

That's why she ran into the obvious trap. She led me into Mason's dragon den out of desperation. Because at any moment, she would keel over like Irena did.

Zurie compromised the mission. She put my, Irena's, and her own life at stake out of pride. She lied to me, told me she was fine, that only Irena was affected—all so she wouldn't have to give me any information.

Because God forbid Zurie tell me *anything*.

Lies. Every time Zurie's name comes up, another lie is revealed. I debate being here. I debate letting her die after all. I debate leaving entirely and giving up on this rescue.

But there's *so* much at stake.

If I'm going to save Irena, I need her help. And if I'm

going to survive in this world that hates me, that hunts me, I need at least one powerful, human ally.

I need Zurie's pardon because if she dies and Irena is still unconscious, Diesel becomes the Ghost.

And I sure as hell don't trust *Diesel*. Even if he granted a pardon to my face, he would probably send Spectres after me for the rest of my life. It would be an eternal war, one that would go on and on until I either destroy the entire Spectre organization or die trying.

No, letting Zurie die would become a bloody death sentence for me.

Furious, I try to swallow my anger. "And where will I be visiting with her later?"

"Oh, we have a nice little room set up for the two of you on the south end." Mason turns another corner, finally starting to head down the path beneath me. "It's lovely. Shackles, electric containment units, the whole nine yards. You even get a window. You'll love it."

"Sounds divine." My eyes gloss over as I mentally recount what little of the facility I know from my brief run through the maintenance tunnel. I think I know which area he's referring to—on the way in, we passed a sign pointing toward the south tunnels.

He could be bullshitting me, but Mason's one weakness is his arrogance. When he feels cocky, he lets little secrets through when he banters, never realizing I'm smart enough to read between the lines and piece together the clues.

Mason is quickly approaching the decoy walkie talkie, and I figure I've learned all I can from him. It's time to end this.

"You know, as nice as that sounds," I say, "I have a confession."

"What's that?" he asks, eyes locked on the next opening between the crates, where the sound of my voice is booming through the decoy walkie talkie.

"I hate you, Mason, with every fiber of my being. The only way you're leaving this room is in a body bag."

He turns the corner to find a dead end, empty except for the walkie talkie I set on the floor. He gapes at it for a moment, and that's all I need.

I aim for the back of his head. My sleeve rustles, sliding down my arm.

His ear twitches.

I pull the trigger, and the bastard *ducks.*

The bullet hits the crate behind him as he lunges toward me, knocking over the stack of crates I climbed. They tumble beneath me, and I roll across the floor to soften the fall.

He's on me in seconds.

Mason kicks me hard in the gut, and I fall onto my back as pain splinters through me. Straddling me, he locks his hands on my throat and squeezes. I see stars.

Screw *this.*

I punch his nose, breaking it. His once-pretty face is

ruined. Blood streams down his mouth and jaw, but he doesn't move. It only seems to fuel his anger. He glares at me, squeezing harder.

White spots dance along my vision.

Choking, gasping for breath, I punch him hard in the gut, and he finally groans in pain. With a deft twist of my hips, I flip us over until I straddle *him*.

And I punch the ever-living *shit* out of him.

My fists fly against his face, my knuckles bleeding, breaking his skin as I unleash my anger on the man who tried to kill me. A surge of energy pulses through my body, hot and bright, and I pause.

For a split second, I try to swallow the rage so that the magic doesn't surface.

It's all the time he needs.

He draws a gun from a second holster on his belt. With an experienced twist of my hands, I bend it out of his grip. He thrusts his pelvis upward, throwing me off balance, and I fall. Seconds later, he knees me hard in my side, the sharp pain loosening my grip. The gun slides across the floor, out of reach.

Yet again, the magic boils within me. And yet again, it distracts me from the fight.

He kicks me hard in the gut. I fall backward and slide along the floor, coughing as the pain shoots through me. He grabs my neck and lifts me, my feet dangling off the metal floor as he pins me against a stack of crates. Jolts of pain crack through me as my jaw and spine take the full force of his rage.

Bloody and savage, Mason looks at me with an unhinged expression. He's like a rabid animal, his eyes wide and wild, his fingernails digging into my skin.

"You're lucky the Boss wants you alive," he seethes. "Because I would love nothing more than to tear you apart, limb by limb, finger by finger, nail by nail."

"And you're lucky I needed info, or I would have killed you the moment you walked in." I grit my teeth, glaring at him as sparks of my magic dance across my arms in a misguided attempt to protect me. Begrudgingly, I try to rein in the power so I can continue my damn fight.

"You've got spunk, kid." His grip tightens. "It's going to be fun to break your spirit, at least."

"Good luck." I kick him hard in the stomach, and he doubles over. I drop to the floor and, without missing a beat, launch my knee into his face. He falls back, and I grab the nearest gun off the floor. I cock it and aim at his head.

He laughs.

Caught off guard, I momentarily pause.

"You're *insane*." I shake my head in disbelief, wondering how these psychos find their way into my life.

"On the contrary." He points up at the catwalk. "I just have leverage."

Any sane Spectre wouldn't look.

Even if it were me up there, Zurie wouldn't turn her head. She would fire at Mason, and she wouldn't care about the consequences.

But Tucker's up there.

I look.

A massive bald man, easily six foot six and broad as a door, holds Tucker by the neck. The shifter has him dangling off the edge of the three-story catwalk above the shattered boxes. Tucker grits his teeth, his hands around the man's wrists, feet kicking as he tries to regain control of the situation.

If Tucker falls, he'll break his back or get impaled on the wooden shards.

"Let him go," I demand. "Safely. Don't you dare drop him."

"Put the gun away," Mason counters, looking me dead in the eye.

Damn it.

Damn it!

Furious, frustrated, seething, I take a few steps back and point the gun at the ground.

This is why Zurie forbids romantic connection. Love. Devotion. On the battlefield, she sees it as a weakness.

But I don't care. Without Tucker's help, I wouldn't have made it this far at all.

He's worth it. Levi's worth it. They're my men, and I'll do anything for them.

As I retreat, Mason laughs harder. "You softie."

"Shut up and free him."

"As you wish." Mason shrugs and nods to the man above us.

The massive man lets go.

"No!" I scream.

In my terror, time slows. I holster the gun so that I don't accidentally shoot Tucker and run toward him as he falls. He briefly looks down at the shards, realizing how bad this is going to be. I leap for him, wrapping my arms around his waist, using my own force to change his momentum. We fall together, hitting the floor just beyond the shards, landing inches from a massive spear of splintered wood.

We roll to soften the fall. As we skid to a stop, I end up on top of him. I frantically check his face, his pulse, his arms, wondering if he's dead—but he groans.

"Tucker!" I gasp with relief.

He grimaces. "Not to complain about your hobbies, babe, but can I plan our date next time?" He winces. "Ow."

I laugh and shake my head, relief flooding through me, and set my head on his chest. "Thank God."

"That might be a little premature." Mason says from down the path, a gun in each hand as he smirks down at me.

My moment of joy gone, my smile fades. I stand. Tucker slowly follows suit, wincing as he puts weight on his left foot, and I hope he hasn't broken anything. We're not out of this yet, and he's going to need to run sometime soon.

I can still win this. The gun in my holster weighs at my hip, and I wonder if he's forgotten it, if Mason—

"Unbuckle the holster," Mason commands.

Damn.

Briefly, I gauge the distance, wondering if I can grab it before he can shoot me.

"Now, Rory!" Mason scowls and aims one of his pistols at Tucker. A red dot appears on my man's forehead, and I silently groan.

Damn it.

I oblige him, my fingers itching to grab the gun anyway, but I don't want to gamble with Tucker's life. It drops to the ground, and I kick it over to Mason.

"Good girl," he says patronizingly.

I wrinkle my nose in disgust at this man. With Mason before me and no weapons to my name, I once more debate my options.

Every crate has something inside, likely something useful, but it's doubtful I'll find something I need fast enough for it to actually help the situation.

I spot the crate I used to store my failsafe—the rocket launcher. My heart does a happy little leap, but it's still about twenty feet away. The lid sits ajar so I can easily reach in, but I'm not entirely sure how I can get over there without tipping off Mason.

"You know..." the Vaer shakes his head. "Rory, you are the biggest pain in the ass of my entire career."

"Thanks," I say dryly. My shoulders relaxed, my entire focus on Mason, I slowly inch toward the crate. Every movement looks like I'm merely shifting my weight. It's painfully slow, but I can't let him know what I'm doing.

"You would be impressive if you weren't so annoying." Mason shrugs. "But you're my ticket out of smuggling, and nothing will stop me from being the one to hand you in. You realize that, right? Even if you and Zurie get out of here today, I will hunt you until you break. I will never stop."

"I know." There's so much more I want to say—to put this asshole in his place—but I need to keep him talking while I make my way toward the crate.

Each step feels agonizingly slow and drawn out, but that's the point. He can't realize what I'm doing until it's too late.

If he does, I'm screwed.

"But that's the fun, I guess." Mason grins. "That's what—"

The radio on his belt crackles, and a man's panicked voice squeaks through. "Mason! Code red! Code *fucking* red!"

Mason stops dead in his tracks and, to my surprise,

closes his eyes in frustration. In anger. "You have *got* to be joking."

The radio crackles. "Thunderbird and a fire dragon —the biggest one I've ever seen in my life! Get your ass up here!"

To my surprise, a flurry of gratitude wells within me. Joy. Excitement, even. I didn't want either of them to know where I was or what I was doing—but Jace and Drew came.

I'm astonished at how happy that makes me feel. These controlling alphas constantly butted heads, but they put aside their hatred for each other to help me.

Me, of all people.

Mason grabs the radio, scowling, and growls into it. "You're panicking over *two* dragons? What the hell is wrong with you?"

The man is already speaking when Mason lifts his finger off the talk button. "—a *thunderbird*, Mason! He's going to destroy—"

"Squads ten through twenty-four to base," Mason orders, interrupting the man's panic. "Kill them both!" He briefly looks toward the staircase, probably in the general direction of the building's command center, and that's the distraction I need.

I bolt toward the stash and throw off the crate cover. Seconds later, I hoist my shiny new rocket launcher onto my shoulder.

My first instinct is to aim it at Mason, but that

would start a chain reaction among the crates and probably kill all of us.

Instead, I aim it at the ceiling.

If Jace and Drew want to join the fight, I figure I'll give them a front-row seat.

I fire, and the rocket propels toward the ceiling. A blast of heat and flame erupts through the air, spiraling into the sky as a massive hole tears through the roof. Overhead, the silhouettes of several dragons soar past the opening as the flames recede and debris rains down on the warehouse.

Mason aims one of his guns at my head. "What the hell—"

I grin. "Like I said, Mason, you're leaving here in a body bag."

I toss the rocket launcher aside and pull out two handguns from my secret stash.

"You're just begging me to kill you." Mason's seething, gun trained on the space between my eyes, and I can tell he wants nothing more than to pull the trigger and end this nightmare.

But I want to do it first.

Before I can shoot him, two dragons crash through the roof behind Mason. A red dragon and a dark thunderbird land on several crates, crushing them to splinters. As they face us, the two of them let loose an ear-splitting roar that's made louder by the confined space.

Mason doesn't miss a beat.

In moments, he shifts, and my guns aren't going to work well against his dragon. He grows in size, crushing a dozen crates beneath his feet, and roars back at the newcomers.

In seconds, Tucker and I are surrounded by dragons —both above us and in the room itself. The massive warehouse becomes suddenly cramped, and everything here—including me and Tucker—are at risk of being flattened.

But I don't care about myself. I care about revenge.

I grab Tucker's arm, looking him square in the eye. "Tucker, get to safety and tend to your injury."

"I'm not leaving—"

I press my lips against his, interrupting him with a rough kiss. When I'm done, I glare at him. "Do it, and don't you dare die!"

"So damn *bossy*," he mutters, trotting off toward the edge of the room.

With Tucker safe, I hook the sword's sheath over my back and stare up at Mason's massive dragon. He, Jace, and Drew snarl, bodies tensing, ready for war as they size each other up.

This is a fight Mason started, but it's one I intend to finish.

I meant what I said. Come hell or high water, the only way Mason will leave this room is in a body bag.

CHAPTER FORTY-SIX

With a stolen pistol in each hand and my new sword strapped to my back, I roll out of the way of Mason's tail.

He's on a warpath.

So am I.

Around us, more dragons funnel into the ware-house. They snarl and snap at each other, and a cascade of fire shoots overhead as a green dragon sticks his head through the hole in the roof. Mason roars in the dragon's direction, snarling in his fury.

It's an admonition—*don't set this building on fire and kill us all, you idiot.*

The green dragon plunges into the room, followed by seven more. They descend on Jace and Drew, and briefly, I wonder if the two of them can handle being so outnumbered.

Jace digs his teeth into the first one before it can even land. The second and third drag their claws across Drew's back, but he knocks them out of the air with a flick of his powerful tail. One by one, the dragons fall as the two of them fight together.

For shifters that hate each other so much, they fight in perfect harmony.

It's clear those dragons are just a decoy, though. As Mason returns his attention to me, I brace myself for the real fight. Guns raised, I aim at his chest. The pistols I stole are of a decently high caliber, but one or two bullets won't do enough damage unless I get a really lucky shot.

I need a freaking miracle to win this.

I wish I could use my magic, but it's too wild. I don't want to kill us all. Just Mason.

He snaps at me, and the battle rages on. I fire at his chest, unloading both of my clips into his body. The bullets hit. Every. Single. One. He shrieks in pain, and blood begins to pour out of the wounds.

But he doesn't stop.

"Crap," I mutter as his tail swings toward me, toppling several stacks of crates. I barely duck out of the way in time. Apparently, he's committed to destroying whatever it takes to get to me.

Freaking awesome.

With no more ammo, the guns are useless. I toss them and bolt through the warehouse as they slide across the floor. Mason follows, his massive body carving through the crates, knocking them effortlessly aside as he chases me.

It's not entirely clear what his end goal is or how he plans to detain me in his dragon form, but I'm sure it involves a lot of pain and a lot of blood. I don't really want to find out.

The best way to kill a shifted dragon is to cut off his head. Not the easiest thing to do. The weight of the sword on my back is somewhat reassuring, reminding me I have a weapon that can probably cut through his hide.

Probably. No real guarantee there, but I've worked with worse odds.

At this point, the sword is my only hope. Pistols are useless, and as far as firearms go, anything short of a mounted machine gun would be futile.

Mason quickly closes the gap between us and attacks, his claws scraping across my legs. I grimace as the pain shoots up my body. Every step aches. It's torture.

He hits me again, his claws gouging my back, and this time, I fall. I hit the ground hard, rolling several feet as the stinging agony burns through my body, numbing my brain, making it hard to think.

In seconds, he's above me, snarling, his lip curling as his razor-sharp teeth get closer.

He sneers, those teeth uncomfortably close.

There are a few daggers still hidden in my clothes, and I draw one from a hidden pocket. With a grunt of pained effort, I dig it into his nose. It's the only thing I can reach. With all my energy, I shove the blade down to the hilt and hold on for dear life.

I don't want to be trampled, and as much as this sucks, it's the next best thing.

He shrieks, and a blast of hot air soars past me as he shakes his head, desperate to knock the blade loose. Try as I might to hold on, my fingers slip off the handle, and I fly through the warehouse.

As the ground looms closer, I wince. This is going to hurt.

When I hit, I can't help but groan in agony. I tumble over the floor, trying to soften the fall, but the damage is done. I try to lift myself, but my arms shake. I collapse, grimacing, eyes squeezed shut as I try to filter out the pain.

Run, Rory, I tell myself. *Get up.*

It's just pain.

I've done this before.

I can do this again.

Gritting my teeth, I force myself to my feet and limp for cover, dipping behind a stack of crates as Mason claws at his face, desperately trying to rip the dagger from his snout.

Despite my own pain, I snort derisively at him. Ha. Asshole. Serves him right.

I take a moment to recline against a crate, hidden in a shadow. My head rests against the wood, and for a moment, all I can do is just breathe. Breathe through the pain. Breathe through the surging adrenaline.

Breathe.

Okay, Rory. Time for a plan, and it had better be a damn good one.

Blood soaks through my pants, and the gashes are deeper than I thought. I should wrap my legs and use pressure to avoid excessive blood loss, but I don't have any gauze or fabric.

Really, what I have to do next is simple—just not easy. I'll use my sword to cut off his head. To strike an effective blow, however, I'll need to jump from a great height in order to get enough momentum to help with the swing. With a dragon as beastly as Mason, I'm going to need all the force I can muster.

Time to go.

Trying to ignore the stinging torment rippling up my leg as I move, I bolt into the maze and toward the tallest stack of still-standing crates. It almost reaches the catwalk, and it's as good as I'm going to get.

Moments later, Mason finally rips the dagger free. Crap. I don't have quite the head start I wanted, but I can still make this work.

He races after me, snarling, his claws digging into the floor and ripping apart the metal with every furious step. As he nears, he snaps at me once more, his teeth missing me by inches, and I start to wonder if he's actually trying to kill me.

Maybe not. I guess they don't need my arms and legs to access my magic—they can cripple me and still get what they need.

I grit my teeth and push myself forward, trying to ignore the thought. God, I can be so *morbid*.

As I run, I try to figure out how to scale the crates with a rabid dragon trying to eat me on the way up. My mind races, filtering through a few possibilities, but I end up with a simple one—stab him until he stops.

Straightforward, not entirely elegant, but *eh*. It'll work.

I jump onto the crates, scaling them as quickly as I can. He growls and reaches for me with one of his claws, and I swing my legs out of his reach a second before he can snare me.

He snarls in frustration and digs his claws into several of the crates. The tower leans, threatening to topple. Without another option, I draw my sword and slash at his face.

The blade carves a deep gouge across his nose, almost catching his eye, and he screams in agony. He lets go, and mercifully, the tower doesn't fall. I scale upward, but it's slow going with only one free hand.

Mason draws his head back, ready to grab me in his mouth this time, and I debate jumping the two stories to the ground.

I refuse to let him win, however much the odds are stacked in his favor.

Before I can move, Mason is dragged backward. His wings block my view of whoever is behind him, but as he struggles with his new attacker, I slowly catch glimpses of red scales. Mason roars in pain, twisting as he tries to see who's behind him.

Drew.

The red dragon's teeth are buried in Mason's back, drawing blood as he glares daggers at Mason. Even as Mason wriggles and writhes, Drew is immobile. Unshakeable. He never once takes his eyes off his enemy, never once falters or flinches.

Drew radiates hatred.

Fire.

Power.

He snarls as Mason finally wriggles free, tearing a good chunk of his hide in the process. Blood drips along Drew's mouth as he slowly stalks toward the Vaer we both despise. Mason's head hovers low, cowering beneath the superior fire dragon, but I know a feint when I see one. He's going to charge—and from the way Drew tenses, he knows it.

Drew's just buying me time.

Oh, I am going to kiss him on his freaking *face* when all this is over.

Grateful for Drew's help, I sheathe the sword and scale the side of the crates as I haul myself onto the top.

All that's left now is a seven-foot stretch of empty air between me and the edge of the catwalk. Beneath me, my tower begins to sway, and I don't have long before it falls.

I can do this.

As dragons roar around me, I leap into the air, my fingers stretched for the metal railing.

My stomach churns.

My pulse thuds in my ear.

Suspended in the air, seconds from falling to what would probably be a painful death, I hold my breath.

My fingers brush the metal. And, mercifully, I grab the bottom bar.

The world rushes back once I grab hold, and I let out a relieved little sigh as I begin to hoist myself onto the catwalk.

At the far end of the elevated walkway, a Vaer guard who hasn't yet shifted spots me. Gun raised and aimed at my head, he quickly closes the distance between us.

But I am in *no* mood for this nonsense.

I roll between the gaps in the railing, the sword on my back catching awkwardly on one of the posts as I try to maneuver myself onto better ground. Grunting in frustration, I slip the dagger out of my boot and throw it. It hits him square in the chest, and he staggers backward before falling over the railing. Seconds later, a loud crash and the splintering of wood tells me what happened to him.

Standing, I adjust the sword on my back. This thing is *huge*.

I take a moment to survey the chaos below. Dozens of motionless dragons lie across the warehouse, covered in blood, and I suspect that's the trail Drew and Jace have left in their wake.

Drew circles Mason below me while Jace fends off four Vaer dragons at the far end of the gigantic warehouse. Most of the crates lie in ruins, their contents crushed to dust beneath the massive claws of the dragon shifters.

Above us, silhouettes stream by the hole, but no one enters. I squint, trying to figure out what they're planning—only to see ice along the edge of the opening. Seconds later, a familiar blue dragon takes his guard by the entrance and roars into the sky. Shards of ice shoot into the air, and several of the dragons take evasive action.

Levi.

My shoulders relax, and my body is flooded with relief. My ice dragon is alive. For the moment.

I can't get too excited. We're not in the clear just yet.

With his back to me and the rest of the warehouse, Jace corners his four targets against a stretch of empty wall at the far end of the massive space. Wings spread, his powerful body taking up as much space as possible, the veins in his wings begin to glow with blue light.

My eyes go wide. He isn't—not in here. Not with all these explosives so close.

Jace is going to do it. He's going to use the legendary thunderbird magic, the magic so many fear. The magic so few know anything about.

I want to time my own attack on Mason, but I can't —not if the warehouse shakes, not if what Jace is about to do affects the rest of us. I wait and I watch, warily telling myself Jace isn't going to put us in danger.

He has more control over his magic than I do, after all.

His whole body hums, glowing brilliantly, and he shoots off a blast of blue light similar to mine. It cuts through the dragon nearest to him like a bullet through fabric, and the dragon doesn't even have time to scream before he dies. The entire building trembles under the might of the blast. The catwalk shivers beneath me, and I hold on to the railing to brace myself. The wall behind the dragon lies in ruins, nothing but rubble and sparking electrical wires.

Nothing explodes. Good sign.

"Whoa," I say under my breath, caught off guard. I've never seen thunderbird magic before—and Drew wasn't kidding. If anyone can understand my wild magic, it's Jace.

Jace angles his head toward the remaining three Vaer soldiers. His movements are subtle. Slow. Controlled. It seems as though he's entirely devoted to the battle, consumed with the fight. The remaining three dragons press themselves against the wall where he has them cornered, snarling even as they lower their heads in submission.

They can't seem to decide whether or not to surrender, likely because they're not sure who they fear more—Jace or Mason.

I briefly study the destroyed wall as the loose wires within it spark and fizzle. They should definitely fear Jace more.

A piercing roar beneath me steals away my attention. Mason and Drew swirl and snarl below me. Each blow, each swipe of their claws or tail is lightning fast, their duel drawing blood on both sides.

Right.

I need to end this.

Below me, Mason is briefly in the perfect position. He pauses and snaps at Drew's face, but the moment is gone too quickly. I jump onto the railing, drawing the sword, my eyes locked on Mason's neck.

I will only have one chance.

One shot.

I can't fail.

I've never faced a dragon as large as Mason. I don't know if this plan will work, but it's everything I have.

This is dangerous. If Drew moves under me as I swing, I could hurt or even kill him instead of Mason. I pause, silently wishing he would look up at me to confirm he knows I'm here. To confirm he knows what I'm about to do.

As if he can read my thoughts from afar, his eyes briefly shift toward me. Nothing else moves, nothing else gives away a hint of his concern except that subtle motion. I get the feeling he's been doing that all along, and in my pained daze, this is just the first time I've noticed.

Our eyes lock, and I lift my sword in warning. He gives me the barest nod. With a few strategic snaps of his powerful jaws, he herds Mason toward me.

The Vaer dragon backs up, once more in the perfect spot.

This is it.

Sword raised above my head, I leap.

The world around me slows. I feel the rush of air over my face, feel the flurry in my stomach as I fall from a great height. The sword's center of gravity shifts as I lean forward, about to deal the final blow.

Mason pivots his head toward me. He roars, his fire burning deep within his body, casting an orange glow along his throat.

There, below me, is his neck.

With the full force of every last ounce of strength I have, I swing.

The blade hits his scales, slicing him open. Blood oozes along the metal as I cut deeper. My momentum, my strength, and the sheer power of the sword can't be stopped.

Not even by him.

My blade goes clean through him. As I reach the floor, Drew's tail catches me. It's a brief movement, just enough to soften my fall, and my momentum carries me onto the floor. With a pained groan, I hit the metal and roll, skidding the last few feet. As tired and bloody as I am, my sword props me up as I look back at the dragon who has destroyed my life.

The one who tried to kill my sister.

The one who stole my mentor from me.

The one who left me to die in a pit.

The man I hate with such a fury, he drove me to war.

His head hits the ground, still frozen in his final roar, and his body topples soon after. Crates shatter beneath the giant dragon's weight, while his limp wings knock aside entire towers of uniform boxes filled with priceless things.

A white glaze covers his eyes as the last of his life fades.

Mason Greene is finally dead. I let out a slow breath, almost unable to believe it's true.

Drew digs his claws into the metal floor and roars into the sky. It's a cry of victory, of pride. His wings stretch into the air, casting shadows over me. At the other end of the warehouse, Jace joins in. The powerful thunder of their voices tears through the room, and I look over to find them both watching me with pride.

My victory is theirs, too. We did this together.

As a team.

It's such a strange thought—to have a team. To have people I can show my back to, who will watch out for me come hell or high water.

And these men—these two growly alphas—they've proved themselves capable. Hardheaded, perhaps, but worthy to at least be considered as permanent fixtures of my life.

Levi pops his head through the giant hole above us and roars along with them, the deafening sound filling the space.

I did it.

I won.

I wipe the blood off my sword and sheathe it. There's one more task at hand—to find Zurie. To talk her down. To win her over.

To make her admit she owes me a favor—and to make it clear how I want to cash it in.

"Oh, my god. Thank goodness." Tucker grabs me and holds me tight, letting out a long sigh of relief as his hand cradles the back of my head.

I chuckle. "We're not out of the woods yet, Tucker."

He laughs. "Damn it, woman, can you savor *one* victory?"

"Yeah, when this is over," I confess.

His smile fades, and he nods. "I'll keep the guys busy here. You sneak out and find her."

"So bossy." I smirk and hand him my sword. It's not going to help me against Zurie, anyway. I'll find a pistol or two on my way to save her.

He winks. "You love it."

"I'll *tolerate* it. This time." I jog off, playfully smacking his ass as I disappear into the shadows.

I need them all to stay here. As horrible as it sounds, they're safer in a warehouse riddled with explosives than they are with Zurie.

And I will *not* let them die.

CHAPTER FORTY-SEVEN

As I run through the maintenance tunnel toward the south end of the compound, I'm on edge. Not because of the dragon shifters funneling through the halls, raising their guns at me. No, I'm concerned for what Zurie's going to say when I rescue her.

If she'll see reason.

What she'll do.

What *I'll* do if she won't listen to me. If she tries to hurt the men I care so deeply about.

As I round a corner, I fire three bullets at the three dragon shifters racing toward me from the other end. Each bullet hits its mark, and the shifters fall to the floor as I charge past them and up a flight of stairs, into the main building.

With a war raging outside and in the warehouse, with Mason dead, this is not the time for subtlety.

There's no telling which of them might try to step up and take over in a time when I need them to cower in fear.

I charge around the next corner, my boots sliding over the tile as I run. Gun lifted, I aim for the next shifter—the only one around this bend.

He raises his arms and drops his gun. As it clatters on the ground, he whimpers, a look of utter terror on his face.

This man doesn't want to die. Well, maybe he can at least be useful.

I grab his collar and throw him against the wall. "Where is the Ghost?"

"T-there!" He points at a door at the far end of the hall. His body shakes beneath my hand.

Oh, good.

"How many guards?" I demand, brow furrowed, channeling my full rage and anger at the entire Vaer family into every word.

He stutters. "T-t-ten left of twenty-three, but I keep seeing them d-d-defect."

"Traps? Cameras? How's she contained?"

"This will get you p-past everything!" He fumbles in his pocket, and I cock the gun, ready to shoot him if he does anything stupid.

He pulls out a white keycard and hands it to me, nearly dropping it twice as he trembles.

I take it. "Anything else?"

"P-please don't kill me." He closes his eyes, at my mercy.

Zurie would.

But I'm not Zurie.

"Run." I command.

He happily obeys. With a sigh of relief, he charges off the way I just came, not bothering to grab his gun as he races through the hallways. In seconds, he disappears around the corner.

My grip tightens on the keycard, admittedly relieved by my stroke of luck in a whirlwind of things not really going my way. As I stare at it, I can kind of understand why Zurie tortures people. It's faster than figuring it out on her own. Easier. Quieter. But it's also cruel and, in the end, unnecessary. I'm good enough at what I do that I don't need to hurt people.

And, frankly, so is Zurie. It makes me wonder if she has a compassionate bone in her body—or if any compassion she once had was beaten out of her after a lifetime of training and missions.

I brace myself. Time to find out.

I pass the keycard over the access panel and impulsively take cover. A hail of bullets sails through the portal the second it opens, and I roll my eyes.

Amateurs.

There's a momentary pause, likely so they can reload, and I take my chance. A quick peek inside reveals seven of the aforementioned ten still at their posts, and I fire a bullet for each one. Each shot hits its mark, and they crumple to the floor.

Beyond them is a dark hallway with floor-to-ceiling glass along one entire side. The glass reveals a large room with a white floor and ceiling. In the middle, a woman lies on a metal slab, her arms and legs restrained with thick metal shackles. An IV is hooked into one of her arms. Four computer screens hover behind her head, attached to a series of metal rods that stick out from the slab she lays on.

I step over the dead soldiers and scan the glass wall as the door automatically shuts behind me. In seconds, I find the way into this strange new room. All I have to do is stand in front of a second door in the glass, and it slides open—which sets off warning flags in the back of my mind.

The steady beep of a heart rate monitor greets me. The woman on the slab is facing away, but I recognize Zurie's face in the reflection on the window across from us.

Her eyes are shut. Face, pale. Body, impossibly still. If it weren't for the steady pulse of the monitor, I would think she's dead.

My heart in my throat, I cautiously enter, looking for any signs of a trap. I don't want to let my guard down when I'm so close to this whole thing being over.

As I walk toward her, my mouth goes dry. I've practiced what I would say in this moment, but I forget all of it. She looks so weak. So drained. So unlike the Zurie I remember.

There isn't much time, so I hunt along the monitors for an access panel. One sits behind the first screen, and I swipe the keycard, hoping the coward I took it from has the authorization level to release her.

He does.

The light flashes green, and in seconds, the bars around her wrists and legs click as they open.

And all hell breaks loose.

One moment, Zurie is lying on her back, still as a stone. The next, she's on her feet, her hand on my throat as she pushes me backward into the glass wall. Her pupils are dilated, and for a moment, I wonder if these Vaer bastards did something to her. If they wiped her mind.

But her body relaxes.

All at once, her expression softens. Something clicks in the back of her mind, and her eyebrows tilt upward in recognition.

Most surprisingly of all, she smiles.

To date, I don't think I've *ever* seen my mentor smile. It freaks me out, if I'm being honest.

"Rory," she says softly. "You came for me."

I nod, not yet ready to say anything. I want to play these cards right, and I can't allow for a single mistake.

Not one.

Her smile widens, and she sets her hands on my

shoulders. She watches me with pride, with a hint of relief and joy, and we simply stand there for a moment in silence.

"I knew you would." She nods, almost like she's reassuring herself, and I quietly debate how much she believed that. Tenderly, she sets her hand on my cheek. "What did you have to sacrifice to do this? I'll double it. Name your price."

Ah, there she is. The woman I remember. Nothing done out of kindness or devotion—everything is a favor.

Luckily for her, I have my price. She just won't like it.

"Freedom," I say simply.

Her smile fades. She scans my face, no doubt searching for the deeper meaning.

"I saved your life, Zurie." I narrow my eyes. "You owe me, and you owe me *big*. My palms are clammy, but I never lose my grip on the gun in my palm. "That's my price. A way out. I want to leave the Spectres, and I want a full pardon. I'll help you find and heal Irena, but after that—"

"No." Zurie lowers her hands, shoulders back, her face expressionless. In one fluid motion, she rips the IV out of her arm and leaves it to dangle, dripping slowly onto the floor.

"You just wrote me a blank check, Zurie." I hold her

gaze, unwavering, refusing to back down. "Well, that's my price. That's what I want."

Quick as a flash, she grabs the gun from my hand. My heart skips beats, wondering what she plans to do, but she simply aims it behind her. Without looking over her shoulder, she fires two shots. Glass shatters, and two bodies fall to the ground.

Two Vaer agents lie on the floor beyond the glass windows, the door to the hallway open again.

Damn it. As lost as I was in my nerves, I didn't even hear them come in.

"Dragons are evil, Rory." Zurie takes an ominous step toward me. "I think, perhaps, you've forgotten that."

In the past, I would have lowered my gaze. I would have submitted to the clear superior—the Ghost, the finest Spectre in the world, the woman who could destroy an entire country if she set her mind to it.

But Zurie doesn't own me anymore.

"Dragons are vile, dangerous things," Zurie continues, lowering her voice as she leans toward me. "They burn, they pillage, and they kill. It's all they'll ever know."

"You're wrong," I say quietly, lifting my chin in defiance. "I've seen kindness, compassion, trust—"

"*Trust*," she says with disdain. "My God, Rory, what have they done to you?"

I bite my tongue to keep my temper in check. The

things I want to say to her would only burn this bridge when I need to keep her on my side.

"The vessel," she says with disgust, shaking her head in disappointment. "It's gone to your head, hasn't it? All this nonsense?"

My heart pangs, and I narrow my eyes in confusion. "How could you—"

"Mason is a talker." Zurie scowls, her eyes glossing over as she privately relives a memory. "He told me all about what you've been up to, Rory. About how you went to a *dragon* embassy. About how you've been making *friends*." She sneers. "Honestly, child, I assumed you were using them, not actually going off to find yourself dragon allies. Didn't I teach you *anything*?"

"You taught me plenty," I say, not bothering to mask my contempt.

"Never mind all that." Zurie cracks her neck, shaking out her arms to loosen them up, and I wonder how long she's been strapped to that slab. "We'll fix all of this. The Vaer. This vessel garbage. All of it."

"And what does *that* mean?" I eye the gun in her hand, wondering if I can move fast enough to pry it from her palm.

If I catch her off guard, then yes. I can.

"I mean you're initiated." She looks me dead in the eye, waiting for me to react.

I balk, entirely caught off guard. "I'm... you mean..."

"You're a full Spectre, Rory." She looks me over briefly. "Like you always wanted."

Before, yeah, that's all I wanted.

Before I realized what it meant to be truly free. After all this time in the sun, however, I never want to live under Zurie's shadow again.

The edge of Zurie's mouth tilts slightly downward, revealing only the barest hint of true the depths of her disappointment. "As a full Spectre, however, you can possess no dragon magic. We will have to find a way to remove this foreign energy from you, but that shouldn't be too difficult. I have a few contacts who can help us."

My body cringes at the thought, and I'm horrified. Horrified it's possible. Horrified she's so confident she can do it. The sensation is like nails on a chalkboard, and I can't hide the brief rush of revulsion at the idea of having this power dragged out of me.

"That's what I thought," Zurie says with a dissatisfied sigh. "They've toyed with your brain. A short spell with the dragons, and suddenly you've forgotten a lifetime of loyalty to your own kind."

I wrinkle my nose in disgust. "A lifetime of obedience, you mean. Of compliance. Submission."

"Not anymore." Zurie's face is deadly serious.

"Explain," I demand.

Her eyebrow twitches briefly in annoyance, but I won't back down. Not now. Not anymore.

Zurie frowns deeply. "You're my heir, Rory. Not Irena. When I die, you will lead."

Blistering chills race through me. The implications are massive.

Me.

The Ghost.

"No, wait." I shake my head, trying to figure out what game she's playing. "Irena was already named your heir. For me to get it she would have to be—"

"Dead." Zurie nods, utterly emotionless as she delivers the news.

For a moment, I can't breathe. The shock burns through me, heavy on my chest, agonizing as it cuts me open from within.

The grief.

The sadness.

The loss.

It's worse than anything I've ever felt, worse than any broken bone, worse than any horror I could ever imagine.

I gape, studying Zurie's face, unwilling to believe her.

And then I see it.

The slight twitch of her left eye, the way her mouth bends ever so slightly upward, a sign of victory she's barely able to contain.

She... she just *lied* to me.

About *Irena*.

Rage boils within me, fast and hot. My God, I want to rip her throat out. To toy with me this way—it's beyond cruel.

I scowl. "Why are you lying?"

"I'm not. The disease spread to her—"

"Stop *lying*, damn it!" I hit my fist hard against the nearest pane of glass, and it shatters the entire window. As glass rains to the ground, the shards cutting small rivets in my skin, I never once break eye contact.

Zurie shifts her weight. It's a subtle movement, but it tells me everything I need to know. Before, she was relaxed—now, I'm a threat. She's evenly balanced and ready to spring.

"Speaking of liars," she says, her grip tightening on the gun in her palm. "Care to tell me why there's a thunderbird here?" She reaches under the pillow her head had been laying on and tosses a radio toward me.

I step aside and let it clatter across the floor. She made her point. "You were listening?"

"Courtesy of Mason, yet again." Her nose wrinkles in revulsion as she says his name. "Like I said, he's quite the talker. Wanted to make sure I got all the updates of your little rescue attempt."

"Successful rescue attempt," I correct her. "One you very much owe me for."

"Rory, why is *Jace Goodwin* here?" Her voice drips with anger. Accusation. "What did you *do*?"

"I saved the Ghost." I narrow my eyes. "Are you going to make me regret that choice?"

"You really are infuriating." She shakes her head. "Obstinate. Obnoxious. But you're the only legacy I have left, Rory. I won't let you leave. Even if I have to take you into the dungeons and reprogram this shit out of your brain, you're coming back."

My heart stutters at the memory of the dungeons. Of the torment. Of the weeks blending into months as I'm left in the darkness. Of the injections. Of the hallucinations. Of sobbing myself to sleep until my throat hurts.

"Don't make me kill you, Zurie." I slowly ease my last dagger out of my back pocket, one just thick enough to slit a throat. "There are other Spectres. Other recruits that actually *want* the job. All I'm asking for is a pardon." I tense, trying to get my full proposal in before she attacks me. "We don't have to be enemies. You don't have to waste your energy on this. On me. You tell your Spectres to leave me alone, you stay away, and I won't tell my new dragon allies anything I know about the organization. About you." I pause to drive my point home. "About how to destroy *all* of you."

"Stubborn girl," Zurie says softly, clicking her tongue in disapproval. "So wicked. You'll make a great Ghost."

She swings her fist at my neck, and I barely duck out of the way in time. Seconds later, she aims the butt of the gun at my temple, and I once more duck to avoid the blow. She rips the dagger from my hand, and it clatters onto the floor.

Zurie moves like lightning, quick and brutal, the onslaught of attacks overwhelming. It's all I can do just to block them—there's no chance to throw in a punch of my own.

I slide out of her reach and kick out her knee. She falls, and I punch her in the face. She takes the hit like a pro, never wincing, never so much as grunting in pain despite the blood trickling from her nose. With a powerful tug, she grabs my leg and throws me onto my back.

Coughing, the wind kicked out of me, I gasp for air. She lands a knee in my chest. I see stars as the pain shoots through my body, reactivating the wounds I got while fighting Mason.

Her sharp and angled face looms over me, and she sneers. "We'll fix this, Rory. But first, I need to clean up your *mess*."

With that, the butt of the gun comes down on my temple, and my world goes dark.

CHAPTER FORTY-EIGHT

I wake to the pounding thunder of a headache.

My vision blurs, but the world around me slowly comes into focus. Boxes. Shattered wood. Beige and black blurs. Streaks of red.

"Just let me check on her!" Tucker shouts.

"She's fine," Zurie says coldly.

I shake my head, groggily trying to sit up as more of the sounds hit me. Dragons snarling. The crackle of fire. The buzz of exposed wires as they spark. The cold metal beneath me. The click of a gun cocking. The creak of skin on a trigger.

My blood runs cold, and I use what little strength I have left to lift my head.

Though everything is blurry, I can make out Zurie standing between me and Tucker. Levi, Drew, and Jace loom behind him—my dragons.

Everyone glares at Zurie and the rocket launcher on her shoulder.

It's aimed at Drew, but true to form, he doesn't blink. I don't think he can even feel fear.

Tucker stands between them. He lifts his hands, trying to placate both Zurie and the dragons even as his eyes are trained on her.

"Don't do this," Tucker pleads, his eyes wide as he tries to reason with my mentor. "Rory doesn't want—"

"You know too much, boy," Zurie says with a hint of amusement. "I think I'll kill you, too."

Like *hell.*

She lifts her elbow to better balance the massive weapon. With what little energy I have, I lunge. I throw my whole body into the attack, throwing off her aim. The rocket launcher points toward the hole in the ceiling as her finger pulls the trigger, and it sails harmlessly into the sky.

Seconds later, a massive explosion rips through the air.

Still fuzzy, my world still blurred and broken, I don't see Zurie's hand until it's too late. She backhands me, but instinct takes over. I grab her wrist and snap it backward. Something in her arm cracks, and she grimaces in pain.

Her other fist lands hard in my gut, and I fall to my hands and knees. I groan, gritting my teeth through the blow, and grab the empty rocket launcher from where she dropped it on the ground.

With everything I have, I hit her across the face with it.

She falls to the ground, panting. My body stings. My lungs burn. The splitting pound in my head is agonizing, but I don't care.

No one touches my men.

My *team.*

I toss the empty rocket launcher aside and try my best to remain standing as I glare at her. "Don't you fucking *dare.*"

Behind me, my dragons growl in approval. Hot air rolls over my neck, my legs, my back—they're pleased and proud.

Without asking, Tucker gently grabs my hand and lifts my left arm around his neck so he can help me balance. I want to tell him to stop, to go away and stop undermining me, but I can't. Mostly because I could topple over at any moment.

When Zurie hits, she hits *hard.*

My mentor pushes herself to her feet and cracks her neck, glaring at me with newfound rage. "Name Rule Number One."

I stand up straighter on impulse at the command. It's a familiar order, more like habit at this point after so many years of conditioning. Irena and I would be told to name a rule at random, and we had to recite it effortlessly. Instantly. With authority and confidence—all while standing at attention. Anything less than perfection was viciously punished.

But here, now, I don't salute Zurie. I won't. Never again.

And even though this is the easiest rule to recall, I don't answer.

"Name Rule Number One," Zurie repeats, seething.

"No." I try to stand on my own, to drive home the point that she doesn't control me anymore, but I can't. My knees give out, and if not for Tucker holding me up, I would fall.

"I *own* you, Rory." Zurie lifts her chin, looking at me like I'm a bug she could squash at any moment. "You're my legacy, the only one I have left. You don't *get* to leave. The longer you defy me, the more painful your reconditioning will be."

"I'm done," I say simply. I want to yell at her, to scream, to point out how this could have all been so easy and simple if she could feel anything other than self-righteous pride, but I don't.

Every breath hurts, and talking is about all I can handle at this point.

"You think they'll accept you?" She points to the dragons behind me. "Once they know what you are, don't you think they'll kill you?"

My jaw tenses. I know what she's about to do. To say.

Don't. Please, don't.

"They fought hard for you today, sure," Zurie frowns. "But if they had known you're a Spectre, do you think they would have fought at all?"

My heart shatters. I briefly close my eyes, my secret exposed just like that. She knew this would be the one blow I couldn't block, and she didn't hesitate.

Behind me, the dragons rumble. In my periphery, Jace and Drew both turn their intense glares on me. The blue light within Jace glows, and black smoke coils out of Drew's nose. Only Levi continues to glare at Zurie, and I wonder how much of this he really understands.

I glare at her. "Low blow."

She shrugs. "I'm the only one who will ever accept you, Rory. The sooner you learn to appreciate that, the better your life will be."

Drew snarls, his claw digging into the metal platform I'm standing on, and I wonder if he's going to attack me. His gaze is once more on Zurie, though, and I suspect he simply wants to kill us both.

Zurie doesn't give him the chance.

She draws a gun hidden beneath her shirt and shoots a propane tank roughly two hundred feet away.

Shit.

It explodes, flinging debris in every direction. Without a word, she bolts into a nearby hallway as the fire catches another propane tank, setting off the chain reaction I was trying to avoid in my earlier fight with Mason.

We need to get out of here.

Tucker guides me toward another exit, but neither of us get very far.

Black claws wrap around my waist, ripping me from Tucker's grip. He yells for me, but seconds later, Drew's red claws grab him and lift him into the air. Levi snarls at Jace, trying to keep up as the thunderbird bolts through the air like a bullet.

Jace soars off through the opening in the roof and into the skies. Drew and Levi chase after us as fires rip through the Vaer compound. They clear the roof moments before the remains of the building go up in flames, and a ripple of heat shoots from the compound as one last massive explosion renders it to charred rubble.

Snarling, furious, Levi races through the sky toward me. He cuts through the air at full speed, pouring everything he has into every powerful beat of his wings, but Jace is faster.

Still weak from the blow to the head and my fight with my mentor, I can barely keep my eyes open. I have no idea where he's taking me—or if I'll survive what's coming next.

They know what I am, now, and Zurie's right. No dragon will accept me if they know the truth. The heartbreaking realization tears through me as Jace's painfully tight grip constricts my movements.

Zurie knows that, even weakened, I'll probably be able to escape. She took a gamble. She wants this to be the thing that breaks me, the moment that makes me crawl back to her. To see the people I care about turn on me once they discover what I am.

But I won't go back to her. I'm done.

No matter who I lose.

CHAPTER FORTY-NINE

Jace is like a jet through the night, so fast we nearly lose Drew and Levi several times during the getaway.

His grip never once loosens. He never looks down at me. His tense body nearly trembles with fury, and I honestly have no idea what he'll do when we land. For all I know, he could drop me at any moment.

We finally descend into a clearing far from the Vaer lands. He sets me gently on my feet, my boots barely touching the grass before he shifts back into his human form. Furious and stark naked, he pins me against a tree.

In any other situation, I would twist his arm and regain the upper hand. But right now, I have to conserve every last ounce of energy I have in the very real chance this goes south.

And judging by the livid expression on his face, it just might.

"A *Spectre*," he says the word with hatred. Disdain. Disgust. "You're a *Spectre*."

"Was," I correct. My muscles burn. Everything stings. It takes everything in me just to stand, but I won't back down.

This is too important.

He tries to say something but can't seem to form the words. He agonizes over the realization, scrunching his brow as he looks away.

His disappointment hurts me worse than his anger ever could. I want to fix this, to ease the betrayal I see in his face, but I just don't know how.

He presses his warm body against mine, his forehead resting against my brow, and my skin sizzles with impulsive, unchecked need at his touch. The connection we share burns between us, and I wonder if that alone is keeping him from killing me.

"A *Spectre* for a mate." He grimaces, as if the thought alone is breaking his heart. "I just… I can't…"

"I'm sorry," I say softly.

I mean it.

He looks at me, then, finally pausing long enough in his anguish to look me in the eye. His tortured expression guts me, like he can't decide whether to kiss me or break my neck.

"Why do you hate us?" he asks quietly. "After every-thing you've learned about us, how could you hate dragons enough to be part of an organization that only exists to kill us all?"

"You act like I had a choice," I snap at him. I can't hide my feelings, not right now. My mask is worthless, and for the time being, he gets to see the real me. I glare off into the dark forest, trying to suppress all the horrors of my childhood. "You act like I got to sign up for this, Jace, like I had any say at *all*."

"Didn't you?" He frowns, pressing the issue, daring me to disagree.

"Not even *close*." I push his chest, and he staggers a few steps backward. The white glow of my magic snakes across my skin as my anger rises. "I don't remember anything before the Spectres, Jace. It's my first memory. It's my childhood. My entire life, I've been trapped in a training cage, or a locked room with a rabid dragon, or—" I squeeze my eyes shut, trying to suppress the memories of the dungeons, of the punish-ments I would get for not obeying fast enough, *hard* enough, *well* enough.

Jace gently holds my arms, his touch hot and sooth-ing. I open my eyes to find him watching me with concern, the anger slowly melting away as I speak.

"I was born into this, Jace." I scan his stormy eyes, wondering if he really understands. "I never wanted to be a Spectre. I never wanted to go on any of those missions. I never wanted to kill anyone. If I didn't, I was tortured. And if I still refused, I would have been killed in my sleep."

"Oh, Rory." His voice is soft and gentle, the look of utter horror on his face a sign that yes, perhaps he might understand.

A silhouette cuts through the air above us, and seconds later, a roar tears through the trees. I tense on instinct, wondering if a Vaer followed us, before Levi lands. The ground shakes beneath him. He bellows at Jace, his teeth exposed as he prepares to eat the man whole in order to protect me.

Drew lands a second later, dropping Tucker uncer-emoniously in the grass as he lands between Jace and Levi. He snaps at the ice dragon, snarling as he breaks up the fight before it can start.

Levi growls, pacing, ready to take them both on at once if he has to, but Jace just sighs and releases me.

My skin goes cold as he lets go, and now that the moment is broken, he won't look at me again.

Levi's head pivots toward me. He takes a wary step backward now that I'm free of Jace's grip, though he's still riled and ready for a fight.

Apparently satisfied that there's not going to be an all-out brawl, Drew tilts his massive head toward me. His golden eyes study my face, sharp and accusing.

Black smoke coils out of his nose, and the low growl building in his throat betrays his absolute rage.

"Shift back, idiot," Jace snaps.

Drew snorts, the black smoke rolling over the thunderbird. Jace just flips him off and paces through the grass, staring up at the sky.

Tucker pushes himself to his feet, never once looking at the others, his entire attention focused on me as he races closer. "Are you okay?"

"I'm fine," I lie.

I teeter a little off balance, and Tucker catches me. He pats me down, and for a second, I think he's looking for broken bones or injuries. That is, until I feel a dagger slide into my back pocket, and the weight of a small handgun slide into the space between my pants and the bare skin of my lower back.

He's arming me in case this all goes to hell.

As he returns his warm hands to my face, I smile weakly at him.

"Thanks," I whisper.

He nods.

Behind him, Drew shifts into his human—and very naked—form. The broad and muscled man is every bit as rock solid as he looks with clothes on, and I can't hide the heat burning my cheeks as my eyes naturally drift to his crotch. I don't know if it's just a dragon thing or what, but they all seem to be hung beyond belief.

Drew, however, is not in the mood to be modest, cocky, or anything other than angry. He glares at me, and it's just surreal how unfazed dragons are by nudity. He and Jace are stark naked, but both glare at me expectantly, waiting for answers.

"Now can we please—" Tucker turns around, only to finally notice the two naked men behind him. "Jesus, guys! Could you put on pants?"

"We left in a bit of a hurry to save your ass," Jace says curtly, arms crossed. "Sorry we couldn't pack a day bag before we left."

"Explain!" Drew shouts, interrupting the banter. His voice rings through the trees. He's glaring at me, the full brunt of his anger trained exclusively in my direction.

The fact is, I don't have to. I don't have to say a word. I could just leave, and they might not move a muscle.

In the past, I probably would have. I would have said screw it—they don't understand me. I don't have to put up with this.

But these men nearly died for me.

When I needed them most, they put their lives on the line without asking why I was even there. They simply showed up. Had Zurie not revealed what I am, they might not have demanded anything of me at all.

I sigh. I don't *have* to give them answers, but I *want* to.

"I was born into the Spectres, and I never had a choice in the matter." I scan each face in the clearing, wondering what they'll do when they learn the whole truth. "My mother died on a mission when I was little, and I never knew my father. We don't keep track of that kind of thing in the Spectres, but the man Zurie suspects is my father died in the same mission as my mom." I pause like I always do when I recall these things, wondering if I'll feel sadness one of these times. I never do—I never knew them—so I press onward. "Zurie raised me. My sister Irena and I are Spectres under Zurie, the Ghost."

As we stand in the darkened meadow, I share everything. Everything about Zurie, about the Spectres, about Diesel, about Irena's illness. I share it all, and to my surprise, it feels kind of good to get these things off my chest. They're truths I've hidden all my life, truths I was sworn on pain of death to keep to myself. It's a relief to not bear the burden alone anymore.

When I'm done, I cross my arms and look each man in the eye, waiting.

"Why would you rescue the *Ghost*?" Jace asks accusingly. "Could you not bring yourself to kill her, should the need arise? Should we be concerned?"

"It's the only chance I have to keep the Spectres from coming after me," I say more curtly than I intended. I pause to re-center myself and soften my tone. "No one leaves the organization. A defector takes precedence over all other missions. Everyone, in every corner of the globe, rallies to kill them. Besides, think about what would happen if I did kill her."

He gestures wildly, inviting me to continue.

I frown. "Irena has to be conscious to inherit the role of the Ghost, which means Diesel would get it. He would hunt us both down immediately to tie off loose ends. So, by saving Zurie, I can save Irena—and, at the same time, I had the best chance of getting a pardon. Without one, I face the full wrath of the entire Spectres organization." I pause. "*Forever.* They don't stop, and they don't forgive."

"Holy shit," Tucker says quietly.

I nod. "It's no joke. They hate defectors more than any dragon."

I study the hard lines of Drew's face, and then shift my attention to Jace. Both men watch me with unreadable expressions, and I wish I could read their minds. Levi watches me as well, never blinking, his fierce gaze suggesting he's picking up more of this than I previously realized.

"Are you going to kill me?" I finally ask, crossing my arms.

They can't, of course, even if they want to. What I'm really asking is, *are you going to make me leave?*

Levi snorts in annoyance and rests his head on the soft grass. I can swear he's smiling, and I can't hide a small chuckle of gratitude.

Jace and Drew, however, don't move. They're still as statues, and I briefly wonder if I should reach for the gun Tucker hid beneath my shirt.

Drew is the first to relax. He lets out a slow breath, arms crossed as he stares at the ground. "I meant what I said."

Whatever you really are, Rory, you have my respect. I stand a little straighter, trying not to hope too fiercely.

"I figured you were special forces," he says with a chuckle. "Maybe ex-military with a few too many enemies. Worst case, I figured you were a Knight. I never could have guessed you were a Spectre."

It takes everything in me not to look at Tucker. To not betray the secret we share.

Drew sets his hands on his hips and studies my face. "You defied the Ghost, of all people, to save us. I know enough about the Spectre code to understand that's a death sentence." He pauses, catching my eye and smiling gently. "And you did it without hesitation."

I weakly smile back, grateful he understands.

Drew looks at Jace. "What about you, asshole?"

"Oh, shut *up.*" Jace groans and rubs his face. "Rory, I couldn't hate you if I tried." He absently scratches his jaw, eyes scanning me as he debates something internally. "I'm still not sure how I feel about this whole Spectre thing, but the mate-bond never lies. There's good in you."

I nod in thanks, not entirely reassured.

"Zurie will be back." Drew paces the small meadow. "She thinks you've been brainwashed, Rory. She'll try to kill us and capture you. Something about reconditioning."

I involuntarily shutter, and none of my men miss it. They all watch me with concern, and I quickly look away in an effort to regain my composure. I don't want them to know how much the idea of the dungeons gets under my skin.

"We won't let that happen, Rory," Drew says gently.

"We'll need to kill Zurie, though," Jace says, watching me to gauge my reaction. "She can't be allowed to live."

"Because she's a Spectre?" I lift one eyebrow in defiance, wondering where he really stands on this issue.

"Because she threatened *you*," he corrects me without even blinking. "No one touches my mate."

Beside me, Tucker bites his lip and looks away with a playfully guilty expression, and I want to smack him.

"Thank you, Jace," I say softly. Sincerely.

"Can you kill her?" the thunderbird asks pointedly.

"If we have to kill her, we—" My voice breaks at the thought of killing my mentor, of watching the light fade from the eyes of the woman who raised me, and I hate how torn I feel.

She's cruel. She delights in breaking people, lied to me about Irena's death for reasons I still don't understand. She has never once been upfront or honest with me, and she uses me to her own ends.

And yet… she's still the closest thing to a mother I've ever had. I hate how the sense of loyalty she instilled in me protects her from the full depths of my hatred.

I want to say yes. Deep down, I know I could. I just don't know what it would do to me.

"I think that's enough for one night." Drew clears his throat and walks toward me, setting his hands on my shoulders. "Are you okay?"

"I've been better," I confess with a shrug.

"She needs a medic." Jace is instantly at my side, glaring briefly at Drew as he angles me away from the fire dragon. "We need to get her back to the embassy."

"Are you sure?" I pause, taking a step back, looking each man in the eye. "I'm a Spectre. Dragons kill us on sight, without asking questions, without—"

"Rory, you're not a Spectre." Drew shakes his head. "Not anymore."

I let that sink in, let the weight of the realization settle on me. The idea that I'm really free. I don't ever have to go back. Zurie's hold on me is gone, and I get to choose what happens next.

It's the truest joy I've ever felt.

"You're right," I say with a smile.

The shackles are off—but more importantly, I'm no longer alone. As I look at the four men before me, my heart warms. The soft, gooey part of me briefly takes over, and all I can feel is gratitude.

Zurie is going to try to take them from me—and no matter what it takes, no matter how fiercely I have to fight her to save them, she's going to fail.

CHAPTER FIFTY

As the sun rises on a new day, I sit on the edge of a cliff overlooking the dojo. Bandages cover my arms, and most of my torso and legs are wrapped in gauze. I wear a loose-fitting uniform provided by the dojo, since my clothes were ripped to hell, and I kind of like the way the breathable fabric lets in the breeze.

I sigh contentedly and lean my back against a rock, happy to have found a quiet little alcove. As the sky burns red and yellow, I close my eyes.

Really, I shouldn't be this at ease. I don't have a home anymore. I have no headquarters, no place to return to when the craziness dies down, and for some reason that doesn't bother me.

I peek through my eyelids at the dojo below me, and I realize that's not totally true. This isn't exactly home sweet home, but the embassy is a haven. Here, for the moment at least, I'm safe.

Safe. It's still such a surreal feeling.

As I look out over the ocean, I almost can't believe we did it. We stormed a Vaer stronghold—one that was *expecting* me, no less—and killed the man who tried to murder everyone I cared about.

We.

I pause, marveling at the idea of having a team. A family, of sorts. Growing up, I was taught trust is a weakness, something the feeble did to give up their power and make themselves feel better.

Huh. Makes me wonder what else Zurie got wrong. Because Jace, Tucker, Drew, and Levi—they have my back. And I have theirs.

With my magic and my men, I'll figure out my new place in the world, no matter who comes for me.

Or *what.*

My mind wanders back to the voices in the mist, what feels like ages ago, and my smile falters. I still have no idea who they are or what they want from me, but deep down, I know it isn't good. With a flicker of doubt, I also get the feeling it's not a matter of *if* I meet them, but *when.*

Footsteps crunch along the gravel behind me, but I recognize the gait. "Hey, Drew."

He chuckles and sits down beside me. "How do you do that?"

"Spectre-sense." I chuckle, liberated by my shared secret.

"You really shouldn't say that here." His smile fades, and he briefly glances down toward the dojo.

True. There's no telling when someone might be listening, or what devices they may set up to capture audio remotely. "I checked the area. It's clear."

"Yeah, but—"

"I know, Drew." I smile at him, not wanting him to ruin my happy moment. "I'll keep that in mind."

He sits with me, watching the sunrise in silence, and I appreciate how he doesn't have to fill the quiet with noise. He and I can just sit and be, enjoying the day.

I feel the gentle brush of his knuckle along my face, and I open my eyes to find him watching me. He smiles, and his eyes drift down to my lips. Sparks fizzle through me, and I wonder what he'll do.

"You certainly like to test me," he says quietly.

I grin. "Guilty."

"Well, two can play that game." He leans back against the rock, a cocky smile on his lips as he toys with me.

I roll my eyes and chuckle. "Fine. Then I guess I owe you this."

Without a moment's hesitation, I press my lips against his. His mouth is warm and tantalizing, and I hold the back of his head as I deepen the kiss.

Though he pauses for a moment in surprise, it's not

long before he wraps his arms around me and pulls me close. He cradles my head, giving in, his fingers strong and thick as he holds me tight.

I break the kiss and grin as he searches my face, confused.

"What did I do to earn that?" he asks, a little bewildered.

"That's for buying me time to kill Mason." I'm tempted to kiss him again, but I resist the impulse and return to my spot on the cliff.

Just to tease him.

He chuckles, and for a moment, he just smiles and looks out at the ocean in silence. "You're full of surprises, Rory."

I chuckle. "What brings you out here? I assume you didn't just come for witty banter?"

He shakes his head. "Vaer update."

I stiffen, my smile fading as I shift into business mode. "Irena?"

"Nothing." He frowns, staring off at the ocean. "The other three locations you gave me cleared out the moment they got word about Mason's death. Someone else is assigned to hunt you down, now, but we don't have a name yet. They know Jace's identity, but don't know me or Levi. They'll figure me out eventually." He shrugs, and yet again I'm struck by how little I know about this man.

The Vaer will recognize him eventually, sure, but I

still don't know who he is or why people cower under his gaze.

"The Vaer are being more careful." He leans forward, resting his elbows on his knees. "The location you gave me for Irena, specifically, was evacuated underground. We have no idea where they went."

"Damn it," I mutter, running a hand through my hair in frustration.

"We'll find her, Rory," Drew says calmly, reclining once again against the rock. "But when we do…"

My jaw tenses, not entirely liking where this conversation is going. "Yes?"

He sighs. "She's still one of them."

"She's my sister." I shake my head. "She would never hurt me or anyone I care about."

"Your mentor wasn't exactly the nurturing type."

"And I knew that risk going into it." I groan in frustration. "But Irena is different."

He watches me intently, picking up on what I'm not saying, and nods. "Okay."

I hesitate. "Okay? Just like that?"

Drew nods and closes his eyes, setting his hands behind his head and getting comfortable. "I like you, Rory. I told you before—you have my respect. You're a smart woman, and you're not going to let nostalgia get the better of you. You know what you're doing."

I smile. "Thanks."

Two more sets of footsteps crash along the path behind us, both sets lighter than Drew's.

"Hey, Jace. Tucker." I say before the two of them round the corner.

Jace walks out onto the ledge, a slightly skeptical expression on his face as he looks between me and Drew. "There you are."

Standing behind Jace, Tucker grins at me. "Having some quiet time?"

I chuckle. "Trying to."

Jace sits on the other side of me, so that I'm sandwiched between the two dominant dragon shifters while Tucker leans against the rock, pretending to watch the ocean.

As Jace sits beside me, his bare arm brushes mine, sending pulses of electric desire through me. I try to ignore it, but I can't help wondering if he did that on purpose to remind me of what he is to me. Of what I am to him.

My treasonous body aches for him, pulling me toward him, urging me to give into the mate-bond that burns between us. Warmth spirals down my thighs, and I wonder if it will always be like this between us— tense and strange but too powerful to deny.

He can't control me. I can't make him stop trying. It's a wicked back and forth, and I seriously question if this will lead to anything good.

With three drop-dead gorgeous men sitting around

me, it takes a great deal of effort to simply sit there and watch the skies. I sigh. Damn it all, that's why I came out here—to relax. Out of the corner of my eye, I catch Drew and Jace glaring at each other.

A rustle of wind tears through the trees by our little ledge. Moments later, Levi soars overhead as he leaves the forests behind us, tilting in the ocean winds. He dips and spins, roaring into the sky as he enjoys his daily time in the air.

These men surprised me. They gave me hope and family when I thought I had lost both. And even though I don't know who most of them really are, I don't really care. They sacrificed everything to come for me, to stand at my side and fight with me, and I'm smart enough to recognize loyalty when I see it.

Besides, with my abilities, they can't hide *anything* from me for long.

Rory, Levi, Tucker, Drew, and Jace are back in *Fate of Dragons*, out now!

Read it now on Amazon.

Read on for a special note from the author.

AUTHOR NOTES

Hey, babe!

It has been such an absolute delight to share this world with you. Thank you *so friggin' much* for taking a risk and picking up *Reign of Dragons.*

I hope you enjoyed this world, the characters, and this new take on the immense power of dragons.

This series has been banging around in my head for a few years, and I've loved getting to know Rory as I designed the world, the magic, and her adventure.

Her story is one I think we can all relate to—a capable woman who wants *more.* A woman who knows there's more out there for her, but who doesn't know how to get it. Her purpose and destiny feel just out of reach, forever at the tip of her fingers, until it's very suddenly *not*.

Until she's forced to face it. To face herself, her doubts, her fears. And to overcome.

Because you and I, babe—we overcome.

I love Rory because she represents us. She's who we aspire to be: strong, beautiful, resilient, powerful, smart, capable, clever, resourceful.

Brave.

And, as we watch her grow, we grow with her.

I know, I know—that's all super gooey. I promise I won't do that too often! Give me these little moments of mushiness.

Mushiness aside, let's talk about hot guys.

So, I have to ask—who's your favorite of her men? I know, it's such a difficult question to answer, but if you *had* to choose just one?

Do you love Tucker the most? His adorable antics always have me in stitches. He can say or do just about anything and get away with it. It's that goofy charm, I swear. He brings her laughter, delight, and joy in a world that's full of darkness.

How about Drew? The handsome, brooding leader who knows so much more than he shares. That man is full of secrets, and I firmly believe we'll never learn them all. He's dominating and authoritative, but he meets Rory as an equal. They're both powerful, and they know it.

There's also Levi. Sure, he's a feral dragon right now, but we've met the man trapped inside. That boy is *gorgeous*—inside and out. He's heartfelt, emotionally connected, and deeply protective. He's Rory's silent protector, and he would rather die than let anyone lay a hand on her.

And Jace... oh, Jace. Our resident bad boy. There's a lot more to him than he lets on. He's a General, a warrior, and he never once suspected he would fall in love. With the mate-bond connecting them, what's going to happen between him and Rory?

There's so much at stake. It seems as though Rory's magic can be taken from her, and there are dozens of people who want it. The Bosses are after her. The Spectres are after her. The Knights are after her. Her sister is still in the hands of the Vaer. There's so much she doesn't know about her magic—so much she still has to learn about not only her power, but herself.

There's a delightful adventure ahead for you, just waiting for you to take a deep breath and dive in. I hope you sink into Rory's journey and lose yourself in the magic, action, love, steaminess, and above all—the *dragons*.

Because what's life without a little danger to spice things up?

Good news—the next book is out now! **Grab your copy** & make sure you **join the exclusive, fans-only Facebook group to get the latest release news & updates.**

Until next time, babe!
Keep on being your beautiful, badass self.
-Olivia

PS. Amazon won't tell you when the next Dragon Dojo Brotherhood book will come out, but there are several ways you can stay informed.

1) **Soar on over to the Facebook group, Olivia's secret club for cool ladies,** so we can hang out! I designed it *especially* for badass babes like you. Consider this as your invite! We talk about kickass heroines, gorgeous men, our favorite fantasy romances, and... did I mention pictures of *gorgeous men?*

2) **Follow me directly on Amazon**. To do this, **head to my profile** and click the Follow button beneath my picture. That will prompt Amazon to notify you when I release a new book. You'll just need to check your emails.

3) **You can join my mailing list by going to** https://wispvine.com/newsletter/olivia-ash-email-signup/. This lets me slide into your inbox and basically means we become best friends. Yep, I'm pretty sure that's how it works.

Doing one of these or **all three** (for best results) is the best way to make sure you get an update every time a new volume of the *Dragon Dojo Brotherhood* series is released. Talk to you soon!

ABOUT THE AUTHOR

OLIVIA ASH

Olivia Ash spends her time dreaming up the perfect men to challenge, love, and protect her strong heroines (who actually don't need protecting at all). Her stories are meant to take you on a journey into the world of the characters and make you want to stay there.

Reviews are the best way to show Olivia that you care about her stories and want other people discover them. If you enjoyed this novel, please consider leaving a review at Amazon. Every review helps the author and she appreciates the time you take to write them.

www.ingramcontent.com/pod-product-compliance
Lightning Source LLC
Chambersburg PA
CBHW031019030726
47497CB00004B/916